If they found out he was part unicorn, his magical body parts would be portioned off throughout the Reason. Best-case scenario, they'd take him at his word that he was a faun and he'd end up playing the flute in some wealthy family's summer home. Gary had learned never to underestimate a human being's capacity for cruelty. He'd been a toddler when the Reason Coalition formed, but his mother had been on the first generation ship to meet alien life on their way to a new planet.

It didn't matter that the alien Bala had familiar shapes known to humans through centuries of myth and legend; unicorns, fairies, and elves. Or that they offered to use their magic to help the colonists survive in their new home. The humans fired the opening shots in what would become a hundred years of war between the humans and the Bala. Growing up, Gary watched a ragtag collection of starving humans become a highly efficient colonizing machine. War galvanized them and gave them the will to live. Humans were never more persistent than when they were in the wrong.

T J BERRY

Space Unicorn Blues

ANGRY
ROBOT

ANGRY ROBOT
An imprint of Watkins Media Ltd

20 Fletcher Gate,
Nottingham,
NG1 2FZ
UK

angryrobotbooks.com
twitter.com/angryrobotbooks
Magic in spaaaace

An Angry Robot paperback original 2018

Cover by Lee Gibbons
Set in Meridien by Argh! Nottingham

Distributed in the United States by Penguin Random House, Inc., New York.

ISBN 978 0 85766 781 6
Ebook ISBN 978 0 85766 782 3

Printed in the United States of America

9 8 7 6 5 4 3 2 1

For Dave.
I may have lost the bet,
but we both won in the end.

CHAPTER ONE
The Bitter Blossom

When the murderer Gary Cobalt trotted into the Bitter Blossom, he nearly gave himself away as half-unicorn within thirty seconds. His prison-issued pants were hiked up so high that his hooves stuck out the bottom, clopping across the tile, calling all sorts of attention. He'd hoped people would mistake him for a common faun, but the bartender let him know that he wasn't fooled.

"Why the long face, son?" asked the barkeep pointedly, holding a glass upside down to catch the liquid flowing out of a bottle of Gravitas. He shoved the cork in, set the glass rim-down, and slid it to a uniformed Reason officer at the end of the bar. The officer caught the drink and tipped it slightly sideways with a practiced motion. A stream of Gravitas rose from the edge of the glass and into his mouth.

"Another," said the officer. Heads turned. Gravitas wasn't cheap. Even high-ranking Reason officers didn't carry around enough cash for more than one glass. The bartender obliged and turned his attention back to Gary.

"Just released from the Quag?" he asked.

Gary nodded and tugged his baseball cap low over his forehead. Ten years in prison for murder had taught him the value of lying low. That officer's freshly laundered Reason uniform did not bode well for him. Prison guards from the nearby Quagmire wore the same basic uniform, but their trousers were encrusted with mud and waste from a dozen races, both human and other. You smelled corrections officers before seeing them. This was no CO at the bar. A well-dressed Reason officer on a dead-end planet like Earth was either here for an official inspection or a resource collection. Gary hoped it was the former, because if it was the latter, the "resource" in question was likely him.

Everyone in the employ of the Reason government, whether filthy or clean, wore the same embroidered patch on their left shoulder. A trio of red spheres: one filled with a five-pointed star, one with a seven-pointed star, and the center one with a twenty-four-spoke wheel, not unlike a space station. Each sphere represented one of the three nations – the United States, Australia, and India – who came together to form the Reason. Everyone called that flag the "spheres and tears," but you'd never say that to an officer's face. Not unless you wanted to end up in the Quag on charges of sedition. Reasoners didn't have much of a sense of humor about their flag.

Nor did they care for even the gentlest ribbing about polluting their planet until it became a hot, uninhabitable marble in space. Humans were touchy about being forced to flee their home world en masse in hastily constructed generation ships. And the people left here on Earth – people deemed too sick or too poor for a chance at a new life – were the angriest of all. Gary didn't blame them one bit. Mostly, he kept his head down and tried not to attract any notice, but today he needed to navigate the labyrinth of human rage.

"I need to see Ricky about my stoneship." Gary kept his voice low and slow. He'd been a free man for less than an hour, but it wouldn't be difficult for a CO on break in the Blossom to find a reason to throw him back into the Quag. Or worse, they'd declare him a natural resource and he'd find himself on the business end of a bone saw. "I was told he bought it at auction–"

The bartender slammed a silver bowl onto the counter to cut him off. Liquid sloshed over the edge and sizzled onto the bar's high-gloss varnish. His eyes went right down to Gary's hooves.

"If you mean *Miss* Tang, then *she's* hosting the game table," said the bartender, lighting the bowl on fire with an ember perched on a golden fork. The flaming drink smelled like crushed limes and wax crayons gone soft in the sun.

"I'm sorry. I have apparently misspoken," said Gary. "The last time I was here, Ricky was a–"

"A charming host who you will find at the game table," finished the bartender firmly. "*Miss* Tang will be pleased to see you again."

The sharply dressed Reason officer studied their conversation over his second empty glass of Gravitas. Gary dropped his face toward the floor, but there was no hiding the line of his powerful jaw; strong enough to crush bones into powder. His stomach rumbled. It had been a long time since he'd crunched through a bone bigger than a rat's femur. Unicorns in the wild primarily ate trisicles – palm-sized chitinous beetles that thrived in the cold vacuum of space – but he could eat any type of bone or exoskeleton in a pinch.

The officer opened his mouth to speak and Gary turned quickly toward the game table. He had to make this fast. Whatever that man came to do, it wouldn't be good for Gary to be here when he did it. If they found out he was part unicorn, his magical body parts would be portioned off throughout the Reason. Best-case scenario, they'd take him at his word that he was a faun and he'd end up playing the flute in some wealthy family's summer home.

Gary had learned never to underestimate a human being's

capacity for cruelty. He'd been a toddler when the Reason Coalition formed, but his mother had been on the first generation ship to meet alien life on their way to a new planet. It didn't matter that the alien Bala had familiar shapes known to humans through centuries of myth and legend; unicorns, fairies, and elves. Or that they offered to use their magic to help the colonists survive in their new home. The humans fired the opening shots in what would become a hundred years of war between the humans and the Bala. Growing up, Gary watched a ragtag collection of starving humans become a highly efficient colonizing machine. War galvanized them and gave them the will to live. Humans were never more persistent than when they were in the wrong.

Gary scanned the game room. In addition to the main table where Ricky Tang presided, there were a few dozen low-stakes games going on. Most of the players were off-shift correctional officers, but there was a single table of Reason officers playing poker among the COs.

Gary saw the simmering heat of disgust between the officers and the COs. Every so often, a CO would walk a little too close to the officers' table and the whole party would look up, daring the glorified Bala babysitter to talk to them. The CO would eventually turn away, but always made sure to hesitate a moment to show the spot on their uniform that bore the largest tear or burn – a souvenir from some violent skirmish in the Quag. Most of the officers hadn't seen a day of combat since the Siege of Copernica Citadel ended fifteen years ago. They might wear the same uniform as the COs, but there was a galaxy of difference between them.

Gary tried his best to walk like a full human. His equine bottom half – two-legged like a faun's – was suited to soft dirt and not slippery tile floors. He skidded across the slick surface, trying to look more like a drunk human than an awkward part-Bala. The hem of his pants collected tumbleweeds of sparkling elf hair and more ogre toenail clippings than could possibly be sanitary in a food-serving establishment.

As he neared the game table, his right hoof slipped in a puddle of dusky brown dwarf blood. He caught himself before he fell, but a few COs snickered. A headless blemmye, pale and doughy, looked over at them with the face embedded in its chest. Gary sniffed the air, trying not to flare his nostrils. Something about it was familiar – a flowery scent that wasn't the usual damp ichor smell of a blemmye. It made the fur on his legs stand on end.

Gary stood behind a pair of neofelis cats at the main table. The cats pushed their furry heads together and played one hand as a team. One studied their cards as the other swatted at a dancing light on the leather tabletop. A group of COs near the window cackled each time the cat reached for the reflection coming off their buddy's watch.

In the chair next to the cats, a fairy sat forlorn, his transparent wing hanging broken and twitching. To be out here in public, wings exposed, meant this Bala was desperate. Indeed, most of Ricky Tang's clients were.

The blemmye bent over its cards, considering for a long minute before placing a vial of angel tears into the pot. As it moved, the floral scent wafted in Gary's direction again. Memories flooded back so powerfully that he had to grab the back of a cat's chair to keep from swaying on his feet. That was Jenny Perata, the woman who had held him captive for nearly two years. That lavender soap she used would forever be associated with the feeling of a knife digging around in his skull, searching for slivers of horn to power her ship. *His* ship, that the Reason had confiscated and awarded to her for defeating him in battle.

The blemmye was a particularly competent disguise. Really, he'd expect no less from Jenny Perata. The thick, coarse robes even covered her wheelchair. She was one of the fiercest adversaries he had ever faced. His gut clenched when he realized he was now vying against both her and Ricky for control of his ship, because there could be no other reason why Jenny was here, in the Bitter Blossom, from which she had been banned for life.

Ricky Tang shook the vial of angel tears, researching its value on her ocular display. The blemmye held its breath while she came up with an answer and Gary knew for sure that its appearance was a subterfuge. Blemmye didn't have lungs.

A wooden girl, kneeling on her chair to reach the game table, looked up at Gary with a wrinkled nose.

"Half-breed," she muttered. She took a drag from her cigarette and blew the smoke in his direction.

In the dealer's chair, Ricky's head snapped up at the slur. Her face moved from ire to joy before the smoke had cleared.

"Gary!" she cried, tossing her hand into the air. The other players threw down their cards in disgust as her voided hand landed face up on the table – three, seven, jack, ten, and king.

"I hoped you'd show up today," said Ricky, tossing a strand of dark hair over her shoulder. "It's been ten years and you haven't changed a speck."

"You have changed quite a bit," said Gary. Everyone at the table froze, but Ricky waved off his words with a calm smile.

"Oh you know, the outside caught up with the inside," she said. "I expect you're here to join the game?"

"I'm here to collect what's mine," replied Gary, raising his voice louder than he intended. His tones were deep and powerful from the generations of royalty in his ancestry. A few heads rose to look in his direction. He quieted both his volume and his mind with a slow breath. "My stoneship does not belong to you," he said calmly.

The damaged fairy looked up at Gary through bleary eyes.

"Leave while you still can," the fairy lisped. His tongue slid past the spaces in his jaw where teeth used to be. Razor-sharp fairy teeth were harder than diamonds and invaluable in the Reason drill bits that cored Bala planets for their minerals. From the oozing, it looked like this fairy had been betting his teeth all morning.

"Don't be a downer, Cinnabottom," said Ricky. "You got a fair chance. Gary can play if he wants to."

"I'm not here to play. I'm here to collect my ship," said Gary. The table of Reason officers had stopped playing and were now openly staring at him, but the officer at the bar was still seated, gulping down another gravity-defying drink. This transaction with Ricky had to go down fast, or he'd be taken back into custody. Gary didn't prefer to fight, but he would if he had to. And he almost always had to.

"Have you even seen it yet... since you were released, I mean?" asked Ricky with delight.

She flicked her eyes up and left to raise the shades on the back windows of the bar. In the distance, on the city's highest landing platform, sat a Halcyon-class stoneship with the terrible aerodynamics of unicorn deep space design. The *Jaggery* looked like a chunk of rounded stone as large as a planet-killing asteroid. It cast a shadow over half the city. A crew of workers was painting an enormous pink blossom onto the stoneship's hull.

The Reason was supposed to return his property to him upon release from the Quag, but they'd shoved him out of the gates with barely a word. The ship had gone to auction this morning and the only person with enough liquid cash in Broome City to buy even a heavily discounted stoneship was Ricky Tang.

Gary took a step toward the window and swiped a hand across the stubble on his chin. Seeing the *Jaggery* again, it felt, for an instant, like he might cry. He slackened his face into an unreadable mask that was the result of years of practice. Ricky already knew how much he needed his ship; he didn't need to broadcast it to everyone in the bar.

"The ship was supposed to be returned to me upon my release," said Gary. Ricky shrugged. One strap of her dress slipped down her shoulder and she let it hang there.

"The laws have changed since you went in." She fixed him with a gaze that was also a warning. Of course he'd noticed that the laws had changed. He'd seen more Bala come into the Quag for minor offenses like incorrect immigration documents in the last few years. Those who came in stayed longer or ended up in a harvesting center for parts.

"I'm just the buyer, Gary. You want to file a grievance about the logistics of the property sale, talk to one of those people."

She gestured toward the table full of Reason officers. Their game had ground to a halt. Gary shoved his hands into his pockets and hunched back down. Officers wouldn't be fooled as easily as a drunk CO.

"How much?" he asked quietly.

"Oh Gary. I have waited years to negotiate with you. I'm honored." She pretended to wipe a tear from her eye. "But my ship is so pretty, I don't think you can afford it. In fact," she flicked a fingernail at each of the beings seated around the game table, "none of these quags can afford it either."

One of the neofelis cats stood up and hissed at the insult. Her empty chair made a whirring sound, not unlike a timer. The other cat gasped and pawed at her to sit back down. After a loud click, a dozen silver needles sprayed out of the chair, piercing the cat's thick fur and burrowing into her flesh. She screeched in anguish and clawed at her back. Her partner pawed ineffectually at the piercings.

"The game is not over until I say it's over," Ricky said to the yawling cat. "Get out. You're bleeding all over my upholstery. But your kittyfriend has to stay."

The neofelis slunk out of the bar growling under her breath, "Ricky Tang, you suck." The remaining cat licked her wounds without taking her eyes off Ricky.

"Damn right I suck," said Ricky with a saucy smile. She turned back to Gary. "If you'd like to play for your ship, a seat has just become available at my game table."

"No game. A straight offer to buy."

"Oh Gary. What do you think this is, Myer? We don't *sell* merchandise here." Her head tilted toward the tidy Reason officer sitting at the bar. "That would constitute illegal black market dealing in Bala goods. And no one's doing anything illegal in here." She waved at the bartender to pour a fourth round of Gravitas for the officer. That explained how he was able to afford such pricey drinks. Ricky was trying to appease him.

"What do I have to do to get my ship back?" snapped Gary. He bit the inside of his lip and willed himself to be calm, because no one won a fight in the Bitter Blossom except Ricky Tang.

"Well, what do you have, kid? The Quag lets you out with two hundred and a shuttle ticket. Two hundred wouldn't curl my hair and I certainly don't need a shuttle ticket now that I own that beauty out on the platform."

"A private ante," said Gary, lowering his voice until it was nearly a growl. He hadn't been alive for thousands of years like his father, but he was still old enough to be Ricky Tang's grandfather.

Ricky dropped into her chair and let it spin in a lazy circle. Gary wondered if this was her tell. She seemed thrilled beyond speech.

"Gary, Gary, Gary…" she whispered. "That is a bold move, my friend."

"I am not your friend," said Gary.

"You used to be," she said, and Gary heard a hint of sadness in her voice that evaporated like alcohol a moment later. "Anyway, I doubt you have anything worth a ship that fine."

Gary snorted, a sound so close to equine that his hand involuntarily twitched upward as if to stifle it. Ricky's cheeks plumped and pinked with the spread of her smile. She wasn't even trying to bluff any more.

"My ship has been in storage for ten years. It may not even run," said Gary. He was losing the upper hand in this negotiation. The others in this room might be clueless, but both he and Ricky knew that you could bury a stoneship in the core of a planet for a millennium and it would still run like new. Especially if the dwarves stayed on board to maintain the ecosystem.

Ricky shook her head.

"I did a walkthrough this morning. Boges kept everything in working order. Well, as much as she could."

And this is where he had her.

"Everything but the FTL," said Gary pointedly. Ricky paused to wipe her palms down the front of her dress. She nodded, searching his face for any clue to the location of his horn. He didn't know where his horn was – he hadn't for quite a long time. The only horn he had was the tiny shaving of growth under his hat that he'd been working on for years eating vermin bones in the Quag.

He had eaten thousands of rats and rabbits in order to grow enough horn to power the *Jaggery*'s faster-than-light engine. The tiny shaving wouldn't get him far, but a few AU in any direction was better than sitting on Earth. He'd had a full horn when he was younger, like any other unicorn. It had been sawn off so he could hide better among humans. It was a big enough piece of horn that he might go anywhere in the universe, but his mother had hidden it to keep him safe.

He didn't feel particularly safe without it.

Ricky opened her mouth to speak. She stopped when a furry paw reached across the gaming table toward the ante. She flicked her eyes across her ocular display and the second neofelis cat howled and clutched her backside.

"I don't think so," said Ricky. She pointed to a sign mounted above the table.

ALL BETS ARE FINAL AND NONREFUNDABLE

The neofelis hissed and yowled.

"Fine then, go. I'm not into pussies anyway." The cat limped off after her partner and Ricky settled back into her chair.

"Is this private ante in the form of a liquid or a solid?" Ricky asked.

"Liquid," said Gary.

Ricky looked dissatisfied and drummed her fingers on the leather tabletop. The wooden girl lit another cigarette and picked splinters out of her teeth.

"Nothing solid at all? A shaving?" Ricky asked. Gary knew better than to admit it.

"Not a lot of bones in the Quag."

"I hear you ate well before you went in, though," said Ricky, staring intently at the front of his blue baseball cap. Gary balled his fists, resisting the urge to come back with a hasty reply. Ricky's words were always calculated. She was trying to goad him toward making a mistake by bringing up Cheryl Ann's murder. He heard a soft sigh from the table. The blemmye looked distressed. The elfin magic that had been used to craft the disguise was starting to drip down its face in the warm room.

"Fine. Five liters," said Ricky cryptically. Gary knew what she meant. Even the notorious Ricky Tang didn't dare say the phrase "unicorn blood" out loud. If the clientele figured out that he wasn't a faun trying to trade wishes for food, they'd be clawing over each other to tear him to pieces.

"That would kill me. Two liters," said Gary.

Unicorn blood healed most wounds and was one of the most precious substances in the universe. The last place he wanted to be was in a bar full of desperate people who knew who he really was. There was also a healthy contingent of planetbound xenophobes who had never made peace with the fact that the first aliens humans had encountered were an envoy of talking unicorns who offered to teach them farming. Within a few generations, most of the Bala races had succumbed to the human doctrine of manifest destiny. If there was one regret Gary had in his lengthy life, it was that he'd had to watch so many of his friends die in a pointless fight for galactic supremacy, when cooperation had been offered from the start. Then again, he'd never had just one regret.

"I don't care if you're dead. My ship's not worth less than five liters," said Ricky.

"Three," said Gary.

Ricky looked out the window, considering for long enough that the blemmye risked wiping away the slimy wetness collecting on its chin. The wooden girl narrowed her eyes.

"I don't know why you let a blemmye sit at your table, Ricky," said the wooden girl. "Everyone knows they suck the luck right out of the room."

Jenny might not have been an actual blemmye, but the puppet didn't know how right she was. If Jenny Perata had risked Ricky's wrath by coming back into the Blossom, things were about to get contentious.

The blemmye lifted a doughy middle finger and grunted. The wooden girl spat a wad of dry sawdust back. It settled on the table.

"Everyone is welcome at my games," Ricky said to the wooden girl. She turned back to Gary. "Four liters. Take it or leave it." She flicked her head toward the Reason officers. "This is your only chance to get out of here. The laws have changed. On any Reason-controlled planet you'll be picked up within minutes. Your very existence is illegal. It's only professional courtesy that they've left you alone in here for this long."

A pair of COs recognized Gary from the Quag and spat slurred curses in his direction with all of the intensity they could muster after complimentary glasses of larval eggwine. The dark purple secretion seared the throat on the way down and shredded the esophagus on the way back up, but during the twenty minutes in between, the drinker stood in the presence of their god. The COs looked disappointed to be back in reality, but were very much enjoying heckling what they thought was an ex-convict faun. He'd gone by his mother's surname, Ramanathan, while in the Quag. The name Cobalt was synonymous with unicorns and he hoped neither Ricky nor Jenny would be foolish enough to use it in here.

"You have no other options, Gary. Four liters is a gift. A welcome back present from me to you," said Ricky, blowing him a kiss. Her brown eyes crinkled at the corners. For a moment, it truly did seem like a fair deal. Then his blood kicked in and removed the toxin that she had just puffed into his face and the deal seemed just as raw as ever. But it wasn't as if he had many other options.

"Fine," said Gary.

"I'm so excited," Ricky stage-whispered to everyone seated around the table.

"What about the blemmye?" whined the wooden girl. The blemmye shrank back in its seat, pulling up its hood to hide its face.

"Your luck problem isn't the blemmye," said Ricky, training her laser focus on the wooden girl, who shrank back in her chair. "The problem is the ancient card counter installed in your brain."

The doll's eyes went wide.

"Don't think I didn't notice the freshly cut access panel behind your ear. Or the gears creaking inside your head. They're louder than a fairy's orgasm."

The wooden girl's eyes were suddenly sticky with sappy tears.

"I would never cheat. I just need to win enough to bail my fairy godmother out of the Quag." She batted lashes that looked like toothpicks.

"You are a cheater and a liar and I know all about the money you owe the Sisters. You're never going to win, but if you want to keep playing, I'm happy to keep taking your money," said Ricky.

The wooden girl's eyes went from wide, innocent hollows to narrow slits dripping with anger instead of sap.

"I guess that means I don't need to pretend you're a girl any more." The doll dropped her cigarette onto the table where it smoldered on the sawdust she'd spit at the blemmye. Ricky picked up the stub and blew the ashes off the leather. She took a long drag and the ember glowed hot. She let it out with her eyes closed as if this was her first cigarette in years. The noise in the room died down to a murmur as everyone waited to see what Ricky would do. She'd killed people for less.

"When you come into a person's place of business and deliberately call them something they are not..." she paused to exhale a perfect ring of smoke and her eyes flicked up and to the left, "...you give the impression that you have no respect for that person."

The air in the room disappeared as the regulars sucked in their breath. A chair scraped across the floor. Ricky took the doll's hand into her own, tenderly, like a woman consoling a friend. She stubbed the cigarette into the tiny wooden palm.

The doll screamed and tried to pull away. Ricky's slender fingers clenched around her like a vise. Gary watched as Jenny pushed her hidden wheelchair away from the table, the blemmye disguise running down her face in little rivulets of moist magic. Straight brown hair showed through the blemmye's shoulder and the outline of a human face replaced the blemmye's blank expression. The eyes crinkled at the edges, like someone who laughed often. Gary had looked into those steely eyes many times. They looked tired now, ten years since he'd seen her last.

Anger tightened across his chest like a hand squeezing. All the nights he'd imagined what to say if they ever met again, and now here she was and he found himself at a loss for words. He looked away, pretending not to recognize her, but kept the wheelchair in his peripheral vision. Jenny was a formidable opponent who had bested him in the past. And unlike Ricky, who would use her wits to outsmart him, Jenny would have no qualms about besting him in a physical fight.

The chair under the doll clicked and popped. A strange creature skittered across her lap. At first it looked like a moving blanket snaking its way up her torso, but some of the blanket broke away into lines that led down her arms. Tens of thousands of insects swarming out of the upholstery and marching in unison up the girl.

"What are th… No!" The doll writhed and screamed, bugs skittering into her open mouth. The tendons in Ricky's forearm tensed as she held the girl in place on the chair.

"You think you can come into my bar," said Ricky over the agitated humming of insects, "try to cheat me and lie to me, not to mention speak to me in that manner? You have no heart, you dry-rotted, hardwood bitch."

The doll choked up clots of insects. A few clumps carried timing gears between them. Bugs wandered out of her eyes

and ears, slow from eating their fill of macerated wood. Ricky
let go of her hand. The doll tried to wipe away the invaders,
but they swarmed too quickly.

"One time, a missionary came into my bar and asked if a
creature like me had a soul, or if it had burned away when
I turned against God," said Ricky. "Would you like to know
what happened to that man?" She ran her free hand across
the leather surface of the gaming table. "You've been playing
on him."

The broken fairy lifted his head up off the leather and
crinkled his button nose. The wooden girl slumped in her
chair, her eyes two empty caverns. An undulating group
of insects climbed out of her slack-jawed mouth, holding a
small bit of dark wood. They marched across the tabletop
and dropped it in front of Ricky. She picked it up and twirled
it between her fingers. It was intricately carved into the
anatomical shape of a heart.

"This will make a lovely necklace for a lovely lady," she
said, sliding the wooden heart into the pocket of her dress.
She swept the rest of the ante into a slot in the table and
waved the rest of the players away.

"Game over. We have a private ante that takes precedence,"
said Ricky.

No one dared to move.

"Ah, right," she said, eyeing her ocular display. There were
audible clicks from all of the seats at the table. With a flick
of her eyes, Ricky's voice was amplified throughout the bar.
Gary was about to find himself in the spotlight – anyone who
hadn't noticed him yet was about to.

"Beings of Bala and humans of Reason," said Ricky,
addressing everyone. "I apologize for the violence done here
today. I take full responsibility for the incident. You see, it
was my choice to *cedar* at the game table."

She flashed a saucy grin and everyone in the room began

to breathe again. Ricky took Gary's hand into hers, squeezing his fingers reassuringly.

"You ready for this?" she whispered, looking up at him and pulling down his cap playfully. She ran a finger down his nose and he pulled away. "I forgot how big you are in person. Another time, another place, you and me could have..." Gary backed away. Ricky's face froze. "Oh. Are the legends really true? Unicorns are asexual? My apologies."

Gary stared at her for a long moment. He appreciated her beauty – and the way she carried herself with the surety of someone with a dozen traps hidden on their person – but unicorns did not often experience sexual urges. Most immortals didn't, or the universe would be overrun with the offspring of eternal beings. Of course, sexuality and love formed a complex spectrum and individual unicorns experienced it differently, which is how Gary was conceived by a unicorn father and a human mother. Though he did not experience sexual attraction, there were many beings in the universe that Gary admired, and even a few that he loved fiercely.

Ricky turned back to the crowd.

"Gentle beings and jewels of every gender, today I bring you a spectacle like none you have ever seen in any corner of the Reason. This man has offered to compete in a game of skill in an attempt to win my new stoneship." She gestured outside to the *Jaggery*, which now sported a pink flower the size of a building. "The ante he has put up is private, known only to him and me. It will be revealed at the conclusion of the game. Aren't you curious what this ex-convict owns that could be worth as much as my pretty new ship? Probably something Bala..." she teased.

The crowd pressed in close. The servers moved through them, ready to take orders.

"If Gary survives all three of my challenges, he will win my ship. If he fails at even one, I receive his private ante.

Creatures both Reason and Bala, you're going to want to see this ante. Buy your drinks now so you don't miss a moment."

Hands went up and servers flicked their fingers across tablet screens with practiced speed. Bottles clinked as the bartender moved double time.

"Gary, do you agree to the terms of the game?" asked Ricky, waiting to record his verbal agreement on her ocular display.

"By the lengthy strides of Unamip and the hardy gallop of Fanaposh, the reverberating snort of Finadae, and the piercing whinny of Hulof, I invoke the strength of Arabis and the–"

Ricky slapped her hand over his mouth and rolled her eyes to the crowd.

"Pantheists, am I right?" she asked, who chuckled as they waited for their drinks to arrive.

Gary knew he'd have to negotiate for the *Jaggery*, but he had naively assumed it would be a private deal, not a public game of skill. Unless he was incredibly careful, he was going to out himself as a unicorn and end up back in the Quag before the game finished. He pried Ricky's hand off his face and adjusted his cap again.

A server dropped a plate of broiled cow meat at one of the tables. Gary smelled the roasted bone nestled inside the seared flesh. His knees nearly gave way from the wave of hunger that gnawed at him. Ricky grabbed his elbow.

"Steady there, big guy," she whispered off mic. "No fainting until I get my blood."

He looked for Jenny. She'd wheeled herself into a back corner where no one would notice as the disguise continued to slide down her face. She was clearly a human and not a blemmye, but everyone was so transfixed by Ricky's announcement of a game that no one saw as she wiped off the last of the elf excretions with her sleeve. It gave Gary the tiniest bit of pleasure to know that magic like that only came from elf semen, which she'd had to smear all over herself. The indignity of it was a small consolation, but he had comforted himself with those for a long time now.

Ricky reached under the table and pulled out a faded canvas bag printed with an elaborate script. It read, "The Atlantic & Pacific Grocery Company," an artifact from her sideline trade in Earth antiquities.

"For the first challenge, we use the baby bag," said Ricky. "Gary, choose your fate."

Gary reached in and dug into the bottom of the bag. Ricky often rigged the more difficult tasks to jump into players' hands. He pulled out one from deep in the corner, covered in crumbs.

Ricky took the tile from Gary and read it. She blew a low whistle that reverberated throughout the bar.

"Oh, this one is going to be fun. Who here wants to experience the moment of their death?" A few inebriated hands went up. Mostly Bala for whom magic was as familiar as breathing.

"Well you just got your chance." She held the tile above her head so everyone in the room could see the bird carved into its surface. A man in the back gasped. A corrections officer shuffled out the front door muttering that there was no way she was going to watch this shit. The rest of the crowd was riveted on Ricky.

"The Sixian parrot!"

Being half-unicorn gave Gary a better chance of survival than most people, but the Sixian parrot was by no means an easy challenge. There were entire institutions filled with humans who thought they could face the bird safely. He braced himself. He hadn't come all this way to end up trapped in the vision of his own death.

CHAPTER TWO
The Sixian Parrot

The crowd parted for a server wearing three pairs of welding goggles over her six eyes. One long tentacle held a covered cage the size of a human child far out in front of her. She set it on the game table and Ricky flicked her microphone on.

"Our challenger must stare at the Sixian parrot for a full sixty seconds. Does anyone know the secret of the parrot?" she asked.

"It shows you the moment of your death," said a human girl bursting out of a too-small sundress near the front of the room. She was likely a child in town to visit her parents in prison. There weren't many humans locked up in the Quagmire, but consorting with a Bala being could get someone a thirty-day stint. If Jenny's dryad wife was here, they were both in danger of incarceration. And if Jenny was arrested for being married to a tree spirit, they'd take her wheelchair as a potential weapon. It would be hard to maim her attackers from the floor. Not impossible, but hard.

"The young lady is correct," said Ricky. "Gary must watch the moment of his death. Now you may be thinking to yourself, 'But Ricky, how is that a challenge? He sees his own death, he feels a little sad, no big deal.' But it is a big deal. Can anyone tell me why?"

"Some people go insane," shouted a man from the back,

slurring "people" into "pee-ooh." He was deep into the drink.

"Is that Lieutenant Cy?" asked Ricky.

"Yeah," said a ruddy-cheeked human not too far from Jenny.

"Lieutenant Cy is also correct. I see you're drinking the larval eggwine. What did your god tell you this time, Cy?"

"He said I should have gone to the library today," said Cy. The room erupted in laughter. Ricky smirked.

"Probably true for all of us," she mused. "But reading patriotic textbooks and watching old television shows isn't going to pay the piper, so here we are. In any case, Lieutenant Cy is right. You don't simply see your death, you experience it. You'll feel the sword's blade piercing your heart. You'll gasp for air as seawater fills your lungs. You'll smell your own flesh crackling as fire consumes you." She mimed all of these horrific deaths, her nails clawing at her throat.

"Two-thirds of all creatures who stare into the eyes of the Sixian parrot will lose their minds." A few people moved toward the exit. Ricky waved them back.

"Don't worry everyone, our Bitter Blossom servers will pass out glasses to protect you from the effects of the bird. Just ten dollars for the rental."

Servers distributed eye protection in various configurations matching each of the represented species. Ricky pulled a pair of glasses out of a pocket, encrusted with gems and giving off the distinct glow of magic. Eyewear like that would protect her from more than just a Sixian parrot.

"Everyone ready?" asked Ricky. Gary lifted his cap just enough to give him a clear view of the parrot. A weak assent went through the group. Ricky cocked her head.

"That's not nearly good enough for the Sixian parrot. Are you ready?"

"Yes," screamed the crowd, shading their eyes despite the glasses.

"Lads, lasses, and every combination in between, I present to you... the Sixian parrot."

Ricky yanked the cover away from the birdcage with a flourish and Gary crouched into a fighting stance, holding his face inches from the bars.

"Go!" shouted Ricky.

The bird was not there. Or rather, it was there, but it existed as a void in space and time. Looking into it was like looking into a hole in reality. Gary opened his eyes wide and stared into the bird. Purple light focused directly into his pupils in two pulsating lines. It suffused his brain with energy. He could no longer think of anything but the bird. Far in the distance, Ricky counted off the seconds.

"One, two, three, four, five..."

The room slid away from him, and he careened toward a handful of tiny lights within the vantablack outline of the bird. The parrot trilled and one of the dots zoomed closer, faster than the speed of sound. Gary fought the urge to tear his eyes away. He leaned into the fall, expecting to hit the floor, but he continued to drop into blackness.

The girl in the front row whimpered.

"Six, seven, eight, nine, ten..."

Gary's jaw clenched and his hands balled into fists. A humming sound emanated from the bird in a multipart harmonic. It wove its way into everyone's brain and vibrated the teeth in Gary's jaw.

The dot grew in size until it eclipsed everything else in his vision. It was a star, a red dwarf, old and dim. Orbiting it was a planet ringed with spiral wisps of pink gas. It was not a world that he recognized. He flew toward the planet like a ship coming out of orbit.

"Eleven, twelve, thirteen, fourteen, fifteen..." Gary could still hear Ricky counting in the bar.

The bird leaned forward and opened its beak. The harmonic

filled the room and every creature resonated with the sound.

The vision brought Gary to the clouded surface of the planet. It was lush and damp, similar to the Bala worlds that had been colonized by the humans. Pink-leaved vegetation towered as high as a Reason skyscraper. He came to rest near two figures kneeling together in the loam. One was his future self, fully bearded and hair grown long and shaggy. The other was a woman, swathed in blue fabric from the top of her headscarf to the hem of her sari. Mud soaked their knees as they knelt in the grass.

"Sixteen, seventeen, eighteen, nineteen, twenty..."

Spittle dripped down Gary's chin and his entire body shook with the effort of keeping eye contact with the bird. A puddle collected beneath him. The odor of hot urine filled the room. In the back of his mind, he felt like he was back in the Quag.

"Twenty-one, twenty-two, twenty-three, twenty-four, twenty-five..."

The bird added one additional note to the harmonic and someone in the front row vomited onto the floor. A few people staggered out of the bar, clutching their heads.

In the vision, future Gary's voice was high and strained.

"I can't," he said.

"You must," said the woman, sounding calm. She placed her hand over his. "It was foreseen."

Gary realized that his future self was holding an object about two feet long and pointed at one end. His horn. He instinctively reached for it before remembering this was only a vision. He was at the mercy of the parrot to move his body where it wanted him.

"Do it," the woman commanded, an edge creeping into her voice. Future Gary began to cry in ugly sobbing gasps. He had never seen himself so distraught.

"I can't," he said between gasping breaths. "I've failed you."

"You are the bravest person I have ever met," the woman said. "The Pymmie are humbled before your sacrifice. Succeed in this or all is lost." She let her hands fall back into the dirt at her sides and waited.

"Twenty-six, twenty-seven, twenty-eight, twenty-nine, thirty... This is where it usually happens!" cried Ricky.

Gary's mouth opened wide in a throaty scream that added a baseline to the harmonic. Future Gary clutched the horn and raised it as if to strike the woman. She reached up and grasped his shoulder, fingers digging in to hold herself steady. She looked over future Gary's shoulder and stared directly at him.

"Are you here?" she asked. Her eyes didn't quite meet his, but she seemed to know that he was watching. "I know the parrot brought you here. You must tell the Pymmie to eliminate all of the humans. Leave not a single one alive. And Gary, this is most important. You *must* kill Penny. Remember. Kill Penny."

In the bar, Gary ran out of air and the scream became soundless. His fists flailed at his sides, pummeling the air like an invisible enemy as he fought the bird for air. Ricky's voice cut into the vision.

"Are you dying? Don't die," she whispered to him. "A stoneship without fuel is just a floating rock in space."

Someone was about to die, but it certainly wasn't him. Future Gary raised the horn above the woman, closed his eyes, and plunged the point into the woman's chest. It slid in easily. Gary heard a crunch as the wide end cracked her ribs apart. Future Gary pulled the dripping horn back out. Blood pulsed out of the woman's body like a fountain.

"Thirty-five, thirty-six, thirty-seven, thirty-eight, thirty-nine, forty..."

Future Gary dropped the horn and let out a yell that startled the trees. They retracted their pink leaves until only pale bare branches remained, pointing at the sky. The woman dug her fingers into the dirt, clawing for something to hold on to. She gurgled and a mouthful of blood ran down her chin. In the gaping chasm of her chest, Gary saw a heart muscle flutter.

Gary's future self doubled over. His screams echoed throughout both the pink planet and the Bitter Blossom.

The crowd at the front of the bar stepped back and covered their ears, but there was no escaping the pervading sense of impending doom. Creatures held onto each other and wailed. The girl at the front had sunk to the floor. Ricky still counted, but her voice quavered ever so slightly.

"Forty-one, forty-two, forty-three, forty-four, forty-five…"

The bird sat back on its haunches and the harmonic dropped an octave, rattling everyone's intestines hard enough that a scuffle broke out between patrons racing for the bathroom. The moment seemed to never end. Gary wondered if he was going to be one of the people who became trapped in their vision.

The image finally began to pull away from the planet. Gary floated numbly on the bird's tickling current, back toward the bar. He was supposed to have seen his own death, and yet he'd seen himself murder someone else… again.

Unicorns weren't technically immortal – they could certainly be killed in the right circumstances – but they wouldn't succumb to disease or moderate wounds. Did this vision mean that he would never die? With no vision to show him, perhaps the bird had substituted the closest approximation, a future time when he would kill another person. If there was any consolation at all, it was that at least he knew his horn still existed and someday he would find it.

"Forty-six, forty-seven, forty-eight, forty-nine, fifty… almost there!"

Coming back into his body, Gary shook so hard that his hooves clattered against the floor. With great effort he managed to stop yelling and take a single gasping breath.

"Fifty-one, fifty-two, fifty-three, fifty-four, fifty-five..."

The parrot tilted its head in that curious way that birds do and its ultraviolet beams shifted to deep blue. Gary panted as if he'd just run for his life, but did not break eye contact with the bird. Ricky Tang was a stickler for rules and he would not look away until she said so.

"Fifty-six, fifty-seven, fifty-eight, fifty-nine... sixty!"

The parrot that was not there chirped and hopped back onto its perch, pecking daintily at a cup of seed hanging off the bars. A server locked the door and threw the cover back over the cage. Gary took two steps backward and dropped into a chair that had been vacated by a terrified patron. He rested his face in his hands and wiped away a mix of saliva and tears.

The creatures in the room found themselves clutching each other and laughed sheepishly as the terror dissipated and they let go. COs helped fallen friends to their feet and razzed them for being weak. Servers circulated among the guests, offering refreshed drinks and discounted uniform trousers.

Gary checked on Jenny. Her disguise was completely gone, washed away by the tears she tried to swipe away discreetly. Smug satisfaction blackened Gary's heart. He wanted to see her suffer, after what she'd done to him and what she'd forced him to do.

His father's voice cut through his self-pity.

Each of your actions must stand alone by the reckoning of Unamip.

His anger dissipated like an angel after a miracle. Harboring silent resentments was like stabbing yourself and hoping the other person died. He could only serve his own penance for

Cheryl Ann's death, not exact punishment from Jenny as well.

Jenny lifted her eyes to meet his while Ricky was distracted chirping orders to servers about cleanup and refills. There was something in the look she gave him. Not quite contrite, but definitely not hostile. She lifted one finger and pointed it first at him, then at herself, and finally let it rest on the *Jaggery* outside the window. It seemed she was making an offer. Gary did not respond.

This was a woman who had wrestled him into a cage and kept him locked there until he was nearly mad with hunger and thirst. She'd dug into his skull for remnants of horn until he'd begged the gods to strike her down and end the pain. She'd placed him into the devastating position of having to eat the bones of someone he loved. He had been working on letting go of his anger toward her, but it was going to take him a minute to follow her into battle.

Ricky, oblivious to the negotiating going on between Gary and Jenny across the room, stepped in front of the crowd, tiptoeing over new puddles. They merged with the old puddles, reinvigorating the smells.

"That was very impressive, was it not?" Ricky asked. "The first challenge has been won!"

The crowd cheered, sounding less like enthusiasm for the game and more like the relief of having survived a traumatic ordeal together.

"Don't worry," said Ricky, "The last two will have decidedly less audience participation."

She winked and a weak laugh went up from the room.

"The human race will become extinct in a prison of its own making," said a high-pitched voice. Ricky frowned and looked down at the sundress girl, sitting on the floor.

"What?" she asked, forgetting to mute her microphone. The little girl stood up and faced the room.

"Human strongholds will turn to sand. We will feel the wrath of the old gods when we are stranded in a desolate corner of the universe. The only survivors will renounce Reason and beg to join the outcasts in their new home. I will starve in the street while the Reason decays."

Ricky reached over and pulled the protective glasses off the girl's face. She held them up to the light. Down the center of one lens was a hairline crack. She grabbed a server by the shoulder and whispered to him. The crowd murmured its concern as the sundress girl was led away into a back room. Ricky held up her hands to soothe the tittering audience.

"Everything is going to be fine. You must excuse our young friend. Regrettably, she looked upon the Sixian parrot and it has scrambled her thoughts. If this strapping bulk of a man barely made it through his journey to the future, then a child..." She trailed off and raised her glass, pivoting to a more solidly rousing topic. "To the survival of man!" she called.

"Manifest destiny!" echoed the officers in the room by rote, gulping down whatever was in front of them.

"Don't think we forgot about you, Gary," said Ricky, pulling him out of the chair. His soaked trousers stuck to his crooked equine legs, making it even more obvious that he was not fully human. Ricky lunged under the game table and came back with a purse embroidered with a bouquet of roses; temperamental plants that only grew on two planets in Reasonspace these days, neither of which was Earth.

"Are we ready for the second challenge?"

The crowd, emboldened by their death-adjacent experience and feeling the tingling rush of new drinks, cheered loudly enough that Ricky smiled over them like a benevolent dictator.

"This bag contains a set of slightly more difficult tasks. I'd say about half the creatures that pick from this bag get a survivable challenge. I hope the odds are in your favor, Gary!"

As Gary reached into the flowered bag, again going deep into the corner for an unrigged game piece, he stole another glance at Jenny. She flicked her head toward the window and he again made no indication that he agreed. Her entire upper body slouched in exasperation. She had a fair bit of hubris to assume that he would simply submit to her demands after all this time.

His fingers grazed a dusty item in the corner of the bag. He made a valiant effort, but it jumped away from him. In this second challenge, every piece was rigged to Ricky's advantage. She was giving him exactly the challenges she wanted. And he understood why. No one with any sense would leave the fate of a stoneship to chance.

Ricky held out her palm to take the game piece. Customers leaned forward to see the tiny bit of orange plastic in her hand. She held it aloft and her ocular display projected an enlarged image into the air for everyone to see. She turned the hollow triangle in different directions, but the confused audience did not react.

"Are you all too young to remember this?" she asked. "It's an old game token. Trivial Pursuit, it was called. Well, today's pursuit is not so trivial."

Gary mused how one of the galaxy's leading pre-exodus Earth historians was a game hostess in a dive bar. If universities had still existed, Ricky Tang would have been the star of an anthropology department. Now she served drunken government officials who would have arrested her long ago if not for the fact that this was the only decent place to get a drink and have some fun on the continent besides New Sydney.

"But what does the pie slice mean? Any guesses?"

"Singularity pie!" shouted Lieutenant Cy, his uniform

shirt soaked with something brown and oily.

"That's right," said Ricky. "A gut-busting slice of singularity pie."

Jenny cursed into the momentary silence and a few people laughed. Gary saw her pull out a tablet and begin typing. He said a lengthy silent prayer to Unamip to give him strength. The odds were not in his favor.

CHAPTER THREE
Singularity Pie

Six servers – heavyset dwarves thick with muscle and of indeterminate gender – pulled a wagon into the room. The wheels groaned under the weight of a single dessert plate resting in the center of the bed. Ricky patted the top of Gary's cap in mock affection. He pulled away. She was checking for sharp bits of horn, not being friendly. She turned to the crowd.

"Felines and waterfowl, this is a single slice of incredibly rare singularity pie forged in the depths of uninhabited openspace. There's a little bit of black hole goodness baked into each bit. It takes six strong dwarves to move it anywhere. Gary will need to eat an entire slice and keep it inside himself for at least a minute."

Singularity pie was intended to nourish universe-builders and demigods. Gary had never tasted it himself, but he'd seen it as a child, on a banquet table set for the unicorn gods of Bala before most of them had been hunted out of existence by the humans. A single bite could turn a human's insides into a pile of innards on the floor. It was a prolonged and messy way to die. Gary prayed to Unamip, hoping that he would intervene if he still existed in some form.

Ricky patted his chest as if he was a pet.

"Poor Gary. The pie itself is so dense with gravity that the steel plate would crumble if we lifted it. He'll need to lean down and eat the pie face first."

Gary gave Ricky a long look. That last comment about the plate was a lie, meant to up the showmanship of the game. Bala bodies had been degraded for spectacle throughout the last century, and today would be no different. Ricky returned Gary's stare, daring him to object. Gary knelt next to the wagon silently, his wet pants slapping the floor.

"Hands behind your back, just like an old-fashioned pie eating contest," goaded Ricky.

The crowd did not react. They could barely remember pies, let alone county fairs and corn dogs. Ricky had probably only seen images of them on old tapes and in stories the surviving humans told at the bar. Gary had talked to actual humans who had been there.

"On your mark. Get set. Go!" she yelled.

Gary opened his mouth and bit down on the pie. The filling looked soft and pliable, but it was impossibly heavy, like leaden gel. He tried to chew, but it dragged at his teeth, threatening to wrench them out of their sockets. He tilted his head back and let the pie slide down his throat. It burned with cold, prickling and bubbling down his esophagus. He grabbed the side of the wagon and held on as it slammed into the pit of his stomach. His face twisted into a grimace as he tried to keep the pie from tearing through his internal organs.

A full unicorn would have completed this challenge as easily as eating an ordinary dessert, but a half-unicorn was made of just enough human meat that the outcome was questionable. His healing blood would try to repair the damage as fast as it could, but he might bleed out if it couldn't keep up.

He took a deep breath as the pie popped through something vital in his gut. He saw motion from the back of the room; Jenny held up a single finger to someone outside the window. Gary dipped his head, pretending to strain under the effects of the pie, and looked to the side to see who she was signaling.

An old man stood outside the Blossom's back window. Gary's insides twisted, and not just from the pie. It was Cowboy Jim, and he did not look pleased.

"One bite down, three to go," said Ricky, nudging Gary with the toe of her shoe.

Gary tightened his grip on the wagon and went back for a second bite, grabbing it and flicking it to the back of his throat in one quick motion. He sagged sideways toward the floor.

Seeing there was no threat to themselves this time, the patrons crowded close. Lieutenant Cy pushed ahead of everyone. His officer status silenced any protests from the COs, but they still shot dirty looks at his back.

Gary swallowed a third bite. The sound that came out of him was a mix of whinny and whimper. The pie was tearing through his insides. Even as they healed moments later, the sensation was agony.

"The final bite. Can he do it?" asked Ricky.

Gary shoveled the final piece of the pie into his mouth and tilted his head back. It went down and so did he, lying face up on the floor, helpless. He told himself that getting horizontal was not a weakness, it was a smart strategy. The pie was less likely to tear through thick abdominal muscles than delicate intestinal tissue.

Ricky pointed her ocular display at Gary and his strained face appeared above the room at triple its normal size. His breathing was quick but controlled, like someone giving birth. He groaned as the pie moved inside him. The audience cheered and clapped. Ricky tapped a timer into the corner of the projection that counted down from a minute.

"That pie is tugging at your insides, Gary," said Ricky, flashing a grin at the patrons. "Stretching your stomach until it's about to tear at the seams. It will bathe your organs in acid and bile, eating them away." Gary winced and the crowd laughed.

"You can let it come out if you like. Just hang yourself over the wagon and it'll fly back out the way it came. No more pain," offered Ricky.

Gary groaned, laid his arm across his eyes, and curled his legs up to his chest, forgetting for a moment that his hooves were in full view. Lieutenant Cy stumbled past him and over to the bar where he spoke with the Gravitas-drinking fellow. Gary dropped his legs and cursed his carelessness.

"Thirty seconds," called Ricky, tapping her foot on the floor impatiently, waiting for him to fail.

The crowd salivated at his agony, especially now that they could all see that he wasn't fully human. Only a handful seemed to understand that he was not just a common faun. Gary could pick them out by the way they inched toward the wagon with a sudden alertness. The prospect of striking it rich had sobered them up with remarkable speed. Jenny rolled closer as well, nudging people out of the way with her footrests.

There was more interest than usual in leaving Earth these days. This was the year of the Century Summit; the hundred-year anniversary of the end of the war between humans and Bala. Though both sides knew those words were hollow and devoid of meaning. The Reason had continued the battles long after the omniscient Pymmie had put an end to the open hostility. Gary often wondered why the Pymmie would bother imposing a false peace knowing that it would be broken the moment they left.

In any case, the all-powerful Pymmie were scheduled to return in less than a day to take account of what had happened during their hundred-year absence. Bala throughout

Reasonspace were attempting to find passage to Jaisalmer for
the meeting to plead their case for assistance. And humans,
in true human style, were treating the visitation as an excuse
to hold a party. Gary would wager that more than a few of
those around him were hoping to win enough to attend the
Summit. For those who figured out what he was made of,
even a tiny piece of him was a shuttle ticket to Jaisalmer.

"Forty-five seconds."

Ricky rested one sparkling shoe on his chest, digging the
heel into his pectoral muscles. It left a footprint on his ragged
prison shirt in someone else's blood. Some of the audience
clutched their stomachs in sympathetic pain.

"One minute. Gary has done it! No one gets this far very
often. Give him a hand for completing the second challenge,"
she called out with decidedly less enthusiasm than before.
There was a halfhearted smattering of applause from around
the room. Gary remained on the floor, huffing and wincing
as the pie shifted in his abdominal cavity.

Ricky lowered her voice so everyone in the room had to
quiet down in order to hear. She paced in front of Gary as the
servers wheeled the wagon away.

"We have arrived at the final task. We've seen so much
together today. I feel like we're family now. Did you wake up
this morning knowing that you would be standing mere feet
away from a Sixian parrot? Or come within striking distance
of a slice of singularity pie?" asked Ricky.

She put her hand out to steady a swaying Lieutenant Cy,
walking back from the bar. The Gravitas-drinking officer had
stayed put. Gary nurtured a spark of hope that they weren't
here for him after all.

"That's why you come to the Bitter Blossom, isn't it?"
Ricky continued, pulling on the uniform lapel of the next
closest corrections officer, a slight woman spattered with
green vegetal liquid that probably belonged to a dryad. "To

experience the unexpected. To witness the extraordinary. And to drink." Ricky held up her glass. "Let's toast to Gary, who has demolished two of my three most difficult challenges and is about to win back his stoneship."

Servers refilled glasses and charged accounts as fast as their limbs could type.

"To Gary!" Ricky shouted.

"To Gary," the crowd echoed weakly.

Gary propped himself up on one elbow, the pie having settled itself somewhere in his torso. He pulled himself up into a chair with a grunt. Jenny rolled up to the front row and tried to catch his eye. This time he pointedly ignored her. He was minutes away from winning back his ship. If he could simply complete the third challenge, victory was within his grasp.

Ricky reached under her game table and slid something behind her back. Whatever it was, there was nothing she had in the third bag that could possibly deter him.

"The final task – and make no mistake, nearly none of our guests get this far..." Ricky looked pointedly at Cinnabottom, who sat crumpled against the wall, sucking on ice. "This challenge comes from the ultramarine satchel."

From behind her back, Ricky pulled out a heavy sack covered in short hairs dyed a vibrant shade of blue. Gary's heart pounded. His hands shook as he took it from her.

The hairs stood on end as his fingers touched the bag. The material itself seemed to shift under his hand, drawing itself closer to him. His insides felt like liquid. This was a unicorn pelt.

"Anyone you know?" asked Ricky softly with a smirk.

Not only did Gary probably know the previous owner of the pelt, they were most likely related by blood. The unicorn family tree was small and tightly interconnected. There were rituals one could perform to draw a unicorn's name out of a piece of their carcass, but this wasn't the time or place. He let his prison mask come down and pretended that his chest didn't ache with the agony coursing out of that scrap of skin.

"Secondhand, of course. I don't have a permit to hunt unicorn," said Ricky with an innocent shrug toward Lieutenant Cy.

"You're a monster," said Gary, clutching his abdomen with one hand and the bag with the other. The audience watched eagerly for Ricky's response. Would she launch a barrage of throwing stars from the wall? A cascade of molten rock from the ceiling? People prepared themselves to run in case the punishment inflicted any collateral damage.

Ricky held his gaze with her own glittering brown eyes.

"As if you should talk. At least I didn't eat my girlfriend," she said off mic. She blinked and her voice rose above the crowd.

"Pick already, big guy."

Gary's fingers pawed through the bag. The balls inside pinged and resonated like metal bells. He spent a long time fishing around, grabbing a ball and bringing it halfway out, only to have it fall from his hand and another jump into its place.

In the front row, Jenny tried frantically to get his attention. From under her hood, she glared at him. When Ricky looked away, she waved. He steadfastly refused to acknowledge her. He was so close.

"Pick now or forfeit the game," said Ricky, annoyed at his insistence on finding an unrigged ball. Gary sighed, pulled out the trick ball, and handed it to Ricky.

"What a surprise... dealer's choice!" she announced, holding the ball up for the room to see. "Ah Gary. How could I possibly select from the list of delights and deviations at my disposal? Any suggestions from the audience? You drink for free if I pick your challenge."

There was no way she would let a patron choose. Ricky already had a task in mind that would guarantee the *Jaggery* would stay with her and she would win his ante.

"Make him fight the twinzels!" called a CO.

"Good choice, but they're in heat right now. I can barely separate the pair, let alone get them to fight. Next?"

"Supernova surfing!" shouted the woman covered in dryad sap. Ricky rolled her eyes.

"Delightful! But how would we get everyone up to Pegasi? The fuel alone would eat up my margins. Anyone else? Lieutenant Cy?"

"Sixian parrot," mumbled Cy. Ricky pointed at him in mock disbelief.

"Really? Cy baby, have another drink. Maybe it'll bring you back around to coherent." Cy's friends laughed.

"All right. I gave you kids a chance, but you're not thinking big enough." She turned to Gary, putting her back to the audience for the first time. "No, I have the perfect challenge in mind for old Gary here. Something he'll avoid at all costs, unless he wants to go back to the Quag... or worse."

She was quiet for a moment, allowing the room to fall silent behind her.

"Gary Cobalt, take off your hat."

CHAPTER FOUR
Take Off Your Hat

Ricky waited for the crowd to roar, but the spectators at the front grumbled and frowned at her final challenge. They hadn't waited here through the piercing cries of the Sixian parrot or the ozone stench of singularity pie just to have the final challenge be something so simple as Gary taking off his hat. A few people sat back down at their tables, restarting their card games with disappointed grumbles.

"What kind of task is that?"

"What a ridiculous waste of time."

"This place gets worse every year."

Ricky waited patiently for the patrons to settle down. She put a hand on Gary's shoulder, whether to keep him from running or to reassure him, he couldn't tell.

On his part, Gary was beginning to think he might need Jenny's help after all. This challenge was more complex than it seemed. If he left his hat on, he would lose the challenge and the *Jaggery* was forfeit – not to mention Ricky would take most of his blood and leave him out on the street to die. On the other hand, if he took his hat off and the crowd saw the divot in his skull that shimmered with the faintest hint of horn growth, they would claw apart every precious scrap of his body.

Ten years ago, he would have flung his hat off defiantly

and torn every creature in the room to red-blooded bits with his teeth and hands. He had more than once felt the crunch of a human skull under his hooves. Today, he was feeling more circumspect, not to mention tired of fighting. Ten years in the Quag could do that to a man.

Gary considered his options carefully. He let Ricky become distracted by the jeers arising from the crowd. Feeling betrayed at the simplicity of the final challenge, they began to root for the underdog.

"Just take off your hat, man."

"Yeah, win back your ship."

"Do it."

Ricky tried to stem the tide of pro-Gary sentiment.

"A round of drinks on me if he loses," she announced. It barely made a difference. People were starting to realize that they stood a better chance of brokering a deal to get off the planet with Gary than with Ricky Tang who had fleeced them for years.

Gary sucked in his breath and clutched his gut. The pie was looking for a way out, and so was he. He looked behind him, and Cowboy Jim was still standing outside that back window. The last time he'd seen Jim, the old man had sworn bloody revenge on Gary and all his kin. He looked just as irate as ever.

Jenny inched forward and tapped him with her chair.

"Take off your hat," she said, just like every other heckler in the room. Her instructions couldn't possibly have been clearer. He shook his head at her.

"Jesus, Mary and Joseph. Just take off the bloody hat," Jenny said. Gary belched and hot ozone gasses seeped out of his mouth, escaping from the pie. Jenny winced and turned her head.

"Why don't you take off your hat?" sloshed Lieutenant Cy, leaning on another officer.

"I don't get it," said a filthy CO, punctuating her words with a spray of spittle. "You can't take off your hat in exchange for an entire stoneship? What's wrong with you?"

The realization descended on Ricky's face like a sunset. She had badly miscalculated, thinking the largely human crowd would hope to keep the stoneship away from him. She'd neglected to take into account the deep desire of everyone *on* this planet to be *off* this planet. They were rooting for him to win because it gave them hope that they too could beat one of Ricky's games.

"Just take it off, man. Get out of here."

One of the few sober creatures in the room began a chant of "Take it off." Ricky lifted her hands to quiet them, but she'd lost control.

"Everyone settle down. A round of drinks on me, but only if you're sitting at a table," she called.

A handful of people found chairs and sat. The rest of the group pushed forward.

"What if I pull his hat off? Do I get the ship?" asked Cinnabottom from the sidelines, suddenly interested in the proceedings. Creatures inched forward on all sides.

Jenny glared at Gary and raised her hand in a "what are you doing?" gesture.

"Take it off. We have a plan," she whispered from under her hood.

Gary had been caught up in some of Jenny's previous plans. They usually involved all manner of nefarious dealings, up to and including torture and murder. He wanted no part of that life again. He intended to get the *Jaggery* and travel as far away from Reasonspace as his horn would get him. If he could just figure out how to get the ship without dying.

She rolled up to him, footrests knocking into his shins. He turned to face her and the pie shifted. His eyes unfocused for a moment as some internal organ popped, then re-formed around the piece of pie.

"Come on Gary, let's get the hell out of here," said Jenny, dropping her hood.

Ricky Tang's mouth dropped open.

"Aiyā, Jenny fucking Perata. You are not allowed in my bar," she yelled.

She shoved Jenny's chair back with her foot and Jenny put out her hands to stop her wheels. Gary tensed. Jenny hated when people moved her wheelchair without asking. He'd seen her bloody a man's nose for trying to help her cross a street. She tapped the tablet in her lap and ducked. The gaming table beside them exploded. Pieces of wood and metal hit the windows, shattering them. The COs hit the deck and the Reason officers drew their weapons. Someone flipped a table for cover.

Ricky squealed and picked shreds of the leathery table out of her hair.

"Lockdown. Go on lockdown," she yelled to the servers, who ran for their riot gear. Jenny motioned to Jim to get inside before blast doors came down. Instead, he used his elbow to knock the remaining glass out of a window and strained to get his foot up over the waist-high sill. Jenny grabbed the front of Gary's shirt and yanked him down toward her. He grunted and burped out a stream of protomatter that smelled like sulfurous eggs.

"Take off your hat, Gary. Jim and I will get you out of the Blossom if you take us with you," she yelled over the chaos.

Servers sprang into action, activating the heavy metal shields that began to slide down over the windows and doors. The customers scrambled for the exits, unwilling to be locked in with a pissed-off Ricky Tang. Ricky herself was climbing through the wreckage of the game table, picking out valuable items and stuffing them into her pockets.

Gary sat calmly, conversing with Jenny as if they were meeting for tea.

"I will not go with you. Your dealings are criminal, you kidnapped and tortured me for nearly two years, and your companion swore blood revenge against me and my family," he replied.

She shook him with one hand while keeping the other poised above her tablet.

"That is all true, but this is our... *your* one opportunity to get back into the *Jaggery*. We help you now or they tear you to shreds."

She flicked her head toward the patrons who, in the absence of a clear opponent, had started fighting amongst themselves. A bold CO had taken a swing at an officer in the melee and was paying the price for it as the officer and her cohort kicked him into submission. Other corrections officers jumped into the melee, realizing that they had numbers and chaos on their side.

Lieutenant Cy had gone back to the officer at the bar and the two of them were pulling out their weapons. Even if he escaped the patrons, those two would absolutely pick him up for resource harvesting once he removed his hat. One of the patrons stepped up to him and Jenny and drew a knife as long as a child's arm. A useful weapon here in Broome City where the fauna were as likely to kill you as the Reason.

Jenny tightened her grip on his shirt and pulled him closer.

"Ten years is a long time, Gary. Please." It sounded, for all the world, like Jenny Perata was begging for his help. Which couldn't be right. This woman had laughed when he had bitten her hard enough to shatter her bones. She'd punched out a necromancer who had attempted to turn her inside out with magic. This woman didn't beg. Perhaps ten years was a long time.

"And you, Jenny Perata." She flinched as he said her name. "Once again, you need my help."

Jim pushed his way through the people clambering out of the back windows and knelt next to Jenny's chair.

"Ready to go, Jen?" he asked, reeking of the cheap pipe tobacco he'd been smoking outside.

"I am, but Gary's not so sure."

Jim and Gary sized each other up. Jim looked like he was about to be sick. Gary's rage softened with pity. Ten years hadn't been kind to Jim. He'd already been old when Cheryl Ann died, subsisting primarily on pipe smoke and grilled cheese sandwiches. Now he was a dried-up shoelace of a man. Jim saw the change in Gary's expression and he turned away, ashamed.

"To hell with this, Jen. Let's just take the ship ourselves," he said, standing.

Jenny gave him a look that could have cooled a booster rocket. They'd had ten years to steal the *Jaggery* out of evidence storage. If they hadn't done it by now, they weren't going to do it without his help. Even if they managed to get the ship into orbit, without unicorn horn, it was stuck within the Solar System. These days, the space around Earth was filthy with orbital pirates and low-level Reason officers looking for a way to get noticed. Without a working FTL drive, they'd be captured within hours.

"Cowboy Jim, are you telling me that you can't make a dent in a room of two dozen spheres-and-tears creeps?" Jenny asked, tapping on her tablet and stopping the blast doors halfway down. Infiltrating the Blossom's computer systems was one of the many reasons that Jenny was banned from the bar. Gary had rarely seen her without a tablet in her hand, tinkering with some snippet of code that she slid out of view as soon as she noticed someone looking.

Ricky stopped treasure-hunting long enough to yell at

the servers to lower the doors manually. She also pointed to Gary.

"Get him in the back room, and get Jenny Perata out of my bar," she said.

Jenny rolled toward the remnants of the game table. Her wheels crunched over wood and glass.

"I'm on my way out, Ricky. And if you had a single goddamn wheelchair accessible door, I'd be gone already. But... one thing before I go."

She looked up at Gary.

He offered up one last prayer to Unamip to guide him. An itch formed on his scalp, close to where his horn should have been. He took it as a sign. He reached up and removed his hat.

"Fuck me," said Ricky, looking at the ceiling in exasperation.

Embedded in a nest of short, curly hair was an excavated circle of pearlescent bone, like a sinkhole in Gary's head. Only those closest to Gary noticed at first, then the realization passed through the room like a wave. Jaws set or slackened, depending on the person and their intent. Weapons, both human and Bala, emerged from belts and boots.

"Unicorn!" shouted a Reason officer, bringing the butt of his service weapon down on the shoulder of a server who happened to be standing between him and Gary. The only thing more valuable than a unicorn was the off-planet promotion a Reason grunt received after capturing one. The officer stepped over the server and shoved the barrel of his firearm firmly into Gary's chest.

"By the authority of the Reason, this magical creature has been remanded into custody for resource harvesting. You will... *oof.*"

Jim barreled headfirst into the officer. He may have been stringy, but the man was like an overwound spring. The officer hit the floor and Jim began raining punches down on him.

Ricky flattened herself against the wall and used her ocular display to launch a barrage of throwing stars into the room. Jenny let go of Gary and ducked as far down into her chair as she could. Gary caught a star in the arm. It sank in with a pop, then fell to the floor. Silver blood soaked through the thin fabric of his shirt, attracting even more attention from the patrons fighting their way toward him.

"Lean over the back of your chair," said Jenny, peeking out to see if the throwing stars had stopped. Gary wrenched himself to his feet with a gasp. He knelt on the seat of the chair and leaned over its high back. Jenny wheeled herself behind his legs.

"Kick up," she said.

He lifted his legs into Jenny's lap, probably leaving bruises on her thighs where his hooves dug in. She grabbed his ankles and pushed them above her head. Gravity did the rest. Four bites of singularity pie slid out of Gary's open mouth onto the floor. They cracked the tile and sat there, attracting dust in little orbital patterns on the stone.

Jim left the first Reason officer and stepped up to a second, swinging a left hook and connecting with a fragile human jaw. The officer crumpled to the floor and Jim straddled him, landing punches with the ferocity of a man who had nothing to lose.

"Jim, clear a path out the back," Jenny called, dropping Gary's legs back to the floor. Gary stood up and stretched like a predator waking up after hibernation. The wound on his arm had already closed, the raw pink scar darkened by the second. The same thing was happening inside him as his body healed the damage from the pie. He stepped in front of Ricky, a full head taller now that he was no longer slouching in pain.

"My ship," he said, holding out his hand as if she was going to give up the set of keys. A thick dwarven woman launched herself at Gary's stump, dagger drawn. He reached out and slapped her out of the air with a thud.

"You didn't take off your hat within a minute," said Ricky, her eyes frantically moving across her ocular display.

"There was no time limit on the third game," said Gary. He was right. In her haste, Ricky had forgotten to add any caveats to the offer. A dozen Reason officers had witnessed the contract. While they had no love for Gary's kind, they'd also lost enough to Ricky's rigged games that they just might arrest her for voiding a contract. The Quag would not be a friendly place for the woman who'd made most of its current inmates destitute.

Ricky's eyes stopped jerking back and forth. She blinked twice and Jenny's tablet pinged.

"Fine. You have your ship back, Gary. But one thing."

Jenny looked down at her screen. A grin spread across her face. A sight which Gary had learned was very bad for everyone in the vicinity.

"The new laws say Bala are prevented from owning property," continued Ricky. "So I took the liberty of transferring the *Jaggery* to your good friend Jenny for safekeeping."

Gary growled. A deep, rolling sound that never should have come from a human-shaped mouth. Ricky paled.

"Good luck getting out of here alive," she said, reactivating her microphone. A line of servers clad in black riot gear filed into the room, forming an impenetrable line around Ricky.

"Lads, ladies, and lovers of every persuasion, we seem to have a unicorn in our midst. Anyone know the going rate for a liter of his healing blood? First person to bring me a chunk of him gets off this rock and might even make it to the Summit on time."

Every creature in the room surged toward Gary.

CHAPTER FIVE
Bitter Blossom Brawl

Jenny's entire body tensed as Gary took off his hat. She wasn't afraid of a bar fight. Far from it; beating a few COs bloody would be good for her spirits, and for Jim's as well. He'd been moping for months about her plan to add Gary to the team. She'd barely been able to coax him into eating. She couldn't even tempt him with a grilled cheese made with real honest-to-goodness bread and cheese, not the crunchy freeze-dried garbage they packed on shuttle runs. No, it wasn't the fight she was afraid of, but what came after when she had to get into that ship with Gary Cobalt by her side.

She'd locked that man up and dug into his head more times than she could count. He'd agreed to come along, but there was still a fair chance that he would take the opportunity to exact his revenge. But she had no choice but to trust him. It had been a lean bunch of years while Gary was locked up. With the *Jaggery* in evidence storage she and Jim had no access to a ship with a faster-than-light drive. Between them, they had barely scraped together enough cash to rent a cargo ship to shuttle between Earth and the handful of inhabited stations in its vicinity. The rental payments took up most of their profit each month, with a little left over for food and drink. Saving up for an FTL ship was impossible.

As the tenth anniversary of Gary's arrest rolled around,

Jenny realized how little they'd accomplished while he was away. Their grand plan to set up a hauling business on a planet outside of Reasonspace had amounted to nothing. They'd frittered away a decade of their lives delivering coffee and condoms to Reasoners. The plan was to convince Gary to let them join him on the *Jaggery*. It was beyond her wildest dreams that Ricky had deeded the ship directly to her. As long as she and Jim could get Gary out of the Bitter Blossom alive, they were on their way. It seemed like Jenny's luck was finally turning around.

She even had a brilliant hauling job lined up. A quasi-religious group called the Sisters of the Supersymmetrical Axion had contacted her a few weeks ago requesting her hauling services. A simple cargo run from Earth to Jaisalmer. The pay was astronomical; the only caveat was that they needed to have a functioning FTL drive to make the trip in time for the Century Summit. Gary's FTL-powering horn was going to cinch the deal.

Trouble was, the bar patrons were also keen on snagging a bit of horn. They crowded around Gary and Jenny, landing a hail of blows that were mercifully blunted by the sheer drunkenness of the group. Gary picked a bite of singularity pie off the floor. He braced himself on Jenny's armrest to lift it and tossed the filling overhand into the face of a Reason officer. It hit her cheek and her head jerked sideways. Blood sprayed from her mouth in a fine mist. She stepped back, clutching her cheek.

"Nice," said Jenny, remembering that particular officer from a cargo run in which an entire flat of tomato plants had "disappeared." It had cost their entire food budget for the month to compensate the buyer for the missing seedlings. She never wanted to see a cup of reconstituted chicken broth again in her life.

Jenny wheeled herself between Gary and the onslaught

of patrons, forcing them to climb over her to get to him. She felt under her blemmye robe for her patu – the club her elderly kuia had used to whack colonists away from her home a hundred years ago. It not only had sentimental value, but it was flat, easy to tuck into her chair, and made of wood, so didn't trigger metal detectors. She was glad for the chance to pound it into the heads of the latest batch of imperialists. She brought it down on the head of a CO who was attempting to climb up onto her chair. He yelped and dropped onto the floor.

Lieutenant Cy pushed his way out of the tangle of bodies on his hands and knees, dragging himself up into Jenny's lap. He climbed over her head and shoulders. She hit him as hard as she could, but Cy had drunk enough to be impervious to pain. He leapt onto Gary's back like a jockey on a horse, digging at the horn stub with a fork and dripping a long line of saliva into Gary's hair.

Gary pulled at Cy's arm around his neck, but the desperate man hung on. Cy wriggled the fork into the tender spot where skull met horn. Jenny knew it was tender because long ago she'd dug bits of horn out of that exact spot herself. Gary had always screamed the loudest when her knife went that deep. Jenny told herself that the turning in her gut was regret over what had happened to Cheryl Ann and definitely nothing to do with her treatment of Gary. She backed her chair toward the remaining pie on the floor.

"Gary!" she shouted, lining up her patu next to a silver-flecked bite like a croquet mallet. He held out his hand and she smacked the pie as hard as she could. It was like hitting a brick wall. The force reverberated up her arm. She heard a crack from her club. The pie didn't budge.

"Oh bollocks," she said, running her thumbnail down a hairline fracture in the wood. This weapon had kept wankers at a distance for centuries, but it was having trouble holding together in the face of weird Bala magic. The spiral-tipped ferns carved deep into the wood had started to crack along their stems.

"You and me both, patu," she muttered, slammed its tapered edge into the throat of a soldier taking aim at her with a firearm. He sputtered and fell back. She had this to say about the Bitter Blossom patrons: they certainly didn't treat a woman in a wheelchair with kid gloves.

"Use the pie," yelled Jenny.

Gary crawled over and cupped a piece between two hands. He reached over his head, found Lieutenant Cy's ruddy face and shoved the pie into the largest hole. Cy let go of Gary and hit the floor, clutching his throat and coughing up a spray of blood as the pie tore down his esophagus. Gary stood up and watched over him, looking distressed. Leave it to Gary Cobalt to make it through a stint in the Quag with his strong moral core intact.

"Hey, the pie was coated in your blood," said Jenny, whacking him on the rear with her patu. "He'll be fine. Go." Gary gave her a reproachful look that said he believed she was lying.

The broken-winged fairy Cinnabottom stepped into their path, mumbling in his Bala dialect. Gary reached out and dragged Cinnabottom closer, clamping a hand over his mouth, but this fairy was fully mature. He didn't need to speak the words of the spell out loud for it to take effect. Gary staggered back and collapsed into Jenny's lap.

"Don't do this," he gasped. The fairy raised his arms and Gary's head wrenched sideways at an unnatural angle.

"Ugh, I can't breathe," said Jenny, trying to push him off. But unicorns were nearly as dense as singularity pie and she only succeeded in folding him over in her lap. She was also beginning to suspect that the strong urine smell was coming from his soggy pants.

"I have to get off this planet," said Cinnabottom, holding his open palm over the horn crater. Gary's neck stretched toward it. He strained against the spell and Jenny heard cracks and pops as his vertebrae separated. That fairy could have made a good living as a chiropractor with a little less murderous rage. Then again, she'd been treated by quite a few chiropractors in her day and murderous rage didn't seem to be an absolute disqualifier.

Gary reached out, begging Cinnabottom to stop. The fairy, engrossed in spellcasting, did not notice the hand's proximity to the remaining unbroken wing draped at his side. Jenny did though, and she pushed hard to wheel Gary the last few inches to his target. Gary's fingers closed around the gossamer webbing stretched between the wing's chitinous ribs. Jenny slid her chair backward and Gary pulled; together they caused a sound like thick cardboard tearing, then a snap like the bone of a cooked chicken. The wing came off in Gary's hand, twitching.

Cinnabottom screamed out a curse and the artificial lights winked out, leaving them all bathed in the yellow glow from the windows. The fairy collapsed at Gary's feet. Jenny gripped her wheels and pushed as hard as she could toward the back of the room, Gary's head lolling grotesquely over her shoulder. It was slow going, but at least fewer people were able to land their blows accurately in the dark. A silhouetted figure stepped in front of her chair and put a shiny-toed boot on her footrest to stop her from rolling forward.

"This creature has been placed under arrest."

Jenny looked up to see the officer who had spent the morning downing Gravitas at the bar. He was a tall pink guy whose close shave had speckled his cheeks with tiny cuts. This close, she could finally see the insignia and name tape on his jacket. Colonel Wenck. She should have figured. He carried himself like someone ranked high enough that protocol no longer mattered.

"I've come to collect the fuel source," said Wenck, looking a little off balance. Gravitas went right to your head. Literally.

"He's my fuel source. The ship is mine," said Jenny, jerking her chair to the left to throw him off it.

"This resource belongs to the Reason," he said.

The bloody Reason was always confiscating everything of value and leaving the rest of the galaxy with the leftovers. Under Gary's ass, Jenny tapped out a message on her tablet, hoping the intended recipient would open and read one of her messages for the first time in ten years. She grasped her patu, ready to seize any opening that presented itself.

Cinnabottom ignored the Reason officer and clamped his mouth down on Gary's pant leg, biting through fabric and flesh with the sharp bits of his remaining teeth. Gary lifted his head, wobbling it around like a baby on the separated vertebrae that were still pulling themselves back into position. He slapped Cinnabottom away, but not before the fairy got a mouthful of his blood. Cinnabottom grinned up from the floor, silver dripping down his chin. Damp baby wing nubbins unfurled out of his back. Tiny, but whole.

Ricky yelled from behind her protective phalanx of servers, "You can't confiscate property from inside my bar. We have an arrangement."

The officer used his eyes to flick on his transcript recorder. No one bothered to implant grunts with ocular displays, but a colonel would have full access to all Reason technology. He was about to make an official announcement. Jenny turned her head so that his camera wouldn't pick her face out of the crowd. She didn't think she had any outstanding warrants, but it was never smart to let the camera catch you.

"All Reason-based arrangements with this establishment are null and void. Regulation 56 of the Reason Regulatory Code was enacted at daybreak today. Humans like you," he sneered at Ricky, "are no longer permitted to own property. Let the records show that the Reason has subsumed the Bitter Blossom into its collective holdings and Mr Richard Xiaowen Tang has thirty minutes to vacate the property with his personal belongings."

Ricky's face froze in an expression of disbelief. She clutched the fabric of her dress and balled it up in her fists. Her servers looked back and forth between her and Colonel Wenck, unsure of what to do next. One of them touched her shoulder. She blinked and seemed to come back to herself, smiling calmly at the server and patting his arm.

"I'll be fine. Keep your job for as long as you can, kid. Save up and get off this planet." Ricky stepped toward the officer, her eyes flicking furiously. She was probably moving money out of Blossom accounts and into her own before the Reason locked it all down. That's what Jenny would have done.

"I'll go quietly. Just give me five minutes to pack a bag. A woman's gotta have her shoes, you know." Ricky darted into the back room.

In the Bitter Blossom, now under Reason control, all bets were off. COs that had a moment ago been brawling each other to get near Gary, instead lined up near Colonel Wenck to plead their case for a transfer. The job of bar manager had just opened up, which was far more preferable than guarding prisoners. The few Bala in the room slunk off toward the windows and doors, ducking under the half-lowered blast shields before their bodies could be claimed and confiscated.

Jenny scooted around the colonel, heading for the windows with Gary still on her lap. Wenck dragged her back by the handles of her chair. She saw Jim off in the corner, still struggling with two COs. That man would never pass up an opportunity to punch an officer of the Reason. She gave him a whistle, which meant to get his ass over to her pronto. Whether he did that or not was a 50/50 shot.

"You're not going anywhere," said Wenck, spinning her to face him. "This Bala creature is the property of the Reason. I'm taking it with me."

"It belongs to me," said Jenny. Gary made a low growl at her phrasing. She flicked him in the ear and he went quiet.

"Not for long," said Wenck.

Lieutenant Cy staggered out of the crowd. His uniform jacket had a Rorschach test pattern of blood on the front, but he was alive thanks to Gary. With the price of unicorn blood these days, it was likely the last time that man would ever taste it in his life.

"Sir, I'm not sure if you're aware, but this is the Hero of Copernica Citadel," said Cy, in a surprising display of chivalry.

Wenck didn't miss a beat.

"I don't care if she's the Reverend Fucking Mother of the Sisters of the Supersymmetrical Axion. This Bala is coming with me."

Jim sauntered over to Jenny's side, wiping the blood off his knuckles and onto his denim trousers. Wenck and Cy sized him up instantly as a harmless old spacer without a rank. They were kind of right, but also not. Jim could be dangerous. Most often when he didn't mean to be. It wasn't as if she kept him around for his winning personality.

Gary's neck had reassembled itself and he sat up. Jenny shoved his head back down so she could get a good view of Wenck. He had apparently come all the way here from Reason Command at Fort Jaisalmer to pick up Gary personally. The unicorn should have been flattered. These high-ranking guys never traveled to shitty planets like this. Especially not with strict horn rationing in effect. Turns out, if you slaughter all of the unicorns, you won't have horn to power your FTL drives. Simple math.

The tablet in Jenny's lap vibrated. She couldn't see the response under Gary's rear end, but she knew it was good news when the entire bar lit up with a bright light from outside. She could see every shaving nick on Wenck's face as beams of light roved over his body and came to rest on the ribbons right above his heart.

"What is that?" he asked, shading his eyes.

Jenny pulled Jim down to the floor by the back of his shirt.

"That's our ride," she said. Her tablet buzzed again and this time she reached under Gary's ass and tapped it. She pushed her face into Gary's back and held Jim's head below the level of her armrests.

Everyone standing, including Colonel Wenck and Lieutenant Cy, flew back into the far wall, landing in a pile of tangled bodies on the floor. It was a nonlethal blast – because Jenny did not have the time or energy to outrun a murder charge – but everyone in that pile would be coming out a little toastier than when they started. In the chaos of the blast, the bartender slipped out the front door with two immense bottles under his arms.

"Get up. Time to go," said Jenny, pushing Gary off her lap and rolling toward what remained of the Blossom's back wall.

Jim looked up at her.

"I need a little help," he said. Jenny rolled her eyes and motioned for Gary to take Jim's hand and pull. The men looked at each other without moving for a couple of seconds that they did not have to spare.

"Dammit you two, we need to leave *now*," she said. Gary held out a strong brown hand. Jim put his bony pale one into it and pulled himself up with an unsuccessfully stifled grunt. There weren't too many more years of life left in Jim, but she intended to keep him moving for as long as possible. It was the least she could do to make up for what had happened to his wife, Cheryl Ann.

Jenny wheeled through the mess of glass and blown-out wood. The full brightness of the *Jaggery*'s spotlights blasted them in the face. She waved at the ship and the exterior lights snapped off. A line of six purple circles dotted her vision. Jim stepped around the corner of the building and picked up the two duffel bags that contained everything they owned in the world. She liked to say she was a minimalist, but really they were simply too poor to have much to their names. There had been a time, not too long ago, when they'd sold off used clothes and food stores to make rent on the shuttle. But things were about to change. She could feel it.

The *Jaggery* hovered a few meters off the sandy ground, leaving the air around it silent and undisturbed. Stoneship design was an engineering marvel. No other species in the galaxy could understand, let alone replicate, it. It looked like a giant rock, but the internal mechanics were so complex and enigmatic that most humans couldn't determine if they were based on technology or magic. As far as Jenny was concerned, as long as the ship went where she told it to go, she didn't care what powered it.

The *Jaggery*'s passenger ramp lowered to meet them and Jenny nudged Gary forward in front of her. Jim dumped the duffels in her lap and took the handles of her chair to push. She usually told him off for that, but her arms ached from dragging Gary around and whacking at pieces of singularity pie.

Jim leaned down, letting his old man breath waft into Jenny's ear. She tried to stifle a gag and ended up coughing to cover it. She leaned as far away from him as she could, but he insisted on coming closer.

"So he won the ship?" he asked.

"He did, but Ricky put it in my name. Gary can't own property any more."

Jim laughed bitterly. When they'd made it halfway up the ramp, a voice called out from behind them. "I'm coming with you."

Jim let go of the chair and Jenny started to roll backward. She grabbed her wheels and turned around. Ricky Tang struggled to pull four oversized suitcases through the debris of her destroyed bar. Jenny started to wave her off, but the suitcases clinked like a dozen bottles were rolling around inside. Jenny was suddenly interested in the prospect of taking on a passenger.

"How much?" Jenny asked, acutely aware of two facts. Number one, she had leverage over Ricky Tang for the first time in her life. And number two, the Reason officers in the bar were starting to climb out of the wreckage of the Bitter Blossom. Instead of feeling vindicated by her newfound power, it made her nervous. Like she was walking on a tightrope, trying not to fall. Ricky spent every moment of the day negotiating, cajoling, and leveraging. Jenny was far outclassed by that kind of social engineering. She was much better at the whack-and-grab school of negotiation and the unambiguous lines of programming within Reason systems.

"A bottle of angel tears," said Ricky, and Jenny scoffed.

"Those were mine anyway. It goes without saying that I want them back."

Ricky parked her suitcases and rested her hand on one of them protectively. In the stress of the moment, she wasn't being careful with her tells.

"I want that suitcase," said Jenny, knowing she'd hit the jackpot when Ricky's forehead creased. Ricky glanced behind her at the smoking wreck of her bar. Wenck was on his feet, barking orders and climbing over injured patrons. Now that Ricky no longer had the protection of her agreements with the local Reason officers, the bounty on her crimes would be collected posthaste.

"Fine," she said quietly. "But don't open it until we get into orbit."

Jenny spun around and continued wheeling herself up

the ramp. Jim was too mesmerized by the clinking suitcases to help her out, but that was fine. You didn't go fifteen years in a chair without developing a hefty set of biceps.

As Jenny pushed up into the cargo hold, a red-bearded dwarf stepped into her path, joined by two slightly smaller dwarves. She nodded to Jenny; an intentional breach of protocol. She should have been down on one knee for her captain, but Jenny let it slide. She intended to be a kinder version of the woman who'd run this ship last time, starting with the way she treated the Bala who ran it.

"Welcome aboard, Captain. Hello, Cowboy Jim," said the dwarf coolly. No matter how many times Jenny told that woman, she always insisted that "Cowboy" was a title. Jim never complained. He probably liked it, even though he hadn't been an actual cowboy since he was a teenager back in the States. Back when there were states.

"Hey Boges," said Jenny. "Good to see you're still running things around here. I'm sure that means we're ready to take off any second now." The dwarf seemed surprised Jenny had bothered to remember her name.

"Yes, Captain."

Boges spotted Gary and her left knee began to bend. Jenny saw her catch herself and nod instead.

"Welcome home, Captain," said the dwarf, her voice hitching. Gary tugged on one of the dwarf's russet braids that nearly matched the color of his skin. It was tough for humans to tell the female from the male dwarves. They both had braids and they both had beards. It was safest to simply ask.

"It's good to be back, Boges," Gary replied.

"It's been a long time," she said. She kept searching his face, probably looking for signs that he was the same man as the one who was dragged away so long ago. Jenny hoped for her sake that he wasn't.

"Let's get underway," said Jenny, hearing Wenck's voice carrying out of the Blossom.

Boges turned to her with a pained expression. "Should I prepare the restraints?" she asked. Everyone watched for Jenny's reaction. This was a question she had not been prepared for. She assumed Gary would come willingly and be part of the crew. It didn't occur to her that she'd need to restrain him again. Her stomach turned at the idea.

Boges read her hesitation as an affirmative and set her lips in a thin angry line. Gary rubbed his forehead. Jim nodded, clearly willing her to say yes. She needed all of their cooperation to complete the delivery for the Sisters, but she couldn't possibly appease them all. She didn't want to hear Gary's anguished screams again as long as she lived, but she'd understand if he didn't want to cooperate. It would serve her right if he simply ate her out of spite.

Jim stuck an elbow into Jenny's shoulder to nudge an answer out of her. That settled it. If there was one thing you could count on these days, it was that whatever Cowboy Jim decided was probably the worst course of action you could possibly take.

"No thank you, Boges," she said. "Gary has agreed to power the FTL willingly." She looked over to confirm. Gary stopped rubbing his head and nodded. Boges' sausage fingers patted her knee.

"I do agree to power the drive," said Gary. "However..."

"Always a catch," said Jim, shaking his head in disgust.

"I have only enough horn growth to get us halfway through the Scutum-Crux Arm. Unless we don't mind being stranded at sublight speeds near Alicante 8, we will need to stock up on bones or trisicles. Lest we strand ourselves between systems... as we have in the past."

Cowboy Jim spat on the floor of the ramp. One of the smaller dwarves took out a rag and wiped it up.

"Goddamn horse-man," said Jim, "You're just dying to murder someone else, aren't you?"

CHAPTER SIX
FTL Jaggery

Gary stepped into the cargo hold of the *Jaggery* and closed the door behind him. The familiar smell of his stoneship had nearly incapacitated him with a flood of relief. For ten years, he'd dreamed of this moment. It had kept him going when all he'd wanted to do was give up. Of course, he hadn't imagined returning with the two people who had held him captive all that time ago, but, by Unamip, he was home.

Gary ran his fingers across the bare stone wall of the hold. When the ship had been his, there had been a thick layer of moss on the floor and all manner of flowering vines clinging to the walls. All of the ship's foliage had been torn out by Jenny after Copernica, but it still smelled faintly of soil.

Jim rushed toward the cockpit to prepare for takeoff, but Jenny stopped her wheelchair and waited for Gary.

"Come on. We need you up front," she said.

"What do you need him for?" asked Jim incredulously.

"To pilot the ship," she replied.

"That's what I'm here for. Best pilot in the system," said Jim.

Jenny closed her eyes and began again in a softer tone, one reserved for children about to have a tantrum.

"Jim, the ship has been dormant for ten years and I don't know if it'll even talk to the new tablets. I need Gary up front to watch the Bala controls. You and I don't know what any of them mean. Start us on a heading toward the pickup coordinates and we'll be right behind you."

Jim let out a great harrumph and stomped off down the hall. Ricky rolled her four huge suitcases along behind him.

"Where's my room? Is there a suite I can reserve? Or a penthouse? I heard this place has a pool," she said. Jim grumbled something that Gary couldn't hear, but made Ricky gasp.

"You don't have to be rude," she said, tiptoeing over the metal grating on the floor so her heels didn't sink in. Boges' dwarves followed Ricky, pointing out the way to the crew quarters. With only Jenny, Boges, and himself, the cargo hold quieted.

"Do you really want me to pilot the ship?" asked Gary. The last time he was here, Jenny had kept him chained in his room. He wasn't prepared to trust her yet.

"Absolutely. And the Sisters want to speak to you at the pickup location," she said.

"The Sisters asked for me by name?" he asked.

"Yeah. They made it abundantly clear that I was to get you on the *Jaggery* by any means necessary. You don't think I wanted you here for your fashion sense?" Jenny asked, gesturing to his ragged, damp prison uniform. He blinked at her attempt at humor. He didn't find many things very funny any more.

"So you came to my aid at the request of the Sisters," he said.

"Yes, and because..." She faltered and stopped.

It certainly wasn't an apology or even an admission of guilt, but there was an expectancy about Jenny that spoke of a consideration for his feelings that had not been there previously. Last time around, she had barked orders at him. And when he failed to comply, she stopped speaking to him altogether and simply treated him like an animal.

The cargo hold shook as the ship lifted away from Broome City. Boges stayed nearby, watching protectively over Gary.

"No one's getting locked up on this trip," said Jenny. "It's all going down nice and easy."

"Why don't you explain to me how it's all *going down*," said Gary, crossing his arms across his chest. Jenny lifted her hands in mock surrender.

"Listen, I don't even want your ship. You can have it back after we make this delivery. You have my word."

Gary scoffed so hard he nearly choked. Jenny's cheeks went red.

"I get it, I really do. You have no reason to trust me. Back there when Ricky deeded me the *Jaggery*, I could have just rolled out of that bar and left you to Colonel Wenck. But I didn't. I made sure you got out too."

"Along with horn to power your FTL drive," finished Gary.

"There is that. Listen, besides your horn and the Sisters' request, I genuinely wanted you along. I know you only have a bit of horn, but I saved up enough cash to make a stop at Beywey for trisicles. There's just enough time for you to grow us the fuel to Fort Jaisalmer. I have it all planned out to the minute. It'll work perfectly."

"What task have the Sisters hired you for?" he asked.

"A simple delivery. A pair of boxes to Fort J in time for the Century Summit. That's it. Very easy."

Nothing was ever "very easy" where the Sisters were concerned. There was always an ulterior motive. Their order had its own FTL ship and enough horn to power it for several lifetimes. It made no sense to contract the *Jaggery* for such a mission. It meant they were moving people like pieces on a chessboard, getting them in position to coax a particular outcome into being. It was a dangerous game, playing with the future.

Jenny must have seen his skepticism, because she let out a heavy sigh.

"I need you to get me to Fort J." She let her fingertips drift across her tablet, swiping through pages without looking at them. "Last year, during a regular cargo run, the Reason picked up Kaila. They said her papers were out of date, but they weren't. I checked them myself." She rubbed her eyes. All of the exhaustion of the last ten years had gathered there. "I don't even know if she's alive any more, but I have to get back there and look."

"I'm sorry to hear it." It was the truth. Jenny's wife Kaila had been one of the few kind souls who came aboard with Jenny last time. He wished no ill toward the tree spirit, even if she was married to a bully. A lot of families had been torn apart by harsh Reason penalties for intermarriage between humans and Bala, including his own.

"They brought her to the harvesting center," continued Jenny. "With no access to an FTL drive, I haven't been able to get back to Fort J."

Certainly not with horn rationing in effect. No one but the Reason was able to get horn these days. Kaila had been taken from Gymnoverium as a young tree and Jenny had rescued her from an auction. Cheryl Ann had told him every detail about their story. As overbearing as Jenny was, she and Kaila had been inseparable for thirteen years. He'd been there for their wedding. As a captive on the ship, not as a guest, of course.

"Yeah, so. I could use your help getting back there." She twisted her hands in her lap.

"I'll get you to Fort Jaisalmer," he said. "And then you'll give me back my ship."

"Deal," said Jenny, wheeling toward the cockpit. "I need to get up there before Jim flies us into a jetliner or a mountain."

Gary followed her through the stone hallways toward the

cockpit. Boges followed at his heels.

"We attempted to replace all of the flora and fauna while in storage," the dwarf said, apologetically. "But we contracted a blight during year three, which wiped out most of the basic feed crops. We were able to breed a strain of foxberries with resistance, but the pin flowers didn't fare as well. I have seeds in stasis, but it's not worth germinating them until the bayfly population comes back. And they're not surviving on the lake at the moment. I believe the vek population has expanded too far. The gravity load is too much. So we decided to keep the foxberries in the hothouses until we can fix the lake. I'm wondering if it would be prudent to begin replanting the hallways, now that you're back on board."

Gary recognized the last sentence as a question, asked in the exceedingly roundabout style of a subordinate addressing her captain. The delicate dance of her words amused him. He had become used to orders barked in his ear and screamed across rooms. No one had bothered to consider his feelings in a long time. He'd almost forgotten that his opinion mattered at all.

"Yes, replant everything," he replied, continuing to walk. Boges grumbled discontentedly.

"What is it?" he asked, turning to watch her while they walked.

"You speak differently now," said Boges. "Your words sound short and harsh, like theirs." She waved at Jenny, who had wheeled ahead of them. Gary laughed.

"My dearest Boges. I offer you my heartfelt apology. Living among the humans for so long has stunted my capacity for compassion and reason."

They both smirked at his little jab at the Reason. Perhaps he hadn't lost his sense of humor after all, it had simply transformed.

"I may sound like a human, but I am still the same man you knew." Even as he spoke the sentence out loud, Gary realized it was not true. He was not the same at all. Cooperating with Jenny and Jim would have been unthinkable to the man he was before. He would have gotten them on board, then ripped out their soft throats. Today, he simply wanted a change of clothes and perhaps a nap. "Replanting the halls is a splendid idea. The faster we can get the ship self-sustaining, the faster we can head for openspace and leave the Reason behind."

"You realize, Captain, that the living layer on the stone will make the hallways difficult to navigate," said Boges.

Gary knew exactly what she meant. He had agreed to allow Jenny to own his ship, but he had not agreed to make the hallways passable for her wheelchair. He was trying to live forgiveness through all of his actions, but occasionally he still felt like screwing with humans as retribution for their treatment of him.

"Boges, Captain Jenny will simply have to ask Unamip for the blessing of those with limited mobility. A healthy ship requires soil on the floor. I'm sure she will understand. And on your behalf, I will ask his blessing for those with limited resources. I hope that when we exit Reasonspace and I take control of the *Jaggery*, we'll have the opportunity to restock all of our supplies."

Gary knew that Boges did not like when he prayed for her, but she never asked him to stop. She had her own dwarven demigod that she invoked when the situation warranted it. Other than that, she didn't speak of matters like prayer. Dwarves were intensely protective of their private lives, inviting very few people into their inner circle. Cheryl Ann had been the only human asked to join their secret ceremonies in the heart of the ship. It was an honor that even he had only been offered a handful of times.

"I look forward to seeing the blight-resistant foxberries," said Gary.

Boges nodded and opened a dwarf door in the wall, tucking herself into one of the many tunnels and rooms carved into the structure of the ship. The service pathways of Halcyon-class stoneships were sized for tiny folk like pixies and dwarves, but dwarves were the best candidates for maintenance jobs. Pixies and their short attention spans were clumsy with mechanical tasks. Not to mention that their bodies were too fragile for lifting heavy engine parts or tolerating the extreme temperatures of space.

He turned the corner and saw Jenny down the hall, pushing open the cockpit door. She held it open with one hand, scraped her chair through with the other, and let it close behind her. The same hallway also housed the crew quarters, including the room where they had held him prisoner and where Cheryl Ann had died.

Gary had devoted many sleepless nights in the Quag to imagining how it would feel to come back to this spot on the *Jaggery*. He expected all that thinking to have prepared him for this moment, but sadness hit him like a punch, stopping him in his tracks and taking his breath away. He paused with his hand on the wall, not daring to get any closer to the scene of the crime.

Down the hall, the cockpit door opened and Jim came out carrying a tablet with the takeoff checklist. He stopped and called to Gary.

"Aren't you going to settle into your bunk?" he asked with a cold smile. Gary felt the blood drain from his face. Of course Jim would force him to sleep in his old room. He wanted Gary to relive the horror of his crime every time he closed his eyes. What Jim didn't know was that he already relived that night endlessly, no matter where he bedded down. He kept his expression stoic, betraying none of his anger and disgust.

He sauntered down the hallway toward Jim as if lying in murder rooms was something that he did every day.

Jim seemed stymied by Gary's lack of reaction. The wrinkles around his eyes deepened into dark crevices. Even though he knew that humans aged relatively quickly, Jim looked worse than most human men would have in his sixties. The stress of Cheryl Ann's absence had worn him down like water over a rock, carving deep lines into his face. That man had seen some hard living while Gary was gone.

"You'll burn in hell, you vile creature," said Jim, quietly so that the dwarves in the walls would not hear. Even Jim knew it was folly to get on their bad side. He lifted his tablet. Gary thought he was showing him the takeoff checklist. Instead, he slapped Gary across the face with it. Then again, maybe Jim didn't know anything at all about getting along.

Years ago, Gary would have returned the slap with a jab hard enough to put the man on the ground. He would have kicked and bitten until Jim begged for mercy. But today he was tired. Even if Jim made him sleep in a room marked with death and pain, he wouldn't ever go back to the Quag.

"You do what you need to do, Jim. I'll be finishing this delivery," he said. The stinging in his cheek was already gone.

Ricky barreled out of a nearby room, still dragging her suitcases behind her.

"I don't like this room. Aren't there any crew quarters with windows? Maybe a bathtub?" she asked.

"End of the hall, there's one with a view," said Jim. "No bathtubs though. You know we're going into space, right? The big open place without gravity. Hey, I heard some bottles in that bag of yours," he added, following her down the hall.

"You buying?" she asked over her shoulder. "Because this isn't a not-for-profit suitcase."

"I'm buying," said Jim.

"Gary, you come too. I have a gift for you."

Gary couldn't imagine what Ricky Tang could possibly have for him. He was understandably wary after that morning in the bar. It was likely a trick. She saw his hesitation.

"Oh come on, Gary. You can't hold the Blossom against me. I have a business to run."

"*Had* a business to run," said Jim.

"You're a kind fellow, aren't you?" Ricky's words dripped sarcasm.

"I lived one way my whole life, I'm not going to change now," said Jim.

"I have just the drink for you," she said, with a sly smile.

She opened the door to the last cabin in the row and ushered both of them in after her. It smelled like old sweat. The previous occupant had only cleared out about half of their personal items. Soiled clothing was strewn on the furniture, as if someone had packed in a hurry. A few dishes piled on a table had a powdery residue, which might have been food when the ship first went into storage. At this point, it was nearly a living civilization. Ricky wrinkled her nose.

"What a mess."

"They didn't let the dwarves clean the cabins. Evidence of a crime," said Jim with a glance at Gary.

Ricky set her suitcases on the bed and unzipped one. She flicked a dirty sock off the night stand and set down a bottle of dark purple liquid and a small glass.

"Cash or trade?" she asked.

"Trade."

"I'm curious to see what a man like you brings to the table," said Ricky, waiting for the offer.

"Be right back," said Jim, heading toward his quarters.

Ricky opened another suitcase and pulled out piles of clothing. There were more glittering, pointy shoes than Gary had ever seen in his life, and his mother had quite a collection herself. They didn't look comfortable in the least.

But there were also two pairs of spaceworthy boots and a few sets of soft booties that Reasoners preferred in zero G environments.

"You're hovering, Gary," said Ricky, shaking the wrinkles out of a silvery cocktail dress. If a formal dinner broke out unexpectedly, Ricky was prepared to attend. She set it aside and unfolded a crimson flight suit that looked like it had never been worn.

"Is that–" started Gary.

"Never you mind," said Ricky, tucking the jumpsuit away and pulling out the plain khaki overalls of a non-Reason spacer. She had an outfit for every occasion. Whether they found themselves on a spacewalk or at a state dinner, Ricky Tang would be prepared.

"You said you had something for me," said Gary.

"Oh. Right." She dug into one of the bags and pulled out a small box with a crank on top. "I know I only have to pay Jenny for the ride, but it feels like bad karma to keep an item that belonged to your mother and not give it to you."

Gary took the box, unsure of what it was and what to do with it. He pulled open the drawer at the bottom and the aroma of his mother's masala dosa wafted up at him.

"What is this?" he asked, unable to conceal the amazement in his voice.

"It's an old spice grinder. It belonged to your mother during her time on the *Cristobal*. It's possible it came from her mother before her. Sure smells like it."

"And how did you come into its possession?" Gary asked, ready to hear a story about shady backroom deals and poker games gone wrong.

"Just a simple estate sale that I handled through my antiquities business. I ended up with a lot of relics from the *Cristobal* after they renovated the pioneer museum on Chhatrapati Shivaji Station. They wanted big symbols of human space exploration, not trinkets from home. Your mother's job as an ambassador of Earth meant that she had a lot of antiques in her cabin. Incredible stuff."

"What else do you have?" Gary had so few items from his past. Most of them were buried in the wreckage of Copernica Citadel. Ricky could give him access to an entire museum's worth of family history.

"Alas, big guy, I had to leave most of it back at the Blossom when we bugged out. If any of my servers are kept on staff, they'll probably preserve anything that the Reason doesn't use or destroy. Maybe they'll send it along to wherever I end up."

Jim came back into the room with a stack of worn currency. Ricky counted through it with practiced fingers and stuffed half the paper back into Jim's breast pocket.

"This'll do. I'm so grateful for the ride that I'm not even inflating prices that much." She poured out two fingers of a purple drink and handed it to Jim. He moved to take a sip and she put her hand over the rim of the glass.

"Oh no. Not here. Take that to your cabin. Drink it while sitting down. And bring back the glass."

"What is it?"

"Let's just say, prepare to meet your maker." Jim seemed think it was a euphemism. He lifted the glass in a salute and left her quarters.

"I wonder what god Jim is going to see," Ricky mused.

"And I am curious what they will say to him," finished Gary.

Ricky sat back on her bed.

"You know how lucky you were to get out of the Blossom, right?" she asked.

"I don't believe in luck," said Gary.

"Fair enough. But having Jenny there in time to grab you before the Reason swooped in, that was brilliant."

"Wasn't my idea."

Ricky's brow furrowed.

"Huh. Jenny fucking Perata. Considering the situation, it probably went as well as it could have."

"She destroyed your bar."

"That bar wasn't going to be mine after today anyway. I knew that law was coming down from Fort J soon. Why do you think I had my funds liquid and these suitcases packed? I was leaving on the *Jaggery* today no matter who was at the helm."

The intercom system crackled to life.

"Gary, get up here," said Jenny.

"The captain calls." Ricky started pulling old books out of her bag and stacking them on the bedside table.

"Don't let Jenny see those," said Gary as he turned to leave. "She thinks books are a fire hazard."

In the cockpit, Boges had already removed the captain's chair to make room for Jenny's wheelchair. It slid neatly between the co-pilot's spot and the wall. As Gary walked in, she was trying to lock the wheels into place with a set of clamps anchored to the floor. Her fingertips barely grazed the top of the clasp. Jim was nowhere to be seen.

"Would you like me do it?" Gary asked.

Jenny sat back in her chair.

"Yeah. Thanks."

He knelt down and snapped the clamps around her wheels.

"You smell terrible," she said. "You need to change before we meet the Sisters. I think all of your old clothes are still in your room."

She tapped the screen of the tablet that had been jury-rigged to interface with the ship's Bala systems. It was as crude as sewing a ballgown with a chopstick, his mother would have said, but it worked well enough to get the ship airborne and pointed in the right direction.

"Where are we meeting the Sisters?" he asked.

"Out in the Little Sandy Desert," Jenny replied.

"Not a lot out there."

"Exactly."

They were just outside of Broome City. An unbroken line of reddish dunes rolled by on the cockpit viewscreen. Most of the vegetation on this part of Earth had died off when average temperatures climbed past fifty degrees, and that was before the generation ships had departed. Humans stopped measuring after that. It was so hot out there that equipment malfunctioned and melted in the sun, especially machines designed for the deep freeze of space. It was unlikely they'd encounter any Reason patrols in this area.

"I thought the Sisters had a good working relationship with the Reason?" asked Gary.

"Not so much these days. They were accused of helping a faction of anti-Reason activists a few years back. The Reason nearly executed one of the Sisters for the crime. It's been tense since then," said Jenny.

"Are they part of a resistance movement?"

Jenny bobbed her head back and forth indecisively.

"It's hard to tell. The Sisters are playing a long game, but for the amount they're paying to keep this delivery off regular Reason shuttle routes, it's safe to say they're moving something critically important to the Century Summit."

"Hm."

Even in the Quag, the Century Summit was all anyone could talk about. Lifers who had no chance of ever getting there talked endlessly about what it would be like to be at Fort J when creatures from all over the galaxy gathered for the big event. The humans saw it as their chance to prove how much progress they had made in the last hundred years. According to their measure of success, they'd expanded to six new planets in the century since they'd abandoned Earth. It didn't matter to them that those planets were already occupied.

The Bala were equally excited for the Summit. They planned to plead their case to the godlike Pymmie who had brokered the alliance between humans and their kind. Gary heard furtive whisperings that the Pymmie were sure to be angry that the humans had gone back on their part of the deal, colonizing instead of cooperating. The Bala were prepared to demand justice.

For the most part, humans were treating the Summit like a massive celebration. Corrections officers had saved up leave for years in order to head to Jaisalmer for the largest party in the known universe. While walking the yard, the COs had made gleeful bets over which one of them would end up in the hospital first. Gary had intended to stay far away from the Summit and its human revelers. Now, he seemed to be headed right for the center of the storm.

"See what you can figure out from the Bala controls," said Jenny, waving him toward the rear of the cockpit. "The ship feels stiff, but I can't tell why."

The room had been reconfigured for human use, with chairs and a touchscreen connected with wires. When unicorns were in charge, they steered the ship using a series of vials and tubes that had been fused with the wall. Gary tapped a glass tube full of liquid that had the consistency of vomit. It should have been crystal clear. The ship was in bad shape.

"I'm cutting you in on the proceeds of the delivery, a third each to you, me, and Jim. And when we get out of Reasonspace you can have the *Jaggery* back," said Jenny. "After we load the cargo, we'll head into orbit and make a stop at Beywey for some trisicles. If the live animal dealer Bào Zhú doesn't have any we'll have to go all the way out to

Soliloquy Station, which will take days. And we don't have days."

She was right. The Summit was scheduled to begin in twenty-five hours. He understood why she'd planned this mission down to the minute.

"You haven't left much extra time in case something goes wrong," he said. Jenny groaned.

"Don't say things like that. You'll jinx us." She knocked on the side of the carved wooden club she always carried with her.

"I'm simply saying that you can't count on everything going according to plan," he said.

"Then we'll make a new plan."

Gary could see where the interface with the tablet was irritating the ship like an open sore. It appeared as a plume of hot gas streaming past a glass lens in the stone. All of the human modifications needed to be torn out for the ship to operate at one hundred per cent efficiency again, but he doubted that Jenny would agree to that. Before long, however, he'd be able to get the *Jaggery* back to what it once was. Jenny tapped on her tablet and Gary saw the order come through his instruments to increase speed.

"What's wrong?" he asked.

"A few ships took off from Broome City around the same time we did. One of them is following us south," she said, opening the intercom.

"Jim, where did you get to?" she asked.

"He's getting drunk in his cabin," said Gary.

"Bloody hell. We are not on this ship ten minutes…"

"And he hit me," said Gary.

Jenny was unmoved.

"Gary, you ate his wife. You're lucky I packed all of his antique six shooters into my bag. You'd be sitting here with a hole in your head."

"I already have a hole in my head."

She chuckled.

"After the stop at Beywey, we'll use the little bit of horn you have to jump us out of Earth's vicinity. You can eat the trisicles and start regrowing enough horn to get us to Fairyfloss Checkpoint."

"What's that?" he asked. A lot had changed while he'd been gone.

"You can't get into Reasonspace without going through a checkpoint any more. Fairyfloss is the main entry point. It's pretty busy on a normal day. Today, the day before the Summit, it's going to be pandemonium. There's no way they can board and inspect all of the ships coming through. We'll sail into Reasonspace without a second glance. The FTL from Fairyfloss to Jaisalmer is just a matter of hours. We might even have time to spare."

"It's a very ambitious plan," said Gary. If just one thing went wrong, they could lose precious hours fixing the problem. The readouts in front of him showed a ship that was teetering on the edge of malfunction. Stoneships were living biomes that operated in synergy with the creatures living within them. After ten years in storage, the machinery might work fine, but the heart of the ship was sick with loneliness.

"Maybe Boges can find some rats nesting in the walls so you can get a head start on growing horn," said Jenny. Gary cringed. There was an outraged sound from behind the dwarf door in the wall of the cockpit. Boges was still watching over him.

"There are no rats in my walls," called Boges indignantly from behind the door.

"I'm sure there aren't," said Jenny. "Which is why we'd better hope that Bào Zhú has a supply of trisicles."

"Humph," said Boges, stomping away down the hall.

Gary took off his baseball cap and rubbed the rough patch where his horn should have been. There was a little jagged spot that he could feel with his fingertips. A sharp outcropping where his body was attempting to regrow layers of dense horn.

Jenny eased the *Jaggery* to a stop at a desolate spot in the desert. Bare branches of dead trees poked out of the ground like fingers reaching toward the sky. There was no other ship in sight, but the Bala controls in front of Gary hummed excitedly, indicating they were in the presence of another stoneship.

The Sisters of the Supersymmetrical Axion flew the FTL *Redshift*, which was a sibling to the *Jaggery*.

"I don't see them," said Jenny. Her dull human instruments weren't picking up any other ship in the area.

"They're invisible," said Gary.

The two stoneships began conversing in a harmonic language older than unicorns. Gary couldn't translate most of it, but there seemed to be a lot of complaining on the part of the *Jaggery*. Human ears couldn't pick up the frequency, but Jenny tilted her head as if straining to hear someone speaking in the distance. A woman's voice came out of the tablet.

"You're being followed, *Jaggery*."

"Hey there, *Redshift*. I'm aware. Let's meet on the surface before he gets here," Jenny replied.

"No time. We'll teleport the cargo directly onto your ship."

Jenny sat bolt upright.

"No, that is a bad idea, *Redshift*. The last time we tried teleportation–"

"Boges knows what to do. Have Gary meet us in the hold," replied the *Redshift* and the comm clicked off.

"I guess that's the end of the discussion," said Jenny. Boges came over the ship's intercom.

"Gary, the Sisters are in the cargo hold. They say you have sixty-seven seconds to join them in here before the apocalypse starts."

CHAPTER SEVEN
The Sisters of the Supersymmetrical Axion

Gary had once been advised that if he inadvertently found himself in a room with the Sisters of the Supersymmetrical Axion, the best course of action was to stand very still and hope that he was not the one they had come to kill. He ran to the hold as fast as he could, dodging dwarves who had already started laying fresh soil in the hallways. The Sisters were known to be volatile and capricious. Their objectives were often so far in the future that their present actions did not always make sense.

They were ostensibly a religious order, which gave them exemptions from searches, seizures, and the majority of Reason laws; however, their allegiance was not wholly transparent. They undertook a significant number of jobs for the Reason, but Gary was under the impression that they only did that to direct scrutiny away from their tiny cloister on the waterlogged planet of Varuna. In reality, their loyalty rested with the Pymmie. The same almighty Pymmie who had brokered a tenuous peace between the humans and the Bala one hundred years ago and who were arriving in just over a day.

All beings, no matter what planet they hailed from, harbored a deep inborn dread of the Pymmie. Which was a shame because, as far as Gary could see, the Pymmie harbored no ill will toward anyone. They were simply scientists. Granted, they could also disintegrate a galaxy with a single thought, but they were rigorous in their data collection just the same.

Survey a thousand cultures from throughout the universe and each would have terrifying stories about thin grey aliens with huge black eyes who visited their planet to poke at them. The Pymmie were only a meter tall, but able to control space, time, and matter with alarming proficiency. You could see the intelligence behind their murky eyes, but also a horrifying indifference. They simply went about their grand experiments without concerning themselves with trivial matters like suffering. The Pymmie were not particularly clandestine with their experiments, the same way that an entomologist would not bother to conceal her presence from an ant.

Humans had encountered the Pymmie throughout their history, but it was not until a hundred and fifty years ago, around the time of the mass exodus from Earth, that the Pymmie had endeavored to make direct contact. They offered plans for generation ships to a human culture that had barely started to harness the power of the sun and wind. Predictably, the results were less than optimal. Most of the ships failed due to engineering mistakes or because two hundred thousand lives were placed in the hands of the lowest bidder.

Gary's mother had been on the *Cristobal*, one of the first ships to leave Earth. It limped toward a habitable planet for decades, only to find that a faster generation ship – one that had left after them – had made it to the new planet first. The *Cristobal* arrived to a tense situation as human colonists wrangled with the planet's magical Bala natives. His mother had stepped in to mitigate tensions between the two civilizations, but the divisions eventually escalated to open warfare. The Pymmie again stepped in and forced an uneasy truce, vowing to return in a hundred years to evaluate the progress of the alliance.

Gary had grown up watching his mother's attempts to steer humankind toward cooperation until she finally gave up and simply joined the Bala in the fight. He hoped the Pymmie would realize the destruction humans had wrought in the last century, but he was not confident that their solution would be pleasant for anyone.

Boges waited in the cargo hold. She chattered instructions as Gary walked to the back of the room where the Sisters stood at attention.

"There are just four of them, but they are decidedly on edge. Do not make any sudden moves. We already locked the cargo down, but the Sisters have a message for you that they insist on delivering in person," she said.

Gary stopped next to two immense boxes that had been tethered to the floor. Four Sisters waited for his arrival, all wearing crimson flight suits and matching red veils. The Sisters could see out, but no one could see in. Three were bipedal and the fourth had a human woman's torso atop a horse's body. Centaurs were renowned for being devastatingly powerful fighters, but they were mercurial and rarely followed orders. They also disliked unicorns with a red-hot hate.

"You called for me?" he asked.

The smallest bipedal Sister stepped up to him, holding out a red envelope.

"Gary Cobalt, this message is for you."

Gary's heart pounded as he took the heavy cardstock. No one used paper to convey messages any longer, and certainly fancy cards like this were a thing of the distant past. One of the few people who had continued such a wasteful practice after the ships had left Earth was his mother. The envelope was worn at the edges and warped from dried water damage. It felt fragile, as if the paper might snap in half if he folded it. He held it by one corner as if it might bite him.

The handwriting on the outside of the envelope was the proper tidy cursive of his mother's hand.

Do Not Open Until Christmas

"How long have you had this?" he asked.

"It has been in the possession of the Sisters for sixty-nine years."

"Nice," said the centaur. The tiny Sister's veiled head tilted at her.

"This is my mother's writing. Which Christmas does she mean?" asked Gary. "Now or sixty-nine years ago?"

The small Sister shrugged. "Our instructions say to deliver the card to you in person, on this ship, at this location, along with this specific cargo."

"I don't know what's in these boxes. They're not mine," he said.

The Sister looked up at the largest Sister, a tall and broad woman who stood with arms across her chest. She made a small motion with her hand.

"They sort of are yours. Don't open the boxes early, but you should be there when the locks pop," said the smallest Sister.

"You mentioned an apocalypse?" he asked, trying to sound casual.

"It's coming," said the small Sister. "But the form it will take has not yet been determined. As arranged, this cargo must make it to Fort Jaisalmer in time for the Century Summit. The temporal geolock on the boxes is not to be tampered with or there will be injuries. The boxes will open automatically if they are in the correct location at the appointed time."

"You could deliver these yourself with far less trouble," said Gary. "We barely have enough horn to make it out of this system."

"The tenuous relationship between the Sisters and the Reason has broken down. The *Redshift* cannot even fully materialize in this universe without being fired upon. You'll have to do the best you can with what you have," she said.

"Of all foreseeable futures, the best outcome results from you, Captain Perata, James Bryant, and Ricky Tang all being aboard for the trip to Jaisalmer," said the tall Sister. "But the outcome is tenuous and ever-changing. Do your best, work together, and perhaps most of you will live."

There was a soft buzzing from near the Sisters.

"We need to leave," said the centaur. The tiny one lifted her hands to shoulder level, palms upward. Purple lightning streaked from her fingers and encased all the Sisters in a glowing electric cage. Gary stepped back. This was necromancer magic, absolutely illegal throughout the Reason. Not even the Bala wanted to be near it. All the necromancers had supposedly been slaughtered during the Siege of Copernica Citadel. Well, all but one, and this definitely wasn't him.

All four Sisters stiffened as the lightning grazed their flight suits. Even benign necromancer magic was not painless. With a crack and a flash, they were gone. Boges stood on tiptoes to check the geolock on the cargo boxes. It glowed a remaining time of 24 hours 23 minutes, along with a set of coordinates for the delivery location.

"If the Sisters are hiding from the Reason, what chance do we have of making this delivery?" Boges asked.

"The Sisters base their decisions on the reverend mother's knowledge of future events. They wouldn't have given it to us if we weren't the best chance of success."

Boges ran her hand over one of the boxes. Gary felt a shiver down his spine.

"Whatever is in here, it's certainly large, Captain," she said.

The boxes were nearly three meters high, made out of an opaque white synthetic material that the Reason had concocted in a laboratory. But it was also suffused with a charge of Bala magic. Gary didn't even want to touch it. He suspected that was by design. Technology was excellent at locking up valuables; magic was good for making you forget they ever existed.

Gary knelt down in front of the dwarf so that they could speak eye to eye.

"Boges, you need to stop calling me Captain," said Gary.

The dwarf drew herself up to her full height.

"I will never," she said indignantly. "Humans cannot be trusted. They will always act out of greed and spite, even if it's not in their own best interest. If you were to give the word, the *Jaggery* would be yours again. All of my kin agrees."

"I've rarely heard so many words from you. And I have never heard you speak of mutiny," said Gary.

Boges gripped the cargo box and leaned in with panicked eyes.

"I will not stand idly by while you are tortured. Not again."

"You aren't responsible for what happened to me," said Gary. Boges blushed.

"I should have stopped it," she said.

"I'm a practically immortal being with healing blood and the strength of ten of them and I couldn't stop it."

"I will not allow history to repeat itself," said Boges, stomping toward the dwarf door.

CHAPTER EIGHT
Orbital Burn

The *Jaggery*'s Bala instruments bubbled and churned behind Jenny. None of it sounded good. The ship was damn unhappy to have humans on board again. Her tablet pinged with a warning that was clear and easy to understand. The Reason ship that had tailed them into the desert was hailing them.

"FTL *Jaggery*, this is the RSF *Arthur Phillip*. On the orders of Colonel Wenck, you are to land your ship immediately and prepare to be boarded."

A lazy smile crossed Jenny's face. She clicked open her comm.

"Kia ora, Ondre, is that you? I haven't heard from you since Copernica. You still have that pixie you used to keep in a mason jar?"

If being a war hero didn't bring you fortune, at least it bought you a few minutes of idle chatter with which to stall your pursuers.

She switched over to the internal intercom.

"Gary, speed it up in the cargo hold. Reason's here."

The *Arthur Phillip*'s communications officer answered in hushed tones.

"Is that you, Captain Perata? Man, it's been ages. That's some ship you're flying. You've done well for yourself. Listen, my boss wants to take a look on board. Can you just give him ten minutes? He's searching for some half-unicorn that we have to bring back to Fort J. I don't know why he thinks it's with you."

"That's really weird," said Jenny, feigning innocence. "All right. Let me get this rock landed. I won some rich guy's stoneship in a poker game this morning and I barely know how to fly it. Do you know where I'd find the attitude controls?"

Ondre launched into a detailed explanation of stoneship control mechanisms. Jenny had learned that while blasting your way out of situations worked middlingly well, the best way to extract yourself from under a man's control was to pretend you needed his expertise. You could stall for hours with a few well-timed uninformed questions.

She turned down the comm volume, leaned back in her chair, and closed her eyes. Her lower back ached and her right arm was still sore from hitting the singularity pie. Also, her brain was tired. She'd been trying for years to break onto this ship. Now she was here, in the captain's seat, but she didn't feel the vindication she'd been hoping for. The fear in her core hadn't dissipated one bit. In fact, thinking about the task ahead, it had intensified.

Jim came in, reeking of cheap cigars and larval eggwine, and holding a small plastic baggie in his hand.

"Don't smoke on board," she said, not looking up from her tablet.

"It's all I got left, Jen." Which was what he said when she asked him to stop any of his ridiculously annoying habits. Like spitting, or drinking while flying, or demanding grilled cheese sandwiches on space stations that hadn't seen bread in a generation. It was the way he shut down every argument that he didn't want to have.

In the background, Ondre paused for breath. Jenny flicked on the comm again.

"But wait, where is the main engine on this thing?" she asked, and turned the mic off while he tried to explain that there wasn't a conventional engine on board stoneships.

Jim opened his baggie and poured a bit of water from a flask in his coat pocket into the hard orange pellets at the bottom. He resealed the bag and started moving the stuff inside around with his fingers.

"Do you really have to rehydrate your cheese at this very moment?" asked Jenny. "I am trying to stop the Reason from boarding. You could help, you know."

"It'll take a few hours to be ready. I wanted to get it started now," he said, shaking the bag to make sure that the water touched every little cheese shred. This man was exhausting.

"Did you hit Gary?" she asked.

"Might've." He finished working his cheese and put it back into his pocket for later when he could get the dry bread out of storage and make himself a grilled cheese sandwich. Jim would be thrilled that Boges would allow fire on board. Jenny had had fire safety drilled into her brain when she was a Reason officer. She didn't allow so much as a stick of wood on her ships. Well, with the exception of her wife, of course.

She was grateful that Gary hadn't been judgmental about how long it had taken Jenny to get back to Fort J to look for Kaila, but the huge distances between planets were only navigable when unicorn horn was plentiful. Now that it was a scarce resource, communications and shipping routes had started to become strained. They'd even stopped holding annual voting for elected officials because the distances were too great. Or so the Reason said.

Truth was, Jenny lay awake every night wondering if Kaila was all right. She woke from dreams in which Kaila was still with her and rolled over only to find that half of the bed empty and the guilt hit her all over again. But with Gary on board, she would finally be able to make good on her promise to find her wife.

"I know you and Gary have a history, but try to keep it together until we can finish this delivery and get paid," she replied.

"I don't like being back on this Bala abomination of a ship," he said.

She heard hoarseness creeping back into his voice, and without looking up she knew he was about to lose it. Jim cried a lot more these days. He was almost past the point of being useful as a co-pilot. Luckily for him, he was good at other things, like being an able-bodied human man who could get them through inspections and checkpoints just by being himself.

"Stop hitting Gary. Avoid him if you want, but don't attack him. All right?"

"I'm not sitting next to the animal who ate my best girl."

"Then I guess you're not sitting in the cockpit, because I need Gary up here with me."

Her own words surprised her. She didn't really need Gary up in front, but for some reason she wanted him nearby. Some bit of conscience was wrestling to do right by him, whether she wanted to or not. She tried to squash it down deep, where her traumatic memories, like those of Copernica or the day Kaila was captured, waited for her. They always seemed to make an appearance right as she settled into her bunk for the night.

"You can have the co-pilot spot. We'll make Gary stand in the back," she conceded.

"He'll fall right the hell over when we boost up to orbit," mused Jim, momentarily placated.

"Uh, Captain Perata?" came Ondre's voice. She clicked the comm open.

"Yep."

"Colonel Wenck says to set down in thirty seconds or he'll open fire."

"Sure thing, I'll get this thing down on the ground pronto."

Jenny clicked the mic off and returned to the intercom.

"Now would be a good time, Gary," she said.

The cockpit door opened and Gary settled himself into the corner. "The cargo is loaded and tied down for takeoff," he said.

"Everyone strap in," said Jenny.

"Are you sure you don't want me to drive?" asked Jim. "I'm the best pilot in the–"

Jenny hit the launch thrusters and Jim was flattened against the back of his chair with a grunt. Gary leaned against the back wall.

"Go to hell, Jen," Jim said when he caught his breath. She turned her head so he wouldn't see her smile.

The ship calculated velocity and trajectory with almost no input from Jenny. Stoneships didn't have built-in artificial intelligence like Reason ships because they had something better. Real intelligence. There was something alive at the heart of this ship and it made you a little squeamish to feel its power coursing through the walls. Stoneships were one of the few places in the universe that Jenny could feel confident any more. As if the power that infused the ship was contagious.

Not all the time, but definitely when the *Jaggery* was pushing itself at full power, Jenny felt a little taste of its magic. It felt like when you got antsy with cabin fever and just had to get outside. During those times, she could make little things happen. Nothing impressive like a Bala could, but maybe change the color of her nail polish from red to blue or fix a little tear in her jumpsuit just by thinking of it. She hadn't even mentioned it to Kaila, because there was no easy way to tell your wife that you might be able to do just enough magic to be totally useless.

The *Jaggery* pushed its escape velocity to the very limit of human endurance. Jenny felt the edges of her vision going white. Speed was good for escaping Reason ships, but bad for staying conscious. The ship inserted itself into orbit among the space junk. Bits of metal bounced off their rocky hull. They were on the wrong side of Earth for Beywey and had to wait through part of an orbit to get pointed in the right direction. The *Arthur Phillip* would be right behind them.

"Did the Sisters give you any idea what we're shipping?" Jenny called back to Gary.

"Other than the fact that it's in two large location- and time-locked boxes, they didn't specify. They were careful to impress upon me the importance of having them arrive for the Century Summit, so my guess is that they're a collection of historical artifacts and official documents for the meeting."

"It's stupid to take on a cargo where you don't know what you're transporting," grumbled Jim through gritted teeth. Jenny had to agree, but beggars couldn't be choosers. She had to get to Fort J. If Kaila had survived harvesting until now, it would be a miracle.

"And I still don't see why we have to give the ship back to Gary," continued Jim, as if Gary wasn't sitting right behind him. "The ship's in your name. It's yours now. Just keep it." He looked a little unsteady. Zero G didn't agree with him.

"You're getting paid enough to buy your own brand new ship. You don't need this one," she snapped. That cabin fever feeling was building within her as the ship gathered energy for the next burn to Beywey Station. She shook her head to clear it and her hair lengthened by a good ten centimeters. She pulled it up and tied it into a bun on the top of her head so no one would notice. At least the bursting feeling was gone.

Jim rubbed the bags under his eyes. "I don't want a ship.

I'm looking for a little six-cow ranch in the middle of noplace where I can settle down and get some quiet."

The door opened and Ricky Tang floated in. A dwarven crew member hung off each of her arms, trying in vain to slow her down.

"Ma'am, you cannot enter the cockpit."

"Let go, little hairy men, I want to sit in front. I'm a VIP," she said, squirming out of the dwarves' grip.

"They're not hairy men," said Gary, as the dwarves hung back, waiting for instructions.

"All right, whatever," said Ricky.

"No, not whatever. You should know better. If you do not know how to address a particular dwarf, you need to ask," said Gary. "There are nine distinct dwarven genders, and they are more than happy to tell you their closest English approximation."

"Understood," said Ricky, pushing herself closer to the viewscreen and pretending to play it off, but Jenny saw her cheeks flush pink.

Jenny unstrapped herself from her wheelchair and floated to Ricky's level. Zero G was the only time she got to talk to people eye to eye, unless they knelt down, which almost no one did. Ricky had changed into a flightsuit not unlike what Jenny wore, but tan instead of Reason red. She'd also put up her hair to stop it from floating around and hitting everyone in the face during weightless flight.

"Ricky, get into the passenger area," said Jenny. "You can take any of the unclaimed cabins in this hallway."

"I have a cabin already. I want to be up front where the action is," she said. "Also I need to tell you where to drop me off."

"This isn't the intra-system shuttle," said Jenny. "You're going where we're going. No extra stops."

"Well, where are you going?" asked Ricky.

"A quick resupply at Beywey, then on to Jaisalmer. No time for other stops."

Ricky looked aghast.

"You can't drop me at Jaisalmer – they'll murder me there."

"Not my problem. Get in your cabin and don't touch anything on the ship. It's all infused with Bala magic and some of it is dangerous."

Ricky looked intrigued instead of intimidated.

"Surely you're open to negotiation, Jenny," said Ricky.

"We could probably be persuaded to let you off on Amaroq for one of those suitcases full of bottles you were dragging around," said Jim. Jenny said nothing, resentful that he'd stepped over her in the discussion.

"First of all," said Ricky, "those bottles are my only way to set up shop on a new planet. And second of all, wolves are incredibly light drinkers. I wouldn't make a quarter of what I did on Earth."

"I'm not stopping at Amaroq, so the discussion is moot. You can get off at Beywey or Jaisalmer. Those are your options," said Jenny.

Ricky wrinkled her nose.

"Beywey isn't even fully operational. There are, like, ten people up there and none of them have money."

"Then I guess you're coming to Jaisalmer," said Jenny.

Ricky groaned.

"Auntie Nash told me never to let a blemmye in my bar. I break that rule one time and look where it lands me. On my way to freaking Fort J, where I am definitely going to be detained because you might remember that my paperwork is definitely not sorted out so that *Miss* Ricky Tang can travel across the Reason."

Jim scoffed and Jenny smacked the back of his head.

"I completely understand, Ricky," she said. "Kaila and I

are in the same situation. But we're going through Fairyfloss, which is the most lenient of the checkpoints. I have some cash for bribes, and I bet you can spare a few bottles of the drink. With Jim's help, we'll get through all right. As a matter of fact, if you stay on board at the Jaisalmer cargo drop, I bet Gary would be willing to bring you to Chhatrapati Shivaji after we transfer the ship to him."

"I would not," said Gary from the corner.

"Oh, thanks for chiming in, Gary. You're being extremely helpful," said Jenny.

Ricky chuckled.

"He's not happy with any of us," she said to Jenny.

It dawned on Jenny that she was in charge of herding all three of these misfits for the next twenty-four hours and that if she didn't lay down the law early, they were going to bicker all the way to Jaisalmer. She slammed her tablet down on the console hard enough that she heard the plastic case crack. The cockpit went quiet.

"I am trying to make this trip as quickly as possible with as few problems as possible," she said, with deliberate slowness. "None of us wants to enter Reasonspace, but that's the only way we make this drop and head our separate ways. I don't care where you go after or what you do on board, but until Fort J, stay out of my way."

Jim grumbled, but didn't object. Gary was suddenly very interested in the Bala instruments in the corner.

"I want a share of the delivery fee," said Ricky. "I'm taking the same risks as the rest of you."

"Don't push your luck," said Jenny.

"I always do," said Ricky with a wink. "But seriously, I want in."

"This is not the Bitter Blossom and you are not in charge here," warned Jenny.

Ricky's face lost all trace of humor.

"Watch the way you speak to me, Perata. I know some things that would curl your hair," she said, with a glance at Jim. He sucked his teeth and stared straight ahead at the viewscreen.

Jenny allowed herself to float so that she was slightly higher than Ricky.

"You want to fight?" she asked.

Ricky took so long to answer that Jenny began to pull off the blemmye robe that still hung over her jumpsuit. It caught on the greenstone necklace she'd worn since she was a child. The open edge of the spiral koru had become tangled into the loose weave of the robe. She eased the stone out of the fabric and tucked it back into her jumpsuit.

"No, I don't want to fight," said Ricky.

"Then get in your cabin," said Jenny.

One of the dwarves held out a hand to guide Ricky out of the room. Ricky rolled her eyes and took hold of the thick fingers.

"Fine. I'll be in back," she said.

For a moment, the dwarves did not move. Jenny followed their eyes to Gary in the corner, staring intently at the tubes and vials displaying various ship statuses. He looked up at the sudden silence in the room. The dwarves bowed to him. He nodded in return. She kept all traces of frustration off her face. If the dwarves wanted to maintain their loyalty to Gary, that was fine, as long as they still followed her orders.

"It's good to have you back in charge, Captain," said one of the dwarves. Jim tisked.

"Thank you," said Gary. The dwarves floated out of the cockpit with Ricky between them. A heaviness descended on the room.

"I guess you never ate one of *his* wives," muttered Jim.

"Jim," said Jenny sharply. He settled sullenly into his chair. She'd taken the risk of putting these two together so that they could escape the scourge planet Earth. She'd figured that she could keep them away from each other's throats. She might have figured wrong.

She floated over to Gary's spot and examined the colored fluids rising and falling in the glass tubes. She had no idea what she was looking at. The last time they'd been on the *Jaggery*, she and Jim had rigged the ship to talk directly to an off-the-shelf Reason tablet, but it had caused failures all over the ship's ecosystem. From the lack of birds in the hallways to the blights that took out the feed crops, Boges was still dealing with massive species die offs caused when they had connected it all up.

"We... did some stuff," she said to Gary.

"I see that," he replied.

"It works to fly the ship, but..."

"But you instigated a mass genocide across the entire biome."

An apology stuck in her throat. She knew it was warranted, but she couldn't bring herself to say the words. Once she started saying sorry for one thing, where would it stop? At the destruction of the ship's ecosystem, or the enslavement of its former captain, or setting him up to go to the Quag? The litany of her transgressions never seemed to end. She couldn't face all of it at once. The past was a mountain too insurmountable to climb, but the future was a blank slate.

She ran her finger across the bulbed end of a glass tube. The liquid inside was a sickly green, studded with white chunks. It looked, for all the world, like vomit in a jar.

"What does this one mean?"

"It's the measure of overall wellbeing on the ship."

"Of the ship itself or the creatures on board?"

"Is there a difference?" He stared at her. Not hostile, but not friendly either. The kind of guarded look you might give a cellmate.

She pulled her hand back and kept her eyes on the readouts. There was an infinite patience within his eyes that made her squirm to her core – and not in the pleasant way that Kaila made her squirm. It was an "I'm waiting for you to figure out what I already know" kind of look that made her feel like a child. Gary was, after all, a hundred and two years old.

She pushed off from the wall and went back to her much more readable tablet. It didn't have any outlandish Bala measurements like wellbeing or overall happiness. Just normal stuff like pitch, yaw, and proximity. She held it up to Gary.

"It works though. First of its kind. Everyone else has to hire a Bala to pilot their stoneships, but Jim and I can do it ourselves. This says we're twenty minutes from the right trajectory for Beywey."

Gary tapped one of his gauges.

"This says that the human race will face extinction within two generations."

Jenny swallowed the lump that had suddenly appeared in her throat.

"I don't see how that helps you fly," she mumbled.

She spun in the low gravity and checked the supply cabinet under the console for spare parts. Everything they'd left was still in there. Human stoneship captains usually activated the artificial gravity as soon as they entered orbit, but Jenny floated every chance she got. In a weightless environment, she was just as fast and maneuverable as anyone else on the ship. Like she used to be.

"I'm going to go wash up before we get to Beywey." The sticky blemmye robe itched like the devil.

"About that," said Jim, leaning his elbow on the console. "What are you doing wearing elf jizz all over your face?"

"It's a very effective disguise," she said. "Some of us are

willing to take one for the team. Ricky and Gary had no idea who I was until it all dripped off."

"I smelled you the moment I walked into the bar. No one else in the system uses that particular lavender soap," said Gary.

"It's a family heirloom," said Jenny, floating to the door. "Keep an eye out for the *Arthur Phillip*. And I'd better not come back to find any dead cowboys or unicorns in my cockpit."

CHAPTER NINE
Flying Vek

Gary found himself sitting alone with Cowboy Jim, awkwardly staring at the ship's readouts and wondering if he should also leave the cockpit.

"How long did it take?" asked Jim. He spoke so quietly that Gary nearly didn't hear him.

"How long did what take?" Gary asked, but he knew what Jim meant.

"Before she died."

Gary's memory of Cheryl Ann's death was a stone weighing down his soul. Even if he had wanted to share the details with Jim, he would not have known where to start. There had been more red human blood than he had ever seen in one place. But the story really started long before that, with kindness, and friendship, and then love. He knew Jim wanted to hear none of that. He tried to imagine what he would want to hear in Jim's place. Perhaps the truth, softened a bit.

"She slipped away. It didn't look particularly painful."

Jim unclipped his harness and floated above Gary's eye level.

"That's bullshit and you know it. I walked in and saw what you'd done. She was a goddamn pile of skin on the floor." Jim's face went ashen and Gary wondered if he was going to be sick. "Was she still alive when you started eating her? Did she beg you to stop? Or was she immobile by then, lying on that cold stone floor, watching while you sucked out her bones, you filthy bastard? You tricked her into thinking she loved you. You lured her close to the bars where you crushed her life away."

Jim was an old fella, but even weak people became strong when they had nothing to lose. He doubted Jim could actually kill him, but he didn't doubt that Jim desperately wanted to.

"I'm sorry, Jim. I can explain what happened between us if you like."

Jim spat. The glob of moisture floated across the cockpit. Gary dodged it and it landed on the instrument panel, clinging to one of the glass tubes, in its own way also indicating the overall state of wellbeing on the ship.

Gary headed for the cockpit door. He wasn't needed until they jumped to FTL anyway. Better to stay out of Jim's way as much as possible.

"Fucking horsefucker," Jim called after him.

In the hallway, Boges poked her head out of a dwarf door.

"If you get a moment, Captain, Miss Tang is rearranging our handiwork in the garden. If you would be so kind as to have a word with her."

"Of course, Boges," he replied. The dwarves had effortlessly adjusted their soil-laying to the zero G environment. They had secured a finely woven mesh over the dirt to keep it from floating away, but allowing plants to grow through.

The garden was on the outer edge of the ship so that it could receive natural light from any nearby star. He expected it to be barren after years in storage, but the first thing he encountered was the smell of fresh tomatoes. Boges had planted several rows by the entrance, hanging on the wall in lighted hydroponic racks. It seemed even Boges was open to adopting Reason technology in the face of resource scarcity.

Despite Boges' best efforts, most of the old growth trees had died off. The immense room looked empty without them. Back when he was a child, you could walk the paths for an hour and not see a wall. Now the room was like an empty cavern.

He continued on along the path toward Lake Vivaan. The lake was a marvel of creativity and interspecies cooperation, and it relied solely on Bala design. While humans assumed that stoneship lakes contained microgravity drives in the waterworks beneath them, they were actually an ecosystem made up of three Bala species that worked together to keep the water stable in zero G.

First, the lake was lined with squabby sand, a fine substrate that radiated heat and ultraviolet light. When the pond functioned properly, it glowed with a purple-blue light emanating from the depths. Mixed into the water above the sand was a large quantity of fire algae from Kaila's planet, Gymnoverium. They absorbed the sand's heat and each individual microscopic alga generated a minuscule gravitational field. The fields were harmless by the handful, but deadly in large quantities. Many an unwary swimmer had drowned by jumping into a pond when the fire algae were in bloom.

The final layer was a school of vek, a palm-sized fish from the water-covered planet of Varuna. Vek were floating fish that jumped out of the water and hovered for a few minutes to catch small flying insects that hatched off the water's surface. They swam near the top layer of stoneship ponds, their floating hormone counteracting the algae's gravitational field so that the crew could swim without fear of being dragged to the bottom.

When the ecosystem worked, the water stayed put even when the gravity was off. Gary remembered playing a game as a child that involved pushing off the roof of the garden and hitting the water where you felt gravity's tug. Then you swam up as fast as you could, trying to jump out of the water high enough to break free of the fire algae's pull and float skyward again. His father had been terrible at the game, four hooves flying in every direction, scrambling across the ceiling. It was most undignified for a unicorn, but it made Gary laugh, so his father had done it again and again. He had many happy memories of this place.

Findae Cobalt had disappeared along with the rest of the living unicorns over sixty years ago. Gary had searched FTL ships for years, checking to see if his father had been held captive for his horn, but he had never found him or an explanation for his absence. Gary had long since resigned himself to the fact that the Reason might have killed Findae for no good reason at all.

He rounded a bend in the path and came upon Lake Vivaan. Ricky floated over the surface of the lake, using a net made of nylon stockings stretched around a wire hanger to scoop vek out of the water.

"Hey Gary," she said brightly. "Come fishing."

Ricky reached into her makeshift net and plucked out a pair of fish before they floated away. She tucked them into a resealable plastic bag filled with water.

"You can't take those. The fish are critical to the lake. And they're not yours to take," said Gary.

"They're not yours either, big guy. Everything in this garden is fair game until the captain tells me otherwise."

A vek jumped out of the water to eat a mosquito and Ricky tried to dive for it. She landed on the surface of the water, which began to drag her down immediately. She pushed down on the surface, which only pulled more of her under the water as the gravity of the fire algae took hold of her.

"A little help?" she called.

Gary picked up a dead branch and held it out to Ricky.

With his other hand, he hung onto a heavy stump on the shore. She grabbed the branch and pulled hard. His fingers slipped off the stump and he landed flat in the water. He kicked as hard as he could, but his legs went down as if tied to stone. Boges had surely done her best, but the pond biome was far out of balance. The algae had taken over. No matter how hard he swam, Gary began to sink.

"Help!" cried Ricky, just before her head sank below the surface. Her hands thrashed in a futile attempt to push down on the water and raise herself up. There was nothing to grab, no way to fight the pull. Gary could only think of one thing to do. He shouted as loud as he could.

"Boges!"

Even if she wasn't in this room herself, one of her kin was always in the walls listening.

Gary sucked in a huge breath as his head went under. He dropped through the layer of vek. They brushed past him and tickled his face. He felt calm. The pond was quiet and soothing. A purple glow illuminated the water. Occasionally, an algae colony flared red with a burst of gravity. His healing blood would go to extraordinary lengths to keep him from drowning. It might take three times as long as a full human. He wasn't sure if that was a positive or a negative aspect of the situation.

He saw Ricky nearby, struggling in the water. He reached for her and snagged one of the belt loops on her jumpsuit. He reeled her in closer as they both sank.

She didn't notice him until he was right up against her. She tried to get leverage off his body, shoving him down deeper. He pushed her hands down and pulled her tight to him, pinning her arms to her sides so that she couldn't make his situation worse. Her eyes went wide. She thought he was trying to kill her. She fought hard, kicking him in the legs, twisting and pushing to break free. Bubbles streamed from her mouth and nose.

Gary held her firmly until she gave up and stopped struggling. She looked up at the surface one more time, eyes wide with terror. Gary leaned close and put his mouth over hers. She pulled back, startled, until she felt the air bubbles. She moved in and allowed him to form a seal over her mouth, then breathed in as he blew. After a few seconds she pulled away. It wouldn't save her life if they didn't get above the water soon, but it might buy them a few more seconds.

They reached the bottom of the lake. Squabby sand crunched under Gary's hooves. He waved to Ricky and pointed to the glowing sand. She watched as he bent his knees and pushed off like he had as a child. He made it most of the way up through the water. His fingers breached the surface before he sank back down again. Ricky passed him on the way down. She was also just short of getting a breath. The gravity was too strong for them to break the surface.

His empty lungs began to burn. Part of him longed to close his eyes and simply allow the algae to drag him down. Only it wasn't the algae sinking him, it was his time in the Quag, his time locked on the *Jaggery*, the panicked look on Cheryl Ann's face when she realized she was about to die. It was the same look that Ricky had now. She reached for him again, but he had no air left to give. He asked for Unamip's blessing for those who have little hope.

He wrapped an arm around Ricky's waist and bent his knees again. He shoved off as hard as he could and they soared upward. This time, the gravity in the water had shifted. Liquid coalesced into boulder-sized spheres that floated away from them, up toward the roof still marked with scuffs from his father's hooves.

Ricky emerged from a bubble of water and took a great gasping mouthful of air. She gagged and choked, hanging onto an outcropping of stone. Gary filled his throbbing lungs.

They hung on to the ceiling, panting.

"Are you all right, Captain?" called Boges from the controls on the far side of the room.

"I believe so," said Gary.

Ricky shook herself off between coughing breaths. Water beaded off her jumpsuit and spun out in every direction. A bunch of globules hit Gary.

"I'm fine, thanks for asking," she called to the dwarf, who clearly did not care.

Boges soared up to the ceiling. "My most sincere apologies. I neglected to mention that the lake was dangerously out of balance and no one should attempt to swim."

"We should not have been in there anyway, Boges," said Gary, raising his eyebrow to Ricky.

"Don't give me that look, Gary Cobalt. You've been dying to take a swim with me since the moment we met." She leaned closer to Boges and whispered conspiratorially. "He even gave me a kiss."

Boges' mouth opened so wide that a globule of water floated inside. She sputtered and spit it out.

"I was giving you air," said Gary, trying to keep the exasperation out of his voice.

"Mmm hmm," she said. Gary gave up and pushed off toward the floor. He floated through a few globules of water on the way down and landed in the empty bottom of the lake. All of the squabby sand was gone.

"How did you jettison the water?" he called up to Boges.

"Electric pumps at the bottom of the lake. When you hit the emergency shutdown, they turn on and suck the sand into a holding tank beneath the lake. It cuts off the UV food source to the algae. Their microgravity shuts down and the water floats away. Unfortunately, the fish go too." Vek gasped and twisted in the air around them.

"Electric pumps? On which Bala world do you find those?"

He grinned at Boges, who blushed.

"Reason tech is good for solving some problems, you know." She pushed off and catapulted herself back through the dwarf door. "I'll have someone come collect the fish and reset the lake."

Ricky floated down next to him. Her playful smile was gone.

"Hey. Thank you," she said. "What you did... I won't forget it." She put out her hand and he shook it. His large palm nearly enveloped her slender hand.

"My apologies for misspeaking in the bar," he said.

"Thanks. And I shouldn't have embarrassed you up there about the kiss." She pointed to the ceiling, where most of the water had spread out to form a shallow impromptu lake. It wouldn't be easy to clean up.

"I may not enjoy that particular activity, but you should know that it delights me immensely to torment Boges," said Gary.

"Then I guess I'm on the right ship, because I'm in the business of tormenting people." She pulled her hair down and wrung it out. More water bubbles floated up into the garden. "Gary, I'm serious. Neither of us should get off on Jaisalmer. It is not a good place for people like you and me. At best, we'll be locked up within hours of landing."

"The Sisters have asked me to be there when the cargo opens."

Ricky waved away the suggestion.

"You don't have to do everything the Sisters say. They like to play that they know the future, but there are so many permutations that even they can't account for all of the variables."

"You were a Sister. I saw the uniform in your suitcase," said Gary, knowing that a true Sister would deny it.

"I was asked to be, but I declined the invitation. I have no interest in living a nun's life in a run-down castle on Varuna," said Ricky. "Maybe when I'm older and have nothing better to do."

"They would be lucky to have you."

The side of her mouth went up in a smile and she looked genuinely pleased at the compliment.

"I think so too. I'm very good at getting into places where I don't belong."

"Then perhaps Jaisalmer is not as bad a prospect as you imagine," he said.

She seemed to consider it.

"Maybe. But Jenny's idea about Chhatrapati isn't bad. I can get a lot of places from there."

"I'll see what I can do," he conceded. It would be easy enough to make the stop. Chhatrapati Shivaji was minutes away from Jaisalmer. "Please remember that some things on this ship can be dangerous."

"You got that right, Gary." Ricky floated off to tamper with more of the *Jaggery*'s systems and Gary went back toward his quarters. He was soaking wet, freezing cold, and there were vek caught in his trousers.

Hovering in the crew hallway, Gary took a moment before entering his old quarters to survey the scene. Boges had instructed the dwarves to clean the room, but even they weren't able to get the smells of old blood and urine out of the air. The bars were gone, at least. That was a start. And his footlocker was still there, although Reason investigators had pried the lock open and haphazardly thrown his personal items back inside. He peeled off his wet clothes and pulled out a dry pair of trousers and a wool sweater, appropriate for chilly days in deep space. He took his hat off to dry. There was no need to hide his head up here.

At the bottom of the trunk he spotted a pair of gold earrings that had once belonged to his mother. They had been crafted into an intricate filigree that dangled low like a banquet hall chandelier. Seeing them was like a kick in the chest. He had been planning to give them to Cheryl Ann once they got away from Demoryx, but she hadn't made it out of the system alive.

Six weeks before Cheryl Ann died, the *Jaggery* had become stuck between the two smallest planets orbiting the red giant Demoryx. Jenny was captain then, and Gary had been locked into a corner of his room that she'd welded into a makeshift cage. He'd assumed that Jenny had a thorough understanding of how trisicles and horn growth worked. By the time Cheryl Ann told him otherwise, it was already too late.

"Hey, bud," Cheryl Ann had said, sitting on his bed outside of the bars like she did every afternoon. She looked too young to be the wife of an angry old man like Jim, but she was a skilled systems engineer whom Gary would have been proud to have on his crew. Even here on the *Jaggery*, which practically ran itself, she had taken the time to learn all the dwarves' names and ask after their kin. In turn, they had shown her the void at the heart of the ship, something humans were rarely invited to see. "We're a little concerned and maybe you can help us out."

"What is it?" he asked. "Jim pummeling more dwarves or Jenny careening the ship into places where it shouldn't be?"

"More of the latter, I suppose," she said, pursing just one side of her mouth. "We ran out of trisicles."

"Then we're all going to die," he said. It was a flippant comment said in jest, but given how close it came to the truth, he wished he'd never said it. Especially not to Cheryl Ann.

"Stop," she said, waving off his pessimism. "We just have to find a cluster of trisicles or figure out a way to get back to a planet with some food."

"Do you think trisicles just float around everywhere, waiting for people to pluck them out of the sky?"

"No, but they have to come from somewhere," Cheryl Ann reasoned. He kicked the bars of his cage and she jumped. He was so bitter toward her in the beginning, taking delight in making her afraid. But she kept showing up every day, asking questions about his life and keeping him company anyway.

"You're supposed to keep the breeding pair and eat only the offspring," he said, with a cruel laugh.

"I don't think Jenny knew that."

"She was captain of an FTL ship for years. How does she not know how to manage a trisicle inventory?" asked Gary.

"Because the *Pandey* didn't have a unicorn on board. The Reason rationed out bits of horn to her. She'd never grown her own."

He snorted, not bothering to hide the equine sound.

"So, any ideas?" she asked.

"If you have bones of any kind, or even chitinous insects, I can grow a minuscule amount of horn from those."

"All righty. I'll see what we can find. Anyway, I brought you something. Don't tell Jenny or she'll have my ass."

She came up to the bars and held out a parcel wrapped in a cloth napkin. He took it and peeled away the fabric. Inside was a dosa wrapped around potatoes and cheese. After months of Reason rations, the smell was sublime. He sat against the back wall and picked off a piece of the pancake. It was crispy and light.

"I had Boges make it using your mother's recipe. She said it was your favorite. I borrowed some of Jim's cheese. It's a little cold. Sorry. I couldn't get here right away."

He ate in silence while Cheryl Ann sat nearby and waited. When he was finished, he held out the napkin. She reached in to take it and he grabbed her hand. She pulled away, but he held her firmly. Her eyes went wide with terror when she realized her mistake.

"That was the kindest thing anyone has done for me in years," he said, letting her go. She laughed with relief.

"Oh sure. Yeah. I mean, it's ridiculous that Jen has you in here like this, but no one's going to change her mind once she gets set on something. You know her."

He didn't answer and she left. A week after that, they ran out of cow bones. The shaving Jenny scraped out of his head that night was so thin that you could see light through it. It jumped them a quarter of the way to Flavos, the only planet in the system with animal life – and more bones. Going there on conventional power would take them eleven months. Jenny had stockpiled enough food for two.

Three weeks before Cheryl Ann died, she'd stopped bringing him food treats and instead tried to distract him with cups of watery chai. She sat outside of the bars and told him stories about her childhood on Earth and how she'd met Jenny in engineering school. Jim had been one of their instructors – a cocky man who didn't flirt so much as demand attention. He and Cheryl Ann married after graduation and started an interplanetary shipping business. They'd invited Jenny to join them, but she had enlisted in the Reason Space Force instead.

Cheryl Ann asked Gary about Bala life before humans had arrived and coaxed him to tell her stories of his childhood. In return, she shared the ridiculous legends she'd heard about unicorns back on Earth. He'd laughed when she suggested that princesses rode unicorns. As if a unicorn would ever willingly consent to being a beast of burden.

He'd stopped trying to frighten her by that point and she started sitting cross-legged on the floor up next to the bars.

"So the Bala have been visiting Earth all throughout our history?" she asked.

"Yes, my father told me stories of the first expeditions. About how adorable you all were, thinking that dirt protected you from evil spirits. For the longest time you believed your sun revolved around you. Can you imagine a more self-centered bunch of dirt eaters? You thought the entire *universe* revolved around you."

"We still kind of do," she laughed.

"A small number of Bala thought humans should be exterminated before you spread off your little planet, but my father stood in front of the Pymmie and pleaded for your survival, telling them you were capable of great things."

"Hm." Cheryl Ann leaned her head against the bars. "Maybe not, though."

"Yeah, maybe not," he replied.

In the week before Cheryl Ann died, she'd stopped bringing him anything at all and she spent more and more time in his room, sitting in silence.

"What are you thinking?" he asked.

"I don't know how we're going to make it," she said, curling against the bars as he sat on the other side and leaned against her. She had her head on his shoulder and he could smell the old perfume on her unwashed jumpsuit. Their water stores were dwindling. Even Lake Vivaan had been drained for drinking. They'd eaten the vek weeks ago.

"How far to Flavos?" he asked.

"We flew flat-out for a while and made some progress, but then we had to shut down the engine when the redworms showed up. We're dead in space. Even if we went back online, it would take nine months to get to Flavos. Gary, I don't think there's enough food for nine *days*. Jim passed out last night on the way to the cargo hold. He's so lean already, the rations can't keep him going."

"And how are you doing?" he asked.

"You know, tired. Slow." She pulled her head away from

the bars and looked up at him. "I hate to ask. You've given so much already, but do you think your blood could help us?"

"It can heal wounds and diseases, but it's not nourishment, any more than a shell or a bone." He knew this firsthand from the Siege of Copernica Citadel where thousands of Bala had gone hungry within the walls after the Reason stopped all shipments coming into the fortress. His blood had helped the sick and injured, but the starving kept right on starving.

"I just don't see a way out," she said, resting her head again.

And she had been right. There was no way out for her. Eight days from that afternoon, she would be dead and he would eat her bones to save the ship.

Gary was devastated to be back in that room, infused with the memories of Cheryl Ann's life and death. He rested his head on the lid of his trunk and for the first time in a decade, he allowed himself to cry.

CHAPTER TEN
Orbital Pirates

Jenny looked up as Gary entered the cockpit and took his spot near the wall. His eyes were red and bleary, as if he'd had a good cry. She couldn't blame him; being back in that murder room would have brought her to tears too.

"You can change rooms if you want," she said, "There's no need for you to be in there."

"It's fine," said Gary, though clearly it was not.

Jim dozed in the co-pilot's chair. Jenny went back to monitoring their progress toward Beywey on her tablet. She smelled the heady toasted marshmallow odor of wood smoke coming off Jim's sweater.

"You smell like a bloody campfire," she muttered.

"Probably from the time we were on Flavos," he replied, shifting to a more comfortable sleeping position.

"Flavos? You're telling me that you haven't washed that sweater in years? It has to be incredibly ripe." She leaned over and sniffed the yarn – and then she understood. The tiniest hint of Cheryl Ann's perfume wafted out of the threads. She didn't know how Jim could stand to smell that all day long. "You're just an old dirty bastard," she said, so he wouldn't know that he'd been found out.

It didn't work. "It's all I got left, Jen," he said softly, and she had to stare at her tablet to keep from losing it. Jim always forgot that when he'd lost his wife, she'd lost her best friend. Jenny had actually met Cheryl Ann first. They'd even had an accidental first date.

Jenny had been in a Cascadian bar during her second year of engineering school. She'd watched the perky little brunette from a back table for a while. It took her a good fifteen minutes to work up the courage to take the seat next to her. The woman seemed genuinely pleased to have company. Jenny had a good feeling about this prospect. She was probably one of the incoming class of pilots in training. First-years, especially those from tiny towns in the middle of the country, were always eager to try out big city bars and sample the local cannabis culture of the region. As a second-year, Jenny was happy to play tour guide. Especially when the first-year in question was as adorable as this one.

"Hey, love," said Jenny, hopping up onto the stool. "What are you drinking?"

Cheryl Ann lifted her glass and studied the contents warily.

"A martini," she said. Then she leaned in close. "It's not that good."

"Here, let me try." Jenny reached over and took a tiny sip. The drink tasted fine.

"What's wrong with it?" Jenny asked.

"Is it supposed to taste that way? It's the first one I've ever had. Everyone in the movies drinks them, but it's not as sweet as I thought it would be." Jenny understood. This woman wanted a sugary cocktail, not a blast of alcohol. She ordered a cosmopolitan for her new friend and offered to take the martini herself. She was usually more of a beer drinker, but now they both had a glass in hand. That was never a bad way to start things off.

The woman took a sip of her cocktail and smiled.

"Oh that's exactly what I was looking for. Thanks. I'm Cheryl Ann." She extended a hand.

"Jenny." They shook. "You a first-year?"

"Yeah. That's a cool accent. Are you from Australia?"

"Aotearoa."

"Is that even a country?" asked Cheryl Ann.

"It's what you call New Zealand," said Jenny.

Cheryl Ann nodded, but Jenny knew she probably wouldn't be able to point to it on a map. People knew where the Aussies lived, but they always thought Papua New Guinea was New Zealand.

"How about you?" asked Jenny.

"Oh, a little town named Townsend, Georgia. We're known for having the smallest church in the country," said Cheryl Ann.

"A small church is a good church," said Jenny. Cheryl Ann laughed.

"So... are you interested in hanging out?" asked Jenny.

"Sure!" She was so excited that Jenny started planning out their entire evening in her head. First, a walk along the pier, maybe they'd stop for some seafood. The two of them would watch the sunset over the sound and then head back to Jenny's apartment for dessert. It was her tried-and-true date formula.

They walked toward the ocean. Jenny showed Cheryl Ann all of the classic Cascadia sights. She had this tour down pat. She knew to start with Great Earthquake Memorial Park. She used to do that last, but it made for an awkward pivot to making out after seeing a monument to thousands of dead people. She now began her tour with the monument, then stopped for drinks at the largest coffee shop in the country. She and Cheryl Ann got cups of hot chocolate to keep them warm in the cool breeze coming off the water. A date with frozen hands could either end up with snuggles on a bench or one of the parties giving up and going home. Jenny no longer took the chance.

Next, they stopped on the main boardwalk to watch the sunset. It was a clear evening and they could see all the way out to the mountains. The sky flamed with oranges and reds. It could not have been more perfect. When the sun had dipped behind the peaks, Jenny put her hand on the back of her date's neck. She leaned in and brushed her lips against Cheryl Ann's, teasing and daring her to kiss back. Cheryl Ann froze for a moment, then pulled away. She covered her mouth with her hand.

"What's wrong?" asked Jenny. She could feel her face getting hot as Cheryl Ann laughed.

"Um. Do women kiss women in New Zealand?" Cheryl Ann asked.

"They do if they're lesbians," said Jenny pointedly. Cheryl Ann looked confused.

"Why would you think that I'm a lesbian?" she asked.

"Because we met in a gay bar. I didn't think it was that much of a stretch."

Cheryl Ann looked horrified. Jenny's stomach dropped right down into her knees when she realized the mistake Cheryl Ann had made.

"That was a gay bar? Oh my god, I'm so sorry. I totally did not mean to lead you on. I have no idea how to figure out which bars are for gay people. They should put a sign outside. So people know," said Cheryl Ann.

"You didn't see the six rainbow flags hanging from the roof?" asked Jenny, staring out over the water, dejected.

"I thought they were just being festive," stammered Cheryl Ann. "Lots of people like rainbows. I like rainbows. Leprechauns like rainbows."

Jenny burst out laughing.

"Well, you know, that was in fact the name of the bar... Lesbians and Leprechauns: A Bar for Rainbow Lovers," said Jenny. She couldn't help the cheeky comment. Not after what had just happened.

"And for prisms," said Cheryl Ann. "And weather forecasters."

"Hey, since you mention weather forecasters, what do you call oral sex with a meteorologist who has a vagina?"

"What?" Cheryl Ann looked genuinely curious.

"Cumulolingus," said Jenny.

They both laughed until their stomachs hurt and tears ran down their faces.

"I'm sorry this wasn't the special night you were hoping for," said Cheryl Ann when they had caught their breath.

"It's fine. To be honest, it's already been more fun than most of the dates I've been on recently."

Cheryl Ann got serious. "So let's keep hanging out. I mean, I'm not going to have sex with you, but if we're having fun, why end it?"

"All right," said Jenny. It had been a long time since she'd been out with a woman simply as a friend. "Let's get dinner."

They shared a seafood boil – the kind that the servers dumped onto the table. They tossed shells into a bucket and talked until they were stuffed. Jenny learned how to properly pronounce "pecan," and Cheryl Ann learned where to find New Zealand on a map.

They walked back to Jenny's apartment and watched movies on the couch, talking through each and every scene until they both fell asleep on opposite ends with their legs a jumble in the middle.

It was the best first date Jenny ever had in her life and it was also how she had met her best friend in the entire universe. When she thought of Cheryl Ann, it was that version of her – the one laughing on the pier over weather-related oral sex jokes – which she remembered. Not the gaunt shell of a woman that she found dead on the floor of Gary's room.

Jenny looked up from her memories. Gary was still standing near the back wall, adjusting those Bala ship controls that defied comprehension.

Jim was now asleep in the co-pilot's chair. It had only been minutes since they'd left Earth, but he was at that point in his life where he fell asleep anywhere and at any time. She had even caught him asleep once in an airlock – a habit that was likely to catch up with him in a bad way someday.

The *Jaggery* had nearly reached Beywey Station, but every few dozen kilometers the ship jerked forward, like a colt straining against the bit, trying to break into a run. It was as if the ship knew Gary was back on board and wanted to stretch its legs and go for a gallop. With every jerking motion, Jenny felt jittery and cooped up.

"Can you tell it to calm down?" Jenny asked.

"It prefers to operate at full throttle," said Gary.

"So do I," said Jenny, zipping her jumpsuit against the cool air in the room. Gary had swapped out his prison-issued clothes for a warm wool sweater and thick work trousers. Stoneships were basically a temperate rainforest biome, a little too chilly for a girl raised in a maritime climate.

They passed through a gauntlet of local ships on routes between the handful of colonies left in this worn-out system. Besides the stragglers still eking out their survival on Earth, most of the residents of the solar system lived under plexiglas domes and pressurized canvas on a handful of fabricated moons and non-orbital space stations.

The *Jaggery*'s immense asteroid shape – now emblazoned with a giant pink flower – made her conspicuous in a sea of private rigs painted with the flags of long-dead nations. Jim started awake just as they passed one ship painted with dozens of white stars above a set of stripes. He put his hand over his heart.

"You don't need to salute that flag any more," said Jenny.

"That nation doesn't exist."

"I will never stop saluting the flag," said Jim. "You see your flag?"

"We've got stars and stripes too, but made up in a different way. You probably won't see it up here. People from Aotearoa prefer to stay on the planet for the most part. But what you might see is the Tino Rangatiratanga. It's a white wave between red and black. There are lots of Māori in space."

"Drawn skyward by the allure of interplanetary travel?" asked Gary from the back.

"Actually, we wanted to stay on our land, but it became uninhabitable. Flooded, too hot, and poisoned by invaders," said Jenny. "Even then, we tried to stay and fix it, but the Reason rounded up most of us for forced resettlement on one of their shiny new planets."

"Sounds familiar," said Gary.

Jim snorted, sounding both affronted and amused.

"Eventually, we pooled our funds to buy our own ships and start independent colonies free of the Reason," continued Jenny. "A bunch of us have a community on Gymnoverium. We coexist peacefully with the Bala there. Everyone works together."

"I know that place," said Gary.

"The Reason calls it Heritage Bay, but its real name is Tūrangawaewae," said Jenny.

"Is that where you're taking Kaila after you find her?" asked Gary.

"Yeah. It's the closest thing to a home we have. We have it all planned out. A little house in the woods near her family."

A small two-seater streaked by them, doing a flyby to ensure the *Jaggery* crew knew they were being watched.

Most of the ships in the area belonged to the Reason. Their designs spoke of buildings full of engineers tasked with imposing efficiency and their un-patched hulls indicated very few run-ins with geodesic pirates. Everyone gave Reason ships a wide berth, preferring not to attract their attention.

"Do unicorns have a flag?" Jenny asked.

"The banner of my clan is cobalt blue, with silver stars noting each member within the family."

"Neat."

"If the League of Nations could take a recess for a moment, it looks like we're being followed," said Jim, pointing to a star-spangled ship that trailed them by a few dozen kilometers.

"Wow. No subtlety whatsoever," said Jenny, scrolling through weapons menus. "I just want to get away from this damned planet. Gary, find out what they want while I get the guns ready."

"This ship has no guns," said Gary.

"Well, it didn't used to…" replied Jim, switching on the comm. "Unidentified ship, this is the *Jaggery*. State your reason for following us."

"Or be blown out of the sky," said Jenny before Jim could switch off the microphone.

The voice that came back over the comm was contrite in an exaggerated way that made everyone in the room doubt its sincerity.

"Oh sorry, *Jaggery*, we just happened to be going your way. Go ahead, we don't want any trouble with a big stoneship like yours."

"Thank you," said Jim, clicking off the mic.

"That's it?" asked Jenny, incredulously.

"Is what it?" replied Jim.

"You're going to take their word for it."

"They have no reason to bother us."

"You are way too trusting," said Jenny. "No reason except that this is an asteroid-sized Halcyon-class ship with about a billion dollars' worth of cargo on board, not to mention that we're about to stop at Beywey, meaning we're probably stocking up on provisions to go FTL as soon as we get clear of the local traffic."

"I don't think–"

A blast rocked the rear of the *Jaggery* and the ship skidded sideways toward a freighter. Jenny adjusted thrusters so that they didn't slam into anyone else.

"Take evasive action," said Gary from the back, sounding for all the world like he thought he was the captain of the ship.

"I've got this, thanks. These kids are in heaps of trouble. Fire at will," said Jenny. Jim tapped out the command to release two missiles toward the aggressive ship.

All three of them watched as the missiles hit the other hull, tearing a gash in the side and ejecting glittering bits of debris into the vacuum surrounding the ship.

"Any casualties?" asked Gary.

"No bodies floating," said Jim, squinting at the screen.

Another blast shook the *Jaggery* from a different direction and propelled it forward as air vented from a breach at the rear of the ship. They drifted until Jenny adjusted the thrusters and slowed them back to a crawl.

"Two ships firing on us now. The cargo hold has been breached," said Gary, resting his fingers on a pulsating muscle-like string of fibers on the wall.

"Anyone in there?" asked Jenny.

Gary nodded solemnly. Dwarves were always tucked into every nook and cranny of the walls and floors.

"Jim, get on the horn and talk to these clowns. They're under your flag," said Jenny. Jim opened his comm.

"Hey, what gives, you guys? A guy from Wyoming can't get any love from his fellow Americans?"

Both ships were quiet for a moment, no doubt conferring with each other as to the veracity of Jim's claim.

"Why aren'tcha showing the stars and bars, friend?" asked a voice from the second ship.

"Yeah, why you decked out all girlie?" chimed in someone from the first ship.

"My wife," said Jim. "She won a bet and I had to paint a giant pink flower on the side of our ship."

"That's a mighty big boat for two people," said one of the voices.

"Manifest destiny," said Jim, in a voice that sounded like he was evoking some holy goddess.

"Mmm," said one of the captains. "And the survival of man."

"What was the bet, buddy?" asked the second voice.

Jim looked up, panicked, and started to take his finger off the button. Jenny slammed her hand over his to keep the channel open.

"I bet him that I could tell what he was writing on my clit with his tongue. Turns out that man lost the county spelling bee seven times in a row."

Jim's cheeks turned pink and Gary gave Jenny a somber look of disapproval. Across the channel, the two captains hooted with laughter.

"Hey buddy, that's a good one. But you could toss a fellow a bone from that fancy ship of yours. Help a brother out."

Jenny zoomed her monitor in on the items spilling from their cargo hold and spotted half a dozen sealed yellow barrels rolling end over end in zero G. She pointed at them and Jim nodded.

"Those yellow barrels spinning toward you are filled with clean, potable water. Have at 'em, boys. And have a blessed day."

There was no answer, but both ships hit their thrusters so fast that the second one nearly scraped their hull in the race to pick up the water barrels. There were probably people on each ship shoving themselves into EVA suits as fast as they could to tether out and grab the bounty.

Jenny maneuvered the *Jaggery* away from the scuffle. As she backed away, several other ships headed for the debris field.

"Go, go, go," Jenny said to the *Jaggery* under her breath as the hulking beast of a ship pulled away from the gathering crowd of flyers. The dwarf door opened and Boges floated in headfirst like a torpedo. She stopped to whisper to Gary and then catapulted herself off the wall back into the miniature hallway.

"Two dwarves missing from the cargo hold and presumed dead. Six injured. We've sealed the breach temporarily, but it will need a permanent fix before we jump to FTL," Gary reported.

"The dwarves can speak directly to me, you know," said Jenny.

"They like him better," said Jim with a smirk.

"I don't care if they like him better," she said to Jim, then turned to Gary. "I'm the captain and I suggest you let them know. Unless you'd rather sit in your room for the rest of this trip."

Jenny regretted snapping the moment she spoke, but you couldn't make words go backward.

"Yes, Captain," said Gary quietly.

"There's my old Jen," whispered Jim, and Jenny suddenly felt as if she might be sick.

CHAPTER ELEVEN
Beywey Station

Jenny brought the *Jaggery* close to Beywey Station – or what was left of it after construction was halted when the economy crashed for the third time in a generation. Some corporation was probably going to buy up the remains and restart construction eventually, but until they did, Beywey was host to a thriving underground market for hard-to-find goods.

Jim struggled to unclip his harness. Jenny stopped him. "Stay here, Jim. Gary and I are going to handle this one."

He looked up, first surprised, then upset, and slammed his hand onto the console defiantly.

"I can do it, Jen," he said.

"I know you can. But if I take you and leave Gary alone he'll probably run away with the *Jaggery*. We can't have that."

"No, I wouldn't," said Gary, waiting just outside the door.

"You're always so very helpful, Gary," said Jenny flipping him her middle finger. "Trust me, Jim. You're better off here."

Jim settled back into his seat and crossed his arms, refusing to look at her. She opened her mouth to coax him back into a good mood, but thought better of it as a projectile passed by the view screen. The smaller ships were fighting over the dropped water barrels. Things were desperate out here.

Every moment they sat parked was another moment closer to being boarded by pirates or detained by the Reason.

Jenny pushed off and led the way to the airlock, pulling herself along on the rocky outcroppings of the ship's walls. Gary followed, more graceful in weightlessness than clopping over solid ground. It was almost as if both of their bodies had been optimized for space travel.

"Hey Gary," she said, giving herself a push.

"Yes."

"Do all unicorns live in space?"

"Technically, every being lives in space."

"You know what I mean," she said.

"No. We developed space travel many millennia after our origin."

"Is there a home planet of unicorns?"

"Not exactly. Unicorns are born in the heart of a kilonova."

She'd heard that term back in engineering school. Kilonovas were rare instances when a neutron star and a black hole came into contact with one another.

"I guess you don't get a midwife for that sort of birth," she quipped.

"Actually, the Pymmie attend to unicorn births."

"But you weren't born in a kilonova."

"No, I was born on this ship." Gary seemed unwilling to elaborate, and they were at the airlock, so Jenny didn't push it. This had been his father's stoneship originally. The *Jaggery* had been an important part of the battles between the humans and Bala. Usually on the side opposite humankind.

The ship's airlock was stocked with EVA suits in a half-dozen body configurations. Jenny found one that was probably for a fairy, with generous room in back for folded wings. Gary grabbed a well-worn suit that fit him perfectly. Sometimes, she forgot that he'd lived here for most of his life before the Reason had stolen it from him. Her wheelchair was waiting next to the airlock door. Boges was a miracle, getting it here from the cockpit before her. Rusted over and no longer able to fold, it didn't even fit in the access tunnels, but Boges knew all of the shortcuts.

Jenny struggled to get her legs into the EVA suit. Her knees didn't bend easily and she couldn't clear the edge of the seal. Gary came over and held out the suit as she maneuvered her feet down into the legs. When one floated off to the side, Gary spoke up.

"May I?" he asked, holding his hand above her ankle.

"Yeah, stuff it in there. It's not always easy for me to get these things on."

He guided her foot down into the suit and helped her lock it closed in front.

"This is why they booted me out of the Reason Space Force. If you can't suit up and bug out in under a minute, they have no use for you," she said, with a rueful laugh. She immediately regretted sharing something so personal, but he looked at her with complete understanding.

"It was unconscionable for them to discard you due to your disability."

"Jesus. No need to pack a sad, let's go already," she said, locking her helmet on. She hooked one end of a tether to her wheelchair and the other end to her belt. Beywey sometimes had a little gravity and sometimes they went weightless, depending on if the equipment was working and if they had the juice to power it. Unless she wanted to be carried or drag herself along the floor, she had to be ready to get back in her chair.

Gary locked his helmet and Jenny hit a button for the airlock to count down from thirty. The door hissed open and they both pushed off toward the station. Gary went ahead. Her chair was tricky to maneuver in space. The tether between her and it tightened and slackened, slowing her down and jerking her back and forth. She used her thrusters to make slow and careful adjustments so that the metal floating behind her didn't pull her off course.

"You've become more skilled at maneuvering," said Gary, waiting on an exposed support beam. She'd forgotten that they'd walked in openspace together, long ago. That time was a lot more frantic and they nearly didn't live to remember it.

"Ten years of practice," she said. "I've been doing cargo runs in rental ships while you were otherwise occupied. You always have to get out and make repairs on those cheap ships."

"That is not a very lucrative business," he said.

"Tell me about it."

She reached out a hand to catch the beam. They'd come in on the unfinished side of the market, facing away from Earth. This wasn't the official entrance to the station, but it was the one Jenny knew best. The one where you were less likely to be ambushed by whatever gang had control of the Beywey today.

They climbed through the girders and struts. She pulled her chair close so it didn't snag on the metal beams.

"Hey Jen," said Jim in her ear from the *Jaggery*.

"Yeah?"

"The dwarves say the cargo hold will be fixed in thirty."

"All right. We'll make it quick."

She tugged her chair around a corner of the structure toward an expanse of glowing white canvas stretched across the beams. They floated through the vacuum toward a plexiglas bubble set into the canvas. A footrest on her chair snagged on a beam and jerked Jenny back.

"Ooof, shit."

She disentangled it and caught up with Gary. The airlock was one of those cheap jobs you bought preassembled and popped into your tent or dome or whatever separated you from the vacuum of space. It was a circle of plexi, just big enough for a couple of people. This one was brand new. Not the same one Jenny had come in and out of on her most recent visit.

Gary went in first, then Jenny floated inside and tried to yank her chair behind her. It stuck on the edges of the airlock, too large to fit. Gary grasped the tether and pulled as well, but it was too wide for the new doorway, especially since she couldn't collapse it.

A face appeared at the inner door and a worn cardboard sign appeared against the plexi.

NO VISITORS

Jenny switched to the public comm channel.

"It's Jenny," she said.

"Jenny. Get in."

"One sec. Your new airlock is too bloody small. Do you have gravity today?"

"Nope."

"Good."

Jenny went back out of the airlock, unclipped the chair's tether from her suit, and locked it around a girder.

"Is it safe to leave it out there?" asked Gary.

"It's not as if I have a choice. The gravity's off. I don't need it."

She locked the outer door closed and gave a thumbs up through the window of the inner door. A hiss of air filled the capsule. As the inner door opened, their visors fogged over from the change in temperature and humidity.

They removed their helmets and were immediately bathed in the festering moisture of unwashed creatures living with substandard air filtration. Gary looked shocked during the first few seconds on board. The tendons in his neck went rigid.

"Smells like the Quag, huh?" asked Jenny. She pushed off away from him.

It was a considerable accomplishment that Beywey had survived this long. Raids by Reason ships and orbital pirates, plus system failures and gang wars had reduced the once-bustling market to a single hallway of airtight tents. Each time Beywey blew out of the airlock, someone floated back to rebuild it. Moisture dripped from every surface and collected on the floor. Without functioning dehumidifiers, all the water that perspirated and respirated off of warm bodies floated in the air and collected everywhere.

The oxygen level was lower than optimal, too. Jenny took a few fetid breaths and still felt lightheaded.

"It's like a goddamn outhouse in here," she said.

"Scrubbers are offline. Have been for a while," said a damp man holding the cardboard sign. He folded it and tucked it into his patched flight suit. "Welcome back, Jen. That your new ship?"

Jenny was careful and cagey around these folk. Some of them were former Reason like her, but that didn't obligate her to answer truthfully. Information was currency in a place like this.

"It's the one I'm hitching a ride on for the moment," she said. "We have a mess of ships on our tail right now, so we don't have a lot of time to shoot the shit."

"Gotcha. Reason raided a couple of weeks ago, so this is what's left. General store's moved over there in the corner. Bar's gone… floated away real fast out the hole. Saved a few bottles that didn't freeze and burst if you're thirsty."

"No, thanks. Just package goods this time."

They floated by what passed as a hospital up here; an airtight tent with a clear plastic door. A thin-boned elfin woman lay spreadeagled on an exam table, the bulbous head of a baby crowning between her legs. On the table next to her, a man lay face down, the skin of his back open for spinal surgery. The same doctor attended to both procedures. Three of his hands were poised to catch the baby and three others held traction and a scalpel for the back surgery. The elfin woman's head came up in a grimace. Her tiny sharp teeth were brown and cracked. The grimace turned into a smile and she waved at Jenny.

"Baby time, Jen!" she cried, then groaned as another contraction seized her and liquid dripped from around the baby's head. Gary looked away to be polite, even though the woman didn't seem to care who watched.

"Good luck Mymo, you're doing great," said Jenny, pretending not to be slightly nauseated at the glimpse of the elf's distended bits. Kids were a pain in the ass and definitely not worth wrecking your fanny over.

They moved past a vendor trading engine parts. Some of them were scorched by the plasma torches used to pry them out of pirated ships. Others were damaged by the missiles that had blasted their previous owners out of the sky. On a regular day, Jenny would have picked over the parts. Fixing up salvaged ships and reselling them paid better than hauling cargo.

Their guide went down to the far end of the hall where the air smelled fresher and the slightest bit sweet.

"This here is where we moved the exotic items after the blowout. You'll find what you need here." The man pushed off toward the airlock.

Gary hadn't even cringed at the word "exotic," even though it was only ever used as a euphemism for Bala. He'd probably heard much worse in the Quag. Or maybe he'd learned to nod along with the insults so no one guessed he was "exotic" himself. You really couldn't tell when he was all suited up. As long as he kept his pants on, no one would notice that he was part unicorn.

Jenny breathed in the smells of the Bala stalls. Fruit floated under plexi domes anchored to the table that kept them contained in zero G and were airtight in case of sudden decompression. A loss of all this produce would likely bankrupt someone living up here on a razor-thin margin.

"How much for these?" asked Gary, resting his hand on a dome filled with fuzzy pink fruits. The scaly vendor drew himself up until he was higher than Gary, undulating like a pennant in the wind. His face pulled back in a reptilian smile, but he did not answer. Jenny gave him credit, trying to negotiate with a grootslang. They were almost as ruthless as Ricky Tang.

Gary started to move on, but a small voice called out from another tent.

"He's talking to you in your mind."

Gary frowned and appeared to concentrate for a moment.

"Sixteen of something?" he said.

"He said he attended a formal dinner with your family once, when he was a hatchling. He says it's good to know that there are still unicorns alive in the universe. It gives him hope that someday the Bala might rise again." The translator said the last bit in a flat voice, devoid of emotion, as if she didn't believe a word of it herself. The grootslang unsealed one of the domes and held out a fruit to Gary.

"How much?"

"He says it's free," said the translator.

"I couldn't."

"You should. He never gives things away. Take it before he changes his mind."

Gary bowed.

"It's my honor to have met you."

The grootslang turned six shades of blue in succession and settled back into his booth looking satisfied.

The market wasn't large and the conversation had been overheard. So much for no one knowing Gary was part unicorn. More of the Bala vendors came out of their tents to have a look at him.

The young translator looked like an elf mixed with some other being that gave her oversized feet and hands. She floated in front of Gary and explained to the group, "This is Gary from the House of Cobalt. His father is Findae. Gary is the one they say will lead us out of the cold darkness of Reason."

The group murmured and conferred. A few of the older beings genuflected in the manner of their species. Jenny hung back, wary of being surrounded by potential hostiles. She got her back up against a wall out of habit.

"Thank you all," said Gary. "I'm humbled by your welcome. But it is not necessary. I am simply Gary Cobalt now. The Bala nobility no longer exist. I am the same as all of you."

The translator piped up from her stall.

"Let them fawn over you a bit. It's a rare day that they get to practice the old customs." She held out an empty bag. "For all of the tributes they're going to give you."

"No, I couldn't..."

But the vendors were already crowding around, handing him anything they could spare from their tents. Hastily written notes were slipped into his bag to be read later. Most of them were probably pleas for Gary to help imprisoned relatives or enslaved friends. A fairy flapped her wings. The breeze she created smelled like roasted lemons. The translator crossed her arms and waited.

Jenny waved Gary over to the live creatures stall when he seemed nearly finished. He gently extricated himself from the group and joined her.

"Ready, your highness?" She was delighted to learn that it was possible to make a unicorn blush.

Bào Zhú, the animal dealer, had set up tanks for each of the different edible creatures. At first glance, he looked like a squat old man. But when you let your gaze unfocus a bit, there was definitely something magical about him. There was a dark shading around him like an aura. He was probably mixed with at least a little Bala. Bào Zhú floated curled into a ball – legs pulled up tight to his chest. He wheezed with the respiratory disease going around the stations with substandard air filtration. Jenny found herself wishing that she'd kept her helmet on.

In the tank below her, shiny, snakelike animals burrowed into a dark wet substrate pinned to one side of the cage by a mass of chicken wire.

"Glitterslips are in stock, Jen. I know you like to keep those on hand," said Bào Zhú. "Best price all year."

Glitterslips were tasty when charred over an open fire, but more than that, they gave you the ability to hear the thoughts of creatures around you for as long as they took to digest. You just had to make sure you didn't buy the females of the species, who laid eggs in your abdomen which later ate you from the inside out as they matured.

Jenny nodded and held up one finger while moving on to the other tanks. Bào Zhú put on a pair of white cloth gloves and plucked a glitterslip from out of the substrate and tucked it into a tiny floating sphere.

Jenny passed another tank that appeared to contain floating bubbles of wet sand. As she watched, a set of tiny animal tracks imprinted themselves onto of the globs of sand. A huvelon. They were useful if you could train them to fetch, but a pain to locate if they escaped their cage.

"Twenty for that one," said Bào Zhú, hovering over her shoulder. "We don't get deliveries as often as we used to." Jenny looked around at the shredded, floating canvas of his tent – no repairs had been done since the blowout. He was probably hurting for cash and would take any little trinket she offered.

Jenny floated to the back of the tent where a pair of trisicles huddled against each other under a dome. They were a mature breeding pair with a couple of sucklings attached to each of them – exactly what she needed for Gary. They'd need to get more to maintain a fully functional FTL drive, but this was a promising start.

Jenny passed by the trisicles as if she didn't see them. If Bào Zhú got as much as a whiff of her interest, he'd quadruple the price in a hot second.

"Captain, those are the trisicles we need," said Gary, floating into the tent. "And a breeding pair with sucklings. Fortuitous indeed."

Jenny cursed under her breath. Everyone within earshot now knew they were looking for trisicles and that the *Jaggery* was Jenny's ship. She was willing to bet that prices on this station just jumped by a factor of ten. Bào Zhú's mouth opened in a smile, then he froze as he noticed Gary, staring in horror.

"You two know each other?" asked Jenny.

"No. We've never met," said Bào Zhú, far too quickly to be true. "But I have heard of you. Welcome, Gary Cobalt."

Gary watched Bào Zhú carefully, but did not answer. There was something going on between the two of them that Jenny wasn't quite understanding.

"Those are a very fine pair of trisicles," Bào Zhú exclaimed, changing the subject. "Harvested from a fresh colony recently discovered in the rings of Saturn. They are fully mature and have already bred six litters in the time that they've been here."

"They are already breeding, Captain, this is exactly what we need."

Jenny held a finger in front of Gary's face to silence him. He was quiet, but some glint in his eye made her think he'd called her bluff on purpose. Maybe to mess with her.

Or maybe to ensure that Bào Zhú got a good price for his goods. Those magical beings had a tendency to stick together against humans, and there seemed to be a history between these two.

"How much? And keep in mind I just spent my last dollar getting off that hellhole of a planet," she offered as the opening salvo in her negotiation.

"We don't take Reason currency here any more," said Bào Zhú, flipping himself around in a circle to distract her. His left hand was curled up to his body and his face was marked with dozens of small scars as if he'd been hit at close range by a shotgun blast. Everyone had their war wounds.

"You're legally required to accept the official currency of the Reason," she said.

"After the last raid, they reasserted their right to Beywey and threw everything out into the vacuum. Only those of us with self-contained tents survived. And some of us," he gestured to the shredded tent with his uninjured hand, "only made it by the skin of our teeth. None of us want their dirty cash now. You want to spend dollars, go back to the front of the market where the humans are."

"But why come back to Beywey at all? You know the soldiers will eventually return. They'll clear you all out again. Over and over. The Reason never gives up," she said.

"And where would we go?" Bào Zhú asked, suddenly angry. Minuscule pinpricks of electricity crackled around him. Jenny backed away. "Do you think it's so easy to leave when you're surrounded by openspace?" He growled and turned back to the tanks, which vibrated with the muted screeches of the creatures inside.

Jenny pulled a vial full of creamy white liquid from her suit and held it out to Bào Zhú.

"Angel tears. Three full ounces. You can–"

He slapped it out of her hand and the vial went spinning

away into the market.

"No one wants your tears. We want a way off this station."

Jenny kept her eyes fixed on Bào Zhú while tracking the trajectory of the vial in her peripheral vision. Her angel tears were one of the few valuable things she had left – they were a gift from a former lover and she didn't want to leave without them.

A few of the Bala vendors had gathered near the back of the market, listening to the conversation. Bào Zhú turned to Gary.

"The Cobalts were a good and honorable family. Surely you can offer safe passage to one of the remaining Bala worlds for those of us who have survived?" he asked.

Gary looked at Jenny and waited.

"I'm the captain of the *Jaggery*," she said to Bào Zhú. "It's me you want to negotiate with."

Bào Zhú continued to speak only to Gary.

"I beg of you, your highness. Have mercy. They'll surely kill us all the next time they raid the station. They took my son the last time they came. They said he was a 'natural resource.' I don't know where they took him."

The translator came forward, holding out a necklace that seemed to be made from thick finger bones.

"They killed my husband during the raid. Sliced out his heart with a laser scalpel while they held him down in front of me. He was still alive when they started cutting into him."

Another Bala creature spoke in a language that Jenny couldn't understand. The others listened and nodded along sadly as the creature's voice crackled like a bonfire, then dissolved into a sound like the rain.

"I'm sorry about your family," said Gary.

Jenny stayed close to the trisicle bubble that had been forgotten in the larger conversation. She wasn't going to leave without them, but it was getting a little close in here.

All the Bala were getting riled up and crowding around both of them. It made her squirrelly.

"Well, Captain. What is your decision?" asked Gary, folding his arms in front of him. At moments like this, she could see why unicorns used to rule the universe. When he looked at her like that, she felt petty and small. It took all of her will not to flip him the finger and head for the airlock with the trisicles.

"Is the group making an official request?" she asked, stalling. "If there's a formal request, I need to hear it."

"We, the Bala of Beywey, request formal asylum from the captain of the *Jaggery*," said Bào Zhú. A handful of creatures nodded or waved, as was their custom. A couple verbally agreed in English.

Jenny reached over and grabbed the vial of tears that had become stuck to one of the few functioning air vents. She tucked it back into her suit pocket and looked around at the creatures waiting for her answer.

There was certainly room aboard the ship. There was enough space for ten times this many refugees. And if she asked for some of their wares in exchange for transport, say thirty per cent, that would leave them each a little nest egg to restart their business elsewhere. Financially, it was a sound plan.

The only problem, and it was a significant problem, was having all of these Bala tagging along with her through the Reason. Even through the relatively easy checkpoint at Fairyfloss, it presented a huge risk for everyone.

"As the captain of the *Jaggery*," she said, twirling her helmet in her hands and drawing out the words so she could weigh the options for a few seconds longer. "I'd like to ex–"

The airlock exploded in a burst of light. The air in the market was sucked out into openspace. Jenny's muscle memory of boot camp emergency decompression training kicked in. She slammed on her helmet and locked it. As the suit pressurized, she instinctively turned to help the soldier next to her, except no one was there.

Gary had been sucked backward and ended up stuck against the wall of a tent. Luckily for him, the canvas had prevented him from being pulled out of the blown out airlock that now vented into openspace. She noted in dismay that his helmet was still clipped to his side. He had only a few moments before he suffocated and froze.

Reason officers floated into the market, suited up in their dark red zero G riot gear. Their faces were obscured by visors, making them all look like giant beady-eyed insects. They began throwing everything into openspace that hadn't already been sucked out of the broken airlock. Including the vendors.

Jenny landed next to Gary. She unclipped his helmet from his belt and slapped it onto his head. She latched it shut and the suit pressurized automatically.

"Good?" she asked.

"Yes," he said between panting breaths. "Get the others."

"That's a negative," she said, pushing off and unclipping the trisicle tank from its shelf. They barely seemed to notice the sudden drop in temperature. Trisicles were accustomed to the rigors of deep space. The thick, chitinous shells that kept them functional in a freezing vacuum also made them the perfect meal for bone-hungry unicorns.

Bào Zhú had tucked himself into a large airtight tank. He sat on a perch, curled into himself, presumably hiding until the officers left. His lips moved as if he was chanting. All of the air had emptied from the market and goods floated freely. The Reasoners were coming closer as Bala in EVA suits fought to get away. Bodies floated frozen and stiff among the shreds of tents and bits of debris. The translator's hair undulated around her frozen corpse like snakes across sand.

"Gary, follow me," Jenny said into her comm. She tossed him the tank of trisicles. They floated through empty hallways that used to be full of vendors.

Jenny pulled the lever on an airtight door at the end of one hallway and floated into a dark section of the station that had never been finished. She wound her way through exposed girders, looking back to make sure that Gary was keeping up.

"Where are we going?" asked Gary.

"There's a control room in the back that always has pressure and gravity, even when the power's out. We can hide back there until the Reason leaves."

She gave a hefty pull off a girder toward a light ahead of them in the darkness. They crossed a large atrium that was in the central gathering space of the station. The control room would have looked down over a dozen floors of shops, docking ports, and living quarters. There were even plumbing pipes at the bottom which indicated the design of an elaborate fountain in the center. It had all been left to decay in the freezing darkness.

Jenny typed a code into the airlock on the control room door. She stuffed the trisicles in ahead of her, then shoved Gary inside while she squeezed in last, pulling the door shut. They were jammed up against each other with the trisicles somewhere below her feet where she couldn't see them.

The interior airlock door opened and gravity kicked in. They all spilled into the room in a heap. Someone reached down and unlatched Jenny's helmet.

"Well, well, well," said a familiar voice. "What do we have here?"

CHAPTER TWELVE
Unamip's Blessing

Gary cringed at the string of profanities coming out of Jenny's mouth. Being deferential to Reason personnel didn't always help, but swearing at them never did. It was hubris driving her to spit every foul word she knew at the officers instead of trying to negotiate for their release. The senior officer drew his weapon and held it against Gary's forehead. The junior officer unholstered hers as well, but with trembling hands. Seeing that, Jenny quieted. Thankfully, she was smart enough to know that a nervous person's finger could easily slip on the trigger.

"We are not in violation of any statutes," said Gary. He hoped to mitigate Jenny's inflammatory comments by appealing to the little "r" reason in these people. "We don't intend to interfere with your sweep of the market. Go about your confiscation and we'll be on our way."

"Are you out of your bloody mind?" said Jenny. It was a moment before he realized she was speaking to him and not the officers. She pointed up at the taller one. "Don't you see who that is?"

Gary stared at the humans in front of him. Unless he looked closely, all the pink fleshy men looked alike. The junior officer was brown, like him, but the peach one was sporting a fresh burn in the reverse outline of a hand. As if he'd put up his palm to shield his eyes from a blast. He realized this was the officer from the bar, Colonel Wenck. The one they'd shot. So much for little "r" reason.

It was interesting to Gary that though the three nations that had come together to form the Reason were ostensibly equal, the officers were almost always pink people. It reminded him of the way Bala made the distinction between unicorns and centaurs. They were very close in everything but a few small cosmetic differences, but you would never find a centaur at the seat of government.

"You have no right to detain me. I was released this morning," said Gary.

Wenck spoke only to Jenny. "In accordance with the FTL Fuel Conservation Act of 2249, this fuel source is property of the Reason and will be confiscated."

"He's a man. Leave him alone," she replied.

Wenck nudged the plexi tank full of trisicles with his boot.

"If he's a man, why does he need a whole family of trisicles?" he asked.

"He's a xenobiologist," said Jenny.

"And I'm Santa Claus," said Wenck with a smirk. "I'm here to pick up a present for all the good Reason girls and boys who need to get into FTL for Christmas." He grabbed the edge of Gary's suit and yanked him forward until he could see down into the crown of his head. "Mmm, there we are." He let Gary go and crouched in front of Jenny, his gun resting on his knee, but still pointed in her direction. "But what about you 'Captain Perata'?" Gary could hear the quotes around her name and title. Wenck clearly didn't think much of Jenny.

"I've been commissioned to deliver a cargo. All legal. Check the paperwork," she said.

Jenny slowly moved her hand to the keypad mounted on the arm of her EVA suit. Wenck's eyes unfocused for a moment as he received a data dump on his ocular display.

"No warrants, no irregularities. I guess I have to let you go, Captain Perata."

The second officer, a thick woman with a wide neck that barely fit into her EVA suit, reached for Gary's head. Gary grabbed her hand by the wrist and held it there. He could afford the risk. If they shot him, he'd heal in minutes.

"Colonel?" asked the officer, with a slowness to her voice that echoed the speed of her dawning realization. "I think we've got a uni-corn here." She broke "unicorn" into two words like he'd heard Jim do occasionally. It was a funny thing humans did when they were uncomfortable saying the word. Unicorns had been mythical creatures on their world for so long that a large number of people had a hard time believing in them. Even when face to face with direct evidence.

Wenck continued reading Jenny's records without answering. The junior officer went on.

"He doesn't look like a uni-corn, but I think it's at least part uni-corn. The bottom part. Because he doesn't have hoof hands. Where's his horn?"

The woman looked genuinely confused by Gary's mixed appearance. Wenck sighed heavily.

"He's a half-breed, Gakhar. Part human, part Bala. Probably sold his horn for cash, but he'll grow a new one. Count on it."

Gakhar wound her hand around in a circle until Gary had to let it go. She used the muzzle of her firearm to push Gary's head down so she could see for herself.

"There's a little bit of horn left, but it's smaller than I thought it would be," said Gakhar, peering down over him. She pushed on the spot and Gary felt pressure on the top of his head. "And sharp, too." He could have kicked her into unconsciousness in half a second. At the very least, they seemed to have no interest in taking Jenny along. If they took him, she was clever enough to come up with a plan to get him back from the Reason. She was excellent with loopholes in regulations. And if she was properly motivated, she had the ability to access Reason systems and find him.

"I'll go peacefully," said Gary.

"What are you doing?" Jenny said in a low voice.

"I'm sure you'll figure out a plan once you're back on the *Jaggery*," said Gary, emphasizing the last four words.

"I'm not going back to the *Jaggery* without you," she replied, equally emphasizing her last two.

"Don't worry about your stoneship," said Wenck. "It won't be there to go back to."

"What do you mean?" asked Jenny.

"The *Jaggery* will be impounded into evidence. You are a suspect in the destruction of a Reason-owned bar in downtown Broome City this morning. We're not sure who gave the order to fire, but a review of the ship's communication logs will clear that up pretty quickly." He stood up and stretched his lower back. "If I were you, Perata, I'd take this very brief moment before you are a wanted woman to find a ride out of Reasonspace and not come back."

For once, Jenny seemed to be at a loss for words.

"Let the records show that the Reason has subsumed the stoneship *Jaggery* into its collective holdings. Captain Geneva Perata has thirty minutes to vacate the property with her personal belongings. It pains me to do this, because you are the hero of Copernica Citadel, but–"

"I'm not *on* the property, you jackass," said Jenny. "How can I get my belongings and vacate it?"

Wenck looked lost for a moment. Jenny tapped on her arm pad while he stammered.

"I suppose we could bring you back for a supervised visit to collect your personal items," he said.

"That's right, you can bring me back there. But you'll have to speak to the new owner about getting permission for a search. Law says you can't take a man's ship if he's not suspected of a crime."

She flicked a gloved finger across the pad to send a file to Wenck. He read the first few lines and flinched. Wenck had recognized Jenny in the bar, but hadn't given a second glance to Jim after dismissing him as a useless old spacer. She was betting that he had an order to detain her, but not Jim and his property. Wenck scanned through the rest of the document quickly, his eyes flicking back and forth. Doubtless, he was trying to find some loophole that Jenny had missed. Gary knew that if Boges had prepared the transfer of title, even in haste, no loophole would be found.

"That's right, mate," said Jenny with a grin. "The *Jaggery* now belongs to one James Bryant, who is a fully human, able-bodied fella, without a speck of magic in him. You can't have it." She shoved Gakhar's firearm away from her face.

"Well look at that," said Wenck, rubbing his irritated cheek thoughtfully. "You managed to take that beautiful rockship away from me."

"And the unicorn is coming with me too," she said. "You can't confiscate the fuel source for a ship on a Reason-sanctioned mission. I have a delivery commissioned by the–"

Wenck blinked slowly to shut off his ocular display, as well as the incident-logging camera built into it. In the Quag, those cameras were always turned off right before a CO was about to do something they didn't want recorded. Eventually, inmates learned that when you saw that slow blink, you ran.

"Jenny…" warned Gary.

"Shoot her and take the unicorn," said Wenck. "We'll claim she shot first."

"You can't just kill a citizen," said Jenny, holding up her hands in surrender. Gary scanned the room for weapons and exits. Even if he could get to the door, Jenny wouldn't be as quick as usual in the gravity of the control room, and he didn't think he could carry her fast enough in their bulky EVA suits.

"I'll go with you willingly. Just leave her here," said Gary. He had felt the wrath of men like Wenck in prison. They were humans so sure of their place in the world that they believed themselves to be above the law. Not even a perfectly executed dwarven contract would stop a man like this from getting what he believed he was entitled to. But Gary could at least save Jenny's life. "You get back to the ship and work on getting me out," he said to her. She shook her head.

"Don't give these bloody wankers one inch or they'll–"

"Shoot her," Wenck said to the junior officer. Gakhar hesitated.

"Don't shoot," said Gary, keeping his voice as calm as he could in light of the pounding of his heart. "She can stay here and I'll go with you."

"Private Gakhar, is it?" asked Jenny. "Listen. Back off for one minute and let me talk to the Colonel. You're not disobeying orders, we're just going to have a chat, him and me. 'Kay?"

"Be quiet," said Gakhar, pleading. "Don't talk while I do this." Gakhar closed her eyes and Gary knew she was about to fire.

"Stop," he yelled in his best booming unicorn voice – the one he'd used when he'd commanded his own troops. Gakhar jumped and the gun went off. The plastic bullet pinged off the wall, shattering into pieces that rained down to the floor.

"You missed, you idiot," said Wenck.

"Kind of not," said Jenny. She reached a gloved hand up to her head. It came away red. She looked up at Gary and blood began to pour down from her hairline. The sharp edges of the bullet had sliced open her scalp. Nothing fatal, from what he could tell, but humans always bled quite a bit from head wounds. It gave him an idea.

"Unamip has granted you a moment to reconsider your actions," he said to Gakhar. "You have a second chance to do the right thing."

Using slow and deliberate motions, he unlocked the sleeve of his EVA suit and set it on the floor. Gakhar was solely focused on Jenny, hands shaking and eyes wide. And Wenck was looking only at Gakhar while spitting orders at her.

"To hell with that. You have a second chance to avoid Reason military court by shooting this useless spacer," said Wenck. His neck had turned from pink to splotchy red. "I'm willing to forget that terrible first shot, Private. But you'd better get the second one right. Get closer, hold your gun with two hands, and squeeze the trigger, don't pull."

Gary reached up and ran his fingers through his hair as if it was a nervous tic. The skin snagged on the jagged bit of horn he'd been growing for months. He dragged his hand against the spot until he felt the sting and pop of the skin on his palm opening.

"Let me see," he said, closing his fist and reaching over to Jenny, pretending to examine her head wound. She bent down and he smeared a palmful of his silver blood into the gash in her scalp. The bullet had sliced deep. He could feel her skull bone under his fingertips. By the time he pulled his hand away, his own cut had already closed.

"Oh my god," she whispered, looking up at him in wonder. The blood was already having an effect. He hoped it would be enough.

Wenck separated the two of them with a kick to Jenny's side. Gakhar lowered her weapon as Wenck stepped between them.

"No need to get rough. We're good here," said Jenny. Gary

could hear the giddiness in her voice from the interaction between his blood and hers. He prayed to Unamip that if it didn't heal her completely, it would at least stop her from dying alone in an abandoned space station.

"Shoot or I'll bring you up on charges," said Wenck, grabbing Gakhar by the shoulder and positioning her directly in front of Jenny.

"This is completely unnecessary," Gary said. "Just leave her here."

Jenny sat up straighter and stared back at Gakhar.

"I know you're going to shoot," she said. "And I understand why. Just know that I have no ill will toward you. I know what it's like to follow orders. I just have to ask." She unlocked the center seal of her EVA suit and pulled the thick fabric open. "Do it here." She pointed to the center of her chest. "Not my head. For the funeral you understand... my kuia wouldn't like to see a mess like that. You wouldn't make your gran look at your busted open head, would you?"

Gakhar nodded and aimed her weapon at Jenny's chest.

Just as he'd hoped, Jenny Perata knew her way around unicorn blood, probably from her time on the front lines of the war. Unicorn blood could heal a lot of wounds, but neurological pathways – especially those in the brain itself – were complex and easy to botch. The blood could spur the regrowth of heart or lung tissue far more easily than it could reconstruct the complicated pathways of the human mind. You could theoretically bring a person back to life after their brain was turned to pudding, but they might not be the same human. Or they might return to consciousness a blank slate; childlike and helpless, but in the body of an adult.

Gakhar closed her eyes again.

"Eyes open, Private," yelled Wenck. "I'll tell you, when we get back you're going to be reassigned to a garbage transport on the freaking moon."

Gakhar cringed and pulled the trigger.

Gary wanted to turn away, but he could not stop himself from watching. The gun fired and this time nothing pinged against the wall. The bullet hit Jenny just under her collarbone. The hole was as small as a thumbnail. She jumped as if she'd been startled. A second later the bullet fragmented internally and she bucked as if she'd been kicked in the chest. She collapsed forward, palms on the floor. Blood welled out of her mouth and splattered on the tile. Gary reached out and Wenck kicked his hand away with his shiny boot. The colonel held out Gary's helmet to Gakhar.

"Finally. Lock him up tight. If we lose him on the way back to the ship, it's coming out of your paycheck."

While the private tucked Gary's arm back into his EVA suit and clipped his helmet on, he watched Jenny to see if his blood was having any effect on the gunshot wound. If it wasn't enough, she'd die right here in front of him. That wasn't even the worst case scenario. If it didn't quite heal her all the way, she might lie here in agony until someone from the *Jaggery* came into Beywey to fetch her. Her hands slid on the wet floor and she crashed cheek first into the tile. She lay there, coughing up mouthfuls of blood.

Her eyes tracked upward, just for a second, before she closed them. She lifted her hand in a weak thumbs up. He almost laughed. He might be the immortal one, but Jenny Perata would probably outlive all of them.

Gakhar shoved Gary toward the airlock. They were going to lock him up on board the *Arthur Phillip* for the rest of his life – which would be a very long time if they didn't kill him in the process. He'd been locked up by Jenny and again in the Quag. The fear, the filth, the chains. He couldn't do it again.

Gary had no intention of letting his kidnappers get him on the *Arthur Phillip*. He had been abducted a handful of times over the years. Humans had stolen his horn, his blood, and everything of value on his body. He'd learned never to let his captors get to the second location. Escape was significantly more difficult once he was locked up tight.

As the outer door opened, Gakhar pushed him through the atrium. They sailed back into the remains of the market, Wenck taking up the rear. Beywey was a frozen graveyard. Priceless Bala treasures floated freely in the air as Reason officers tore apart tents and smashed furniture, looking for stragglers.

Gary passed the tent of the grootslang who had once dined with his family. The lizard now floated stiff and unseeing among his frozen fruits. Gary stopped at the stall and touched a gloved finger to the creature's head, asking a blessing from Unamip upon the kind stranger who had died. Unamip's blessings were many and varied. There was one for every occasion.

He requested one more blessing before Wenck caught up to him. It was the blessing for a man about to take his own life in the service of a greater good.

Gary unlocked his helmet.

CHAPTER THIRTEEN
Race to the Jaggery

Jenny lay on her side in the control room, not sure whether to pray for life or death. She didn't even know toward which gods to direct her prayer. On the upside, she was able to breathe again. On the downside, the searing pain of two dozen plastic shards embedded in her internal organs washed over her as Gary's blood stabilized her shock symptoms.

Her rapidly healing body pushed the plastic bits out of her tissues. A few of them pinged against the inside of her suit. A couple of the higher ones emerged inside her throat. She coughed them up and spit them onto the floor. They were sharp and multi-faceted like little plastic diamonds, designed to inflict maximum damage on organic tissue while leaving steel bulkheads intact. You could shoot anyone on a ship in space without fear of explosive decompression. They were slow, painful, and quite effective. Jenny didn't need medical training to feel her body failing in various, serious ways.

As the bullets tried to shred her insides, Gary's blood was simultaneously trying to knit her back together. She had no idea how the magic of it functioned, only that her cells craved more as they worked to stem the cascade of failures. She put her head down on the cool floor and breathed, letting the pain pierce her. She'd learned years ago, after Copernica, that leaning into the pain worked better for her than fighting it. She couldn't always make it stop, but she could let it burn within her like a fire.

People who weren't in constant pain could fritter their lives away with meaningless delightful activities. But when you hurt all the time, you had to make every single motion count. Going out with friends? You might need to push yourself a quarter mile uphill to the bar. Those drinks better be top notch. Sitting up to read a book? It better be worth the ache in your lower back in the morning. Every day was a complex calculus of tradeoffs, but she was used to spending pain like currency to get what she wanted.

The room around her was quiet... except for Jim's voice coming from her helmet nearby.

"Jen, do you hear me? Goddamn it woman, answer me."

She tried to answer him, but she couldn't catch her breath. The healing was slowing down. The viscous glob of blood Gary had smeared on her head like an anointing oil had stopped the worst of the bleeding, but her lungs were still full of liquid. She coughed forcefully and another mouthful of it came up.

"Jen? I hear you. Are you shot?"

"Mmmm," said Jenny.

"Aw shit." His voice became muted as he spoke to someone else in the cockpit. Probably Boges.

"Reason," gasped Jenny. She gagged and coughed a clot out of her throat. It jiggled on the floor like a dessert they made her eat in school.

"I know, Jen. They have us boxed in. They can't take the ship, but I can't get to you until they leave. Can you hold on for a bit longer?"

Jenny pushed off with one arm and got herself to somewhere between hunching over and sitting. There was a lot of blood on the floor of the control room, but none of it was silver. They'd taken Gary unharmed.

She took a shallow breath in and it felt like her lungs were wet and full. She pulled the helmet closer and leaned down toward it.

"I'm fine," she whispered, because that's what she always said, even if her heart was beating slightly out of rhythm because the muscle fibers were still knitting themselves together.

"You don't sound fine," said Jim. "Hang tight."

She sat and listened to Jim and Boges argue about whether to start firing on Reason ships. Jim, of course, wanted to blast his way into the station and stage some dramatic rescue, but Boges convinced him to wait and see if they could grab Gary when the Reason officers came out of Beywey.

"Why do your ships have no goddamn shuttles?" asked Jim. His voice was as high and tight as his haircut.

"Because we don't feel the need to take over every planet that we see," said Boges. Jenny had never heard her so agitated, not even when they'd locked up Gary for all those months.

She lifted her helmet and yelped. Her pectoral muscles spasmed, ejecting a few more bits of plastic into her EVA suit. Boges and Jim went quiet.

"Jen, are those guys messing with you again?" he asked.

She dropped the helmet over her head. His worried voice was right in her ear now.

"They're gone," she panted.

"Wait. Here they come," said Jim. "Six in riot gear, two in EVA suits. No Gary."

"They'd only leave him behind if he was dead." Boges' response was punctuated by the sound of tapping on Jenny's tablet. She was scanning the station for signs of life. Which is what Jenny would have done in her place.

"Aw shit," said Jim. "He was our ride."

"The *Jaggery* says that there is one other person-sized

being alive aboard the station besides Jenny."

Jenny noticed Boges had already dropped "Captain" from her name. She leaned on her arm and buttoned up her EVA suit. It was a risky bet that Gakhar would shoot her in the chest and not the head. She'd seen soldiers come back from point-blank shots in the brain. Even with unicorn blood results were mixed. Her company had seen more than one zombie-like private before they'd stopped trying to resurrect people with head wounds.

"Where?" she asked. She coughed and sprayed the inside of her helmet with a fine spray of red droplets. She could still see, mostly. And it might have been her imagination, but it felt easier to breathe. More like the sharp ache of cracked ribs digging into your side than the burning sear of a stab wound. Jenny knew both from personal experience.

"Maybe," said Boges. "I can't tell who it is. But I assure you, Gary did not come out with them."

There was a screeching tone as the *Arthur Phillip* hailed them with a message. Jim boomed out over the comm. "Gentlemen, what can I assist you with?"

"Sir, we will need the documentation for the cargo in your hold immediately. If you can provide Reason-only provenance, you will have satisfied legal conditions of ownership and we will be able to depart." Ondre's voice was slow and deliberately formal, trying to intimidate Jim into compliance.

Jenny knew bigotry couched in legalspeak when she heard it. The bottom line was that if Jim could prove the boxes had belonged to a human and were going to a human, he could keep them. She heard him tapping, slow and unsure, to bring up the documents on her tablet.

"I sent it over. Passage booked for two large shipping containers by the reverend mother, Lady Nashita Naveen, Sisters of the Supersymmetrical Axion."

That gave them pause. Though not an official priest of the Reason, Lady Nashita was the closest thing they had to a prophet.

"*The* Lady Nashita?"

"The very one."

"And she put you in charge of her time-sensitive cargo?"

"I'm the best pilot in the galaxy."

There was a sound like a cough mixed with a chuckle. They must have read Jim's service record. He was barely the best pilot in a room full of dryads and their years-long reaction times.

"She and I have been friends for a long time," he protested, sensing the slight to his reputation. Jenny willed them to move along. If they teased him about his driving enough, he was sure to start an argument. That man would lose an entire stoneship over a bruised ego.

"Sure, old man," Ondre said. "I get it. She's helping out an old friend who's down on his luck. Moving relics from one planet to another."

"No," said Jim. "She entrusted us to get these boxes to Fort J in time for the Summit."

Ondre paused for a long moment. Any cargo headed to the Summit under orders from the Sisters was likely to be important. If Jim let him stew for just a moment longer, Ondre was bound to let the *Jaggery* move along. But, of course, Jim would never do that.

"We're getting paid a pretty penny to–" he began.

"Dammit Jim, shut up," Jenny muttered, forgetting that the comm was open. All sounds from the cockpit stopped.

"Who was that?" asked Ondre.

"Just one of my buddies fixing some hull damage from the orbital pirates. How's it going Chexy?" asked Jim. Jenny took the biggest breath she could without coughing. It wasn't much, but it seared her lungs.

"Almost done out here, boss," Jenny said, trying her best to sound both exasperated and nonchalant, like a real maintenance grunt. Thankfully, her voice rasped and crackled and sounded nothing like her own. "Pirates tore us a new one."

The comm went quiet again, but they seemed to come to the conclusion that she was legit.

"We'll be leaving now, sir, but take care that you don't let this ship fall into the wrong hands again, if you know what I mean."

"Yeah, I gotcha. You won't find no Bala filth on my ship. Except the dwarves, of course, but they don't count. They're part of the ship."

Jenny knew he was blowing smoke for cover, but it still stung to hear him say the slur. That was her wife he was talking about. She pulled herself to sitting with a groan once she was sure the Reason officers had closed the open channel.

"They're departing, Captain," said Boges.

"Thanks," said Jenny and Jim in unison. Jenny was starting to fully grasp the magnitude of turning over the ship to Jim. She'd done it in haste to save their ride, but now there was nothing stopping him from simply turning around and flying away. She hoped he didn't realize that before she got it back.

"Jenny, can you move?" asked Jim.

"Just about. Gravity's on. One minute."

"Go fast because they backed off, but they're still within visual range. None of us over here can EVA over to you without attracting attention. You have to make your way to us."

Which wasn't entirely true. Jim could spacewalk over to her, but he would never agree to that. Jim would sooner die than float around in openspace.

"'Kay," Jenny replied. She pushed herself all the way up to sitting, arms shaking with adrenaline. Her bones ached, especially her lower back and hips. Her bone marrow was going into overdrive making red blood cells to replace what she'd lost. She was suddenly incredibly thirsty, but there was no unaccounted-for water hanging around in an isolated station like this. Every drop was in use.

Jenny got hold of the edge of the door frame and dragged herself toward the airlock. The button to open the door was placed at shoulder height for standing people. Even before getting shot in the chest, it would have been a feat to get up there. Now, it looked like scaling a mountain. She pulled herself halfway up onto a rolling chair next to the control console. The bottom of her diaphragm rested on the edge of the chair and pressed painfully into her lungs. She couldn't get more than a sip of air. She dropped back down to the floor with a yelp.

"Dammit."

"What's wrong?" asked Jim.

"Can't open the airlock."

"Oh no, Jen. You have to," said Jim. "I can't come out there."

Jenny wondered if there was a Boges-sized suit on the *Jaggery*. She went to wipe the blood off her face and her arm thwacked into the plexi of her helmet. Her brain wasn't working. She made sure she hadn't cracked her arm tablet and it dawned on her that she could use it to open the airlock.

She pulled herself back up onto the chair, digging the edge into her guts again. She nudged it over to the console and thanked her lucky stars that the keypad was low enough for her to reach. She turned the power key and let the console boot up.

Beywey's computer system was so old that even her tiny EVA suit tablet was exponentially more powerful. The problem wouldn't be getting into the system, it would be convincing her lightning-fast tablet to talk with such an ancient behemoth. The console practically creaked as it started up. The screens were old two-dimensional readouts, not even touchscreens. She loaded up a little program she'd come up with while laid up in bed after Copernica. A little bit of code that let her log into any Reason system using her old credentials. She couldn't get through keycard door locks, especially on planets within Reasonspace, but these deep databases out in the middle of nowhere didn't always have updated personnel deactivation records.

The computer pinged a welcome to her.

"Jen, you out yet?"

"One minute."

"Because there are a few orbital pirates who seem to be mighty interested in us," Jim said.

Jenny made sure her helmet was secure and hit the command to open the inner door. The outer door shut and a thirty-second countdown started until the airlock was pressurized again. She looked behind her and realized she'd nearly forgotten the globe of trisicles. She inched the chair closer and grabbed the handle.

As much as she wanted him to be, Jenny couldn't quite believe that Gary was the single lifeform that Boges had detected. Wenck would never have left Beywey without his unicorn. They'd tear the station apart rather than leave such a valuable resource. The only way they'd leave him was if he was dead. Which brought her to an important question. How could anyone kill a unicorn? As far as she knew, it would take something akin to a complete dismembering. Even multiple shots to the head would only net you a slightly less coherent and decidedly more pissed-off unicorn.

If Gary was dead, she hoped he was at least somewhere inside of Beywey and not floating around outside the station. Once a projectile got going in a particular direction in openspace, it would just keep going forever. It could take days to find his body among the debris. Dead or alive, she wasn't leaving the system without him. Even dead, Gary still had at least a small sliver of horn left on his head. Enough to get them at least part of the way to Jaisalmer. Maybe Soliloquy Station, where she could trade something for a sliver of some other unlucky unicorn's horn. The Reason had locked down most sources, but Ricky probably knew where to get some.

The inner door pinged and Jenny pulled herself and the bugs into the airlock. The pull of gravity was less strong in here. About half of Earth. Whatever generator or spell they were using only had a radius of the room. Depressurization was fast – less than ten seconds. The outer door of the airlock opened silently and Jenny floated across the atrium to the market door. Though zero G had the unfortunate effect of shifting her lacerated organs around and making it harder to catch her breath.

The market door was open. Pieces of canvas floated around like ghosts in the darkness. The soldiers had broken anything of value that couldn't be thrown out of the airlock, lights included. Jenny flicked on her headlamp and pushed through floating objects, ignoring everything smaller than a body. She kept seeing little flickers of motion out of the corner of her eye, but on turning, there was only debris.

She came upon their Bala translator, skirt flared in the vacuum to reveal a worn-down blue-green tail fin instead of legs. It had to have been hard up in space for a part-mermaid, in a place where water was rationed so strictly. She passed the grootslang that had spoken to Gary, splayed out in a climbing position. Probably trying to crawl back into his airtight tent when the door was blasted open. These creatures were prepared for slow leaks, but no one could outrun an explosive decompression.

She floated on toward the medical tent. Her friend Mymo

floated inside, a frozen infant clutched to her chest. The doctor and his other patient were dead as well.

"Fucking Reason," she said. Not all the pangs in her chest were from the shrapnel.

"Jen?" asked Jim.

"Coming," she replied.

"Hurry up there kiddo, before you bleed out." Jim said, with an anxious laugh. They'd been working together for so long that she could hear the worry he was trying to keep out of his voice.

She turned out of the medical tent. A huge object caught her eye up near the ceiling. She grabbed a shelf and pushed off. It was Gary's body. He was frozen solid like the others, holding his helmet out in front of him like a beggar's cup. She pulled him closer. The last little bit of pearlescent horn had been dug out of his head. At least he was probably already dead when they'd hacked away at his skull. Even she hadn't been that considerate.

"Found him," she said into the comm, breathless.

"Thank god," said Jim. "Tell him he's an ass for not answering me."

"He's dead," said Jenny. She heard a tiny gasp from Boges.

"But the single lifesign–" began Jim.

"Not him." Jenny hung onto Gary's suit and looked around. Someone else was alive in here.

"Well, tether him in then. Go fast, the Reason ship is waiting, but the pirates are getting antsy. A few of them have done flybys already."

Jenny let the trisicles float nearby and reached up to slide Gary's helmet back onto his head. Her sternum crunched like a packet of crisps and she groaned. It took all her willpower to keep her arms up long enough to latch the lock. His suit pressurization headed toward normal.

"Are you all right? I can send Boges to come get you," said

Jim. Boges protested in the background.

"Dwarves don't go out there. Hills and mountains only," she whispered furtively.

"This is an asteroid," said Jim, as if that explained anything.

"It's practically a mountain," she replied.

"We can't leave yet," said Jenny, gasping from the exertion of suiting up Gary.

"Why the hell not?" demanded Jim.

"There's someone else alive in here."

"Sounds like their problem."

Jim waited for her to reply, but Jenny didn't answer. She shoved Gary and the trisicles into the hospital tent and floated past the other booths. Jim seemed to understand that she wasn't coming.

"Whoever it is, find them fast," said Jim. "I'll get as close to Beywey as I can, but you're not going to have a lot of cover as you come across."

She saw a frenetic motion out of the corner of her eye, faster and more urgent than the languid floating of the discarded objects around her. It was Bào Zhú in one of his own spherical animal tanks, waving to her frantically, his mouth open in a soundless cry. She pulled herself toward him. Her torso spasmed and she curled inward, veering off into one of the ransacked stalls. A metal tent pole snagged on her EVA suit and left a couple of pinprick holes across her upper arm.

"Fuck me," said Jenny.

"I do not like to hear that," said Jim. "What's going on?"

"Got a little rip. It's fine."

Fine was her favorite word for when things were going to complete and utter shit, and Jim knew it.

"Just come back now," Jim said. "Forget whoever is still in there. They'll figure it out."

"Found him," said Jenny, watching her O_2 sink. It was

a tiny trickle of a leak. Nothing she'd even need to patch for at least an hour. And she was planning to be back on the *Jaggery* in a few minutes. She reached out and took the handle of Bào Zhú's container. He pressed his hand against the plexi in gratitude.

A boom sounded through the comm.

"Damn, which one did that?" asked Jim.

"The Cascadian cruiser," replied Boges.

"Huh. They're usually so mellow," said Jim. "Jenny, get back here now. We're taking fire from pirates."

Jenny floated toward the exit, dragging Bào Zhú behind her. He was heavier than he looked.

"On my way," she said.

A second explosion sounded in her helmet and this one rocked through Beywey too.

"Just come back," Jim's voice cracked. He wasn't up to this shit any more.

"That's the plan," she replied.

Air trickled out of the break in Jenny's suit and the backup O_2 tank ran continuously, but the readout gave her plenty of time to get back to the *Jaggery*. She reached the hospital tent where she'd left Gary and the trisicles floating. She grabbed the handle on the back of Gary's suit, which was perfectly designed for dragging unconscious companions. There was no way for her to drag Bào Zhú, the trisicles, and Gary at the same time. She braced herself against a strut and launched Bào Zhú toward the gaping doorway. She grabbed the trisicle ball and pushed it and Gary toward the exit, allowing their momentum to carry her. "Coming out, I have everyone," she said.

A constellation of tiny red spheres floated in front of her. They were little frozen balls of blood emerging from the three tiny holes in her EVA suit. She was bleeding inside it. On the upside, the frozen blood was stopping up the air leak.

A group of folded papers floated by like a flock of birds. It was the notes that the Bala had passed to Gary with their prayers and tributes.

"Um…" said Jim. "We have a problem."

A pained whine sounded over the open channel. Almost like… a whinny. She yanked on Gary's suit to turn him so she could see into his helmet. Something wet in her chest tore open and her vision went white around the edges. She took a couple of slow breaths. As long as you stayed awake, you could just keep going.

Gary's cheeks had thawed from bluish gray back to his usual russet brown. His eyes were closed, but he shook his head as if to clear it.

"Pirates are on all sides of us, Jen. They know we don't have all of our crew on board yet. They're waiting for you," said Jim.

"Wake up, Gary. Help a girl out," she whispered.

"Unnnghhh," he replied, in agony as his core began to thaw and burn with the pain of full-body frostbite.

"Hey," she put her face as close to his as she could in their helmets. "Gary, wake up. I know you feel like shit, but we have to cross to the *Jaggery*, and I need your help. At least don't fight me. Yeah?"

He looked at her with confused and fearful eyes, not understanding who she was, let alone what she was saying. She smiled at him and his instinct brain pegged her as a friendly. He smiled back, but without recognition. Unicorn blood worked miracles, but miracles took time. Something she had very little of right now.

"Why do I have to do everything?" she said, taking a wheezing breath in before pushing Bào Zhú closer to the exit. Another explosion sent a cascade of debris back into Beywey. Jenny hung onto a support beam so the blast wouldn't knock her further in. She took the tether from Gary's suit and clipped it to the trisicle sphere. One of them was useless without the other anyway. She reached for her own tether and realized it was outside attached to her chair, that she still had to pick up. This was going to be like dragging a bloody flea market across openspace.

She grabbed Bào Zhú's tank and pulled herself to the edge of the blown out airlock. The *Jaggery* took up all of her field of vision outside of the station. She'd never been more grateful to see a huge pink flower in all of her life. Below the flower, Boges had the large cargo door open and ready for them to come across. The dwarf pressed her face against the interior window, waiting to tell Jim when to pull away. There were at least a hundred meters between Beywey and the stoneship – far too long for Jenny's comfort. She leaned out of the station. Lights of all shapes and colors lit the dark stone of the *Jaggery* from the pirates waiting to ambush her and Gary on their way out. Whoever they captured would be good for a substantial ransom from a fancy stoneship captain.

"Jim, tell them there's a market full of human and Bala goods, plus water and food in the station. They can have it all if they let us get to our ship."

Jim made the announcement over an open channel. None of the lights disappeared, but a few backed away. Orbital pirates weren't famous for embracing logic or compromise.

Jenny pulled herself out onto the shredded beams surrounding the blown airlock, taking care not to tear her suit again. She reached for the tether holding her wheelchair and reeled it in. The nylon strap came back attached to one bent armrest.

"Shit."

"I see them coming in, I'll give you covering fire," said Jim, sounding delighted to finally have an excuse to shoot at something.

"What?" Jen looked right to see a pair of green lights

heading between the ship and the station, coming right for her. The other ships, seeing one of them get a head start, also revved their engines and sped toward Beywey's entrance.

Jim fired in all directions, missing most of the ships, but sending debris from a couple of direct hits flying at Jenny.

"Watch it," Jenny yelled as a clipper engine on full throttle hurtled into the station below her. The beam in her hands jerked sideways and bits of engine pinged against the bottom of her suit. Bào Zhú pointed up and Jenny followed his finger to see Gary's limp body floating up and away in the arms of a pirate who had suited up and climbed across to Beywey.

She pushed off and caught the pirate around the neck, unclipping his helmet with one deft motion and flicking it up and away. It was one of the first openspace combat techniques they taught at boot camp – a frozen enemy can't fight. The pirate clawed at the vacuum, trying to swim to his helmet. She grabbed Gary's handle and tried to push him toward Boges, but without bracing she only managed to move herself back toward Beywey.

A two-person skiff came racing up to her position and stopped close enough that she could see both people inside suited up and ready to jump out. Three more ships arrived, hovering around them in all directions like the hands of a deadly clock.

"Jim?"

"Still shooting," he said, out of breath.

"Right. I'm going to need you to stop that."

"No, I'm hitting a few..."

"Jim," she said in her best captain's voice, the one she used to command people into certain death. "Cease fire."

The blasts around them stopped, except for a few pings from the smaller ships.

"Full thrusters toward Beywey. Hold your position," she ordered.

"We'll crush you," said Jim.

The suited pirates were out of their ship and closing fast. One pulled out a modified Reason gun. One that would tear through flesh and steel. But she'd had enough of being shot today.

"Do it," she barked, stopping to cough up a piece of tissue that looked suspiciously important. She could barely see through the haze of blood in her helmet.

Jenny held onto Gary and Bào Zhú as the hull of the *Jaggery* came closer. She couldn't push off with her legs, but at least she could be in the right position when it made contact.

A few of the pirates saw what the *Jaggery* was doing and slipped out from between the ship and station. Another handful realized what was going on, but didn't have time to get out. Most of them were so fixated on their prize they didn't even notice the four thousand tons of stoneship about to pin them against the remains of Beywey Station.

The largest of them were crushed first, hulls imploding under the immense pressure. Explosions billowed out into soundless vacuum.

Gary ducked away from the fireballs instinctively. Jenny held him firmly in place to keep him from drifting away. The cargo door was large enough for a small transport ship, so getting three bodies and a ball of trisicles into it should have been easy.

But nothing is ever easy.

A spinning engine turbine from one of the Cascadian ships flew at the group. Gary ducked and the piece hit Jenny's helmet, cracking it from ear to ear. The decompression warning sounded and suddenly Jim was in her helmet, demanding to know what was going on.

"Did I get you, Jen? Are you inside yet?" he asked. Proximity warnings sounded behind him and Boges chattered on the ship's intercom, screaming at him to keep going.

Jenny reached up to cover the crack with the back of her hand. Another blast passed over them in a wave of heat and force as a two-person cruiser split in two just a few meters away. A strut careened past, whacking against Bào Zhú's sphere like a cricket bat and knocking him out of Jenny's grasp. He screamed at her soundlessly as he spun away into openspace.

Jenny kept the other hand on Gary's suit and braced for impact. The *Jaggery's* airlock door was just a few meters away. She could see Boges yelling and hear her in her helmet.

"Slow down, you're just about there," she called. "Slower, you'll crush them!"

The girders surrounding Jenny and Gary curled inward toward Beywey against the unforgivingly hard exterior of the stoneship.

Jenny pulled her hand away from her helmet and pushed off from the beam behind her. Pieces of debris from the remains of the surrounding ships pelted them at speeds high enough to break bones. A few hit her in the torso and the world went white around the periphery again. Her suit alarm changed from orange to red. She breathed in, but there was nothing left to breathe. It was cold in her suit. She didn't make a sound as they floated the last few meters into the airlock.

Boges closed the door. Jenny and Gary slammed against the far wall as Jim accelerated away from Beywey Station. Jenny sank to the floor as the ship's gravity gradually came on. The lights in the airlock turned from red to green and the inner door opened. Boges ran to Gary and flicked his helmet off. Jenny heard him thrashing and fighting her. More dwarves ran in to help.

Jenny lay on the floor of the cargo hold as the dwarves stripped off her EVA suit. Tiny hands applied pressure to the places where her insides were coming out. Boges stood among them, her red braids flying as she shouted orders in the old dwarf language. Or maybe it was English and Jenny's head was just not processing it correctly.

She turned her head, making sure that the trisicles had come through. The world slid sideways and she closed her eyes. Boges knelt next to Jenny.

"Thank you for bringing him home," she said, bending down to kiss Jenny's forehead. Jenny smiled back and patted the dwarf's leg.

"I wish someone loved me the way you love him," she said, knowing that this was a dream and in dreams, you could say anything that came into your head.

Boges waved over more dwarves with a wooden stretcher. When they rolled Jenny onto it, she looked down and saw a lake of blood spreading across the airlock floor. It was almost as large as the one that had been under Cheryl Ann. Jenny felt no fear because she was sure this was a dream. She knew it had to be a dream because for the first time in fifteen years, she could feel her legs.

CHAPTER FOURTEEN
Trisicle Drive

Gary awoke in the ship's hospital. His head throbbed in time to his heart, which was thankfully beating strong. He reached up and felt through his hair. The sharp knob of horn he'd grown was gone, shorn down by Wenck after he'd reached Gary's frozen body floating in the remains of Beywey.

Boges sat by his side, kneading her forehead.

"You realize I am self-healing," he said.

She raised her head. Her dark eyes were bleary with exhaustion. Gary sat up and grunted. His insides were tender and raw, as if they had been removed, wrung out, and put back in again.

"How long have I been out?" he asked.

"Not very long. Less than two hours."

Boges held out a cup of steaming chai. It touched him that she still used his mother's recipes after all these years.

"Unamip has blessed us with your continued life," said Boges.

"You don't believe in Unamip," he said gently, taking a sip and letting the hot tea warm his freezing insides.

"In these times, I will pray to any god who will listen," she replied. "How are you feeling?"

"My human half was considering giving up; however, my Bala half apparently wasn't ready to die."

Boges turned up the flame in the lantern on the bedside table. He'd missed the warmth of real fire during his time in prison. Humans loved to live their lives by harsh buzzing lights that ruined the colors of everything and made your eardrums vibrate.

He remembered Jenny and sat up so fast he spilled tea all over the comforter.

"Did you find Jenny? She's in the control room on Beywey–"

Boges held up her hand.

"She's the one who brought you back to the ship." She leaned closer, as if sharing a secret. "You should have seen it. Jim crashed the *Jaggery* right into the space station and managed to take out a good number of the pirates in the process."

"By accident or on purpose?" asked Gary.

Boges shrugged.

"No telling, Captain. The way he pilots the *Jaggery*, you would think he had never spent a day in openspace. You have tea in your beard." Gary wiped it away and dried his hand on the covers. Boges frowned.

"You haven't changed since you were ten years old," she sighed.

"Where is she?" he asked.

"Resting in the next room. She told us how you saved her life."

"As she saved mine."

"She only retrieved your body as fuel for the journey through nullspace," Boges scoffed.

"You see it as well as I do, my friend. Jenny is not the same woman who held me against my will. Humans can change, Boges."

"I have never seen proof of that." Her eyes were hard and angry.

"Perhaps you just have," said Gary.

Boges pulled the cup of chai away and stood to leave. She paused in the doorway, regarding him with a coolness that chilled him like openspace.

"I will not allow these tragedies to occur again," she whispered.

Gary watched her storm out, red braids flying. The entire time he'd been in the Quag, Boges and her kin had stayed aboard the *Jaggery* in evidence storage. A dwarven crew would rather die than abandon ship. They'd farmed as best as they could in the semi-darkness, sustaining themselves on mushrooms and other crops that grew in deep shade. They'd survived for ten years, but at a great personal cost. Gary could feel the bitterness that tinged the very ship itself. He could certainly see it in the instruments in the cockpit. Boges and her crew had lost their faith in the goodness of man, and even their trust in him was becoming strained.

A creak in the doorway startled him. Jenny rolled in, pushing a new wheelchair. It was a wooden marvel assembled with dwarven precision. No nails, only dovetail joints fitted together tightly by a dozen tiny hands in the couple of hours they'd been back. He could still smell the oil they'd used to polish the wood. Her hands flew past carvings etched into the side that told the story of a human who rescued a part-unicorn from the coldness of openspace. Apparently, not all of Boges' kin believed that Jenny was the enemy.

"Hey," she said, resting her hands in her lap. Her dark hair sat like a hippogriff's nest on top of her head. She no longer wore that ever-present ponytail like she had ten years ago. Gary was glad. He took exception to the name. "You look well... considering," she said.

She shifted uncomfortably in her new chair, stretching her side and wincing. This chair had less padding than the old human-made one. Dwarves didn't generally believe in upholstery.

"And you look well… also considering," he said.

"Your blood is a hell of a drug." She rubbed her sternum and grimaced.

"Yes, it can heal even a pointblank shot to the heart." She started to nod, then realized the double meaning and looked away, embarrassed. The first time he'd met Jenny, she'd shot him in the chest to assert her dominance. He'd never forgotten the look in her eye as he realized she was going to pull the trigger. Not the cold disinterest of most Reason soldiers, but a satisfied pleasure in watching terror dawn across his face. Unicorns didn't fear death, but pain was pain, no matter what species you were. Her intended effect has been to make him understand that she was willing to do anything to get her way, and it had worked.

"I think you know I'm sorry for that," she said. There was a definite wheezing quality to her voice and she strained to get the words out without stopping for air. A small part of him wanted to give her just a bit more of his blood to help her breathe. A very small part of him. Nearly nonexistent.

"Do I?" he asked.

"Well, I'm sorry for that."

It was woefully inadequate for someone who had not only shot him, but had kidnapped and tortured him for the better part of two years. He didn't even bother to acknowledge the words. They sat in uncomfortable silence for a moment.

"Thanks for helping me back there," she said eventually. "I'd be toast without it. With all that power, it's a wonder the Quag managed to keep you locked up."

"How did you manage it?"

She blinked at him slowly like a guard shutting off his body cam, but she was just processing what he'd said. Her eyes slid down to the floor. She backed out of the doorway.

"I have to get my ship back before Jim realizes he doesn't need any of us to make this delivery."

"Your ship," Gary said softly, chuckling to himself.

"Listen, I don't want to be here any more than you want me here. We drop these boxes off and I'll hand the *Jaggery* over to you, no strings attached. Jim and I will be out of your hair for good."

"Jim is not going to give up the ship that easily," said Gary, tossing the covers off his legs.

"Well perhaps when the time comes, you and the dwarves will help me convince him."

Outside the door, a man cleared his throat. Jim walked into Gary's room chewing on a small stick from one of the fragile trees in the garden.

"Y'all having a nice little chat?" he asked.

Jenny's cheeks went pink and she plucked the branch out of Jim's mouth and pointed it at him.

"Yeah, I was just telling Gary what a bloody awful pilot you are. When I said to pull the *Jaggery* alongside, I didn't mean to take out half of Beywey in the process."

Jim sucked his teeth and regarded both of them with the countenance of a man sizing up his prey.

"I'm the bloody awful pilot who saved your life," said Jim.

"That's one way of looking at it," said Jenny.

Jim nodded toward Gary. "Is he ready with some horn?"

"I'll need the trisicles and time," said Gary.

"Time is something we do not have right now," said Jenny. "The *Arthur Phillip* is hanging close, probably trying to figure out a way to legally board us. It won't be long before they decide that they don't have to do things by the book way out here. Not to mention three dozen pirate ships trailing us just waiting for a chance to avenge their fallen comrades. Any little scrap would come in handy right now. Even a quick jump would get us away from most of them."

Gary shook his head.

"Look for yourself." He leaned forward so they could see the chasm in his cranium. Jenny pursed her lips.

"How long after you eat can we go?"

"About six hours."

Jim kicked the door frame.

"Well, that's not going to work one bit. You two have been out of commission for a couple of hours and already five ships have tested my patience."

"You're not shooting them down, are you?" asked Jenny.

"Not mostly," said Jim. He noticed her dismay and shrugged. "It's all I've got, Jen."

"Transfer the *Jaggery* back to me and I'll talk to them."

Jim leaned against the doorway.

"I think that would be a terrible idea. Those Reason boys are just waiting for an excuse to impound this ship. They'll be monitoring, and if they see a transfer to anyone on board but me they'll yank it right the hell away from us."

Gary took a mental roll call. Indeed, there was no other creature on board eligible to own the ship right now.

"Besides, I like being captain." Jim smiled, exposing teeth stained by a lifetime of smoke, and plucked the branch back out of Jenny's hand.

Jenny spun her new chair so fast that Jim had to jump out of the way to avoid getting hit. There was a crash from the outer room as she banged into something on her way out. "Gary, eat those trisicles so we can get going."

Jim stood in the doorway, chewing his stick.

"Jenny doesn't want me to lock you up," he said between bites. "But I don't know why I have to listen to Jenny any more. Personally, I'd like to see you back behind bars until you shrivel up and die."

He spoke slowly, disarmingly, the way you talked to a friend, which made Gary more uneasy than if he had yelled.

"You're right, Jim. I wouldn't blame you for incarcerating me again. But I assure you, we both have the same goal. Deliver the cargo and go our separate ways. I'll do everything within my power to make this mission a success."

Jim's chest seemed to deflate.

"You're a monster," he muttered.

"I have done some despicable things," agreed Gary. "But I'm attempting to be a better man."

"She was too good for you." Jim dropped the branch and pushed his hands deep into his pockets.

"She was too good for both of us," said Gary.

Jim turned and wiped something away from his face.

"You eat those bugs and get us underway," he said.

"Yes, Captain."

Jim left the hospital and Gary wondered who was going to be that man's next casualty. Jenny often got the blame as the center of chaos, but she was usually just cleaning up Jim's messes. The last time, Cheryl Ann had paid the price with her life, because there was always a price with a man like that. The only difference was who paid it.

Boges had left the trisicles warming under the lantern. He pried one of the babies off its parent. They were dormant here, pincers tucked in and inert. Back in their native habitat, a murky place that was somewhere between nullspace and openspace, they were vicious beetles that tore through anything softer than they were.

When Gary was a baby, his mother had worried that his humanlike teeth wouldn't be strong enough to bite through their chitinous exoskeletons. She'd asked his father to grind up the shells before feeding. But he was able to crunch through trisicles and had grown horn like any other unicorn.

He bit down on the shell and gave a thought of thanks to the trisicle that was giving its life for their safety. Not that a trisicle's life was terribly interesting. They absorbed light and used it to fuel their internal processes, building layer upon layer of shell that was dense with energy. In that way, they were very nearly a plant and not animal. Or that was what unicorns liked to tell themselves.

The trisicle's shell shattered between Gary's molars, crumbling to powder that tasted like toasted almonds. He was just about to take a second bite when the effects hit him in a rush, like the disorientation of stepping down onto a final stair that wasn't really there. A short burst of laughter escaped from deep in his belly. He hadn't felt this much energy coursing through him in years. His head buzzed with power.

He popped the remainder in his mouth and chewed while prying the second baby off its parent. It would take a couple of days for them to breed again, but what he grew over the next few hours would probably be enough to get them to Jaisalmer. Trisicle shells were concentrated energy, but any bones would do to get them back out of the Reason. If Jenny and Jim could pick up some scraps at Fort J – cows, pigs, even chickens – they would be able to jump back out of Reasonspace right after the delivery.

The trisicles were gone much too fast, but he couldn't eat the parents and leave them stranded with no breeding pair. That was how the trouble had started last time. He tucked them back into their bubble and left it in a dark corner of the infirmary.

Between the pleasant buzz of trisicle shells in his brain and the topsoil that the dwarves had finished laying in the halls, the walk to the cockpit felt almost like the old days. The ship shuddered – a roiling wave like an earthquake through mud. One of the dwarves made an alarmed sound and ducked into a tiny door. Gary hung onto an outcropping in the wall until the ship settled back down.

He opened the cockpit door to chaos. Jenny was trying

to steer the panicked ship with her clumsy tablet while Jim shouted into the comm at whoever was attacking them. Ricky leaned over Jenny's shoulder, offering what she probably thought was helpful advice.

"Maybe you can hide behind the Moon," she said, pointing to the gray disc in the distance.

"Too far," snapped Jenny, dragging her finger across the tablet. There wasn't any object nearby that would offer protection for a ship of this size.

"More pirates?" Gary asked, squeezing himself past Ricky and into the corner. The biological Bala instruments throbbed with alarms, warning of incoming magic-based attacks.

"They've got some kind of magic weapon," said Jim, which Gary interpreted as a request for his assistance in identifying said weapon.

"They do not. They're normal bullets coated in magic, which gives them the ability to disrupt Bala technology, which this ship runs on."

Human artillery modified with magic was especially dangerous to the *Jaggery*. Conventional bullets pinged off the surface of the ship, but magic-laced projectiles affected its Bala heart. A stoneship heart was difficult to destroy, but the right kind of weapon could confuse it into protective hibernation. Waking a hibernating stoneship could take days... or years.

On the viewscreen, a sleek fighter zoomed past faster than the external cameras could track. In the distance, a handful of larger ships hung back, waiting until the fighter disabled the *Jaggery*.

"What about Jiàrì Park?" asked Ricky, who was clearly familiar with the stations up here. Gary had never heard of it.

"Too crowded," said Jenny. "It's February." As if that explained it.

A second shot grazed their flank. The lights in the cockpit

flickered and a wave of dread went through the room – not the people in it, but the walls themselves.

"Unidentified fighter, we are friendlies, I repeat, we are friendlies. Do not shoot," said Jim into the comm.

"You know not every human is on your side?" asked Ricky. "Most of these quags will kill you for a barrel of water. No offense, Gary."

"None taken." He'd never thought of himself as a quag, even though he'd spent ten percent of his life there.

Jim grumbled and hit the firing mechanism for the retrofitted guns he and Jenny had installed on the ship. A group of projectiles sprayed ineffectively into openspace. It was difficult to aim at a target going that fast in a 360-degree starfield.

"How's the ship doing, Gary?" called Jenny, spinning the *Jaggery* and dropping it under a Mars shuttle like a boulder hiding behind a pixie. He was grateful she'd kept the artificial gravity on. Jenny was as skilled a stoneship pilot as Gary had ever seen, even among full unicorns who could control the ship with their minds. She had a clarity of purpose that the *Jaggery* responded to. As if it wanted to please her. But right now, it whined a bit through a crack in the stone wall.

"The ship is concerned," he replied.

"Me too," said Ricky.

Jenny sat back in her chair and tapped her teeth with a fingernail. The fighter circled behind them and let off another volley of shots. Two hit the *Jaggery* in the rear and the ship bucked like a wild gryphon.

Ricky gasped as the artificial gravity didn't compensate fast enough and she left the floor for a moment.

"Gonna get someone killed out here," she said, hanging on to the back of Jenny's wheelchair.

"Gary, any growth yet?" asked Jenny, spinning them around a water transport ship. Human faces pressed to the windows to watch the stoneship zigzagging across space as if it wasn't the size of a small moon. Gary bent down and showed her that there wasn't a shimmer left in sight. Nothing but grey skull bone.

"Bollocks," said Jenny, flicking her finger on the tablet and sending the ship careening toward a decrepit old station that had been constructed as a mashup between several spacefaring nations. At the last minute, she swiped the ship down and around the station. It wasn't big enough to hide them, but it was a historic monument that the Reason was unlikely to destroy. It might buy them a minute or two. Jim let fly another volley of shots, a handful of which hit a shuttle on its run to the Moon. The shuttle skidded off course and he cursed under his breath.

"If you kill civilians, even you won't be able to dodge that charge," warned Jenny.

"That's not necessarily true," mused Ricky.

"You have to sit through anti-decompression drills on those shuttles before takeoff," said Jim. "I'm sure everyone there knows what to do. They have oxygen masks and such."

A pair of Reason ships sidled up to either side of the *Jaggery*.

"FTL *Jaggery*, prepare to be boarded," said Ondre from the *Arthur Phillip*.

"You're not doing anything," Ricky said, waving at Jenny's tablet. "Do something."

Jim looked expectantly at Jenny as well. Jenny lifted her hands.

"There's nowhere to hide around here. Can't jump to FTL. I don't know what else to do."

The fighter screamed past one more time and fired another set of shots at the *Jaggery*. All of them hit and the ship moaned like whalesong.

"We are so dead," said Ricky.

"Come on, Jen," said Jim. "You always have something."

Jenny's brow furrowed and her brown eyes looked troubled.

"I have one idea, but no one is going to like it," she said.

"I bet I'll like it," cried Ricky, as the Reason ships inched closer so that the *Jaggery* was pinned between them and the historic station.

Jenny looked over her shoulder at Gary.

"Go put one of your trisicles in the FTL drive," she said.

"Oh hell no," said Jim, grabbing her chin and forcing her to look at him. "That is not an option." She slapped his hand away.

"I'm entertaining suggestions," she said. The cockpit was quiet. "No? Then this is all you've got."

For once, Ricky looked to be at a loss.

"What does running on trisicles do?" she asked.

Once Gary's stomach unclenched, he spoke.

"It thrusts you into the tormented realm where trisicles spawn," he said.

"But it also punches you out of this space and into theirs," finished Jenny. "We just need a second or two. Enough to get us out of here."

"And end up where?" asked Jim, wagging his finger at her. "The ass end of nowhere."

"You would prefer the Quag?" she asked. Jim set his mouth in a thin line. "I didn't think so."

She hit the ship's intercom.

"Boges, put one of the trisicles into the FTL drive. We're going to turn it on up here, but stand by to shut down the drive if we can't turn it off." She turned off the intercom. "You can never tell if the ship is going to freak out in bugspace. But even if I can't shut it down here, Gary can try from back there, and last resort Boges should be able to just yank the trisicle back out of the drive and we'll come out somewhere in openspace."

No one spoke and she looked up at everyone, questioning. "What?" she asked.

"You are going to kill us all," said Jim, with a touch of awe in his voice.

"Or strand us in a trisicle's fever dream," said Gary, for once in agreement with Jim.

"Excuse me?" said Boges incredulously into the intercom.

"Boges, do it," Gary said. There was a disdainful tisking from the other end of the intercom before it shut off, but the dwarf did what she was asked.

"Jim, you keep firing, but be sure to miss everyone," said Jenny.

"That shouldn't be too hard," said Ricky, dryly. Jim shot her a dirty look.

"Gary, let me know if we're going to break apart or go into hibernation or anything like that," said Jenny, tapping on her tablet. The ship spun on its axis in its tight quarters between the two ships and a station, thwarting the Reason's attempt to extend a docking clamp toward their cargo door.

"FTL *Jaggery*, do not move or we will fire on you. Prepare to be boarded." The Reason ship maneuvered itself back to the cargo door and the docking clamp extended again.

"Boges?" called Jenny, letting them drift ever so slightly away from the clamp. The *Jaggery* shook as a plain old explosive shell hit its surface from a few meters away. The Reason was forced back from the inertia of the blast.

"Idiots," said Jim, tightening his harness.

"Ready, Captain," came Boges' voice. Jim's eyes went wide as Jenny's finger hovered over the tablet. She glanced around the cockpit, letting her eyes come to rest on Gary.

"Shut it down if I can't," she said. He nodded and she dropped her fingertip on the tablet. The stars on the viewscreen winked out and the cockpit went dark. The last thing Gary heard was Ricky Tang's scream.

CHAPTER FIFTEEN
Bugspace

Jenny had only been in bugspace once before and she had hoped to never enter it again. As soon as she heard the whispering chirps of a billion billion trisicles on threat alert, all the fear from last time came flooding back. Ricky's screams were not helping matters.

Jenny's hand shook and she dropped her tablet beside her chair. Even leaning far over the armrest, she couldn't reach it. A crawling sensation spread over her entire body as trisicle spawn, too small to see, landed on her and began to feed. The *Jaggery* had manifested into a miasma of trisicles and their tiny babies. This was bugspace.

She was able to keep it together because of a lesson her gran had taught her. A trick to getting through anything that terrified her. Instead of waiting to feel ready, you looked at the thing were afraid of doing, and you did it afraid. She'd complained and resisted at first, but it was liberating when she finally realized her kuia was right. No amount of deep breathing or counting down from ten was ever going to take away her fear. From that moment on, Jenny acknowledged her terror and just kept on going.

There was no way to get all of the infinitesimal spawn off her without a shower, and a few of the mature specimens had latched onto her legs, digging into her jumpsuit with their pincers. She flicked the larger sucklings off and onto the floor, leaving wet divots in her skin. The ship had burst into their realm unexpectedly and thousands had jumped into the *Jaggery* when it materialized. The bugs swarmed it, both inside and out. Trisicles were able to teleport themselves over short distances, which is why they fueled the transition to FTL so efficiently.

Ricky flailed in the back of the cockpit, not so much dislodging the trisicles, but agitating those attached to her. Jim pried his off with the edge of a folding knife that Jenny hadn't known about. That man had weapons secreted everywhere on his person.

"Damn trisicles eating me alive," he muttered. An alarm sounded and the artificial gravity clicked off. Ricky floated toward the ceiling, banging into walls as she kicked and writhed. The trisicles on the floor floated skyward, latching onto whatever surface they could find. A few popped themselves to other locations. Jenny heard dwarves crying out in the walls.

Jenny hit the touchscreen to deactivate the trisicle in the drive and bring them back into regular space. The tablet did not respond. Jenny wiped her bloody fingers on her trousers and tried again. The tablet confirmed her order, but still the ship stayed in bugspace. She followed the wires that she and Jim had run from the tablet to the console and into the wall. They went all the way to the engine room, tacked along the top of the corridors. Trisicles covered every inch of the plastic-coated wire, gnawing through it in dozens of locations. Too many to fix right now.

"Gary," she said, turning around to find him clawing at his throat. His eyes were round and frantic. He was choking.

"Boges!" she yelled, hitting the intercom button and unbuckling from her chair. "Shut down the drive."

Boges did not respond.

Jenny floated toward Gary, who had his fingers deep in his own mouth, trying to fish out whatever was suffocating him. Tears ran down the sides of his face. He pulled out his empty hand and tried to grab onto the wall. One of the glass vials came away in his hand in pieces. His lips were starting to turn an alarming shade of purple.

"Do you need me to..." Jenny began. He nodded and grabbed her arm, pulling her closer.

Jenny took a deep breath and slid her hand into his mouth. It was as warm and wet as she'd imagined. She cringed and pushed her fingers deeper. Something sharp tickled the tips of her fingers.

"Sorry," she whispered, and shoved her hand forward the last little bit. Gary gagged, but didn't pull away. Jenny got her index and middle fingers hooked around something hard and spindly. She dragged out a mature trisicle as big as Gary's fist, its pincers fully extended and coated in Gary's silvery blood. He sputtered and coughed.

"Thank you," he wheezed.

"Oh sure, any time," she said, flicking his saliva off her hand with a grimace and wiping it down the sleeve of his sweater. A bolt of pain shot down the back of her leg and she hung onto the wall for a minute to steady herself. Everyone except Jim, who was still harnessed, floated toward the ceiling. A caustic smell wafted through the cockpit. Boges burst through the dwarf door, gasping.

"Captain, I had to evacuate the engine room and the bottom three floors of the ship. We're filling with ammonia gas from several small hull breaches caused by the trisicles. And also, we're falling."

Jenny checked the viewscreen. It was still working, but wasn't communicating with the tablet. The exterior cameras were picking up swirls of peach-colored clouds right outside the hull. As everyone had feared, the ship hadn't been able to map bugspace properly and had materialized in the same location as an existing celestial body.

"We jumped into a planet," said Jim.

"No, we jumped into the ammonia rings of a planet. Just low enough to be falling out of orbit," said Jenny, reading external data off the tablet. Sensors were pinging errors as trisicles gnawed through them on the outside of the *Jaggery*.

"I told you so," said Jim.

Inertia started pushing them flat against the ceiling. Jim had to look up at her to deliver his smug satisfaction.

Jenny turned to Boges and Gary. "Seal the doors between the decks."

"There aren't blast doors in here like on Reason ships," said Boges, fighting the gathering force in order to slide herself down toward the dwarf door. "These aren't warships."

"Decompression happens to everyone," said Jenny.

"This is true, it's a common problem," said Ricky. The ship shifted and she slid toward the back wall. Jenny peeled a persistent trisicle off her neck and flung it toward the corner of the room. It was getting difficult to turn her head and her throat burned as ammonia gas seeped into the rest of the ship.

"Can you get us into orbit outside of the rings?" she asked Gary.

Gary pulled himself against the force toward a series of holes in the biological instruments and whispered a few words in a language that Jenny recognized as a unicorn dialect. The ship careened above the surface of the planet, no longer falling, but not rising either. Everyone fell to the floor as the gravity of the massive planet exerted its pull.

"That's not orbit," said Jim, hanging onto his harness with two white-knuckled hands.

Jenny pulled herself up into her chair. The air still burned, but if she was going to smash into the surface of a bugspace planet, at least she would die sitting up. Her eyes filled with tears from the corrosive gas burning her throat and lungs. She tried to take shallow breaths. Boges sat bleary-eyed, half in and half out of the dwarf door. Jim was awake, but stared out at the planet passing underneath them in a daze.

Ricky pulled herself upright on Jenny's chair. She pulled a filtration mask out of her pocket and put it over her mouth and nose and stepped over the piles of trisicles to join Gary at the instrument panel.

"Hey you, ship, get us into orbit," she said through her mask.

"That's not how it works," said Gary, swiping across a clear tube as different colored gases rushed through it.

"It can't hurt," said Ricky. She tapped a section of moss fronds on an outcropping in the rock.

"You just opened the cargo bay door," said Gary, tapping the same spot again. "Stop touching things."

"I don't think any of these baubles actually do anything," said Ricky. She leaned close to the instruments.

A rush of fresh, chilly air blew in from the open dwarf door. Jenny took as deep a breath as she could before her ribs twinged. It cleared her head. Ricky took off her mask.

"You're prepared," said Jenny.

"Gassing everyone was a good way to stop a brawl at the Blossom," said Ricky.

"Bet you picked a few pockets in the process," said Jim, patting his shirt. Jenny made a note to check him for more weapons when they got back to openspace. That man was going to kill someone if they didn't disarm him.

"Good thinking, opening the cargo bay door," she said to Ricky. "It vented the gas in one of the largest areas of the ship."

The corner of Ricky's mouth went up. She playfully punched Gary's shoulder.

"See? I'm helping."

"I will admit, that did vent the majority of the ammonia gas."

Boges lifted her head and listened to the whispering along the dwarf tunnel. With the door open, Jenny heard it too.

"We have two more hull breaches to fix before we ascend to orbit or jump out of bugspace. A matter of minutes," said Boges.

Jenny read the incoming data on the planet. The rings around it were primarily ammonia, but the atmosphere itself had a high concentration of water vapor and oxygen.

"We could land..." she began.

"No," said everyone in the cockpit at once.

"I swear, you are trying to kill us," said Jim.

"Yeah, nah. I was just spitballing," said Jenny, pretending that she wasn't miffed that they didn't consider her perfectly reasonable idea of landing on an unknown, hostile alternate dimension with practically no supplies, a breached hull, and no horn for an FTL jump. Amateurs.

Ricky kicked a few of the trisicles into the corner. They still clawed at everything within reach, but with the planet's gravity pinning them to the floor, they weren't catching much. A few popped out of existence, then reappeared a moment later elsewhere in the cabin, but they fell back down just as quickly.

"Forget orbit where all the trisicles are," said Jenny. "Fix the breaches, get back into the engine room, and pull the FTL drive offline. We can jump back to openspace right from high atmosphere."

"That is a very good idea," said Gary, rubbing the base of his throat. The ship stabilized and hovered over the surface of the planet. It was mostly shades of brown down below. No sign of lights or built objects.

Boges poked her head out of the door.

"Hull breaches are sealed, Captain. One of my kin is heading into the engine room to pull the drive offline."

"Excellent," said Jenny.

"Good," replied Jim at the same time. He leaned over to her and only sort of whispered. "You remember I'm the captain now, right?"

"Then captain something," she hissed right back.

"Take us out of bugspace," he shouted at Boges, even though that was exactly what she was doing.

"Yes, Captain," said Boges, with the tiniest of glances at Gary. To his credit, Gary kept his eyes on the instrument panel. Any reaction at all and Jim would have thrown a fit. Jenny was starting to wish she'd had Gary as a co-pilot all these years.

"Hold onto something," said Boges, relaying a message from further down the tunnel.

The image on the viewscreen compressed until it was a thin glowing line. The ship thrummed with a harmonic vibration, then squeezed in the middle, like when Jenny and her friends had put a bunch of rubber bands around a rockmelon. It took on an hourglass shape right before it burst open. Jenny's eardrums hummed and ached, then the pulsing stopped. On the viewscreen, the ringed planet had disappeared.

"We're back in openspace," said Boges. The relief in her voice was tangible.

"The ship is stable," said Gary, glancing up from the pulsating spot in the wall that looked for all the world like a beating heart.

"See? That worked," said Jenny, with a casual smile that took a herculean amount of effort to muster.

"I should have taken my chances with Wenck and the Quag, because you are out of your damn mind," said Jim. His voice shook with anger. "I can order you to do what I want, you know."

Jenny scoffed at the idea.

"I can drop you back there, if you like," she said. "I'm sure we're not too far from Earth." She tapped to figure out where they'd reappeared. It was outside of Earthspace, which was good, but the nearby natural satellites didn't look familiar.

Ricky stepped over piles of inert trisicles and leaned down over the back of Jenny's chair, squeezing her shoulder.

"Well, I like your driving, Perata. You remind me of my Auntie Nash, who once flew a stoneship so close to Reason Command that she scraped a layer of paint off the building."

"One time, I blew a general out of an airlock for grabbing my ass during an inspection. I mean, he was suited up. I wasn't trying to kill him or anything. Just gave him a ride," said Jenny.

"If I had a dollar for every time I had to break the fingers of some guy grabbing my ass..." began Ricky.

Jim turned to them both, his face stricken.

"You two think this is funny? Look." On the viewscreen, he pointed to several glowing red spots in the distance.

"Oh bollocks," said Jenny.

"What now?" cried Ricky. "What could possibly be happening now that is any worse than pirates, ammonia, falling out of orbit, and being eaten alive by trisicles?"

"Redworms," said Jim.

"Aiyā," cried Ricky. "I take it back, Perata. You definitely have a death wish." She hesitated for a moment, hand on the cockpit door. "I don't know whether to watch this trainwreck from up here, or have a last drink before we're all dead."

"I vote drink," said Jim, starting to unbuckle.

"Oh no," said Jenny, putting a hand over his. "You have to stay up here and go down with the ship, *Captain*."

He sat back with a string of mumbled curses.

"Sorry, guys," said Jenny quietly. "It was all I could think of."

"Well, you're an idiot," spat Jim. "Always making the wrong call and getting people killed. The Reason never should have put you in command, especially after Copernica. Everyone around you ends up dead."

Jenny rubbed a finger across her lips thoughtfully, wondering how many blows she could land on Jim before Gary pulled her off him. Maybe, given their history, he wouldn't pull her off Jim at all and she could break his nose and maybe his jaw before he begged her to stop. Without Jim's help, they wouldn't be able to get through the checkpoints around Reasonspace. She folded her hands in her lap and tried to keep the fury out of her voice.

"All right, Jim," she said, with false brightness. "I'm sorry about what happened to Cheryl Ann. And we can have that out later… for the thousandth time. But for the moment, we need to figure out where we are and also how not to get dissolved by redworm acid."

Gary raised an eyebrow at her.

"What?" Her patience was wearing thin.

"I think you are handling this difficult situation admirably," said Gary, and all her anger dissipated.

"Ta, Gary. Thank you. See? Gary thinks I'm doing a good job," she said.

"No one cares what he thinks," grumbled Jim.

"I care what he thinks," she replied.

"You would take his side," said Jim. Jenny let it go. Leave it to Jim to start a pissing match right before a redworm attack. She rolled her eyes. And took a breath and held it. She was used to rolling with the punches, but she was reaching her limit. Her chest ached, her head pounded, and she was getting that cabin fever antsy feeling again from the ship jumping into and out of bugspace. She let out the breath and her jumpsuit changed from Reason red to cobalt blue.

Jim was too wrapped up in being pissed off to notice, but Gary made an interested little grunt from behind her.

"What was that?" he asked.

She gave him a warning look.

"It was nothing. Anyway. Redworms. All right. We've done this before," said Jenny, squinting at the viewscreen. "See there? They're zigzagging in a grid pattern, which means they haven't spotted us yet. They're just canvassing for food. If we're lucky, they'll miss us in all this openspace."

"We are never lucky," said Jim morosely.

"I am very lucky," said Gary.

"You are not helping right now," said Jenny, turning to him. "Do your little bubble glass thing and steer the ship where I tell you, please."

Gary nodded, but he looked amused. Again she thought she could get used to flying with him. He certainly made a better wingman than Jim.

"Cut the external lights and any heat-generating equipment," she said to Boges. "They'll be less likely to find us if we're cold and dark."

Boges nodded and disappeared down her tunnel. Jenny picked up her tablet. It was still receiving some external sensor data from the ship, which was sent wirelessly. It just couldn't access the control mechanisms, which were the wired connections the trisicles had chewed through.

"Let's see where we are."

The tablet churned through star maps, then announced they were in the Demoryx system. Of course. She didn't bother mentioning it to anyone. No need to bring up those bad memories again.

"How long to Fort J?" asked Jim.

"Thirty-six hours in FTL," said Jenny. Jim made a low whistle.

"Well, that's not enough time before the Summit. We have

twenty hours," he said.

"How long before you can get us into FTL? Even a short hop?" she asked Gary. He reached up and felt his head.

"Four hours."

Jim gestured angrily at the redworm cluster undulating in the distance. They moved up and down, left to right, methodically searching for anything edible.

"We'll never stay hidden from them for four hours. We can either sit here and pray they miss us or we can turn on the engines and run. We might get pretty far before they catch up, but I guarantee it won't be four hours. I give us two hours tops before we're toast. And even if we do stay away from the redworms and by some miracle that guy," he jerked his thumb toward Gary, "grows enough horn to jump us to Fort J, we're not going to make it until after the Summit, so no delivery, no cash, no ship. Good job, Jen. Another successful mission."

"I thought you were in charge," said Jenny sharply. "Fix it, *Captain*."

Jim threw off his harness and stormed out of the cockpit, stumbling over trisicles on the way out. He slammed the cockpit door hard enough that Jenny cringed. She traced the edge of her tablet with a fingernail, ticking through possibilities. She hadn't quite given up yet. She wondered if there was a way to overclock an FTL engine. Or if they put another trisicle back into the drive maybe they could hop to a spot closer to Jaisalmer.

"Don't even think about flying on trisicles again," said Gary. Jenny jumped. For a moment she'd forgotten he was back there. She unclipped her chair and turned it to face him. She was grateful that a cockpit that was big enough for full unicorns was plenty large enough for her and her chair. Reason ships were tightly designed and she often couldn't fit her chair in the captain's spot. It was one of the other reasons they'd given on her discharge papers. "Inadequate accommodations onboard standard vessels." Though that seemed like their problem to solve, not hers.

"I know you were considering it, because I was considering it," said Gary. "But I don't think it's worth the risk. We jumped into the rings of a planet this time, but next time it might be the center of a planet or halfway through another ship."

"There aren't any ships in bugspace," said Jenny.

"Not any good ones," said Gary. Jenny suddenly wished she had time to ask him all of his stories about traveling the universe for a hundred years.

"I bet you have stories," she said, watching with relief as the redworms changed their heading downward, away from the *Jaggery*.

"I'm sure you do as well," he replied. He turned back to his control panel and started shutting down as many systems as they could spare.

"You're a good co-pilot. I wish I'd had you at Copernica." She realized her blunder as the words were coming out of her mouth. Gary had been at Copernica Citadel, but on the ground, directing the assault against her and other Reason troop carriers. Her face went hot.

Copernica Citadel had been one of the last bastions of Bala power. This was long after open battles were over and humans had turned the Bala planets into the collective known as Reasonspace. The remaining free Bala had congregated in the ancient stronghold on Copernica. The Reason had tried to bomb it out of existence during the active fighting, but the city-sized fortress was protected by the spells of a hundred different magical creatures, including five free necromancers.

Jenny's only mission was to shoot down anyone who tried to leave Copernica. The situation had stabilized years before she had arrived, and for the most part, the residents of Copernica Citadel were content to live quietly in their impenetrable castle. They didn't start trouble and they ignored the Reason patrols that dogged their planet. It was a grudging truce that the Reason expected to remain unchanged until they decided to change it.

As the captain of the RSF *Pandey* – with its complement of eleven hundred troops – Jenny's job was to sail her ship on an elliptical orbit between Copernica and the fifth planet in the system. Four other Reason ships followed different patrol routes within the area. Between all of them, there was always a Reason ship within hours of Copernica. Every couple of months, four of the five ships ended up back at Copernica at the same time while the last completed the farthest orbit. For three days they checked in, compared data, resupplied, and partied so hard it took a week for everyone to recover. But in a grunt job, quite a distance from Jaisalmer and far from any sort of recognition, they needed something to get them through the long stretches of nothing. Jenny considered it part of boosting morale.

It was during one such gathering that Copernica Citadel attacked. The Reason captains had assumed that any aggression from the Bala would involve projectiles from the surface. No one had been expecting a direct assault in openspace. The Bala had slipped all five of their necromancers into orbit on the backs of some ridiculous mishmash of an eagle and a horse called a hippogriff. No one had any idea how they'd flown that high or how they were even breathing in the vacuum.

The Bala had hit on day two of their revelry, when most of the crew was passed out in the recreation rooms at the far end of the ship. Necromancer magic crushed three troop carriers before half the crew had even woken up. Jenny's first indication of trouble was on her viewscreen, when the RMF *Armistead* twisted in half like a wrung-out towel. Frozen bodies spilled into space as purple lightning streaked across the vacuum. It took her a moment to realize she wasn't hallucinating from larval eggwine and they were under attack.

Jenny took over the pilot's chair from a swaying helmsman and maneuvered the *Pandey* through the wreckage of her comrades' ships. She dodged violet bolts and ducked behind the largest pieces she could find. She ordered her gunners to fire, but finding the necromancers against the debris flying in all directions was tricky. The Reason ships were built to fight other ships – equipped with huge missiles that missed their tiny Bala targets by a wide margin.

Jenny instructed her crew to target the origin point of the lightning with a wide spray of any small items they could load into an explosive casing – screws, nuts, bolts, whatever. They weren't trying to pierce a hull, just incapacitate a flesh and blood body.

The hardware missiles worked. The *Pandey* took out two of the hippogriffs. The three remaining necromancers focused their magic on the main bridge of the *Pandey*, attempting to tear the ship in two before they could load another shell. Jenny called the order to evacuate the bridge as the first bolts hit, but the ceiling torqued before they got out. The metal cracked and their precious air vented into space. They ran for the door as the emergency bulkhead started to come down and seal off the bridge from the rest of the ship.

The crew members closest to the door got through all right, but the forward bridge crew weren't going to make it in time. There was no override when it came to hull breaches. You saved whoever you saved.

Jenny slid under the bulkhead and stopped herself halfway through. The door came down, catching her on the pelvic bone. It stuck there for a few seconds, pushing with unrelenting force. She felt the bone bend – an unnatural sensation that would haunt her nightmares for the rest of her life. Her helmsman shoved the remaining seventeen people under the door, past Jenny. That door just kept pushing. She thought it was going to slice her in half. But at least her crew would be able to continue the fight from engineering.

She'd passed out from a combination of trauma, shock, and air loss before all seventeen of her crew were off the bridge. They told her that after the door had crushed her pelvis, the helmsman and two others had dragged her out from under the door to engineering. Then they'd radioed the other surviving Reason ship with instructions for building their own space shotgun. Between the two Reason ships, they picked off all the remaining necromancers, bar one who flew back down to the surface and was never found.

Without necromancers to protect the citadel, it fell quickly. The remaining Bala were rounded up and transported to Reason Command on Jaisalmer, which is where Jenny ended up during her recovery. When it was clear she wasn't going to make a miraculous comeback, they'd dubbed her the hero of Copernica Citadel, propped her up in a wheelchair, still dizzy from pain meds, and Reason brass pinned medals on her jacket while taking thousands of promotional photos. There was an entire generation of soldiers raised on the legend of her selfless victory at Copernica.

"How did you get the necromancers to breathe in orbit?" she asked into the terrible silence in the *Jaggery*'s cockpit.

"Mermaids," said Gary. "They're quite proficient at regulating bubbles of air and pressure. We put them on the backs of the hippogriffs with the necromancers."

"Smart," said Jenny.

"How did you shoot down the necromancers?" he asked. "They were trained to avoid your heat-seeking projectiles."

"We stuffed shell casings with metal scraps and chucked them toward the source of the lightning."

"Resourceful," he replied thoughtfully. "I hope we're

never on opposing sides of the same battle again."

"Me too," said Jenny. "I don't have any spare legs to lose."
She'd meant it as a joke to lighten the mood, but the nod he
gave her was full of resigned understanding from a fellow vet
and it bloody well cut her to the bone.

A silver flicker on the viewscreen caught her attention. A
ship had materialized off their starboard side. Jenny zoomed
in on it. It was the *Arthur Phillip*.

"What the fu–" she began.

The *Arthur Phillip* fired on them before she even had a
chance to lock her wheelchair back into place. The *Jaggery*
jerked backward from the force of the purple blasts and
Jenny hit the console hard enough that her teeth dug into
her bottom lip. She hit the intercom.

"Incoming."

She locked her wheels and tapped her tablet before
remembering that it was disconnected from the ship.

"Gary?" she called.

He was back at the biological instruments, moving through
a set of commands from muscle memory. The *Jaggery* soared
up toward an asteroid field in the distance. They'd have
decent cover among the huge rocks and the *Arthur Phillip*
wouldn't be able to get close enough to board them. He
flicked his fingers across the incomprehensible controls and
the ship spun and dodged around jagged outcroppings. He
even managed to keep the artificial gravity steady. Stoneships
were miracles if you knew how to fly them.

Jenny scanned the area using the external cameras.
The *Arthur Phillip* paced them outside of the debris field,
occasionally letting another volley of sparks fly toward the
Jaggery. The purple lightning split the asteroids nearest them
as Gary jerked the ship through the maze of rocks.

Jim barreled into the cockpit and cursed at the image of
the *Arthur Phillip* on Jenny's tablet.

"How did they find us?" he asked. Jenny smelled whiskey on his breath.

"That's necromancer magic," she replied, pointing to the lightning that streaked into the asteroid field around them.

"Partial necromancer, thank Unamip, otherwise we'd already be dead," said Gary, spinning the ship around a giant smooth asteroid that was a dead ringer for a stoneship.

"Even a partial necromancer could track us," she said. "They probably have one captive."

Jim leaned up against the console to get a better look at the *Arthur Phillip*. He pointed at a collection of red specks in the distance that were no longer swimming lazily through space.

"What's that look like to you?" he asked Jenny.

Jenny zoomed in on the area. Six red lines sped toward them in pyramid formation, the largest at the front.

"Redworms noticed the lightning," she replied.

"So much for unicorn luck," said Jim.

A shard of purple lightning slipped past the asteroid field and hit the *Jaggery* full on. A tremor started in the heart of the ship and vibrated outward until everyone in the cockpit was sick with the reverberations.

"That seems bad," said Jenny.

Gary placed his hand flat on his instrument panel and listened.

"It was," he said.

The *Arthur Phillip* made a hairpin turn and rounded on them through a break in the asteroids. The ship threaded its way toward the *Jaggery*, bumping rocks off its hull in all directions. Their pilot was not nearly as skilled as Gary.

"Why Bala don't believe in escape pods is beyond me," said Jim, tugging at the collar of his button-down.

"We didn't need to escape anyone until humans came along," said Gary.

"EVA suits. We could suit up and get onto one of these rocks..." started Jim.

"I'm not leaving the cargo," said Jenny, watching the redworms close in on the light show.

"You don't get to decide. I'm in charge here," said Jim.

"Are you?" she asked, with a single raised eyebrow.

Jim grabbed the zipper of her jumpsuit and yanked her over to the pilot's chair. In her peripheral vision, Jenny saw Gary move toward them.

"Are you out of your mind? No delivery is going to happen. We'll be lucky if we get off this ship before we're eaten by redworms or arrested by Reason. My ass is going to be sitting out there on an asteroid with an emergency beacon before the Reason boards us and throws us all in the Quag."

Jenny resisted the urge to smack his hand away. If Jim left the *Jaggery*, they were not getting through Fairyfloss Checkpoint into Reasonspace. She could not let him go out that door. She eased his hand off her jumpsuit and Gary stepped back.

"Cheryl Ann would have wanted you to stay and fight," she said.

Invoking the ghost of Cheryl Ann was a dirty move and Jenny knew it. But Jim paused at the door, so she kept talking.

"We need you to get through Fairyfloss... and to pilot us," she added, though both of them knew it wasn't true. He hadn't left, but he also hadn't turned around. "You can hate Gary and you can hate me, but you know that Cheryl Ann wouldn't have wanted you to leave us out here again. After everything she sacrificed to save our lives."

Jim turned around, but didn't meet her eyes. He sat down and strapped himself in.

"Jim, she–" Jenny began.

"Shut up and save our asses," he said.

CHAPTER SIXTEEN
Hibernation

Gary felt the *Jaggery* taking protective measures, curling into itself as each bolt of purple lightning struck its side. Hibernation was meant to be helpful – keeping the creatures inside the ship safe until the threat had passed. But it would leave them stranded in openspace for days, until the ship decided it was safe to come out of lockdown. He coaxed it through the asteroid field, hoping they could keep the *Arthur Phillip* at bay long enough for one of them to come up with a plan.

Jim sulked in the captain's chair and for once Gary sympathized. It had been cruel of Jenny to remind him of Cheryl Ann in order to make him stay. Gary didn't think that they needed Jim at all. Let the man float away between the asteroids if he wanted to. It could only improve things on the ship.

"Any horn yet? Even just a sliver?" asked Jenny, craning her neck up to see his crater. He shook his head. He felt the process working: there was a giddiness in his brain and, dare he say it, a frolic to his step that he hadn't felt in years. But it would still take hours to make even enough to jump a single AU.

With a shiver, the ship murmured to Gary that the redworms were about to arrive. Even if they got clear of the

Arthur Phillip, the worms were now focused on them with a singular goal. Eat.

"Let the *Arthur Phillip* board us," suggested Jim. "They'll jump us back to Reasonspace before the worms get here."

"No. We can do this," said Jenny, scrolling rapidly on her tablet. Gary watched to see what she was thinking. As callous a person as Jenny could be, her sense of strategy was incomparable. He'd seen it firsthand at Copernica.

"I should have taken my chances outside," grumbled Jim.

"You're safer inside the ship, even if it goes into hibernation," said Gary. Jenny turned toward him, her face full of realization. He knew immediately what she meant to do.

"Let the *Arthur Phillip* hit us square on," she said, but Gary was already on it. He maneuvered the *Jaggery* into a space between two large rocks and waited.

"What in the hell–" started Jim.

"We have to get the ship to hibernate. Redworms will always head toward a source of heat and light," she said, flicking on the ship's intercom. "Buckle up, everyone." she said. There were no harnesses where Gary stood, but a few shattered unicorn bones were worth the survival of everyone on board. The ship attempted to buck itself out of the way of the incoming lightning, but Gary spoke to it in a soothing voice, convincing it to stay in place with a whispered apology. "By Unamip, I mean you no harm."

"How about praying for us instead of the damn ship?" said Jim.

"I can do both," said Gary, not doing both.

The *Arthur Phillip*'s necromancer saw the opening and cast a colossal spell toward the *Jaggery*. A half-dozen violet bolts struck the ship at once. The *Jaggery* seized, then squealed like a hurt animal. The ship tried to bolt through the asteroid field. It glanced off a rock the size of Beywey Station.

Gary hit the opposite wall. He felt a bone crunch in his shoulder, then pull itself straight. If Jenny's plan worked, there was a chance they could get away. Or end up stranded inside an inert, locked-down stoneship in a remote asteroid field farming mushrooms for years. Which didn't sound half bad, really.

Another shot burst from the *Arthur Phillip*. The lightning this time was a weaker pale lilac, but it was enough to send the *Jaggery* into paroxysms of self-preservation. The cockpit lights went out except for Jenny's tablet, bathing them all in a bluish glow. The gravity clicked off and the trisicles on the floor rose around them like flying scarabs. Gary floated over to Jenny's chair and hovered, watching as she monitored the exterior camera feed. The *Arthur Phillip* rounded on them for a final shot, not noticing the pack of redworms coming up behind them.

"They don't even see the worms," said Jim in the darkness.

"They're focused on us," said Gary.

"Please, please, please," whispered Jenny, in what Gary supposed was a human version of prayer. He wondered if Unamip answered those.

A final shot of lightning hit the *Jaggery*, so pale that it was nearly white. The necromancer was almost spent. The *Jaggery* let out a hiss as it locked down all exterior openings and became, for all intents and purposes, as lifeless and impenetrable as the asteroids surrounding it.

The *Arthur Phillip* finally seemed to notice the redworms when they were a few kilometers away. They fired their aft cannons and one of the worms exploded into chunks. A second one latched directly onto one of the ship's engines, sucking fuel and air out of the puncture wounds from its massive teeth. Redworms could, and would, eat anything that wasn't rock.

The largest worm opened its mouth and belched digestive

acid onto the *Arthur Phillip*'s communications tower. The tower dissolved into bubbles of liquid that floated around the attacking pod. The other redworms drank the frozen slurry of metal and human parts that floated around the ship. Jim put a hand over his mouth. Zero G never sat well with him.

"Do you think they'll see us?" asked Jim.

"We look like all the other rocks out here," she said. "We're fine." But she tracked each of the worms carefully on her screen. Gary heard the edge in her voice, like she was soothing an annoying toddler.

The *Arthur Phillip* spun and dodged, trying to dislodge the worms. They fired projectiles at whatever they could and even had the depleted necromancer cast a few weak bolts. One caught a redworm around the middle and twisted it in half. The two writhing halves were descended upon by the remaining four worms. Nothing edible would be wasted out here.

The *Arthur Phillip* slammed into one of the asteroids head on. Gary couldn't tell if it was a strategy or a panicked error. The ship bounced off the rock. Debris and atmosphere vented out of the crushed hull. Jenny zoomed in and Gary saw more bodies floating free. She let out a pained breath.

"They would have done the same to us," said Gary.

"I know," replied Jenny.

Escape pods jettisoned from the sides of the Reason ship. One of the smaller worms pursued each one in turn, working methodically through the debris. A few pods managed to disappear into the asteroid belt. On Jenny's tablet, a dozen distress beacons activated on a Reason emergency frequency.

The three largest worms spat acid onto the aft section of the *Arthur Phillip*, working their way methodically up the hull. At this rate, it would take them no more than a couple of hours to digest the entire ship.

Jenny turned off her tablet and stuck it into a pocket in

her jumpsuit. She plucked a trisicle out of the air and handed it to Gary.

"Get eating while we figure out how to get a stoneship out of hibernation."

She unsnapped her harness and floated toward the door, waiting for them both.

"You want I should stay here and keep watch on the worms?" asked Jim.

Jenny shook her head, resisting the urge to needle him about deferring to her again.

"No need. If they come for us, there's nothing we can do with the *Jaggery* locked down. I need everyone figuring out how to wake it back up."

Jim still didn't move.

"Even if you magically get this ship restarted, out of East Bumfuck, and back into Reasonspace, we're not going to make it to Fort J in time for the Summit," said Jim.

"You're right. Not if we go through Fairyfloss."

A mirthless laugh erupted from Jim.

"You want to go through Borstal," he said, shaking his head in wonder. "None of you are making it through Borstal Checkpoint. They'd incarcerate a Pymmie if it suited them."

"You have no faith in me. Haven't I gotten us this far?" asked Jenny.

In the distance, the *Arthur Phillip*'s engines exploded, rocking the *Jaggery* like a ship in a hurricane. Another handful of distress beacons popped up on the tablet screen.

Jim unbuckled reluctantly. Gary left his instruments and followed.

"If we get the ship restarted, we should pick up the survivors," said Gary. Jenny pushed off the door frame and into the hall.

"I said I was trying to do better. I didn't say I was aiming for sainthood," she said, without pausing.

The hallways of the *Jaggery* were lit by candles that the dwarves had placed into crags in the stone. Jenny sucked in her breath at the smoky globes of flame. Reason soldiers were trained never to have open fires in space, but Gary was used to it. Stoneships were not as concerned with the spread of fire as the pressurized steel cans that the Reason used for transport. When operating normally, the environment on the *Jaggery* was perpetually damp and the threat of fire spread was low.

Trisicles floated freely around the halls. Gary grabbed one and crunched down on it. He had never seen so many in one place. The dwarves were packing them up into nets for storage. There was enough food here for him to take the *Jaggery* anywhere in the universe after they made their dropoff at the Summit. He was starting to have a glimmer of hope that he might come out of this trip with the ship he had been promised.

Ricky's door burst open and she flew into the hall.

"My window went black right at the good part of the battle," she complained. "What else am I supposed to watch around here?"

"Why don't you put your brain full of tricks, cons, and scams to good use and help us figure out how to get to Fort J in time?" said Jenny.

Boges floated around a corner, holding a lantern.

"Captain, if you're headed for the engine room, don't bother," she said. Gary wasn't sure who she was addressing, because she certainly wasn't looking at Jim. "I have ten of my best kin in there and none of their usual songs are waking the ship. Abattor only knows how long we'll be stuck here." Things were certainly dire if Boges were invoking the dwarven god of axes.

Everyone floated to a stop.

"So, what now?" asked Jim. Jenny shook her head, her

brown hair coming undone and splaying around her like a crown.

"Now, we must use a dwarven strategy for problem solving," said Boges.

"What's that, hammers and pickaxes?" asked Jim.

Boges floated off toward the main hall.

"No. We eat," she called over her shoulder.

Jenny pulled out her tablet. The redworms had eaten about half of the *Arthur Phillip*, but they were getting full and slowing down. One rested on the top of the ship, basking in the light from a nearby star that had just begun to peek around the asteroids and warm the hull. She scrolled through all of the distress beacons in the area, then tucked the tablet away.

"It can't hurt. I need to think for a few minutes anyway," said Jenny.

Gary was grateful for the break. He was ravenous. Besides the trisicle and a couple of sips of chai, he hadn't eaten since the night before. The Quag wasn't in the habit of wasting a morning meal on a man who was about to go free. But it was already late afternoon Jaisalmer time, the night before the Summit. They had less than twenty hours on the cargo clock. This dinner would have to be fast.

The *Jaggery*'s dining room had been closed up during storage. The dwarves preferred to eat in their own tucked-away homes in the walls. The waterfall had been shut off and all of the banners rolled up and tied to keep them free of dust. In the dim candlelight, it looked like a cave.

"Creepy," said Ricky, floating in and hovering near one of the long communal tables.

A group of dwarves floated in with lanterns using pressurized fuel that was much brighter than zero G candles. They hung them in the rafters, illuminating a vaulted ceiling and huge timbers crossing the expanse in geometric patterns.

The wood was primarily decorative, telling the stories of past adventures through carved motifs. Gary recognized a few of his father's more notable exploits memorialized in the wood.

Another set of dwarves came through the far door, carrying platters of food covered in glass domes.

"I apologize for the lack of options. We haven't been able to restock the pantry," said Boges. She shot a glance at Jenny, who had come on board with more mouths to feed and no provisions of her own.

The dwarves set down a tray of roasted sweet potatoes. "Apologies for the lack of butter. We ate the cows years ago."

Jim grabbed a potato out from under a dome and warmed his hands with it. Jenny took hers and floated away from the group, pulling herself around the perimeter of the room in the weightless equivalent of pacing. Gary took one and ate it between bites of trisicle. He needed to grow horn, but his human organs still needed sustenance. This simple potato was better than any of the food he'd had in the Quag over the last ten years.

"I might be able to spare a little wine for cooking if you need it," Ricky said to Boges. "That is, if you have any dwarf artifacts to trade."

Boges bounced with giddy excitement. Locked in here, she had likely not had access to a luxury like alcohol for a long time.

"I do have some antique human clothing you may be interested in. One of my kin crashed his ship during Earth's mid sixteenth-century. Out of the entire crew, only seven of them survived. They were stranded for nearly a year until they were able to mine and refine enough metal to fix their ship."

"That sounds like quite an ordeal," said Gary.

"Not so terrible," said Boges. "They set up a cabin in the woods and made a lovely little life for themselves. There were some unfortunate run-ins with the locals, but they survived."

Ricky leaned close to Boges and they began conversing in hushed tones over the trade value of a magic-infused Bala mirror.

Gary hooked his legs around a bench bolted to the floor and pulled a second potato out from under the dome. He bit off nearly half of it before remembering to slow himself down. He'd picked up the terrible habit of eating as fast as he could swallow.

"What was in the card from your mother?" asked Boges.

"I forgot about that," said Gary, reaching into his back pocket for the card, now bent and torn on one edge where trisicles had bitten through the paper. He slid his finger under the seal and pulled out the card. It was an old one, printed in mass quantities with a decorated tree on the outside. Ricky practically purred as she saw it.

"I'll give you two glasses of larval eggwine for that card." Gary ignored her offer and opened the heavy folded paper. His mother's handwriting was as round and exuberant as she had been. Seeing the loops made his heart ache like no gunshot wound to the chest ever had.

Beta,
   I took something from you long ago to keep you safe. If you are reading this, the Sisters have decided that it is time to return it. Merry Christmas.
   Love forever,
      Ma

She was talking about his horn. She had sawed it off him when he was still a child in order to protect him from the Reason. She'd hidden it and never given up the location – even under torture. Gary tried not to show any of the discomposure he was feeling.

Ricky leaned over his shoulder and read the message out loud.

"A Christmas present, eh?" she asked, chewing.

"We never celebrated Christmas," said Gary, turning the paper over for any hints as to where the item was hidden. The paper was blank.

"What did she take from you?" asked Jim.

"His horn," said Jenny. "She hid it."

Jim leaned all the way forward until he was nearly horizontal.

"Lemme see that."

He grabbed for the card. Gary held it away from him.

"Don't touch my card."

"I'll find out where that horn is," said Jim, pushing off and reaching again. Gary unhooked his legs from the bench and floated upward.

"This is not yours," he said, holding the card behind his back. A half-eaten sweet potato ricocheted off Jim's cheek. Jenny floated near the table, hands on her hips.

"Gentlemen," she said archly, holding a second potato ready to launch.

Jim pushed off from Gary's sweater a little harder than he needed to and went back down to the table.

"He started it," he muttered.

Jenny looked up at Gary.

"Do you want help figuring it out? We all have a vested interest in finding your horn."

"It's not likely to be on the ship. Perhaps it's in the boxes the Sisters delivered."

"They don't open until just before the Summit. That would be spectacularly unhelpful," said Ricky. "Do you think she left the horn with the Sisters?"

"No. They're not exactly Reason, but my mother never

trusted them completely."

"So who did your mother trust completely?" asked Jenny.

Gary looked to Boges.

"Oh," said the dwarf. "I swear on the Hexaxe of Abattor, she did not tell me where she hid your horn."

"She wouldn't risk telling you directly. But she always said you would stay with the *Jaggery* until your final day."

"And I would," said Boges with ferocity.

"So she hid it on the ship," said Jenny. "But the Reason didn't find it."

All of them floated in the dining hall, wondering where one could hide a two-foot section of unicorn horn undetected. The Reason had combed through the ship looking for it after Gary's arrest and had come up empty handed.

"Boges, is there anything left on the ship from my mother?" asked Gary.

"Not much," said Boges. "Her earrings in your footlocker. A few tapestries in storage. A blue sari."

He turned the card over and held the picture up to Boges.

"Does this have any meaning to you?" he asked.

Boges squinted at the picture in the low light.

"It looks familiar. Like I've seen it before, but I can't recall where."

"That's a Christmas tree," said Jim. "For Christmas. You see them all over in December."

Boges frowned.

"No, but I feel like I've seen one recently. I just can't…"

"Elf magic," said Gary and Jenny in unison.

Elves were masters of subterfuge and disguise. What they called a sliding spell could cause someone's eyes to glance right over the thing they were looking for. Gary did not prefer to think about the bodily fluids needed from a willing elf to make such a spell, but his mother was a warrior who would have done what was necessary to protect the horn.

"There are two ways to render a sliding spell inert..." started Gary.

"Water and heat," finished Jenny. "And unless we want to turn up the heat, which we don't because of the redworms, I think we need to make everything a little wetter around here. Are the environmental controls still active?"

"Yes. Hibernation is meant to protect what's inside the ship, not freeze it to death," said Boges.

"Set the foliage misters up to full force," said Gary. Dwarves flew in different directions to set the mist nozzles on high. When the ship was in full bloom, they kept everything watered and lush.

A huge smile spread across Jenny's face. She'd just arrived at the same conclusion he'd reached a moment ago.

"That's how your mother was going to know that you were back in charge of the ship. She knew we humans would take out all of the plants. As soon as you or another Bala took command and started watering and getting everything misty again, the spell would wash off and you would find your horn. Bloody brilliant."

"That she was," said Gary.

Nozzles in the walls began to churn out a fine spray of water. With the gravity off, the mist floated aimlessly around the dining hall, collecting in larger balls of moisture. Gary hoped it would be effective to wash off the spell in zero G.

"I had sprayers like that in the Blossom," mused Ricky. "But for a very different purpose..."

"No one cares to hear about that," said Jim, chewing resolutely.

"I remember," said Boges, pushing off the table and up toward Gary. "Where I saw that tree. It was in your mother's shrine."

Boges pointed to the far wall of the great hall.

Gary sailed to the edge of the room where the shrine was

tucked into an alcove carved into the wall. This spot served as a makeshift temple for his mother, even though she was the only worshipper of these gods on the *Jaggery*. She'd taught him how to pray to these human gods, lighting the lamp and folding his hands just so. But Ganesha, Shiva, and Krishna had never resonated within him the way Unamip had. By the time he was a teenager, he'd already turn his head away whenever he passed the shrine, hoping that his mother would not make him stop to light the lamp. She had chosen a wise hiding place, knowing that he would make every effort to look away from her gods and never even notice his horn under the Bala spell.

Tucked far into the back of the shrine, behind the framed pictures and statues, was a pink metallic Christmas tree. He vaguely remembered seeing the tree, but it never seemed of much importance. The elfin magic had caused it to slide away from his notice. Now it sat, damp and dark within the alcove. It had been sitting there, in plain sight, for nearly a century.

Gary pulled the worn tree off its base. Power thrummed in his palm. He peeled away the glued branches and unwound pink tape from around the trunk. If he had known, he could have saved Cheryl Ann's life. His own life. When all of the gaudy Earth bits had been stripped away, what was left in his hand was the pearlescent shimmer of a unicorn horn.

A hand reached around him and tried to take it. Gary yanked it back and pushed off toward the rafters.

"Give that here, boy," said Jim, coming up after him. "This ship is mine and so is that horn."

"Jim, let him keep it," shouted Jenny.

"I'm not gonna get stuck again," said Jim, panting from the exertion of chasing Gary around the ceiling.

Jim pushed off one of the massive timbers toward Gary, catching him around the neck. Gary felt the old man's cold, bony fingers close around his windpipe and start to squeeze. It felt like a skeleton trying to choke a birch tree. He laughed at the feeble attempt to subdue him.

"Can't quite get a grip any more, cowboy?" he chuckled. Jim pressed harder, barely getting his gnarled fingers around Gary's neck. Gary put his hand onto Jim's chest and pushed. The old cowboy bounced off the rafter with a grunt like a deflating balloon. Gary turned to head back down.

Jim pushed off again. This time he aimed for the base of the horn and pulled, stopping Gary's inertia. Gary spun and faced the dried-up human hanging onto the other end. He put two hands around the horn like a cricket bat and shoved forward until the base hit Jim across the bridge of his nose. Blood bubbled out into the weightlessness. Jim coughed and let go.

"I'm the captain." The plaintive cry was muffled through Jim's hands covering his face.

"Are you?" asked Gary, with a raised eyebrow.

"Bastard," said Jim.

Gary kicked off on the ceiling timbers and floated back down.

"You didn't need to do that," Jenny said to him.

"He shouldn't have tried to take my horn," replied Gary, plucking his mother's card from where it hovered above the table. Humans always tried to take everything of value, then cried foul when you fought for what was rightfully yours.

"That's going to end up bad for all of us," continued Jenny, looking up at Jim trying to wipe the blood bubbles away from his face with his shirt. Anger rose in Gary. A feeling that he'd pushed down for years.

"Good. I am done coddling humans. You are all driven by self-interest and greed and a few more of you need to get your noses bloodied."

He reached toward Jenny, and for a split second fear

crossed her face. She thought he was going to hit her. His anger ebbed and he held out his hand.

"Can I have your tablet, please," he asked, calmly.

She reached into her jumpsuit pocket and passed it to him. The door to the dining hall closed with a bang as Jim slunk off to his room.

"I guess you're in charge now, Gary," said Ricky, taking a potato and floating along behind him, as if to follow. "I'd just like to say that I have always been on Team Gary. You'll remember, I gave you this ship."

Boges tisked at her.

"You shouldn't put a hibernating ship directly into FTL," the dwarf reminded Gary. "None of the guidance systems will work."

"Have the dwarves been able to wake the ship yet?" Gary asked.

"No," said Boges. "Last time it went into hibernation, it took six weeks to wake it."

"We don't have six weeks. Just jump it from hibernation," said Jenny.

"Traveling in the nullspace without guidance, we will almost assuredly collide with another ship in FTL. The nullspace paths are tunnels, not wide expanses like openspace. The guidance systems keep the ships from merging in the null. Unless you would like to partially merge with a Reason officer," said Gary.

"I know how to wake a stoneship," said Ricky.

"Quiet," said Jenny dismissively.

"I'm not joking. I've done it before," said Ricky, between bites.

"You have not," said Jenny.

"Wait," said Gary. Ricky was not bluffing. "Have you really?"

"Yes." Ricky let the half-eaten potato float away. She leaned down and whispered something to Boges, who flew toward the crew quarters. Ricky pushed off toward the engine room. "Do you want to watch?" she asked. Gary followed. He did, in fact, want to watch.

CHAPTER SEVENTEEN
Faster Than Light

"You don't run the best bar on the continent without picking up a few things about stoneships," said Ricky. "Drunk Reasoners are always dying to tell you about the time they woke a hibernating stoneship, captured and sold off its crew, then a got a big promotion."

Gary led them along hallways that Jenny had never seen. This ship was a maze of caves in the center. Boges popped out of a nearby door in the wall, looking horrified by the conversation. She handed a fancy bottle to Ricky.

"Sorry. I mean, we all know they do it," said Ricky. "Doesn't make it right."

They were deep in the center of the *Jaggery*. In the quiet of hibernation, there was still a thrumming heartbeat pulsing throughout the walls in this area. Cheryl Ann had mentioned this years ago. She'd said that the heart of the ship had sung to her. Jenny had laughed at the time, thinking her friend was exaggerating, but now it seemed to be singing to her as well. That anxious feeling was increasing the deeper they went into the ship. Like the little magical tricks she'd been doing wanted to burst out of her. She clamped down on the urge and pulled herself along behind the others.

The tunnel narrowed and the air vibrated with a multi-part harmony. Gary pushed open a door and held it open for

Ricky, Boges, and Jenny. As she passed him, Jenny could see the shimmering whiteness of the horn in his hand. It looked like sunlight sparkling off freshly fallen snow.

Seven concentric rings of dwarves were deep in song around a sphere in the center of the room. They cried out in what sounded like seven distinct rhythms that occasionally came together in a single, elaborate melody, then broke apart again into warring notes. Jenny's head buzzed from the noise, but in a way that left her feeling energized and sharp. It was as if the antsy feeling had intensified to an electric hum of power within her. Boges left her side to join the dwarves in the innermost ring. The dwarves on either side embraced her warmly without skipping a note. Her contralto voice soared above the others, pulling them along with her song.

The sphere glowed gold around the edges, but the center was filled with the darkest of blacks swirled with distorted lines of color like paint on the surface of water. When Jenny was young, an oil spill had washed up onto the beach near her home. It had swirled in the same way; a rainbow of distorting colors that curled into spirals. Her gran had warned her not to touch the oil. She had touched it anyway and her fingers had come away sticky and black.

"What is this?" asked Jenny over the drone of multi-part harmonies.

"This is a stoneship engine," said Gary.

"Why are they singing?" asked Jenny.

"Because that's what it runs on," said Ricky, looking at her like she was a fool. "Did you not know?"

"How would I know that this ship runs on a bunch of dwarves singing? I thought it ran on... I don't know... magical rocket fuel?" said Jenny.

"Spaceships run on rocket fuel. Stoneships run on the power of ancient song sung into the great void," said Gary.

Jenny's mouth opened, but she couldn't think of a single thing to say.

"I know. Just go with it," said Ricky. "When stoneships hibernate, you have to prime the engine to get them started again. Luckily, I brought along some stoneship engine lubricant." She held up the crystal-cut bottle, which looked heavy. The label on the side said "Gravitas".

"You're selling engine lubricant for five hundred a glass?" asked Jenny.

"You wouldn't believe what people pay for coolant fluid," said Ricky.

She floated toward the sphere in the center of the room, uncapped the bottle of Gravitas and let the liquid float out into the void. It curled around the colors within and infused them all with a silvery sheen. Ricky poured out almost all of the bottle, then capped it and floated away from the sphere.

The swirling colors were now tinged by silver and reminded Jenny of the plume of smoke behind the booster rockets of Reason troop transports. She'd been a grunt back then, young and scared. Her hands had quivered in her lap on the shuttle to her first assignment. They quivered now. The energy coming off the void was making her both excited and terrified. She couldn't shake the jittery feeling that they were all waiting for a miracle or a disaster.

"Now what?" Jenny asked.

"Now they have to restart it," said Ricky.

Gary moved to the front row near Boges and joined the song. His voice began low, creeping under all of the dwarves in the room, then it rose above them, daring their voices to meet his. The song became louder until Jenny was carried along with the noise like a leaf caught in a river current. She felt wrapped in it, like a safe, suffocating blanket of sound.

Gary looked back and flicked his head to indicate she

should join them. But she couldn't. She didn't know the song or the words.

"Gary wants you to sing," shouted Ricky over the harmonics. "Stoneships get attached to certain people. I think you should join them."

"I can't," replied Jenny.

She felt a strong sense of disassociation, as if her body and mind were not quite aligned. It was the same sensation she felt when entering nullspace, but this time it didn't dissipate. She was swelling with unspent energy. She was going to be sick from it unless she found a way to release the pressure.

Jenny flexed her fingers and flowering vines bloomed out of the stoneship floor – the size of a dinner plate and thick with fragrance. She took a long breath and the pounding in her head felt a bit better. Ricky moved toward the floor to inspect the blossoms and Gary raised an eyebrow at her. Boges left her spot to float toward Jenny and take her hand.

Boges' hand was calloused and strong. She pulled Jenny along above the plants that had sprung up in the pathway. She pushed Jenny into a spot in the innermost ring and patted her shoulder. They wanted her to sing, but she couldn't. She didn't know the words or the melody and her head was swimming awfully. She closed her eyes and felt pinpricks of power coming off the sphere and landing on her exposed arms. The engine was nudging her. She resisted.

The room slid sideways, and she felt the same dizziness she did after too many beers. She reached out, but there was nothing to grab onto to steady herself. It was like she was falling toward the void in the sphere. Inside of the blackness, past the sheen of colors, there were millions of twinkling dots that looked like stars. There was a sadness in the void. A feeling of loss not unlike the Sixian parrot's hum back in the Bitter Blossom.

And suddenly, she knew the right song to sing.

Jenny began the funeral haka with a guttural cry that caused several of the dwarves near her to startle. She lifted her quivering hands into the air. The words of the manawa wera became entwined with the singing of the dwarves. Sometimes her cries clashed with their melody, battling their words into submission, but other times her harmonies joined with the Bala singers to strengthen and bolster their wails. Jenny had never cried when her family performed a haka, but today her eyes were wet.

The edges of the void turned gold and the entire sphere contracted, then swelled outward in a burst of power. The dwarves allowed their song to settle back down into a calm, quiet rhythm. Jenny finished her haka with a pūkana, widening her eyes and lifting her chin. She drew a breath and rested her tired hands in her lap. The ship waited for instructions. It hummed with power, no longer in hibernation.

"See? I told you I could do it," said Ricky from the back of the room.

A new set of dwarves took the place of a few who had become tired during the song. It looked like they switched over in regular shifts. It would take a lot of singing to power this ship for years on end. Jenny suddenly had an appreciation for how much the dwarves were doing that she could not see. No wonder Cheryl Ann had taken the time to learn their names.

Boges stopped in front of Gary.

"She reminds me of your mother," she said, patting his sweater affectionately and heading into a dwarf door in the wall.

Jenny pulled out her tablet. She still slightly nauseated from the humming of the dwarves around her. The redworms were drifting lazily around the remains of the *Arthur Phillip*, but they would find the *Jaggery* shortly now that it was back online.

"It was good that you joined us," said Gary. "The ship appreciated your song."

"I wasn't sure what to do."

"You did fine."

Ricky was examining the blossoms that had popped up around the room. It almost looked like a fully functional stoneship, with tall grass on the floor and vines snaking down the walls.

"What is all this?" she asked Gary.

"It's very interesting," he replied. "Few humans in history have been able to channel nullspace energy. You seem to have learned the skill."

"It's not a skill. It's just... coming out of me." Jenny lifted her hand. It looked completely ordinary now.

"The Sisters study for years to create even a basic diversion or disguise. What you are doing is advanced magic," said Gary.

"I thought humans couldn't harness Bala magic. It's all locked up in your biological processes," said Jenny.

Gary looked like he was debating whether to say something. He seemed to decide in favor.

"Bala bodies are built for channeling nullspace energy. In general, human bodies are not. But there are a handful of humans who learn how anyway. You know them as necromancers."

"Bloody hell," said Jenny as her breastbone began to ache again. She rubbed it and closed her eyes. "And I shot them out of the sky."

"Yes, you did." Gary pushed off the floor to leave the engine room. Jenny grabbed his arm to stop him.

"One more minute," she said.

"We have to get into FTL–" he began.

"A second. Can your blood heal nerve damage?"

Gary's eyes rested on her legs, hovering above the floor.

"Nerve damage is the most difficult injury to heal. It's not likely that the small amount of blood I administered subcutaneously could bring back your mobility," he said.

"Right now it's just twinges of pain, pins and needles," she replied.

"Then that's likely the extent of the healing you will experience."

Jenny sighed and zipped up her jumpsuit for want of something to do with her hands. This entire conversation was making her uncomfortable.

"Is that bad?" he asked.

"I don't know, Gary. Is it good to feel stabbing pain in my legs, but still not be able to use them? I think it could be better."

"Do you want to use them?"

The answer came more slowly than she expected.

"This is me," she said simply.

"Perhaps the woman who is an impressive fighter in her chair won't be so impressive without it," he said.

"I can't relearn everything again. I'm tired," she replied.

"You're afraid," said Gary.

"No. Maybe." She hedged. "I'm afraid of what Jim is going to do. You set him off good by breaking his nose."

"I'll offer to heal it."

"You know he'll never accept that from you," said Jenny.

"Jim hasn't changed at all. He's repeating the same mistakes over and over and he's going to drag the rest of us down with him," said Gary. "Our only leverage over him is that he wants to get away from us as fast as possible. Knowing that, we need to make this delivery as seamless as possible and let him move on."

"I know. I've been letting him hang on for too long. I guess he reminded me of Cheryl Ann and… the good times before it all went to hell."

"Who's Cheryl Ann?" asked Ricky, coming over with her arms full of flowers.

"I'll explain later," said Jenny. "It's complicated."

"Oh wait, is that the woman Gary killed?"

A pained expression flickered across Gary's face.

"I said later," said Jenny firmly.

Boges poked her head back into the dwarf door. Her voice cut through the humming dwarves in the room.

"Captain, the ship is ready to jump to FTL."

Jenny didn't care whether Boges was calling Gary "captain" any more. But Jim was a powderkeg ready to blow. Gary twisted the horn in his hands.

"You're not going to let that go any time soon, are you?" asked Jenny.

"If you're going through Borstal Checkpoint, I'll have to hide it again," he said. It was a question phrased as a statement.

"It's the only way to get to Fort J in time," she answered.

Boges soared out of the dwarf door and handed Gary a gleaming knife. He shaved a thick sliver off the bottom of his horn and handed the knife and the rest of the horn to Boges. He floated over to an ornate wood cabinet mounted on the wall and pulled open the doors. Inside, Gary blew the remains of a desiccated trisicle out of the FTL drive. He placed the sliver of horn into the gleaming gold mesh of the drive and closed the door. A chunk that big could get them to Fort J five times over.

Boges waved from the dwarf door to get Jenny's attention.

"If you intend for Jim to get us through the checkpoint, you should be aware that he has locked himself in his room."

Jenny groaned and pulled herself toward the cockpit.

"We'll get into FTL first, then I'll get Jim out of his room."

"You know, Perata," called Ricky, gathering up a blossom that took two hands to harvest. "These stamens are worth big bucks in the pharmaceutical division. If you can grow some more, we could–"

"I can't make more. It was a onetime thing," said Jenny.

"It's an incredibly useful skill to have," said Gary.

"Hasn't been useful so far," said Jenny. She pulled out her tablet. The redworms were starting to stir. They nosed at the debris of the *Arthur Phillip*, searching for chunks worth dissolving and finding few. The distress beacons had dwindled down to a handful. It hadn't been pretty out there.

Jenny sailed along the hallways, which were now full of soil. A small part of her wanted to bloom them like she had the engine room, but not with Gary and Ricky watching behind her. In the cockpit, she settled into her chair and Ricky took Jim's seat.

"Going to FTL," called Gary from the back. He touched the instruments to put the *Jaggery* into FTL. For a split second the ship became transparent as it ceased to exist around them. Jenny's consciousness caught up to the ship, but not before hanging free for one fraction of a second within the expanse of space – untethered and exposed to the full magnitude of the universe. If she'd been inside of her own body at that moment, she would have screamed in terror. It was the second best part of traveling through the null.

Jenny loved nullspace. She was still unable to walk in FTL, but she felt calmer and less overwhelmed in here. Like zero G, she had more mobility. The solid rules of logic and physics seemed to fray a little at the seams, giving her the ability to move and think faster.

"Feels like that dream where you're trying to run, but you can't get yourself going," said Ricky, resting her head on the console in front of her.

"Yeah," said Jenny absently. A zing of pain jolted down

the back of her thigh. Those electric bursts were happening more often. They took her breath away.

Gary called out the ship's status via the vials and tubes in front of him.

"Heat, gravity, and water systems are coming back online," he said. "The ship is traumatized, but it is making do."

"That goes for all of us," said Jenny, massaging her leg. She snaked an input cord from her tablet to an outlet on the side of the viewscreen. It flickered to life with an image from the remaining exterior cameras.

"There. Now we can all see," she said.

"Where are the stars?" asked Ricky.

A fuzzy orb glowed in the center of the viewscreen. It appeared as if they were heading straight for an immense woolen sun.

"The eye of Unamip watches over our journey through the null," said Gary.

"Or... it's the Doppler effect from flying past the stars this fast," said Jenny with a shrug. "Whatever your pleasure."

"How long to Reasonspace?" asked Ricky, taking the deliberate breaths of a woman about to heave.

"We'll be at Borstal Checkpoint in less than an hour. And no puking in my cockpit," said Jenny.

"If we're not going to make our rendezvous at Jaisalmer, you can drop me at any space station along the trade route instead," said Ricky.

"We're going to make our rendezvous," said Jenny. She reached under the console and found the stacks of coiled wire and tools she'd stashed there. She grabbed some rolls of coated copper and cutters and floated up to the wires that the trisicles had chewed through.

"There's no need to reconnect the tablet," said Gary. "I'm perfectly capable of flying the ship from right here."

"I know, and you're brilliant at it, but when we go

through Borstal, Jim has to be piloting and he can't use those controls."

She snipped the frayed wires and ran fresh ones to her tablet. Thankfully, the bugs hadn't gotten into the walls and ruined those runs. She twisted a wire onto a connector and plugged it into her tablet. It pinged and buzzed with alerts as it read the ship's status. She saw everything that Gary had already told her, plus dozens of other errors. She muted them all. Reason technology relied on the immutable rules of logic. While they were in nullspace, it would ping her about every strange readout or occurrence on the *Jaggery*. Which would be a lot in this realm that didn't adhere to the laws of physics. Better to rely on Gary and the Bala instruments, which were built to handle the shifting reality of nullspace.

"I still don't like this Borstal idea," said Ricky, lifting her head. "The entire point of going through Fairyfloss is that they're overworked and tend not to do onboard inspections. You go through somewhere else and they're going to comb through this ship like a... like a comb."

"It's the only way to get to Fort J in time," said Jenny.

"But the only one on board who can get through is Jim," said Gary.

"And me," said Jenny. "I am the hero of Copernica Citadel."

"That's not going to get you very far in Reasonspace any more," said Ricky. "Ever since the horn shortages began, things are getting strict near Jaisalmer. Why do you think I only work in Earthspace?"

Jenny tapped on her tablet and pulled up a document.

"I have a plan for the checkpoint. It's going to suck, but it'll get us through. I have working papers for all of us. Real, legitimate papers. Not forged. Jim can get us through as his staff."

"You mean as his property," said Gary.

"It'll get us past inspection. Be deferential to him for a few hours, we'll drop this cargo, and then we can all get on our way."

"I don't see why this cargo is so important to you," said Ricky. "We don't even have to go back into Reasonspace to make some cash. I have my bar supplies and you can make those flowers. Gary can sell bits of horn. Just fly on out of here."

"The cargo is critical to the Summit."

"Is that what the Sisters told you?" asked Ricky. "Because I hate to tell you, they're more fickle than I am. Who knows who they're working for today?"

"No, we are going to Fort J," said Jenny, frustrated. "Even if we miss the Summit."

Ricky narrowed her eyes. Jenny tried to play it off, but she'd said too much.

"What are you hiding?" asked Ricky.

"Nothing," said Jenny. She tapped her tablet to open the rest of the working papers. All she needed was Jim's signature in three places on each and they would be able to get through with a minimum of hassle. She was only mildly concerned that he'd keep them in his service after the delivery. Jim wanted a lot of things out of life, but a complement of servants wasn't one of them.

Ricky was still staring at her.

"What?" asked Jenny.

"I've worked a game table for years. I know when someone is lying," said Ricky.

"Explain it to her," said Gary. "Perhaps she can help."

Jenny closed her eyes for a moment before replying. "They captured my wife, Kaila, on a supply run a while back. They have her on Jaisalmer."

She put her left hand in her pocket so she didn't have to see her wedding ring.

"It started out as a routine cargo inspection and then they went into the crew quarters and grabbed her out of our room. I couldn't stop them," she said.

"Oh shit," said Ricky. "I'm so sorry." She rubbed Jenny's back.

"Thanks. I'll find her. Dryads don't have much in the way of valuable parts, so she's likely being detained in the Jaisalmer harvesting center." She turned to Ricky and couldn't stop herself from asking for reassurance. "They wouldn't bother with a dryad, right?"

Ricky squeezed her shoulder.

"No. I'm sure she's fine. Probably just hanging out in a pot decorating some general's living room," said Ricky.

She pushed herself out of Jim's chair. "Well, I know better than to try to dissuade a woman from rescuing her wife. If we're going through Borstal Checkpoint, I need to go hide some things in the walls." She floated out of the cockpit.

Gary studied the orb for a moment, then bowed his head. Jenny had the distinct sense that he had just said a prayer.

"What did you ask Unamip for?" she asked.

"For safe passage and the strength to endure."

"That's a good prayer."

"You know, in Bala history, I am also called the hero of Copernica Citadel," mused Gary.

"But your side lost the battle," said Jenny, with a laugh.

"We took down four Reason ships before the citadel fell." Indeed, they had.

"Fair. How has life treated you since Copernica, hero?" asked Jenny.

"I wouldn't say they've been the best years of my life," said Gary.

"Me neither. I wonder sometimes, if our ships hadn't taken out those last couple of necromancers, would the whole war have come out differently?"

"I wonder that as well," he said.

Jenny appreciated that he hadn't asked to put the gravity back on. Jim would have been whining her ear off right about now.

"It's fascinating how life comes full circle sometimes," said Gary. "You remember that last necromancer? The one who retreated back to Copernica?"

"Yeah, we never found him."

"Are you aware of who he was?"

"No, who?"

"Bào Zhú."

Jenny turned herself fully around in her chair.

"What? Did he know this whole time that I was the captain of the *Pandey*?"

"I can't imagine so. If he did, he wouldn't have allowed you to live."

Jenny thought of the topographic map of scars across Bào Zhú's body. She'd caused those with shells full of hardware. And then she'd let him go flying off into openspace at Beywey. She'd killed that man twice.

"Well damn. I had no idea," she said.

"I think that was the point. He wasn't keen on anyone on either side knowing he was the necromancer who lost the war."

Another electric zing shot down Jenny's leg. She jumped. Her hand went to the spot involuntarily and Gary noticed.

"Another twinge?"

"Yes, Doctor Cobalt," she said.

"Don't be rude."

She chuckled at his stern demeanor and toggled the intercom.

"Jim, I need you in the cockpit," said Jenny. She turned back to Gary. "When we get to Borstal, you and Ricky need to be in the walls with the dwarves. I'll meet the boarding party in the cargo hold with Jim. There's a chance, with the Summit starting in a few hours, that they'll be skimming through ships quickly without inspections."

"I wouldn't count on it," said Gary.

"I'm not. You stay hidden until they find you. Only then will we try the ownership papers."

Gary made a face.

"I know. I don't love it either." She hit the intercom again. "Jim, get out here."

"I'm good right here," he answered.

"This guy," said Jenny, exasperated. "Get in the cockpit now."

"No," he pouted. "This is my ship and everyone keeps calling you 'Captain'. Well then, you captain it, Miss Fancy Pants."

"Oh for bloody hell," muttered Jenny. "He only pulls out Miss Fancy Pants when he's about to have a meltdown. If I had time, I'd let him stew in there until he got hungry, but we don't have more than thirty minutes until Borstal."

She tapped her teeth with a fingernail and thought through options.

"I have an idea," said Gary. It was rare that he offered a plan. Jenny was intrigued.

"I think you can convince him if you speak to him as Cheryl Ann," he said.

"Oh no," said Jenny. "You said yourself invoking Cheryl Ann before was cruel. Pretending to be her would be awful and wrong and a disguise like that would require a shapeshifter."

"I've seen what you've been doing. Your jumpsuit, the flowers, and a few other things you thought no one had noticed," said Gary.

"Party tricks. I can do them for a few seconds. You could probably do better."

"Shapeshifting is not a skill I possess," said Gary.

"Then have Boges do it," she said.

"Dwarves can't shapeshift," called Boges from behind the dwarf door where she was listening in. She opened it a crack. "It's a learned skill that only a few Bala master. It's unique for a human to have the ability to access nullspace energy at all, let alone shape it into intentional forms. Are you sure you're not part Bala?"

"Definitely not," said Jenny. "Maybe Ricky has some spell up her sleeve." She hit the intercom to Ricky's room. "When you're done stashing contraband, join us in the cockpit."

"I have a few of Cheryl Ann's things in storage," said Boges, disappearing through the dwarf door. Jenny called after her.

"Don't bother. I don't need them. We'll figure out some other way." Boges didn't answer. "Listen, I have no love lost for James Bryant, but this is needlessly sadistic," she said to Gary.

"It is heartless, but not needlessly so. There are beings counting on us to get through the checkpoint. Possibly millions."

"At least one," said Jenny, absently. Her finger paused on the tablet as she lost herself in some memory. Gary wanted to offer a consoling sentiment, but he couldn't assure her that everything would be all right without lying. A flicker of despair shadowed her face like a passing cloud.

"You'll find her. She'll be fine," he said. Jenny made a tiny snort through her nose. It was kind of him to lie.

"Of course," she replied. "She'll be fine." The shadow passed. "What I'm most worried about right now is Jim. When he figures out it's me under there, he'll kill me. No hesitation, no questions, he will straight up murder me where I stand."

"We'll be right outside the door," he assured her.

"I know, but you are nowhere near as fast as a man who has nothing to lose."

CHAPTER EIGHTEEN
The Ghost of Cheryl Ann

"I am deeply uncomfortable with this plan," said Jenny in the cockpit, looking down at the blue dress that used to belong to her best friend. Wearing it, she felt like a centaur on a bicycle. She smoothed down the skirt as it rose around her in zero G.

"How do you keep this thing down?" she asked.

"Wires, sometimes," said Ricky, putting Jenny's hair up. "Magnets work too. Zero gravity couture is a whole subgenre of fashion. Just let it float. It can only help you."

Between the dress, the hair, and the perfume that Boges had dug out of storage, they'd gotten Jenny as close to Cheryl Ann as they could. It was up to Jenny and the nullspace energy to do the rest.

"You could really use some makeup," said Ricky, looking disdainfully at Jenny's bare face.

"Don't even think about it," said Jenny. She was just about at her limit as it was. "I've never done anything like this," she warned. "I made a few flowers grow and changed the color of my jumpsuit. Nothing this complex."

"Then speak quickly," said Gary.

"When you're trying to convince someone, the devil is in the details," said Ricky, slipping one of her sturdier heels onto Jenny's floating foot. "Mention something that will bring back his memories of her. Something he'll remember fondly."

"Again, I am deeply uncomfortable lying to Jim," Jenny repeated. Gary and Boges nodded. Ricky put two hands on her shoulders.

"Don't think of it as lying. Imagine you're giving him the gift of one last conversation with his lovely bride. Let him say the things he's waited ten years to say. If you can get him talking, he'll probably go there on his own," said Ricky.

"How can you be sure?"

"Because that's what I would do," said Ricky. Jenny got a brief glimpse of something pained behind Ricky's unflappable facade before it went up again and she was tucking Jenny's hair behind her ear.

Jenny checked her tablet. They were ten minutes from Borstal. It was now or never. Jenny pulled up the file of Cheryl Ann's engineering school ID and studied the picture. She turned her awareness to the nullspace energy surrounding her. It pulsed along with the ship. She gathered it up like a sponge sucking up water, more than she ever had before. She had that feeling from the engine room, of being swollen with unspent energy. It made her as jittery as seven cups of coffee. She cracked her neck to release some of the pressure building in the back of her head.

"You all right?" asked Ricky.

"Just choice," said Jenny. She imagined Cheryl Ann's long honey-colored hair parted in the middle, her funny little turned-up rabbit nose, and her eyes the color of the twilight sky. She shook her head to move the energy into her features. She didn't need to ask if she'd gotten it right. Gary's pained face said that she had. She practiced Cheryl Ann's toothy grin and the look on Gary's face nearly broke her heart.

"I think I got it, bud," she said in Cheryl Ann's perky cadence.

"Nicely done," said Boges. Gary didn't, or couldn't, say a word.

Jenny pushed off into the hallway. She floated down to Jim's door and knocked. She'd thought impersonating her best friend would be hard, but as soon as that voice came out of her, all the goofy little phrases Cheryl Ann used to use came right back to her.

"Jimmy? I wanna talk," she said. There was quiet within.

"Wakey wakey, eggs and bakey," she called at the door. The voice was uncannily accurate. It sent shivers down her arms and she knew it was fake.

Jim's door opened. He stood there bleary-eyed, his shirt covered in dried blood. She gathered one last breath of nullspace and touched his crusty cheek.

"Oh Jimmy, what happened to you?" she asked.

Jim blinked the sleep out of his eyes. It didn't look like he was fully awake. All the better.

"Damn unicorn hit me," he said.

The real Cheryl Ann would have chided Jim for picking on Gary, but Jenny had an agenda.

"Baby, we need to get that bastard off our ship. Let's drop him at Fort J and..."

Jim's eyes narrowed, like he'd just become aware of what was happening.

"What are you doing here?" he asked, putting his hand over her own and squeezing it to see if it was real.

"We're in FTL, cowboy. Anything can happen."

He pulled her into his cabin and slammed the door shut.

"Did anyone see you?" he asked.

"No." Jenny started to get nervous. He was more frantic than she was expecting. His eyes darted around the room, as if he expected someone to jump out and ambush him. This was a man on the edge of reason.

"Good," he said. "I need someone on my side around here.

I think Gary is trying to kill me and Jenny is helping him. I think we need to strike first."

Jenny had imagined she'd spend most of the time convincing him she was really Cheryl Ann. She hadn't dreamed that he'd accept it right off the bat and pivot directly to murder.

"Oh, bud," she said, as disarmingly as she could. "I think you're jumping to conclusions. They just want to make their meeting time and drop off the boxes. We could really use the cash, hon."

"I don't want to go to Fort J," he said, putting his ear up to the door to listen to the hallway sounds.

"You'll be fine there. You have no warrants and you're not Bala. It'll be a piece of cake."

"But if Jen gets there, she's gonna find out that I turned Kaila into the Reason patrol for the reward money."

Jenny couldn't breathe. She gasped and clutched the front of her dress, which was suddenly two sizes too tight. There was a thunk out in the hallway. Thankfully, Jim pressed his ear up to the door and didn't see as her illusion flickered. For a moment, she was plain old Jenny, floating there, aghast. She got a breath in and reconstructed Cheryl Ann's face around her own.

"You did what?" she asked in mostly her own voice.

"We were low on cash and Jenny had us running on fumes between Earth and Mars. Kaila was always shedding leaves and drinking up all the water. It just made sense."

"Oh," said Jenny. She was afraid that if she tried to say anything else, she'd give herself away.

Jim floated up to her and grabbed her shoulders.

"I've missed you, bug." He leaned in to kiss her and Jenny turned her head away. He left a wet mark on her cheek instead.

"Hey, I can't remember the name of that bull cow who gave you so much trouble. The one that knocked you into the pond?" she asked.

"Tank. We called him Tank," said Jim.

"Ah, that's right. Tank. I was thinking, Jimmy. When you set up shop on some planet with a lot of grass, you should find one of those bull calves that looks like Tank and make a little ranching concern of it. Maybe get a momma cow too so you can have real cheese for your grilled cheese sandwiches. It's been a long time since you had real cheddar."

"Yeah. That's a good idea," he said, a wistful smile spreading across his face.

"It's just what we wanted, bud. And to get that plot of land you're going to need the help of every creature aboard this ship. You can't make this delivery alone. Make the drop, get the cash, move on with our lives. Trust me, bud."

Jim's eyes went wide in realization. Jenny felt victory within her grasp.

"You know what?" he asked brightly.

"What, hon?"

"I can make this delivery alone. I don't need a single damn one of them."

"No, that's not what I said. Just get everyone through Borstal. For me."

"The ship's in my name now. The rest of them can go to hell. I'm not letting you go again."

He reached out and stroked her hair. Jenny flinched and he narrowed his eyes at her. Her disguise flickered, like a flame sputtering. She ducked under his arm and pushed off toward the door. Jim froze with his hand in mid-reach.

"You don't move like my Cheryl Ann," he said.

"It's the null. I can't–"

A bony hand reached out and slammed Jenny against the wall, knocking the breath out of her.

"Which filthy Bala are you under there? One of the dwarves? Gary?"

Jenny wasn't ready to give up just yet.

"Jimmy, stop," she said, doing her best to mimic Cheryl Ann's pleading voice as her heart pounded. She lost her grasp on the nullspace energy and her disguise flickered into nonexistence. She was just Jenny wearing a dead woman's dress.

Jim's eyes hardened into black coals of fiery anger. He lifted his hand to strike and Jenny slammed him in the jaw with her elbow. He grunted and let her go. The door to the room opened so fast it banged against the wall. Two bare human feet kicked out and hit Jim in the shoulder. He flew away from Jenny and rebounded off the far wall. Ricky hung onto the doorway and held out her hand.

"Come on."

Jenny let Ricky pull her along the hallway, back to the cockpit. Jim came roaring after them, an antique six-shooter in his hand.

"I don't care if I bust a hole in this ship as big as a man, I'm going to kill you, Jenny Perata," he shouted, taking aim at her and Ricky. Boges popped out of a door in the hall and tried to block Jim. He floated right over the top of her.

"Where's Gary?" asked Jenny.

"He's a bit of a mess right now. I told him to walk it off," said Ricky.

"Don't move or I'll shoot," said Jim. They stopped and Jenny held up her hands.

"Hey, I'm sorry. We just needed your help and you wouldn't come out. We couldn't think of any other way to get you to open the door."

"So you impersonate my wife?" he cried, dragging himself slowly along the hallway. "That is the lowest. I know the rest of them hate me, but I thought you were my friend."

"You are no friend of mine, James Bryant. You turned Kaila into the Reason for cash. You are a dead weight hanger-on who I only bring along because you can get us through Reason checkpoints. No one likes you, no one wants you, and after this, I'll be delighted to get as bloody far away from you as possible."

The triple-click of a cocking revolver echoed off the stone walls. Ricky grabbed Jenny and shoved her down, bending over her like a shield. Jim pointed his gun in their direction. With no more than a few meters between them, even a shaky old guy like him couldn't miss.

He pulled the trigger and Jenny braced for the impact. There was a hollow click, but no shot rang out.

"Shit," said Jim. The gun clicked three more times. Every chamber was empty. Jenny started to breathe again. Ricky floated away from her. Gary came up behind Jim and slammed him into the stone wall. The old guy floated inert for a moment, then spasmed back to life with a wheeze.

"All of you are dead. Every single damn one of you," he said, pulling himself slowly along toward the cockpit, his face crumpled in pain. He shut the door behind him and the deadbolt slid home.

"That went well," said Ricky brightly.

"How are you doing?" Jenny asked Gary.

"I must admit that I'm feeling more emotions right now than I have names for," said Gary.

"Me too," said Jenny. "Ricky fucking Tang was going to take a bullet for me. Nothing in the universe makes sense any more."

"Maybe you owe me one or maybe you're just starting to grow on me, Perata," said Ricky, with a grin. Jenny turned to Boges.

"I'm curious why Jim's gun, which he keeps loaded at all times, was suddenly and mysteriously empty," she asked.

Boges opened her tiny fingers. Inside her palm were six gleaming bullets.

"I wouldn't let him shoot any of you," said Boges.

Jenny tugged on one of the dwarf's braids.

"Well done, Boges," she said. Boges ducked her head, but not so fast that Jenny didn't see the color creeping into her cheeks. Jenny pulled out her tablet.

"We're five minutes from Borstal. Jim intends to punish all of us by dumping us with the Reason. He's going to make the drop alone."

"So the cargo will get to Fort J," said Gary.

"And so will you," said Jenny. "They'll bring you to the harvesting center."

They exchanged a long look.

"You're just as bad as I am," said Jenny.

"Indeed," replied Gary.

"What am I missing?" asked Ricky.

"Jim is accidentally bringing us right where we need to be," said Jenny.

"Only not in the way that we intended," said Gary.

"Unamip's path is a labyrinth," said Jenny. "Some roads are unclear until the heat death of the universe."

Gary smiled at her – except for his eyes.

"I heard through the door. It's unconscionable what he did to Kaila," he said.

"What did he do?" asked Ricky.

"He turned in Jenny's wife for the reward," said Boges.

"What a shithead," said Ricky. "So how do we keep from getting arrested at Borstal?"

"Don't fight the current of fate," said Gary. Jenny laughed at the ridiculousness of the two of them quoting unicorn gods as they were about to be boarded, arrested, and tortured.

"Go with the flow," she giggled back.

"I don't understand you two," said Ricky, exasperated.

She kicked at the cockpit door, which sent her flying against the far wall. "How are we going to get out of this?"

"We're not. We're going to let the Reason take us to Jaisalmer. Jim is going to take the cargo there too," said Jenny.

"Oh perfect," said Ricky, her words dripping with sarcasm. "We only have to break out of both the rehab center and the harvesting center. People do that all the time. You couldn't have come up with an easier plan."

"You have to admit, it's a very Jenny Perata plan," said Gary.

Ricky pushed off toward her cabin.

"I'm not going to sit around and wait to be taken in. I'm going to hide… and if that doesn't work, I'm going to fight."

"I'm a little overdressed for incarceration," said Jenny, slapping down the gauzy skirt. "I'm going to change, and then wait for the boarding party in the cargo hold. Boges, can you help me out of this?"

"Of course, Captain."

"I'll meet you in the hold," said Gary. "I'll find Kaila at Fort J. You get yourself and Ricky out of the rehab center. If you can get to us on Jaisalmer, good. If not, we'll come to you."

"You sound quite confident."

"It's all I've got, Jen," said Gary.

They both chuckled. Jenny had heard that laugh before – on ships carting away Bala prisoners-of-war from Copernica Citadel. It was the mirthless laugh of fighters who knew they were about to die.

CHAPTER NINETEEN
Borstal Checkpoint

Gary floated over to the cargo boxes. They had eighteen hours to get them to Fort Jaisalmer. He wondered what would happen if they opened while they were in the air. It had occurred to him, with the Sisters' ever-shifting allegiance, that he could be delivering a weapon of mass destruction to the Summit. That would explain why it was so important to have it in the right place at the right time.

Jenny floated in after him. She'd quickly changed out of Cheryl Ann's dress and back into her usual flight jumpsuit and boots. She'd put her nest of hair up in an ornate braid that he suspected Boges had some hand in. Jenny was more likely to leave it floating. She had her tablet out to listen in on Jim's progress through the checkpoint on the public comm feed.

"Unidentified stoneship, this is the RSF *Lady Nugent.* Identify yourself immediately or you will be fired upon." The comm officer at Borstal sounded bored with her job. She threatened the *Jaggery* with a flat affect, reciting it by rote. That was a good sign that they weren't expecting trouble.

"*Lady Nugent.* This is Captain James Bryant of the stoneship *Jaggery.* I'm a human person on my way to Fort J for the Summit."

"We may get through without an inspection," said Gary.

"Just wait," warned Jenny.

"*Lady Nugent*," Jim continued. "I have captured some people and Bala wanted in connection with an attack on the *Arthur Phillip*. You may want to come on board and round them up. Just be quick. I'm on a schedule."

Gary heard a string of dwarven curses behind him. Boges ducked into the dwarf door to warn her kinfolk.

"They'll leave you on board as part of the ship," called Jenny after her. "You'll be fine." She turned to Gary. "We, on the other hand, will not."

"I'll be sent to the harvesting center. They'll take you and Ricky to the detention and rehabilitation center off the coast. Your security will be more lax than mine, so I expect that you'll be able to make your way to me. If you get to Fort Jaisalmer, your first priority is to ensure the delivery of the cargo, then head toward me. I'll find Kaila at the harvesting center and get as close as I can to you," said Gary.

"Yes, Captain," said Jenny, clearly amused that he was giving her instructions for a change, but she looked like she had every intention of following them. She'd saved all of their lives several times – and that was just over the last few hours. No wonder she'd been such a formidable adversary at Copernica. He was glad that for once they were on the same side.

"One last thing," he said. "You aren't going to have your chair."

She squeezed his arm reassuringly.

"I know. I've worked without it before. It's harder to knock people's teeth out when I'm on the floor, but not impossible. I can take care of myself."

"I have every confidence in you," said Gary.

"And you take care of yourself at harvesting. They are not going to let a unicorn gather moss for long. You cannot let them get you into the dissection room. Your best chance of escape is from the holding cells. There are windows on the far wall. They're high up on the wall, but they're not alarmed in any way. That's the weakest link in the security system," said Jenny.

"You're quite familiar with the layout," said Gary.

"I've worked there before," she said, letting her eyes slide away from his. "A long time ago."

The door to the cargo hold opened. Jim floated in and hung back near the door.

"What the bloody fuck-all did you do?" Jenny asked.

Jim raised his hands innocently. "You made me, Jen."

"People are going to end up dead because of you," she said.

"Then those people should have been nicer to me from the beginning. Maybe if we'd just stuck with the way things were before, with me in charge, this whole delivery would have gone a lot more smoothly. You bring in all these weirdos and suddenly a man doesn't have a place in the cockpit any more."

"Is this about your ego? Gary's better at piloting so you have us all arrested?" she asked.

"No, it's just about the natural order of things. I can't say that I'm thrilled about getting you all caught up in this, Jen. I've always respected you. But you've been mouthy ever since we got this ship back–"

"Since *I* got this ship back," said Jenny firmly.

"See? That's what I mean. This is my operation and you keep taking the credit. I just want some recognition for everything I do for you."

"Everything like having me arrested?" Jenny asked.

"Just cooperate, act sorry, and they'll let you go."

"Spoken like a man who is considered the default in every way," said Jenny.

Jim hit a switch on the wall and an alarm sounded. Gary

held onto the shipping crate nearest him as the gravity kicked on. Jenny scrambled for something to grab onto, but she wasn't near anything. She hit the floor from three meters up.

"You all right?" asked Gary, helping her to sit up.

"Choice," she said, with a glare at Jim.

The cargo hold vibrated as the *Lady Nugent*'s docking tunnel clamped onto the *Jaggery*. Gary's stomach clenched. Jim had implicated all of them in the destruction of the *Arthur Phillip*. Reason officers weren't kind to those who took out fellow soldiers.

Jim reached up and opened the airlock. The door hissed and swung open. Several Reason officers ran into the room with stun sticks and bolt guns drawn. Unlike Jim, these people knew the danger of firing off projectiles in a pressurized spacecraft.

"Down on the ground, now!" shouted one of the soldiers, shoving a stun stick into Jenny's ribs, even though she was already on the floor. Her face hit the stone. The soldier grabbed her arm and dragged her toward the airlock.

"There is no need for violence. We will go willingly," said Gary, raising his hands to eye level. The soldiers ignored him.

"Geneva Perata in custody," a soldier shouted to the officer in charge. Jenny pulled a wooden club out of the side pocket of her jumpsuit and thwacked the soldier's knuckles. He let go, dropping her onto the floor. She hit him in the knee and he doubled over.

"Jenny, stop. We're going with them," said Gary, wondering if she'd misunderstood the plan. Two soldiers flanked him, holding their stun sticks at the ready. They seemed unsure of whether to start hitting since he was cooperating.

"I don't have to make it easy," she replied, swinging at the next soldier who stepped toward her.

Colonel Wenck stepped into the cargo hold and marched over to Jenny. His burns had started to scab over around a hand-shaped pink patch. A man of his rank had access to healing spells and unicorn blood. The wound would be completely healed within a day. Wenck put his boot down on Jenny's club. The polished wood split in two with a snap. He kicked the pieces across the floor.

"Acknowledged, Perata in custody," said Wenck, crouching down near Jenny. He laced his fingers into her hair and pulled her head as far back as it would go.

"Just cooperate and you'll be all right," said Jim from the back wall, like a spell to counteract what he was seeing.

Wenck ignored him and stared icily at Jenny. "Well if it isn't the Hero of Copernica Citadel again. I'm impressed that you survived that little bullet wound. Must be that Bala magic you're always playing with. Speaking of which, your little manicorn friend is up and about as well. How extremely convenient for me."

"Suck my dick," said Jenny, through clenched teeth.

"Oh I don't think I'll be the one sucking dicks, Perata. You're headed to rehab. There are fixes for people like you who consort with Bala filth."

He stood up and shouted to his soldiers. "We have Perata and Cobalt. Bonus points for catching Mr Tang, boys."

He knew all of their names, even the old ones that didn't belong to them any more. It meant that they were not going to stop tearing apart the ship until they found everyone. There was no place on the *Jaggery* in which Ricky could hide.

The soldiers flanking Gary took their cues from Wenck's actions with Jenny. They shoved stun sticks into his torso. They couldn't injure him, but it tensed all of his muscles until he couldn't control them. He lurched forward and held onto the cargo boxes. They stunned him again and he hit the floor.

"No," said Jenny, lifted to her feet by a soldier. He tried to get her to stand and she sank back down.

"Ma'am, we can do this the easy way where you come with me willingly, or the hard way where I make your day a little worse. Which one will it be?" asked the soldier.

Jenny lifted both of her middle fingers. If he could have talked, Gary would have told her that was the least productive way to conduct herself right now. She smiled as if gleaning great joy from the experience of flipping off the officers. A small part of him wondered what that kind of insouciance felt like, because he certainly would not have survived it.

"All right, we're going the hard way." The soldier waved over two others. They took her feet and dragged her into the center of the room.

One of the soldiers extended an open palm to Jim. "Papers, sir."

Jim's hand shook as he held out the tablet.

"This isn't the way inspections used to be," he said.

"Old man, a lot of things aren't the way they used to be. It's called progress. Stand against the back wall and let us do our jobs," said the soldier. Jim shuffled against the wall like a chastened child.

"You don't need to harm us, we're coming voluntarily," said Gary.

"You, my horsey friend, are the product of a sicko human and a filthy Bala. I'll do anything I want to you," said the soldier.

Wenck looked up from his tablet. "Don't talk to it. Incapacitate, immobilize, and impound. We have everyone except Tang." He got on his radio. "Anyone find Tang?"

The radio crackled.

"Sir..." There was the sound of struggle from the other end. "Sir, we found him, but he's giving us some trouble."

"Mister, you get that outlaw down to the cargo hold within two minutes or I'll have you brought up on charges."

"Yes, sir. It's just–" There was a loud snap and a groan. A giggle, then a gasp.

"Fine. Fine, I'll come. Just point that somewhere else," came Ricky's voice through the radio.

The soldier came back on, out of breath and with a high note of pain in his voice.

"Tang in custody, sir."

"Good." Wenck switched off the radio and stood eye to eye with Gary, staring straight at him, but speaking to his troops.

"Men, let this day be a lesson to you. Bala filth must never mingle with humanity. We will find every last one of them and contain the threat. To the survival of man."

"Manifest destiny," replied the Reason troops in unison, raising their weapons. This call and response always sickened Gary. Today was no exception. Wenck approached Jim with his tablet outstretched.

"I just need you to sign here for the reward money, sir."

Jim made a mark with his finger and Wenck tapped out the funds transfer. "You're quite the patriotic citizen, Captain Bryant. A man of Reason can practically make a living rounding up Bala filth these days."

Wenck read further. A sickly smile spread across his face. "Oh look at that, you got a few thousand in exchange for Perata's wife a while back. Good for you. If we didn't round these things up for parts, they'd be off frolicking in a forest somewhere. We might as well get some use out of them."

A trio of soldiers burst into the cargo hold with Ricky between them. She had changed into heavy military boots and a red Reason flight suit, trying to curry favor with the locals. One of the men by her side was missing an ear. Blood drenched his uniform shoulder.

"Perata, you look terrible," said Ricky. "I told you this was a bad idea."

"Did you take that man's ear off?" asked Jenny, spitting

out a mouthful of blood from when she'd hit her chin on the floor.

"I might have," said Ricky with a naughty twinkle in her eye. Jenny reached between two barrels of water and grabbed the broken piece of her club. She threw it, spinning, at the other soldier on Ricky's right. It caught him in the eye and he doubled over with a grunt.

"Brilliant!" said Ricky. She and Jenny laughed together. Both of them took a stun stick to the side and their laughter stopped as they flattened against the floor. Gary was glad he wasn't going to the same place as Jenny and Ricky. Between the two of them, they were going to either get themselves killed or take out half of Jaisalmer.

The soldiers took a step toward him. His hands went to the back of his head. The Quag came back to him in little ways. Like how he instinctively kept his eyes on the floor and didn't make any sudden moves.

"No trouble," he said.

"Yeah, you'll find all the trouble you can handle right here," said Ricky, raising her hand to indicate herself and Jenny, lying on the stone.

"Hey," Jenny called out to him. Gary faced her without raising his head. "Meet you at the Summit." She smiled at him with bloody teeth.

CHAPTER TWENTY
Fort Jaisalmer

The Fort Jaisalmer harvesting center smelled just like the Quag. Solid and liquid waste from a variety of species mixed with sweat and mildew to form a foggy miasma hanging over the cells. The sounds were the same as well; the clanging of cell doors, an echo of voices against tile, hushed and furtive with occasional bursts of shouting. Gary sat back against the bars and tried not to make any noise. He'd been brought in during the night and few beings were awake yet. He preferred to keep it that way for as long as possible.

The Reason required English to be spoken in public and private, but Gary heard a few other Bala languages around him as well. Two wolf women spoke in strained whispers, yipping occasionally to underscore a point. An elf dropped the r-sounds out of his words like a human as he told a murmured story to the others in his cell. Even fifty years ago he would have been derisively ostracized from elf circles for sounding so common. It seemed that the harvesting center was a great equalizer.

Gary's father had made sure that he knew all of the Bala languages so that he could converse with any being in the system. It was his duty as a future leader, he had been told many times. His mother, on the other hand, had taught him only two human languages: English and Kannada. She showed him how to assemble sticks and balls to make English letters and how to glide his pen through the undulating contortions of the Kannada alphabet. He had hated writing practice, complaining that no one wrote anything down any more. He had been right. Writing by hand was an art form that would nearly be extinct within a generation.

"Mama, I don't want to be a king," he'd said once, while he wrote. She'd laughed at him, but not unkindly.

"Why not, beta?" She pointed to a word he had misspelled. Her gold bracelets jangled. She was the most extravagantly dressed leader in the Reason resistance. She had once been a curator of Earth's culture and she took her job seriously, always dressing in traditional clothing, even when it didn't quite work under an EVA suit.

"Because when you're a king you have to solve everyone's problems," he complained.

"No, beta. You just have to listen." She had kissed the top of his head, staying clear of the sharp point on his horn. She'd given him a pained look that he hadn't interpreted correctly until much later. He'd thought she was annoyed by his question. It was only later that he realized she was thinking about how he would survive in the world with two feet of the most precious substance in the universe growing out of the top of his head. She'd been right to worry.

In the harvesting center, a pig-like creature grunted in a nearby cell. Something clucked and the pig squealed in pain. Hooves scraped across the floor. There were waking sounds from other holding pens. Gary knew from the Quag that this time of morning was dangerous, when some inmates slept and others woke first.

"Hey, new guy," said a voice from the bench in their enclosure.

In the rising light, a woman drew herself up to a sitting position. Her torso was covered in soft gray fur, but from her hips down she appeared to be a human woman. He didn't like to speculate, but she was likely part neofelis cat. Gary sat on the edge of the cell, away from the other beings. He was almost always the strongest in a fight, but raw strength wasn't always the most effective measure of success.

"Hello," he answered, trying not to wake anyone.

"What are you in for?" she asked.

"I haven't done anything illegal," replied Gary. She laughed.

"That's not what I mean. We're a natural resource, like a stream or a seam of coal. What did they bring you in to take from you? Because you look like a trash faun and those aren't even worth the effort of rounding up."

"I guess they made a mistake, then," said Gary. "Because I'm worth nothing."

The furry woman laughed mirthlessly. "True. They make mistakes all the time. I once saw them mistake a minotaur for a monoceros and try to power an FTL ship on its horn. Do you know where a minotaur horn sends you?"

"Where?"

"I don't know, but you can't find your way back out." She chuckled to herself. It was an old joke, but he didn't mind hearing it. Most didn't know the truth, that putting a minotaur horn in an FTL drive would bring your ship to a remote mountainous planet, atop which an oracle sat. He would let you ask as many questions as you liked, as long as you brought along a bit of candy.

The holding cell was barely three meters on each side with benches along one wall. A waste bucket in the corner attracted flies and other wriggling things. There were six Bala in this single cell and dozens of other cells adjacent to theirs. Gary stood up and tried to figure out where he was in the warehouse. Cells stretched in every direction. Along the far wall, a pair of guards flanked the exit.

"You're serious for a faun. What's your name?" asked the woman.

"Gary."

"I'm Mizzet."

"I'm looking for someone," said Gary.

"You and everyone else." She swept her arm wide. "There's one of everything in here."

Beings of all configurations were starting to sit up and stretch. Gary searched for the wide canopy of a dryad's branches. He listened for the rustle of leaves that would mean trees were here.

"Who are you looking for?"

"A dryad with yellow flowers. Goes by the name of Kaila."

"She'd be over in the flora section. This is fauns, half-breeds, and other bipeds."

Gary stepped up onto the bench to see the corner of the warehouse nearest the wall. There were the windows Jenny had described, too high to reach, even from a bench. The guards had at least put the flowering plants near the windows, which meant they were trying to keep them alive instead of starving them to death in the dark.

"Get down," hissed Mizzet. "No one needs a guard over here."

There was a group of trees in a corner standing on the sandy gray clay that passed for dirt in this part of Jaisalmer. They were clumped together in the center of the cell, their branches commingling for warmth and comfort. He sat down.

"Who is she to you?" asked the cat woman.

"A friend," he replied.

A guard from the door walked down the row and paused at their cage. Gary ducked his head. The woman tucked her legs up and made herself as small as possible.

"What were you doing up there?" asked the guard.

"A mistake, CO. Won't make it again," said Gary without looking up. The guard tapped the bars with his baton and kept walking.

"See that you don't," he said.

"You've been in before," said Mizzet.

"Did some time in the Quag," said Gary.

She let out an awed hum.

"Impressive. Who'd you kill to get stuck there?"

Gary didn't answer.

"That's fine. You don't have to say." She chuckled. "You're half human. I can see it in your face. I bet you tore your mother in half when you were born," she goaded.

"You don't have to be like them. Just because they have you caged, doesn't make you an animal," said Gary.

The guard came back with a younger colleague and stopped at their cell again.

"See, this faun came in on a transport last night. Picked up at Borstal. Some guy rounded him up in openspace. He and a few people were responsible for a whole lotta deaths on one of our ships. I want you to get some practice in with him today."

The older guard unlocked the door and stepped into the cell. He raised his stun stick and touched it to Gary's neck for several seconds. Gary hit the floor, his arms numb. Mizzet hissed quietly.

"They're getting riled up," said the younger guard, with fear in her voice. "Should we gas them?"

"Calm down, Harper. They're acting on instinct. Show them you're the alpha."

The older guard raised his stick and brought it down on Gary's side several times, whacking his ribs and shoulder. He lay as quietly as he could.

"See? Totally docile. You do the cat."

The younger guard approached Mizzet with her stick

poised to strike. She faltered when the cat growled low and puffed out her fur.

"Show it who's in charge, Harper," said the older guard, breathing hard between blows on Gary's back. Harper hit Mizzet sideways across the face. She yelped and curled into a ball. Harper paused and the older guard urged her on.

"Good. But you have to solidify your status. Make it bleed on the floor."

Harper lifted her arm again and came down on Mizzet's ear. She did it a second time. The woman whined and covered her bloody ear with a paw.

"I did it," said Harper, looking sick. The older guard stopped mid-strike and examined her work.

"Not bad." She reached up and wiped a spatter of Mizzet's blood off Harper's cheek. "You always get a little bloody. Wash your coveralls in cold water and dish soap to get the stains out. Keep your uniform clean. Not like the rest of these grunts. You want to move up in the Reason, you have to look the part."

Harsh buzzing lights hanging above the warehouse came on with a loud thunk. Creatures groaned and blinked in the sudden brightness. A set of heavy boots marched down the space between cells. They stopped at Gary's door. He could see them even with his face to the floor; they were polished and pristine.

"There were express orders from Colonel Wenck not to begin any intake procedures on last night's drop off before I–"

She stopped and bent down to Gary on the floor. She smoothed his hair away from his face.

"What the bloody hell," she said, so quietly that only Gary heard. She stood up, the command back in her voice.

"Get him up and into the dissection room. No one touches him until I get there." She marched out of the warehouse with footfalls that woke everyone who wasn't already up. The guards pulled Gary to standing. They prodded him out of the cell, even though he went willingly.

He bit his lip to keep from making noise as his ribs crunched and tugged, his bones knitting themselves back together in time for the next beating. He had never decided if a healing ability in prison was Unamip's blessing or a curse.

"That turkey they fed us last night was garbage. Some kind of lab-cultured crap they keep trying to pass off as meat," said the older guard.

"I heard it was phoenix meat," said Harper.

"Explains the heartburn." The older guard rubbed his chest and belched.

They led Gary past a dozen rows of cells, all filled with Bala and part-Bala in various states of deconstruction. A legless spider, head and thorax only, sat in one of the cells alone. It chittered at him as he passed; a plea for the mercy of death. There were human cells as well, filled with forlorn people who had been caught with their Bala loved ones. He didn't see any children. He wasn't sure whether that was something to celebrate or mourn.

The guards paused at one of the cells near the door. Two centaurs were fighting unrelentingly, their human halves grappling while their hooves stomped and skidded. One of them held the front half of a pig under his arm. The guards opened the cell door and attempted to separate the two without getting trampled.

Gary was as close to the dryads as he was ever going to get.

"Kaila," he called into the tiny forest a couple of cells away.

A set of branches unfurled from the tangle of foliage and a bark-covered face looked out at him. Her green eyes narrowed, then widened in surprise. She stepped out of the circle on bark-covered human legs. Jenny had always wistfully said they "went on for days," and the metaphor seemed apt. Kaila clasped her hands and the long, leafy branches sprouting from her head rustled down her back with excitement.

"Gary Cobalt?" She extended her arms through the bars, but she could not reach him. "Is my Jenny still alive?"

"Yes. She's trying to get to you."

"Tell her not to come here." Kaila's green eyes flashed in terror. Her voice carried and the guards looked up from their centaur brawl.

"She's already on her way. Be ready," said Gary. A bolt of pain coursed through his side as a guard stunned him again. He hit the floor so hard the metal grating cut into his knees.

"Get away from the bars," said Harper. The older guard joined her.

"See? You're getting it," he said.

They pulled Gary up and brought him to a room that would have given the mightiest warrior pause. Examination tables of various sizes were lined up in rows. Each one had straps to tie down a creature, no matter how large or small. A bright movable light hung over each one. Around the perimeter of the room, tidy shelves and racks held tools both edged and blunt. It looked like an armory, or a museum exhibit dedicated to pain. Sharp-toothed saws for carving off limbs hung next to delicate surgical instruments. This was where the Bala were portioned off for parts.

The two tables nearest the door were occupied. On the first, a juvenile redworm lay sedated across two tables, its immense body hooked to a series of tubes that drained its acidic blood. The orange-red liquid bubbled in the collection container. The human technicians were covered from head to toe in protective gear. One of them looked up as he passed. Half her face had been seared by acid, but no one had offered to heal it. She glared at him with her remaining eye.

The next table held a dwarf, strapped down tightly. His

tiny body took up barely a quarter of the massive table. Two technicians stood over his throat, flayed open, examining the vocal cords.

"See here? If we excise these two vocal folds, they can be mounted in the engine room directly."

"How do we keep the tissue from decaying?"

"Biotech is working on a solution of fairy plasma that slows decay."

As they passed the table, Gary noticed the dwarf's eyes were open. He blinked rapidly, and the heart monitor beeped an alarm.

"Push another round of succinylcholine." A tech tapped the controls and the dwarf's eyes stopped fluttering and stared blankly at Gary.

The guards walked Gary to the far end of the room, where the tables were sized for humanoid beings. They tilted one vertical, fixed restraints around his legs and arms, and left him there.

The officer with shiny boots strode in a few minutes later, barking orders without breaking stride.

"Get out," she said. The redworm technicians put down their instruments, but the other two stayed near the sedated dwarf.

"We're in the middle of something," said one of the surgeons.

The officer pulled out her service weapon and shot the dwarf in the head. The heart monitor went flat.

"You're done. Go," she said, heading for the back of the room. The surgeons groaned and tossed their instruments onto a tray.

"Singh, you are the fucking worst," said one, taking off his lab coat.

Gary was surprised to see that he recognized this officer and her tightly wound headscarf. This was the woman the

Sixian parrot had shown him in the Bitter Blossom; the one who he had impaled with his horn. Her face was set hard like other Reasoners, not as kind as it had been in his vision.

She stopped in front of Gary.

"This won't work on you, will it?" she asked, holstering her weapon.

"No."

She stepped up to him.

"Who are you?"

"Gary Cobalt of the—"

"Not that. Why are you in my head?" she asked, searching his face for answers.

"You've had a vision of the two of us."

"Every night, you are in my nightmares," she said, poking her finger into his chest. "Who sent you to haunt my dreams?"

Indeed, she had dark patches under her tired eyes. She walked over to the wall and pulled down a bone saw.

"I'm supposed to supervise the collection of your useful body parts. They say it isn't possible to kill a unicorn. But they don't say anything about a half-unicorn."

"The colonel wouldn't allow you to kill me," said Gary. "I'm far too valuable alive."

He had seen his own kin chained for years in the holds of Reason ships, locked into collection systems that continually scraped a thin layer of horn as it grew. These unicorns were shadows of their former selves. Most of them were atrophied and broken, unable to form coherent thoughts. They made unintelligible sounds and ran themselves in circles when set free. If these were the only unicorns that Reasoners encountered, he could see why humans would consider them animals.

"Who are you?" she asked again, brandishing the saw close to his face.

"We are connected somehow. It's not my doing," he replied.

She furrowed her brow at his lack of fear and dropped the saw onto a tray with a clatter.

"You are exhausting," she said, rubbing her eyes.

"I've heard that before," said Gary. She nearly laughed, then her mask came down again. There was a flicker of hope, if he could just keep her talking. "I don't even know you. Tell me who you are and perhaps we can figure this out," he said.

"I'm Subedar Lakshmi Singh, regimental administrative officer for Colonel Wenck. Why are you in my head?" She asked the question more plaintively than the first time, and Gary realized she genuinely wanted to know why he was tormenting her.

"I assure you, I am not. I have seen the same vision you describe. Yesterday morning, when I stared into the Sixian parrot. You were in my vision of death."

"Yesterday?" she asked. "But I've been dreaming of you for months. Is this some kind of Bala magic?"

"Is it possible you have some... Bala ancestry?" he asked as delicately as he could.

She flinched and shook her head.

"I'm not one of you."

Across the room, the redworm on the table twitched. Singh watched it while she peppered Gary with questions. "Who is Penny? In the dream, we needed to kill her."

"I don't know anyone named Penny."

"And I said that we needed to kill all humans. Why?"

"I don't agree with that sentiment at all," he said.

"Me neither. Obviously."

"I have a question for you, Subedar Singh," he said, using her formal title. "You have seen this dream every night for months. Would you say that you've had this vision at least one hundred times?"

"Yes."

"I ask you. In your vision, did we appear to be adversaries?"

She folded her arms across her uniform jacket and looked at him skeptically. She was decorated with pins for several battles. There was a blue enameled wave for the Battle of Botono Bay, where the Reason had routed the last of the free unicorns from their hiding place under the sea. Another was a snowflake that indicated the Ketewan Uprising, in which the Reason had quelled a rebellion of humans trying to stop the war. And at the top was the pin that he had seen on Jenny's uniform, back when she still wore it – the stylized stone turret that symbolized Copernica Citadel.

"You were at Copernica."

"That's correct." She looked uncomfortable.

"Then you must know Jenny Perata."

"I've heard the name. She wasn't on my ship, but she saved a lot of people on the *Pandey*."

"You're holding her wife in there." He flicked his head toward the warehouse.

"We have a lot of people's wives in there."

"Not a lot of people are the hero of Copernica Citadel."

"Are you asking me to liberate a resource just because it's married to a former Reason officer?" she asked.

"No, I'm asking you to liberate both of us."

Subedar Singh laughed out loud.

"You are bold, my nocturnal visitor."

The redworm by the door moved again and Singh took a moment to walk over and check its vitals. On the way back, she picked up the scalpel that the techs had used on the dwarf. She stopped in front of Gary and picked up a collection vial from the tray of equipment. She dragged the dirty scalpel down his forearm and caught the run of silvery blood that ran out.

"Pretty," she said, holding the vial up to the light. "I just want to try something."

She brought the vial over to the dead dwarf and poured his blood into the wound in his head.

"I wouldn't–"

"Shhhh," she said. The dwarf convulsed on the table, then pulled against his restraints. He babbled in a language that was neither human nor Bala, whispering through his open throat. Singh watched with an unsettled look on her face. She stomped back to Gary.

"Why didn't it heal him?" she demanded.

"It did. My blood can heal the tissues, but not replace the knowledge or memories they contained. You would do well to shoot him again and put him out of his misery." It was a thing that Gary had never imagined himself saying, but he had learned that sometimes the cruelest path was also the kindest.

Singh unholstered her weapon. It was a typical Reason projectile firearm, which meant that this woman worked only on-planet. She drew it, but hesitated.

"You can't bring him back?"

"Not like he was."

She fired a single shot and the dwarf went still again. Singh returned, looking thoughtful.

"What a waste," she said.

"Perhaps if you didn't dissect us, it would be less wasteful."

"I'm not here to debate Reason ethics," she retorted.

"What *are* you here for?" he asked. "Because I am positive that Colonel Wenck does not want me taken apart. I'm sure there's an FTL ship somewhere in orbit with a cage waiting for me."

She pursed her lips.

"When I saw who you were, I thought I could get some answers."

"Those dreams will continue for as long as I live," he said.

"I will continue killing you every night in your sleep unless we determine the cause."

She furrowed her brow.

"That's not the dream I'm having. In my dream, I'm killing you."

"With my horn?"

"Yes. In my dream you're begging me to kill you and I don't want to. You're... a friend. And I feel so terrible, but I have to do it, so I do, but after I'm just gutted and then I wake up an absolute wreck. Like I've murdered my..." She trailed off with a shrug.

Gary was more confused than ever about the vision, but at least this conversation was keeping her from sawing pieces off him. This was the most thoughtful discussion he'd had with a Reason officer in nigh on thirty years.

"We're seeing two versions of the same event," he said. "Which may mean that how it occurs is still uncertain."

"You sound like a Sister," she said.

Gary leaned forward in his restraints.

"A Sister would know what the vision means," he said.

"I can't get an audience. I tried," said Singh. "Pulled every string in the Reason, but they won't talk to me. Especially after that business with the rebels."

Gary let out a single laugh. He felt like a chess piece on the board, slotted into place exactly where he needed to be in order to set up a particular scenario. He felt light and calm. As Jenny would have said, it was all going to be fine.

"Actually, I have a meeting with the Sisters this morning," he said. "If you get me and Kaila out of here, I'll bring you along."

Singh considered in silence. He hoped that she realized how rare an opportunity this was. Meetings with the Sisters were not granted frequently, and certainly not to regimental administrative officers who sat at a desk doing paperwork all day. With him at her side, the Sisters would be willing to listen to her questions. And there was no better group suited to explaining a mysterious vision than the Sisters.

"Maybe," she said, surveying his human upper half. "But taking two of you out is impossible. I cannot drag a dryad out of holding and through the streets without being noticed."

"Not during the Summit. The streets will be at full capacity. No one will look twice at a Reason officer with their faun and dryad heading to the festivities."

"Do you think people just take their trees for a walk?" she asked. "Like you bring it to the store? Sheesh."

"I think you can tell anyone who asks that you're bringing Kaila to the colonel's apartment. That would not be unusual."

"Ridiculous. I can take you, but not her."

Gary noticed the clock on the wall behind her. Between the trip from Borstal to Jaisalmer, and the time he'd slept in harvesting, there were less than two hours before the cargo boxes opened. Even if Singh agreed to take Kaila, he still had to find Jenny and Ricky and get as close to the *Jaggery* as possible before the timer hit zero. He strained toward Singh.

"Please. Where is your humanity?"

"This is humanity," she said, holstering her weapon and repeating back the ideas from a Reason schoolbook. "This is how we've thrived for so long despite our planet dying, and sailing off into openspace, and encountering hostile aliens. We used our tenacity and resourcefulness to survive."

There was one last thing that Gary could try. He recalled the words that Singh had spoken to him in the vision. He hoped that they would stir something in her, even if it was simple fear.

"You are the bravest person I have ever met," he said. "The Pymmie are humbled before your sacrifice. Succeed in this or all is lost."

Singh's fingers clutched at the front of her jacket. Her cheeks flushed.

"I don't know what that means," she stammered.

"Don't you want to find out?" he asked.

He could see that she desperately needed to know, but she was afraid to throw away her future in the Reason by walking out with two inmates. She was hedging so she didn't end up ruining her career over what might turn out to be a simple dream. He had to convince her she was part of something bigger than herself. That would be worth the risk.

"It's possible that you will be part of a great battle in the future. And you will be the one to kill the last unicorn." Gary wasn't sure that he actually was the last, and a full unicorn would have scoffed at the suggestion that Gary call himself a unicorn at all, but Singh seemed taken with the idea. She stepped closer and began to unfasten his restraints.

"Kaila too," he said, gently. She sighed.

"Fine. Which one?"

"Yellow flowers."

He towered over her. She looked up with a hand on her holster.

"I can't kill you with this, but I can probably erase half your fondest memories with one good shot. So no tricks."

He spread his hands wide to show he intended no such thing. She radioed the guards to bring Kaila to the dissecting room and handed him a long white lab coat.

"Put this on. They'll think you're a tech."

The door at the far end of the room opened again. Four guards dragged Kaila between them. They tossed her onto a table where she screamed and lashed out with her most flexible branches.

"Firewood delivery!" said a guard.

"These trees are useless, why did we even drag it in here?" asked the other guard.

"I think I'm allergic to its flowers," said the first guard, scratching her arms.

"No need to strap it in," said Singh. "I'm taking her to the colonel's apartment." One of the guards raised his eyebrow. Singh ushered him out the door with a wave. She moved to the side of the redworm, fiddling with its whirring medication dispenser.

"Gary!" cried Kaila, shuffling over to him at the speed you would expect from a tree spirit. She wrapped her branches around him and planted multiple kisses on his forehead. He hadn't expected her to be so effusive in her welcome. The last time they'd seen each other, he was her captive as well. Seems most of Jenny's group had forgotten their part in his torment.

"It's good to see that you're alive," he said. "I'm going to take you to Jenny."

"I can't believe you're here, rescuing me."

"Neither can I," said Gary, which was entirely true.

Subedar Singh returned, holding out handcuffs and snapping them around Kaila's wrists.

"You need to wear these to get out of here. Struggle against us. Make it look real." She turned to Gary. "Follow me out of the building with her between us. An alarm is going to go off in a minute. When it does, just keep walking."

"What kind of alarm?" asked Gary.

She held up a container of sedative labeled "succinylcholine" and rolled it between her fingers.

"That redworm isn't going to be paralyzed for much longer."

CHAPTER TWENTY-ONE
Barlee Base

Jenny had been hanging from the wall of the shuttle like a side of beef for hours. They'd strapped her in, legs dangling for the long FTL ride from Borstal Checkpoint to Jaisalmer. The straps bit into her hips, right where the damage from Copernica was the worst. Each jerk of the shuttle made her suck in a breath, though she tried not to tip her hand to these grunts.

Ricky had tucked herself between two Reason officers, with whom she was busy negotiating a deal.

"All I'm saying is, look up the files. None of them are classified. You'll see what I'm talking about and where the paper trail leads," she murmured to the soldier next to her.

At least they were in nullspace, which gave Jenny a pleasant head rush. She'd considered trying some kind of Bala mischief to get them out of here, but all her attempts to harness the null were fruitless. All the space that she'd previously used to absorb energy was filled with excruciating pain, not to mention a smattering of remorse about using the null to impersonate her dead best friend. There was no room left in her for magic. At least, if she was seeing right on the displays up front, they were on track to arrive on Jaisalmer on the morning of the Century Summit.

The shuttle dropped several meters, probably to avoid

another ship in the null, and Jenny's lower torso twisted. She gasped.

"Hey, you wankers. Get me down," she called.

The officers in the cabin looked up, but didn't rise from their seats. One young officer stared at her longer than the others. She was young enough to be Jenny's kid.

"Hey, Private. My straps are too tight. I'm going to suffocate. Come over and loosen them a little," Jenny called.

The woman grappled with her harness, as if trying to unbuckle. A larger soldier shoved her hand away from the latch.

"She's messing with you. Trying to get you to go over there."

"But what if she really can't breathe?" she asked.

"Then she dies. They're probably just going to let her rot in a cell when we land anyway." He patted her helmet patronizingly. "Don't stress over it. One less anchor pulling everyone else down. To the survival of man."

"Manifest destiny," mumbled the soldier halfheartedly.

Jenny struggled with her harness, but it was locked shut. This wasn't their first time transporting prisoners. The shuttle hit the turbulence of thick atmosphere. Her head ricocheted off the wall behind her.

"Damn you all," she called out. "Where's the unicorn?"

"All Bala are processed through the harvesting center at Fort J," said the private.

"And where are we headed?"

"The detention and rehabilitation center on the Great Barlee Sea." A comrade smacked her in the helmet to shut her up. She sat back, subdued.

Ricky lifted a finger to her lips for Jenny to be quiet. She was doubtless trying to negotiate their release, but Jenny wasn't willing to let her life balance on whether Ricky traded an exotic item or got someone to believe a wild story.

The shuttle dropped out of FTL. The faces of the soldiers around her went slack with wonder for a moment as they saw eternity stretch before them. Jenny saw eternity as well; it looked long and boring.

Jaisalmer filled the viewscreen, deep in shadow and dotted with artificial lights. Fort J was at the edge of the rising dawn, but their shuttle flew into the darkest black, toward the center of the planet's ocean. Even if an inmate escaped from the detention and rehabilitation center, there was nowhere to go but the water.

The shuttle tilted downward for re-entry and Jenny's legs dangled toward the cockpit, stretching her painfully. She tried not to give the officers the satisfaction of making a sound, even though it felt like a few fragments of the bullet on Beywey were still shredding her from the inside. The shuttle jerked again and a small groan escaped her lips. The private looked up. Jenny made the tremendous effort to extend the middle finger of her right hand. The concern in the private's eyes was replaced by disgust.

The shuttle leveled out and Jenny's torso moved back to where it should have been. She breathed hard. An officer tapped a panel on the wall and her harness popped open. She dropped to the floor, landing hard on her side.

"I thought you wanted out," grinned the officer. Jenny pulled herself up to sitting. They'd left her chair back on the *Jaggery*, just as Gary had warned. She wondered if they planned on dragging her throughout the detention center. Her jumpsuit was already torn. If they pulled her all over this facility, they'd tear her legs to shreds.

They landed with a jolt. The grunts got up and stretched, refastening their uniforms. The side door opened and a cool breeze filled the shuttle. It smelled of salt and fish. Jenny breathed it in – the air reminded her of home on the beach, before the sea reclaimed her town and forced everyone inland and then into openspace.

Two soldiers reached beneath her arms and pulled her down the landing ramp. She stared at the ocean stretching to the horizon in every direction. She knew this wasn't Earth, but it felt like home – blue water, white clouds. Only the reddish sun on the horizon indicated otherwise.

The Reason had built the detention center on pylons above the water line with a series of metal bridges connecting the buildings. They were fine for people who could walk, but too narrow for the two officers to drag her between them. They started down the path and both bumped into the railings.

Ricky whispered something to the officer she was working on and he nodded.

"Carry her," he called out.

The private pulled off her helmet and hung it from a clip on her flight suit.

"I'll get her," she said.

"Piggyback, sir," she said to Jenny, kneeling down and waiting. Jenny locked her arms around the private's neck. She couldn't wrap her legs around her, but the soldier reached behind her knees and hoisted her up. She turned her head so that one eye caught Jenny's.

"No screwing around back there or you'll take us both out. Got it?"

"No promises," said Jenny, watching the waves. She could float just fine, but swimming against a current or in rough conditions would exhaust her quickly. These waves crashed against the pylons, stirred by the brisk wind. This was no public pool.

Ricky marched side by side with her new favorite officer. She whispered in his ear and he didn't pull away. That woman could survive the apocalypse on her wits alone.

Jenny's face was close to the officer's close-cropped red hair. It smelled like rose-scented soap, not that standard issue crap they issued grunts on deployment.

"Someone off-world sending you soap, or did you bring it from home?" Jenny asked into the soldier's ear.

"No talking," replied the private.

"I only ask because I have a stash of lavender soap. Good stuff that my gran saved from before the shortages. If you get me to Fort J, I'll give you everything I have left. Three bars."

She'd been saving it for a special occasion – like when she and Kaila went to meet her family of dryads. She figured smelling like flowers when you met your wife's extended family of trees was simply good planning.

The redheaded officer stepped onto the bridge after her unit. The floor was made of metal grating and Jenny could see the ocean roiling beneath them. She spoke quietly into the private's ear.

"Listen, I was deployed back in the day. I know the garbage toiletries they give you in the outposts. Mess kit, a few tampons, and a bar of soap that dries out your skin and makes you itch everywhere. You probably get a lot of windburn in a place like this. Think of it. Moisturizing soap. All you have to do is 'misplace' me and my friend here before we get to intake."

"Sir, I'm not going to risk losing my job in exchange for a bar of soap," said the private, marching steadfastly toward the intake center. If you got bagged and tagged into a place like this, you didn't get back out. Once she and Ricky passed the threshold, escape would become damn near impossible. Jenny started calculating how hard she would have to throw her body to the side to pull them both off this bridge. She'd have to signal Ricky to jump and hope that Ricky followed her.

Ricky now had two soldiers listening to the story she was telling with rapturous attention. They walked alongside her, helmeted heads cocked in her direction. Every once in a while, she looked back at Jenny with an indecipherable expression, a kind of warning that Jenny couldn't quite figure out. As Ricky glanced back for the third time, Jenny flicked her head toward the sea. Ricky frowned and made the slightest shake of her head. Jenny insistently motioned toward the water. Ricky rolled her eyes and went back to her audience of two. Jenny didn't want to leave her behind, but she couldn't force Ricky to jump.

The private spoke without turning her head.

"You were at Copernica Citadel," she said quietly.

"I was."

"You saved all those people on the *Pandey*."

"I helped out," said Jenny with the false modesty expected of a war hero.

"And you turned the tide of battle in our favor."

"That's what they say."

"So why are you here? I thought they had retirement homes for wounded vets."

"You're walking toward it."

The private went quiet. At recruitment stations, they told new enlistees that the Reason would take care of them for life. You'd do your service and be rewarded with a warm spot by the fire where you could tell war stories to your buddies while you got old. They promised a regular stipend. Not an exorbitant amount, but enough for regular meals, good alcohol, and a little trip to Earth to see your planetbound family now and then. You could go back and visit like a hero so everyone could remember what you fought for.

But if you searched through all eleven thousand pages of the Reason's annual budget, you'd find no line item for veteran stipends. Especially not for the care of soldiers wounded in the line of duty. There was insurance money – a set amount for whatever body part you lost – but the payment was ludicrously small. It was just about enough to fly back to the beach and get a crap job hauling cargo in a rented shuttle while watching the kids in your hometown realize one by one that mankind had left them behind to die. You could always tell when another group of teenagers figured it out because you'd wake up to another building in town with its windows shattered. Or the local secondary school would catch fire again.

That left you with just a handful of choices. You could keep right on baking to death at home, maybe skimming off the Reason to stick it to the man. Or, you could make off with a unicorn and his stoneship and find a planet where you and your wife could get that spot by the lake. If she wasn't dead already.

"They told us we'd be taken care of," said the private, her voice tight.

"Well... I will be taken care of, in a way," said Jenny.

"I can't let you go for some soap, sir. Not worth the risk. I still have years on my time."

"I understand. What's your name?"

"Rassick. Angeles Rassick."

"Angeles. Like the city that fell into the sea."

"Never been there."

"Me neither."

They were silent for a moment, and Jenny waited patiently.

"How would you get off planet?" asked Rassick eventually.

"Not your problem. All I'm asking is that you let us go over the side of this bridge. When we fall into that water, you don't happen to see where me and my friend end up and we make our way to Fort J."

"I'll lose points."

"Gunning for sergeant?"

"Yeah."

"Well I hope you get it. Nothing wrong with trying to do your job well. Lord knows I spent a long time trying to climb that ladder. Just be aware, kid, that there is nothing at the top. You get there and you just fall off into nowhere."

"Yes, sir."

"How about this. Fire off a few shots when we hit the water. Tell them you hit me and I sank. That I couldn't swim. It's an easy story to believe; they already don't think much of me. You'll get credit for stopping an escape attempt. Two, if Ricky jumps with me."

They were less than a minute from intake. Ricky was still talking and didn't seem to be in any hurry to get off the bridge. Jenny's arms tensed around Private Rassick's neck. Come hell or high water, she was not letting them take her into that building.

"Are you with me, Rassick?" asked Jenny.

"I don't know, sir."

"You prefer to take your chances and trust the Reason to do right by you? After what you've seen and what you know?"

Jenny was betting on the fact that Rassick had probably experienced the same climb to the top that she had, with all of the wandering hands and broken promises. The Reason wanted all sorts of bodies to throw at problems, but it was clear which bodies were more valued than others.

"Let me put my helmet on first, sir," said Rassick, unclipping and easing it over her head. "I can't swim."

"Well that's a ridiculous move on an ocean outpost," said Jenny, forgetting she was supposed to be buttering up Rassick.

"I know, sir. Just haven't had time to learn." Her voice was muffled through her helmet.

"On my mark," said Jenny. She glanced down again at the water. The tops of the waves were starting to light up with the dawn. It would be hard to see them for another half hour or so. She yelled to Ricky in front. "Hey, Ricky. Jump."

Ricky turned and shook her head angrily. She wasn't moving. Her choice. Jenny gripped the armor plating on Rassick's suit and jerked them both to the side as hard as she could. Her first attempt didn't send them over, but Rassick put a little lean into it and they tumbled over the metal railing.

For a split second, freefall felt like zero G and Jenny was at home. She pushed away from Rassick and aimed at the water so her legs would hit first.

Jenny made impact. Her knees hit her chin and knocked her teeth together. She felt some of them crack. She resisted the urge to gasp or scream as she plunged under the surface, waiting until she bobbed back up before taking a breath. Blood and saltwater ran down her throat.

Ricky entered the water with a huge splash on her left. She'd hit spread-eagled. That was going to sting. Jenny heard her thrashing and gargling sea water. In her haste to get down here, she'd neglected to determine if Ricky could swim.

Rassick bobbed up at Jenny's side, her suit spraying water from its thrusters. Those things worked in water or in vacuum.

"I'm fine, but the detainees are resisting," said Rassick into her comm. "I may need to subdue them."

She pulled out her service weapon and fired. Close enough that Jenny felt the bullets zing through water next to her, but none of them made contact. Rassick motioned for Jenny to drop below the surface. It was still dark enough that the soldiers above would lose her in the whitecaps.

The cold water helped numb the throbbing in Jenny's jaw. More bullets sped past her, this time aimed in Ricky's direction. She hoped Ricky had the sense not to flail around so Rassick could miss her intentionally. She let her face come up for long enough to take a breath.

"They're both dead. I'm gonna leave their bodies," said

Rassick. "My thrusters can't haul that much weight. Mark them as lost at sea." She shut off her comm.

"Get up that pylon to the shuttle and I'll meet you there. I can get you off the planet," said Rassick.

Jenny tried to answer that they didn't want to get off the planet, just over to Fort J, but when she opened her mouth, her jawbone crunched and a wave of nausea hit her. She breathed through her nose. It was not fun to vomit with a broken jaw.

Rassick activated her suit thrusters and lifted out of the water. A few of the soldiers looked down to watch Jenny and Ricky bobbing limply in the waves, but most of them had continued down the bridge. No intake forms meant some off-the-books R&R time before the next mission. Her and Ricky's lives were not even worth the paperwork.

Jenny lay back on the water and watched Rassick ascend. She tested her limbs. Both arms worked. Legs were the same as usual, except maybe with a bit more of that tingling feeling that she remembered from when her foot had been asleep for a while. It had increased steadily since Beywey and now the occasional electric jolts were strong enough to take her breath away. She'd gone from no pain and no mobility, to lots of pain and no mobility. It was decidedly not an improvement. She'd have to thank Gary if she ever got to Fort J.

Waves crashed over her periodically, and she could only breathe through her nose, but she was alive and not trapped in detention, which was a start. Ricky swam over.

"Wǒ cào, Jenny. I think I'm dead."

Jenny pointed to her bloody mouth.

"Brilliant. Your jaw is broken and my everything is broken. This was another amazing Jenny Perata idea." Ricky flicked her wet hair out of her eyes. "You're ridiculous, throwing yourself off a bridge," she said. "I had them convinced we were Reason agents undercover with the Bala. You ruined it all by jumping. You realize that during my time at the Blossom, I had infiltrated almost every existing Bala cabal and Reason gang. I have protected informant status with three separate intelligence agencies. I have so much valuable information, I could not only have gotten us out of there, we would have had a cushy military escort to Fort J."

"Mmm," said Jenny.

"But, you know, if you prefer the Jenny Perata method of crisis management, we can all just instigate massive bar brawls and toss ourselves off bridges until death finally catches up."

Ricky was on a roll and Jenny couldn't open her mouth to stop her.

"You know why I banned you from my bar, Jenny? Not because you tried to rig my games in your favor, because that I can understand. I banned you because you're a hurricane, creating a whirlwind of destruction everywhere you go. I am a surgeon using a scalpel of chaos and you are a Tasmanian devil, annihilating all of my best prospects."

Jenny pointed to the landing platform.

"I know, I'm going. All this because I decided to be nice and let a blemmye into the bar."

Jenny saw a barely perceptible brightening in the sky. Jim had probably landed at Fort J and dropped off the cargo by now. Knowing him, he'd taken off for openspace without stopping to count his cash.

She spit out a mixture of blood and saliva and swam for the pylon, pulling herself through the water with a crude backstroke. She'd been a good swimmer as a child, but there hadn't been many opportunities to practice after Copernica. She remembered the basics. Float. Use the resistance of the water. Don't breathe it in.

Ricky followed at a slower pace. If she didn't know any better, Jenny would say Ricky was keeping an eye on her. It warmed her hypothermic heart. Ricky swam up and grabbed the ladder bolted to the pylon. They both hung on for a while, catching their breath.

No one had bothered to light the exterior of the buildings on this outpost, where people stayed locked inside most of the time due to the water and the wind. A few of the windows were lit with harsh white LED lights. Soldiers were eating their morning meal gathered in groups behind the glass; troops waiting to be dispatched to their next arrest.

At one of the windows, a lone person looked out at the water. In the light behind them, Jenny saw a shock of red hair. She raised a hand in thanks and Rassick turned away from the glass.

"I can't carry you up thirty feet," said Ricky. "If you wait here, I can–"

Jenny grabbed a ladder rung and hoisted herself out of the water. After years of hauling herself around ships that weren't made for wheelchairs she had developed biceps like a prizefighter.

"Oh, you've got it," said Ricky, following behind. "I always underestimate Jenny fucking Perata."

Jenny pulled herself out of the water. Her legs were bruised, but she couldn't see any bones sticking out. The zinging nerve pain had let up for the moment, but probably only because she was so cold. She'd be quite the sight at Fort J. A space hobo crawling around in a shredded jumpsuit.

Jenny pulled herself up until it became a rhythm. Left hand, pull. Right hand, pull. She shut everything else out. Even Ricky's occasional comments. There were thirty rungs to the top. Her arms shook and her palms burned. If she stopped for too long, she feared that her resolve would evaporate. The skin on her hands slipped and blistered, tearing raw ovals in her palms. She kept going, leaving smears of wetness on each rung. If Ricky noticed, she didn't say so.

Ten rungs from the top, her right hand slipped. She caught herself with her left and yanked her shoulder painfully. Her legs dangled in Ricky's face.

"Don't fall on me," yelled Ricky. Jenny knew that if they hit the water again she might not have the strength to get back out. "If you fall, I'll have to go down after you. You don't even want to know what you'll owe me if I save your life again."

Jenny dragged herself through the trap door at the top and lay on the landing platform. Ricky flopped down next to her. "I hate you so much. Are you all right?"

Jenny lifted one hand and let it fall back down.

"Dear God, I made some promises down there that I don't intend to keep," said Ricky. "Please don't hold it against me."

A pair of boots clomped across the flight deck and stopped in front of them.

"Never mind. Deal back on," said Ricky, raising herself on one arm.

Jenny looked up to see Rassick standing over them in the pink light of dawn. She pulled Jenny up and ducked under her arm to pull her toward the shuttle.

"I'll just walk myself, thanks," called Ricky.

Rassick set Jenny down in the co-pilot's seat and closed the shuttle door behind Ricky.

"How was the climb, sir?" she asked.

Jenny pointed to her mangled jaw.

"Oh man. You'll be all right, Cap," said Rassick, buckling her in. Ricky took the seat behind them.

Rassick settled herself into the pilot's chair and flicked on the comm.

"Rassick to Barlee Base."

"Barlee Base. Go ahead, Rassick."

"I'm making a coffee run to Chhatrapati. Any takers?"

There was a pause. Jenny thought they were caught. The

comm crackled back to life.

"Six with cream and sugar. Two black. And that asshole Marquez wants a milkshake."

Rassick laughed with the mic on so they could hear just how relaxed she was.

"I'll stick my dick in your milkshake, Marquez. Back in an hour."

"Roger, Rassick. Dick in the milkshake. Good flight."

She flicked off the comm and started going down the takeoff checklist. Jenny missed the camaraderie of razzing your people and knowing that someone always had your back. She noticed Ricky checking out the side of her face with a concerned concentration. Their eyes met and Ricky looked away sheepishly.

"Just making sure you're alive enough to pay me back for all this lifesaving, Perata," she said. The smile that formed on Jenny's face hurt like the devil.

Rassick cut in. "Just so you know, I can't bring you to Fort J. That's a twelve-hour round trip over land and I don't have clearance to set down there during the Summit. But I can get you to Chhatrapati Shivaji. You can pay off a ship owner to smuggle you into Fort J with the dignitaries."

It was a quintessentially Reason feat to arrange it so that the easiest way to get five thousand kilometers on this planet was to go thirty-five thousand kilometers up and back.

"But we're spies," said Ricky.

Rassick gave her a withering look and even Ricky knew when to fold her hand.

Jenny closed her eyes and felt the gravity burst of takeoff. Rassick kept talking.

"I can't imagine being at the Siege of Copernica Citadel. You guys must have gotten pummeled by those necromancers. They say some of them made it all the way onto your ships. Holy hell, I would've shit myself coming face to face with a necromancer. Could they really stop your heart with a single word?"

The legends of Copernica were exaggerated, but Jenny couldn't say that now. Even if her jaw wasn't broken, she would have just nodded along anyway. People needed to believe the stories to justify their choices. If she had known the necromancer who had twisted her ship in half was some tiny guy who had a kid at home, she might have thought twice about throwing a shell full of screws at his face. Those were the lies you told yourself to get through war.

Rassick put the shuttle on auto and reached under her seat. She tossed a first aid kit on Jenny's lap.

"Not a lot in there, but there's some analgesic. We don't see a lot of action out here," she said apologetically.

Jenny opened the box and pulled out two injectors. She handed one to Ricky. They pressed the spray to their necks and pulled the trigger.

"Gah, that stings," complained Ricky.

Warm bliss spread from Jenny's neck to the rest of her jaw. This was the good stuff, meant for soldiers in the field who needed to numb up, but still keep fighting. It wouldn't make her drowsy, but it would take away the pain.

Rassick was still watching Jenny.

"You are so fucking tough, Cap. Back at Copernica... and now. I don't know how to get like that. To stop caring."

Jenny wanted to explain that the trick wasn't to stop caring, it was to care so much that nothing else mattered. She'd thought of Kaila in the harvesting center every night, when the lights went out and her dearest love was alone in a cell with hostile creatures. She would never forgive Jim for what he'd done. Just as he'd never forgiven her for the part she'd played in Cheryl Ann's death. She guessed they were even now.

Getting off Jaisalmer took no more than seven minutes

and the ride to Chhatrapati was even faster. As they slid around the corner of the station, Jenny spotted an asteroid-shaped ship with a huge pink flower on the side. She waved to Ricky and pointed to it.

"Look who's here," said Ricky. "That tricky bastard."

CHAPTER TWENTY-TWO
Chhatrapati Shivaji Station

Rassick matched the shuttle's velocity to the spin of Chhatrapati Shivaji Station and eased them toward an open docking bay. Jenny noticed she was flying on her own without computer assistance. The kid was trying to impress her. Usually, she'd ignore it, but today she gave Rassick a little approving nod. The grin that spread across the private's face could have lit up a dark moon.

Jenny hadn't been here in ages. The station had grown to a massive size. It had been constructed out of the wreckage of the generation ship *Cristobal*, one of the first human ships to reach this part of space. The Reason had added rings around the original habitation cylinder for shops, restaurants, and refueling stations. You could barely see the original ship at the heart of it underneath all the new bits.

Jim's parking job was terrible, as usual. He'd gotten so close to one support strut that several maintenance people in EVA suits were out scratching their heads about how he was going to fly back out without destroying it.

"Chhatrapati Shivaji, this is Barlee Base Shuttle Four, docking at gate nine-three-one."

"Roger, Barlee Base Shuttle Four. Gate nine-three-one."

"Hey Raz. Back so soon?" asked a different voice.

"Coffee run. You know we only get the shit stuff out there

in the water."

The shuttle jolted as the dock latched home and the shuttle spun in time to the station. Rotation meant gravity. Jenny wouldn't be able to float herself around and her chair was still on the *Jaggery*. Rassick leaned over and extended a hand.

"I'm going to have to carry you again. Second verse, same as the first."

Jenny reached out and caught Rassick around the neck and pulled up onto her back. They stepped out into the bright lights of Chhatrapati Shivaji. It had been a long time since Jenny had been on a properly functioning station. Nothing dripped rusty water and it didn't smell like feces in the least. It was downright majestic.

They stepped into the gate area where travelers of all kinds departed their shuttles. Most were being wheeled off their transport ships in glowing stasis chambers, still asleep from years-long journeys from faraway planets. A dock worker pushed a family of four off a transport ship in a stack. These weren't the wealthy, who could afford FTL drives and unicorns to power them, but middle class people who had forked over a lifetime of savings to move from one planet to another for a chance at a better life closer to the center of the Reason.

Rassick bounced when she walked, which rattled Jenny's broken teeth. The smell of coffee dominated the atrium – the real thing, not the thick goopy stuff the dwarves tried to pass off.

"Do we have time for a stop?" asked Ricky, peering into the shops on the concourse. She stopped in front of a bookseller's window, bending down to read the titles in the display.

"Drop-off first," said Rassick, walking past. Ricky sighed and tore herself away from the books. Rassick headed down the hallway marked Jaisalmer Shuttle. Jenny tugged her in the opposite direction and pointed toward the hallway where the *Jaggery* was docked. She could tell exactly where it was because people lined up at the windows to get a look at the stoneship. There weren't many left roaming around these days.

"You want back on that ship? After your captain turned you in?" asked Rassick, stopping in her tracks.

"I'm not going that way," said Ricky. "I'll take my chances on the surface." Jenny mimed taking a drink and Ricky's face fell. Everything she owned was on the *Jaggery*. She needed her suitcases full of tricks and bottles.

"Can I borrow your service weapon, Rassick?" asked Ricky.

"No, you may not," said the private, heading down the hall toward the crowd. "But I'll be your wingman for a few minutes."

People stared at the Reason soldier carrying a torn-up woman in a flight suit, trailed by another woman in sopping wet coveralls. Because of her fresh cuts and bruises, Jenny realized her lack of mobility didn't appear to be permanent. To everyone here, it looked like she'd recently been in a skirmish. Throw on a uniform and she'd pretty much be a war hero again.

They reached the *Jaggery* and found the cargo hold open. Jim was supervising loading a crate of dehydrated cheddar cheese pellets. That man never changed one iota.

"Hello?" called Rassick. "Delivery."

Jim looked up and dropped his tablet. The glass shattered on the metal deck. A dwarf hurried over with a dustpan.

Jenny tried to smile at him. A few bits of teeth and saliva fell out of her mouth, but it was worth it for the horrified look on Jim's face. A hundred retorts went through her head, but she could only manage to raise her eyebrows and grin like a jack o'lantern.

"Can't get rid of us that easily, you old fart," said Ricky.

"What the hell did they do to you? I told you to cooperate," he said, his face going white. Jim was never useful in a medical emergency.

"This is what cooperation looks like in Reasonspace," said Ricky, stony-faced.

"I didn't mean for–"

Jenny raised her hand to stop him. Didn't even give him the finger, though by Unamip she wanted to. She'd put her ass on the line for him over and over, only to have him ditch her like trash.

Boges ran up, pushing her carved wooden wheelchair. Rassick set her down into it and stood there awkwardly smoothing her hair.

"So, I'll be off now," she said. "Hope you get where you're headed."

Jenny grabbed Boges' arm and mimed a tablet. Boges handed over her own and read over her shoulder as Jenny typed and held it up to her. The dwarf ran for the crew quarters.

"You guys headed back out to Bala space?" asked Rassick.

Jim shook his head, still watching Jenny warily. "Gotta drop some cargo at Fort J first."

Jenny watched him right back. He could easily call over the authorities and have her arrested again, but he seemed thrown by the fact that she'd reappeared. He looked at her with a fearfulness like she had some Bala magic that kept her coming back. Who knows, maybe she did.

Boges ran back into the hold. She handed Jenny a box, which Jenny held out to Rassick. The private opened the box and the aroma of lavender wafted out.

"Oh," she said, stroking the purple bars with the tips of her fingers. "I couldn't. Not after what you went through."

Jenny put up her palm to insist.

"Man, I'm gonna shower for days. You're good people, Cap. You kept your word after everything."

"You could give *me* some soap, Perata," said Ricky. "I got you all the way up that ladder." Jenny rolled her eyes.

Rassick tucked the box under her arm and walked down the ramp. She stopped at the bottom and turned, coming to attention and bringing her hand up in salute to Jenny. Jenny saluted in return.

Behind Rassick, Reason officers headed to their various ships. Every one with that bloody spheres and tears flag on the shoulder. You could tell the civilians by the furs and flora they wore that had been stripped from the bodies of various Bala creatures. A woman in heels walked by trailing a pixie on a leash. Another man rode high on the back of a centaur. She knew that being ridden was an insurmountable shame to equine Bala. She wondered what they had to have done to that centaur to pummel it into submission. Another man walked past the open door and Jenny smelled the distinctive odor of elf semen. Smeared all over one's body, it really did make a foolproof magical disguise. Jenny wondered who it was under all that elf sperm. Maybe it was a blemmye. She laughed to herself without opening her mouth.

The door started to close and Jenny turned her chair to see Boges at the controls.

"We're about to leave for Jaisalmer," the dwarf said, watching to ensure the door sealed properly. "We have a landing slot scheduled for eleven AM, Fort J time."

Jenny rolled back toward her quarters. A sturdy calloused hand landed on her arm. Boges dropped a tiny screw-top bottle of silver liquid into Jenny's hand. It was no bigger than a marble. She was afraid to drop it.

"This is all I have left, but take it," the dwarf said. "Go find him."

Jenny popped off the cap. Boges' face compressed. Jenny couldn't tell if it was anger or anguish.

"You do this and all debts are cleared," said Boges. Jenny didn't think that was true, but she wasn't about to turn down even a thimble-sized dollop of unicorn blood. Jenny tipped the vial back and let the globule coat the remains of her teeth. She swished it around. It was thick enough that it made her want to gag. In the spots where it touched her mouth, her cuts sealed. Her teeth rebuilt themselves with a sharp toothache that had her seeing double.

"I'LL FIND BOTH OF THEM," Jenny typed onto Boges' tablet. Her tongue was thick and heavy, coated with a metallic tang.

"Can Cowboy Jim be trusted?" Boges asked. Jenny shook her head. The bones in her jaw were re-aligning. She touched her eye with a finger to warn Boges to watch him.

"HOW LONG BEFORE THE CARGO OPENS," Jenny typed.

"Ninety minutes," said Boges.

"CUTTING IT CLOSE."

"It would not have been my first choice." Sometimes, Boges sounded just like Gary.

Boges handed her the patu that Wenck had stepped on and cracked in half. The dwarves had mended it with wood glue and careful sanding. You could still see the crack, but it blended in with the other carvings on the wood.

"Your grandmother would have been proud of how you fought," said Boges. Jenny was suddenly glad that she wasn't able to talk.

A chime sounded and the ship lurched into FTL. Boges slipped back into her maintenance door, leaving Jenny alone in the cargo hold. Jim kept the gravity on. He could care less that Jenny wouldn't be able to get down the dirt hallways in her chair. The pain in her legs intensified, shooting down her backside and into her calves. Her toes curled from it. On the pain chart they'd given her at the hospital, she was the orange face with worried eyes. She was willing to bet that full unicorn blood did the same job with a lot less anguish.

The last time she'd felt this much pain, it was right after Copernica. Her entire company had looked in on her in the hospital. Major Yerkel had come to visit with a basket of fruit.

"You'll be up and around in no time, Perata," he said, ruffling her hair. "You did good, Captain. People lived because of you."

She'd nodded along, high as a kite on the drugs the hospital had provided. She'd spent months in bed, waiting for the bones to heal. They didn't have enough unicorn blood for every vet who came through the doors. After that, they'd moved her to rehab. A few of her best mates had come by every day to cheer her on during a break in the rotation.

"Come on, Cap. Take a step."

"You can do it."

"One foot in front of the other."

But no matter how much she wanted it, her legs would not move. She pulled herself up, hanging onto those parallel bars over and over, but as soon as her weight shifted, her legs collapsed out from under her. The crew was quiet as she reset and tried again. Over and over. Day after day.

After a couple of weeks, her mates started skipping rehab appointments. They'd realized she wasn't going to be one of those miracle cases who ended up running marathons a year after their pelvis and spine were crushed to bits. She was just going to be sitting in her chair while they went back out to the front. She didn't blame them for being disappointed. She was too. When they were assigned to new ships and redeployed, she wheeled herself out to say goodbye to each of them. It was heartfelt – there were tears – but there was a separation between them. She was the one who got left behind.

Most of those kids were dead now. She wondered if her sacrifice had meant anything. She'd bought them a few more months of living, that was all. It hadn't hurt to give her legs for them. It hurt to know that it didn't make any difference in the long run.

Jenny pushed her chair out of the cargo hold and into the hallway. Her wheels sank into the soft earth. The uneven ground made her chair unstable. She wrenched it forward, inch by inch.

She made it to her quarters, stopping every few feet to rest. She had asked a lot of her body over the last twenty-four hours. Gary's blood was helping, but her bones ached and her muscles felt tight and sore. She pulled on some clean clothes and re-laced her boots. She tried to brush her teeth, but her jaw wouldn't open wide enough yet. The bones were no longer grinding past each other, but the joint was tender and stiff.

She tossed a couple of personal items into her duffel. She hadn't even really unpacked yet. A comb. Her patu. A jumpsuit. She traveled light these days. You never knew when you had to bug out of somewhere fast.

"Boges," she called through her stiff jaw. A different dwarf poked his head into the room via the dwarf door.

"At your service."

She opened her mouth to speak and grimaced. The dwarf looked around the slightly tidied room. He anticipated her request.

"Would you like me to bring your bag to the cargo hold?"

Jenny nodded.

"With pleasure."

For once, it sounded like the dwarf was sincere. She thought of Cheryl Ann and the way she had worked to learn everything about each of the dwarves on board. They had been delighted by her interest, inviting her into their inner circle and regaling her with stories of their adventures on the *Jaggery*.

"Wait," she said.

The dwarf's head returned.

"Yes?"

"What's your name?"

For a moment, he looked like he hadn't understood her mumbled request. Then his face brightened.

"Sunder," he said.

"Thank you, Sunder."

"You're welcome, Captain."

She shoved her chair over to the cockpit. Jim was still regarding her like the walking dead. They had thirty minutes to kill before they could leave for Fort J and she wasn't planning to let Jim out of her sight for a minute.

"You look better. A little color back in your face," said Ricky, standing in the co-pilot's spot. She started to step out, but Jenny waved at her to stay.

"You too," said Jenny, trying not to move her sore jaw. She stood near the Bala instruments and tried to read them, but the various bubbling fluids and twirling leaves were incomprehensible. She hummed to the ship and it hummed back to her.

A new tablet was stuck on the console to replace the one Jim had dropped. Jenny pulled up the documentation for the cargo delivery and handed it to Ricky. She was, after all, an expert in contracts.

"Lady Nashita's bill of lading says we have to get the boxes to the planet's surface before they open. Nothing about actually bringing them into the Summit," said Ricky.

"Is someone coming to pick them up?" asked Jim.

"It doesn't say here. They need to be delivered to Fort Jaisalmer before the timer reaches zero. It actually seems pretty easy," said Ricky. "Just drop them at the docking station and that fulfills our end of the contract."

Jenny and Jim did not respond. Nothing was ever easy.

Especially when the Sisters of the Supersymmetrical Axion were involved. It was in one's best interests to follow their instructions to the letter.

Jim looked exhausted and he kept stealing glances back toward Jenny, like he was afraid she was going to jump him or something. She made her eyes wild and wide, like someone showing ferocity to their enemies. Jim sat as far up in his chair as he could to get away from her.

"Why's this ship called the *Jaggery* anyway?" he asked, trying to distract her. "What the hell does that even mean?"

"It's sugar," said Ricky. "A pressed cake of it. Gary's mother named the ship. Or... renamed it really. After she married his dad."

"Who's Gary's mom?" mumbled Jenny. Her jaw cracked and popped when it moved, like the leather seats in a new ship. She knew his father was a full unicorn, but she assumed his mother was just a random human on one of the early pioneer transports.

Ricky tapped a name into the tablet and held out the article for Jenny to read.

"Her name was Anjali Ramanathan. Though you're probably more familiar with her colloquial name – Apocalypse Angie."

"Huh," said Jim.

"Yeah. She led the early rebellion against the Reason when they were just a collection of broken-down generation ships. But before that, Gary's mother was the chancellor of Proxima Centauri." Ricky had slipped effortlessly into antiquities dealer mode. She sounded for all the world like a professor giving a 101-level history lesson.

"Anjali's title was mostly ceremonial, but her job was to preserve as much culture from Earth as possible. Languages, artifacts, history, old films and shows. That's why Gary doesn't talk as formally as the other unicorns. He probably had more of an Earth kid's childhood than most of us did."

Jenny took the tablet. The photo accompanying the entry showed a brown woman in her twenties dressed in a formal sari dotted with shining stones. It was her official photo, but she'd been caught mid-laugh, so it looked like an outtake. She looked genuinely happy. It was hard to imagine Gary with such a young, joyful mother.

As if reading her mind, Ricky reached over and flipped to the next page. The photo was Anjali again, holding a tiny Gary on her lap. His dark hair curled at the base of a horn as tall as her hand and you could just tell that he was sticky. His eyes had the same serious expression that they did now, but his mouth was open to show four tiny teeth.

"How does a woman even make a baby with a unicorn?" muttered Jim.

"Are you asking for an anatomy lesson?" said Ricky archly. "Because it's obvious if you think about it. Unicorns are asexual and there wasn't any sex involved, so..."

"Bala magic," said Jim.

"See? You got there all on your own," said Ricky. "When Anjali's ship arrived at Proxima, three faster ships that started after hers were already having conflicts with the Bala they found there. They thought the *Cristobal*'s people would act as reinforcements. Which is all in the history books, but what they won't tell you is that Anjali fought to keep her ship from joining the war on the side of the humans. She almost had them convinced. The *Cristobal* was this close to siding with the Bala in the fight."

Jenny thought again of the moments that could have changed the tide of war in a completely different direction. If the *Cristobal* hadn't joined the fight, perhaps they would all be living on Bala worlds instead of Reason ones.

Ricky flipped the page. This photo was candid, probably a still from a ship's video feed taken during the first battle for Proxima. An older Anjali leaned over a map, both hands gripping the edge of the table. She looked like she was arguing with the other humans in the room. Her face was set and tired, but her eyes blazed. Ricky swiped again. The final photo was the Anjali Ramanathan Memorial Shrine on Proxima. You could barely see the inscription behind the fruits, flowers, and other offerings left at its base. Bala used to travel from all over openspace to leave her a tribute. The first human to fight for peace between her people and the Bala.

"Amazing," mumbled Jenny.

"Oh, you haven't seen his father yet," said Ricky. She reached over and tapped on the tablet.

"Findae Cobalt," she said. The entry shifted to a much shorter article. The image at the top was an oil painting, not a photograph. Ricky enlarged it.

"Gary's dad is the king of the unicorns. Gary won't ever tell you, but he's actually Prince Gary. And if you ever call him that, he'll turn six shades of red and deny that there's a royal family any more."

"Yeah, he did that on Beywey when some of the locals recognized him as a Cobalt," said Jenny.

"Man, it's a good thing unicorns are extinct or they would be pissed at you for keeping Gary hostage," said Jim, looking at Jenny. "But I guess you did what you had to for the survival of man."

Manifest destiny came the reply in Jenny's head that had been drilled over a lifetime. She tossed the tablet onto the console.

"FTL *Jaggery*, this is Chhatrapati Shivaji. You are clear for takeoff," said a voice over the comm. Jim touched the tablet and backed the ship out of his parking spot. Grunts in EVA suits waved him frantically over to the left. He scraped the hull along the support strut. It groaned along the edge of the stoneship. When they'd backed out, Jenny could see a bent beam sagging toward the station.

"They're going to bill you for that," said Ricky.

"They can try to find me," replied Jim, spinning them toward Jaisalmer.

After a few hours of rest and restocking at Chhatrapati, the *Jaggery* descended through the upper atmosphere and Fort Jaisalmer sprawled beneath them. The fort was located on a dry area of the planet, covered in sandy gray clay. Fort J spanned two time zones on a single continent. It was where the Reason Command trained their armies and planned their conquests. It was the largest concentrated gathering of humans anywhere in the universe, even including Earth.

"FTL *Jaggery* to Fort Jaisalmer with a SSA delivery, requesting a landing site for an eleven hundred scheduled touchdown," said Jim into the comm.

Fort J traffic control did not answer for several minutes. Jim shifted in his seat.

"This paperwork is legit. I don't know why they're not talking to us." He looked back at Ricky and Jenny. "Maybe they can tell you two are aboard."

He looked about to toss them both out an airlock rather than jeopardize the delivery. The comm came to life.

"FTL *Jaggery*, we were not aware that you were Halcyon class. We don't have much room for a stoneship. Do you have a shuttle you can take down to us?"

"That's a negative, Fort J. We need a landing location."

The comm went quiet again.

"I'm going to get my luggage," said Ricky, heading for the door. "Don't leave without me."

Jenny rolled her chair into her spot at the controls.

"You gonna look for Kaila?" asked Jim, without looking at her.

"Mmm," she replied. She wiggled her jaw back and forth and it felt intact. She opened her mouth and aside from a few rough bits of teeth that hadn't quite finished regrowing, it felt pretty good.

"You can take my gun if you want," said Jim.

"I don't want your gun," replied Jenny.

"Wouldn't it be funny if we both ended up with dead wives," he mused.

Jenny was stunned. Something was seriously wrong with this man.

"Like karma, I mean," he continued, digging himself in deeper.

Obviously bored with waiting, Jim dropped them through the atmosphere like a stone. If he didn't ease up on the stick, they were going to slam into the surface. She wasn't sure that it wouldn't be intentional, either. Jenny grabbed the tablet out of his hands.

"Let me drive," she said.

"Still my ship," he said, but he let her have it.

She glided them to a spot just outside of the city and hovered, waiting for landing clearance. Ships were stacked up in a long line, coming out of orbit one after the other with just a couple of minutes between them. Air traffic control would be slammed.

Ricky came back in.

"Perata, the suitcase I traded for passage is in the cargo hold by your bag," she said, watching the ships land.

"I don't need it," said Jenny. "Thanks anyway."

"I pay my debts," said Ricky.

"What if we stop worrying about debts and karma and just be nice to each other," said Jenny. "I give you a ride, you help me up a ladder, it all works out."

"You mean like friendship," teased Ricky. "I've heard of this concept. People doing nice things for each other, for no reason at all. Seems suspicious, but I would be willing to give it a try, Perata." Ricky patted the damp braids that Boges had woven into Jenny's hair.

"I don't want any friends," said Jim, chewing on that damn stick again.

"Oh good, because you have none," said Ricky.

"You two are the mean girls of space, always picking on guys like me," he pouted.

Ricky burst out laughing, and even though it hurt like hell, Jenny couldn't help but join in.

"Oh my god, I am seriously getting that engraved on my tombstone. 'Here lies Ricky Tang, the meanest girl in space.'"

The comm crackled open.

"FTL *Jaggery*, this is Fort Jaisalmer, you can set down in the rugby stadium."

"This day just keeps getting better," said Ricky.

CHAPTER TWENTY-THREE
Redworm Sunset

The redworm reared up as Gary, Kaila, and Subedar Singh tried to inch past it out of the dissection room. Alarms blared throughout the floor, indicating a set of restraints had been broken.

"I may have misjudged the timing," said Singh, pulling out her firearm and aiming it at the worm's head. Gary pushed her weapon toward the floor.

"It will spray corrosive acid if you shoot it." Ridiculous humans, always trying to shoot their way out of problems. "Kaila, get in front of us. It is drawn to heat and you're the coolest of us."

Kaila looked at him skeptically, but extended her branches horizontally to shield them.

"I thought you were here to rescue *me*," she said.

"This is a Jenny Perata sort of rescue," said Gary.

"Ah," said Kaila, in complete understanding. "Then this will get harder before it gets easier."

The door opened and the redworm techs rushed in, stopping short at the sight of a ruddy, five-meter creature hunched over against the ceiling. It turned on them and sprayed acid the color of an Earth sunset. They didn't have time to scream before they dissolved into a puddle of goo. The worm bent down and extended a proboscis to slurp up the nutrients. It was probably the best meal it had seen in months.

"That's the only door," whispered Subedar Singh. For all of her bluster, she didn't sound like someone who had ever been in a fight. She probably just bullied Bala here on Jaisalmer.

"We need to get it away from the exit," said Gary. He scanned down the tools hanging on the far wall of the room. Mostly saws, surgical instruments, and collection containers. But there was one thing. While the worm was focused on its puddle of humans, Gary picked a blowtorch off the wall. Someone had put it away dirty – there were still downy phoenix underfeathers stuck to the nozzle. He tossed a couple of lab coats onto the floor and turned the valve on an oxygen tank mounted to the wall. Cold O_2 flowed out of its attached hose. He laid the end on the lab coats, lit the blowtorch, and held it to the rushing gas. The oxygen hissed into flame, melting the hose and spreading the fire to the lab coats underneath. He dropped the blowtorch on top of it all.

The worm already sensed the heat coming from the far wall. It reared up again, smashing its mouth on the ceiling. It snaked over to the fire, knocking over the exam table with the dead dwarf, ignoring the bipeds in the room completely. Gary pulled open the door and Subedar Singh jumped over the puddle of acid that had already eaten through the tile and part of the subfloor. Some poor human in the administrative offices below was going to experience a searing red rain any moment now.

Kaila stood at the edge of the puddle. She was too heavy and slow to jump in place, let alone across such a width. Gary crouched down to let her onto his back.

"I'll carry you." All of Kaila's branches whipped forward to cover her face in horror.

"You can't expect me to *ride a unicorn*," she said, scandalized.

"Just this once," he said with a smile. She put her cuffed hands over his head and leaned onto him. He used his long gait to step over the puddle. A couple of her longer fronds trailed through the acid and she jumped.

"Ow."

Gary put her down in the hallway. Other techs and guards ran up to join them.

"What's going on?" asked a guard, with a stun stick out.

"Redworm escaped. You'd better get it under control before it gets out of the building," said Subedar Singh in a convincing approximation of imperious anger. The guard nodded and ran into the room, sliding on the puddle. His foot came to rest in a hole in the tile, wedged in the disintegrating subfloor. The acid began to melt his flesh.

"Help!" he screamed to the other guards.

"Get in there," said Singh, pushing the others forward into the room.

By this point, the redworm had realized the fire contained nothing edible and slithered back to the front of the room. It was rather inelegant without the weightlessness of space to help it glide.

The first tech was suited up against acid spills. She stepped past the howling guard and raised a heat gun that was intended to mesmerize a redworm until you restrained it. But this worm had already been tricked once today and it was not having it. It propelled itself forward and sprayed.

Subedar Singh pulled Kaila between herself and Gary and motioned for them both to start walking. More guards arrived and a second alarm sounded throughout the building as the acid dripped into the rooms beneath them. There was a chorus of human screams from behind them as they calmly walked toward the exit.

"This is definitely a Jenny Perata rescue," said Kaila.

"It will take them a while to sort out the body parts. They

might even assume we've all been eaten," said Subedar Singh over the alarm.

A team of armed Reason officers rounded the corner, weapons drawn. Singh stepped in front of Gary and directed them toward the dissection room.

"Two redworms escaped. I saw one go into the ventilation system," she yelled. The officers nodded and ran down the hall. "That will keep them busy for a while."

"But there was only one worm," said Kaila.

Subedar Singh shook her head.

"Trees are so dense," she said.

As they stepped out into the Jaisalmer sun and heat, blast doors came down over the building's exits. That would definitely trap all of the humans inside with the redworm and not stop the worm itself at all, noted Gary darkly. After the chaos of the harvesting center, the street outside felt like a calm respite, even on Summit day. In his lab coat, none of the rank and file gave Gary a second look. Kaila, on the other hand, was a different story.

A patrol stopped them on the street, but Singh was ready.

"Sir, why is this dryad out of the harvesting center?"

Singh patted the curve of Kaila's trunk.

"She's been requested in Colonel Wenck's apartment."

"Very good." The soldier waved them on their way.

An explosion blew out the bottom floor windows of the harvesting center. They ducked as chunks of glass rained down. Kaila extended her branches to cover Gary and Singh from the worst of it. Shredded bits of leaves floated around them.

"You don't think that was the blowtorch?" asked Gary. He'd hate to think he'd caused that.

"No. They're probably trying to flush the 'second redworm' out of the vents," said Singh, making quotes with her fingers.

"But there was only one worm," said Kaila again, clearly confused.

"So, where are we meeting the Sisters?" asked Singh, pulling her uniform jacket down tight.

"I'm not sure," said Gary. She gave him a look that could melt iron.

"If you tricked me out here…"

"It's not that. We have a delivery for them. My stoneship is supposed to land and meet them, but I don't know where."

Singh thought for a moment.

"There's only one place in the city large enough for a stoneship to dock." She pointed north. "The rugby stadium."

"That's not far," said Gary.

Kaila's face shifted from dismay to elation at something in the sky behind Gary to the south. He looked up to see an immense, slow-moving asteroid soaring over the city, casting deep shadows as it passed.

"Jenny!" squealed Kaila.

"She's probably not on board," said Gary. "They took her to detention."

The human faces around them lifted to watch the *Jaggery* fly over the tops of the buildings. People gasped. It was on a crash course with City Hall. The ship rotated on its axis until a relatively flat section was facing the facade. The *Jaggery* skimmed along the side of the building, not disturbing the structure, but skimming a layer of paint off the side of the concrete and onto the asteroid. It came away as a white line above the pink flower. The ship spun again and deposited itself neatly into the concave bowl of the rugby stadium.

Sirens wailed in the distance as emergency services scrambled to contain the redworm threat as well as the fire that had started billowing out of the lower floors of the harvesting center. Gary thought he saw another dryad slinking along the sidewalk, but when he turned to look it was just an ordinary tree, inert and still.

Kaila was transfixed by the *Jaggery*.

"Jim can't drive like that," she said breathlessly. "That is definitely my Jenny."

"Thank Unamip," said Gary, relieved that he wouldn't have to go look for her and Ricky. This might turn out to be easy after all.

"Singh, what in the hell are you doing out here with my unicorn?" called a voice from the far side of the street. Colonel Wenck stepped into traffic toward them. Military vehicles screeched to a stop as he marched across four lanes without looking.

"Oh, bollocks," said Subedar Singh, her hands going from her sides to being clasped in front, then back again.

"The redworms, sir," she said, faltering. "I pulled these two out of harvesting as the redworms began attacking. I thought you might want to ensure the unicorn was out of harm's way."

"There was only one redworm," insisted Kaila.

"Not now," whispered Gary.

Wenck looked skeptical. "Come with me. I'll escort you over to the office. We'll lock him in the storage closet until this mess with the worms is over."

"Yes, sir."

"And get rid of this thing. I don't know why you thought I'd want a tree." He shook his head.

"Get rid of it?" asked Singh.

"Shoot it, or whatever. I'm not slowing down for a stack of timber."

"Oh dear," said Kaila, covering her mouth with her branches.

Wenck started walking toward Reason Command, not waiting for anyone.

"Should we make a run for it?" asked Gary.

"No. He'll radio it in and every grunt within ten blocks will be on us." She took out her weapon and aimed it toward the sky, glancing behind her to ensure that Wenck wasn't looking. She turned back to Kaila. "Fall to the ground when you hear the shot. When we're out of sight, get to your ship as fast as you can. We'll meet you there when we can slip away."

Singh squeezed off a single round and no one around her flinched. Kaila lay down on the ground dramatically, splaying her branches so that people on the sidewalk had to step around her. Singh tossed the keys to her handcuffs on the ground, grabbed Gary's arm, and ran to catch up with Colonel Wenck.

"Get up here, Singh!" called Wenck.

She and Gary trotted behind Wenck toward Reason Command, in the opposite direction to the rugby field.

"How dumb do you think I am, Singh?" asked Wenck without breaking his stride.

"What, sir?" asked Singh, her eyes wide.

"You were trying to steal my unicorn."

"No, sir. I was getting him out of the–"

"Don't bullshit me, Subedar. He's got that lab coat on and his best friend's wife next to him. I am not an idiot. You were springing him from harvesting."

Gary still thought they had a good chance if they made a run for it, but Singh stubbornly kept at it.

"Honestly, sir. I found them together in the harvesting room. I went in there to check on him, like you asked, and he already had the coat on and the tree in there with him. They let the redworms go and tried to kill me. I grabbed them both and got out of the building before we were sealed in. That's when you found us."

Wenck didn't appear convinced. A second explosion boomed out of the harvesting center. A piercing shriek echoed down the street. It was the cry of an injured redworm.

Gary hated to do it, but he knew how he could help Singh and make their way toward the *Jaggery*. He reached out and slid his hand over the back of her shoulders. She looked up, confused as to why he was seemingly being affectionate at that odd moment. He yanked her back toward him and pressed his forearm against her neck, then reached down and unholstered her firearm, pressing it against her headscarf. This was exactly the type of violence that he abhorred, even in jest. But sometimes, the Reason pushed a man so far that he felt he had no other choice. That was the gift of conflict escalation – it just kept on giving.

Singh struggled against him.

"What are you–"

"Shut up," Gary snarled in her ear and he felt her stiffen. She didn't know him well enough to understand this was well out of character for him. All the better. Her reactions would be authentic. Shame burned in the pit of his stomach.

Wenck turned and drew his own weapon, as expected.

"You put her down or I'll shoot."

"Don't shoot," cried Singh. "You'll hit me."

"That is an acceptable risk," said Wenck, taking aim with cool detachment.

As his finger tightened on the trigger, Gary twisted so that his back faced Wenck. The shot rang out and Gary felt as if he'd been punched in the ribs from behind. Singh jerked in his arms and pulled away. Her uniform was coated in silver. She put her hands on her knees and breathed heavily.

Gary's blood pumped out of the hole in his chest for a few seconds, then the opening closed.

"Unicorn blood," he yelled in his loudest voice, pointing at the puddle on the ground. He put his hand on the back of Singh's neck and walked her quickly into the crowd as people ran over to scrape silver drops out of the dirt. Wenck tried to push through after them, but the frenzy only grew as more people fought for the precious substance. A few scrutinized the crowd frantically, looking for the unicorn who had bled into the soil.

They ran two blocks before Gary handed Singh back her firearm.

"I apologize for that," he said. "Were you hit?"

"No."

"Now you have plausible deniability. Tell Wenck I made you come with me," said Gary.

"Oh. Thanks." She still seemed shaken at having taken fire.

A pair of grunts waited on the next corner, looking over the heads of the crowd. Searching for them.

"He radioed it in," said Singh, cocking her gun. Gary put his hand over hers and eased the hammer away from the trigger.

"You don't need to shoot your way out of every situation," he said.

She looked genuinely perplexed.

"But how else…"

He took her hand and pulled her into the closest building. It was a grocery store, packed with tourists in town for the Summit. They pushed through the aisles, past baskets of flying vek held down by nets, and bottles of fizzy drinks made with something called "essence of fairy." One woman was testing a facial cream that smelled like elfin armpits. A rainbow display proclaimed Real Unicorn Meat in chilled, parchment-wrapped packages. An employee was frying up samples on a portable stove next to it. From the smell, it was ordinary cow flank, but these people wouldn't know the difference.

Singh took the lead, pulling him through a swing door into the cold back room. A few employees looked up from their tasks.

"Reason business," said Singh, "Where's the emergency exit?"

A faun in a bloody apron pointed his cleaver toward a narrow hallway. Singh followed it to a door at the end. They burst back outside, blinking in the sunlight. They emerged in a small street between buildings piled high with trash and empty boxes.

"This way," she said, heading toward one end of the alley. Two Reason soldiers stepped into their path, blocking the exit. Singh turned and pulled Gary in the opposite direction. Two other soldiers came around the corner from the other end. Gary moved his hand up to her wrist and held her like he was in charge. If they took him in, at least she wouldn't be charged as an accomplice.

"What do we do?" she asked.

"We let them take us," he replied.

Her hand hovered over her holster.

"I could–"

"No more killing," he said firmly. Her hand fell back to her side.

"Subedar Singh?" called one of the grunts, advancing on them with weapons drawn.

"Yes. Get me out of here!" she cried in mock alarm.

"Unicorn, drop your weapon and get down on the ground."

Gary raised his hands above his head. It seemed like they were in that position a lot these days. He suspected they would remain that way for the foreseeable future. The burden Unamip had placed on him, he had realized, was to live forever, but without self-determination.

A streak of red swooped through the alley from the building above them, knocking down the grunts on the right side of the alley. They lay still. A crack like thunder echoed off the cement walls and the second set of grunts was down, hit by a bolt of purple lightning from above.

Gary squinted into the sky. He couldn't see anything except the roof ledges. When he looked back down, four

Sisters stood next to them, veils perfectly still as if they'd been there all along.

"Follow us," said one of them. It was the tall Sister from the desert with her former companions. It was surprisingly easy to tell them apart, even with their veils on. Each Sister was quite different in body shape and personality.

The two Sisters in the lead stepped over the prone bodies of the grunts who had been knocked down. Their wide, blinking eyes were conscious, but they did not move. Two other Sisters took up the rear, forming a protective barrier between Gary and the crowd. They stopped. The tall Sister motioned for Subedar Singh to come along.

"You have a part in this as well," said the lead Sister. Singh looked surprised, but took a spot in the formation next to Gary.

"Thank you," said Gary, stepping out into the street proper and noticing that no one was giving the Sisters a second glance. They were heady with magic. It surrounded them like a protective halo. There was at least one necromancer in the group and they were able to walk through the street without anyone taking notice.

"Kaila told us where to find you," said the small Sister who had spoken to him on the *Jaggery*. "Without intervention, there was a ninety-seven per cent chance that you were going to be recaptured and miss the Summit."

"Technically, it was ninety-seven point four nine percent which rounds to ninety-seven percent," said another Sister from the rear.

"There is no need for two decimal places in casual conversation," said the tall Sister, and the others nodded in agreement.

"If we helped, we brought the chance down to nine per cent," she said, turning her veiled face to the Sister behind her to see if she was going to offer a correction. She was silent.

"I am so fired," muttered Subedar Singh.

"Actually," said the small Sister, "we're counting on you not only keeping your job, but getting a promotion. It's extremely important to the future."

The tall Sister cleared her throat and the smaller one dropped her voice to a whisper.

"It's going to get bad for a while, but it will be all right in the end. Trust me."

They turned a corner, emerging from between two buildings. Suddenly the *Jaggery* loomed above them, filling the sky. Jenny had hovered it above the stadium like a giant poached egg balanced in a tiny cup. The Sisters led them toward the tunnel that opened onto the playing field.

"My gods," said Subedar Singh, looking up.

"Not just yet," chirped the small Sister, cheerfully. "They'll be here in about fifteen minutes."

CHAPTER TWENTY-FOUR
Seven Sisters

Typical of Reason grunts, Fort Jaisalmer Traffic Control hadn't bothered to clear the stadium before granting landing clearance to the *Jaggery*. As Jenny swung the stoneship over the rugby field, a lone groundskeeper making stripes in the grass looked up and abandoned her lawn tractor at a run.

"Sorry, love," called Jenny softly, easing the behemoth ship into the oval stadium on the halfway line with the cargo door facing the ground. She hovered it about five meters from the grass and hoped that would be close enough for unloading.

An explosion rocked the streets of Fort J. Jenny could see a three-story building billowing smoke a few blocks away. That was the harvesting center. If that was his exit, she might not have to go searching for Gary after all.

Boges popped into the cockpit.

"I'll have my kin unload your personal belongings, Captain," she said to Jenny, then turned to Jim. "Would you like me to have them pack your things, Cowboy?"

"Don't touch my stuff," he said.

"No one wants to touch your stuff," said Ricky.

"We'll leave it for you to collect," said Boges. "You're going to find him, right?" she asked Jenny.

A second, larger explosion shook the ship.

"I get the feeling he's on his way," said Jenny, rubbing her jaw. The bone had gone back into its proper shape, but the ache went all the way up to her ears. Add it to the list of things that hurt; she was a veritable medical diagnosis textbook of painful conditions.

A redworm screeched and Boges ducked back into the dwarf door. On the viewscreen, a contingent of people marched in formation toward the ship.

"Soldiers incoming," said Jim, getting out of his chair with a pained sigh. "You better lose yourself until I get rid of them."

Jenny looked at the viewscreen more closely. Each person was dressed alike, but not in Reason uniforms. They wore crimson flight suits and matching opaque veils that obscured their faces.

"Those aren't soldiers," she said. "It's the Sisters."

"Yes!" cried Ricky, rocketing out of the cockpit.

"Even worse," said Jim, following her toward the cargo hold. Jenny brought up the rear in her chair. Sweat beaded up on her forehead as she shoved herself through the dirt in the hallways. She couldn't tell if Jim didn't hear her struggling, or just didn't care.

The Sisters marched up into the open belly of the *Jaggery* without waiting for an invitation. A woman at the head of the formation lifted her veil and threw it back so it hung around her neck. She was compact and completely bald, like one of those smiling monks who begged for cash in exchange for flowers on space stations.

Ricky threw herself at the Sister, showering her head with kisses. "Auntie Nash!"

The woman embraced her, then held Ricky out at arm's length.

"My dear niece Ricky Tang. You look so good. Maybe gained a little weight. You're doing well for yourself."

"Ugh," Ricky sighed. "Stop with the weight, Auntie."

"My invitation still stands," said Lady Nashita, tugging on Ricky's collar playfully. Ricky waved away the suggestion.

"I'd be terrible as one of your girls. I never follow instructions," she said.

Lady Nashita gave a withering look to one of her acolytes.

"Not all of them are as disciplined as you think." The offending Sister shifted on her feet uncomfortably. "But we have ways of working around that."

Ricky made a face. "Sounds terrible. I'd rather take my chances on the streets of Jaisalmer."

Jim stood stupefied, but Jenny offered a bow.

"Lady Nashita," she said, "We have your cargo." She gestured to the boxes tethered behind her.

Lady Nashita came close to Jenny, smelling of cigars and whiskey.

"Jenny Perata, you have fulfilled the contract," she said, much to Jenny's relief. "But at great personal cost." Lady Nashita reached up and ran a gentle hand down Jenny's jawline. Her hands were soft, but freezing cold. "I did not understate the risks of this task, did I?"

"You did not," said Jenny.

Lady Nashita moved over to Jim, scrutinizing his face and wrinkling her nose.

"James Bryant, my sincere condolences. You have lost your dearest love and your life's purpose. Be assured that you will find one of those again soon." Jim coughed and cleared his throat.

A pair of Reason soldiers approached the loading ramp. Lady Nashita whirled on them.

"This ship is under my protection. You have no need to search it."

The soldiers walked up the ramp. One of them nudged the reverend mother out of the way with the end of her weapon.

"Your protection is not worth as much as it used to be," she said, stepping up into the cargo hold. "Not after you what you Sisters pulled with that escaped political prisoner."

The Sisters' heads swiveled to wait for Lady Nashita's orders. She held up a hand as the Reason soldiers checked the cargo.

"Should I take them out?" asked the tall Sister.

"You should wait like I asked," replied Lady Nashita. "Your willingness to fight is going to come back to bite you."

The Sister stepped back into line as the Reason soldiers came down the ramp.

"It all appears in order, but there's a note here from Colonel Wenck –"

Lady Nashita flicked her head toward her acolytes and the tall Sister's leg shot out so fast that it was barely visible. The soldier hit the ground, out cold. Before the second one could react, another Sister swept his legs out from under him and landed her fist on his temple.

"You were saying, Reverend Mother?" asked the tall Sister archly.

"Hush," replied Lady Nashita, nudging the unconscious soldiers down the ramp with the edge of her boot. They rolled into the grass, limp. "Make sure they stay down while we're waiting for these boxes to open."

The cargo hold's interior door opened and Ricky walked out, rolling two suitcases behind her.

"As for the matter of payment, we will pay extra to compensate for your past and future losses, Geneva," said Lady Nashita.

"Future losses?" asked Jenny. "That sounds alarming–" Her tablet pinged. "Bloody hell, that's a lot of money."

Jim looked at his own tablet as it chimed, then slid it nonchalantly into his pocket. He pulled out a bag of tobacco and a set of papers and started rolling himself a cigarette.

Lady Nashita walked to the cargo and checked the timer as it counted down the final minutes.

"Shall we move these outside, Sisters?"

The Sisters sprang into action, unstrapping the boxes and sliding them down the ramp onto the grass. They looked odd and out of place – two giant plastic crates on the center line.

"Where is Boges?" said Lady Nashita. Boges poked her head out of one of the maintenance doors. She approached timidly.

"Reverend Mother," she said. Lady Nashita rested a hand on her head.

"Is everything ready?"

"Yes, Reverend Mother. I am regrowing most of the flora and repopulating the fauna."

"Good. A shipment of supplies will arrive shortly. You'll need those for the next destination. I don't need to tell you how important they are."

"No, Reverend Mother."

"And where is little Gary?" asked Lady Nashita.

"The Reason took him at Borstal Checkpoint. He's in the harvesting center," said Jenny.

"Oh, that's very close. Just a few blocks from here. I'll have my girls go pick him up," she said, as if they were grabbing him from a shuttle terminal and not breaking into a high security Reason facility. Four Sisters turned and ran toward the stadium exit. Their long veils streamed behind them like contrails.

"Wait," said Boges. "Jenny's wife is there as well."

"No, I don't think so," said Lady Nashita.

Jenny's heart pounded in her ears. The Sisters knew things that others didn't. They saw the future and knew how things would play out in the long run. If Kaila was dead, Lady Nashita would know.

"What do you mean?" she asked, dreading the answer.

"I mean we walked past her on the way here. She's on her way to the stadium," said Lady Nashita, with a grin.

Jenny rolled down the ramp onto the grass, ignoring Jim's questions about where she was going. In the tunnel where the Sisters had entered the field, a tree shuffled slowly toward her. She spun her wheels so fast her hands slipped off the grips.

"Kaila!"

Jenny careened headfirst into branches and bark, nearly knocking her wife over. Kaila leaned down and kissed her, over and over, until the bark started to chafe her lips and her jaw ached from ear to ear again.

"Oh my Sap, I thought I'd never see you again." She hung onto Kaila as if she was never going to let her go.

"I knew you would come," said Kaila, winding her flexible branches round Jenny's waist and settling herself into Jenny's lap.

"I'm sorry it took so long," said Jenny, resting her head in Kaila's flowers. "I'm going to take you home."

"You have a ship?" asked Kaila.

"I'm giving the *Jaggery* back to Gary, well... I'm making Jim give it back, but we have enough cash to buy our own ship now. One of those new ones that practically flies itself. Maybe Gary will give us a bit of horn so we can get there fast, or maybe not and we'll just enjoy the ride." She ran a finger along the edge of Kaila's ear. The dryad shivered with an autumnal rustle of leaves.

"Sounds perfect," said Kaila, and they kissed again.

Someone at the far end of the hallway cleared their throat.

"You're going to end up with a mouthful of splinters like that," said Gary. He looked nearly as happy to see them together as she was.

"You don't know the half of it," said Jenny, grinning so wide that her new teeth throbbed. "Get over here." He walked over flanked by two Sisters. There was a Reason officer with him as well, but no one else seemed concerned by her presence.

Jenny pulled him down by the front of his sweater and whispered into his ear. She was so giddy with the smell of Kaila's flowers that she'd kissed him on the cheek before realizing it.

"Thank you for bringing her back to me." He nodded and moved away, but she held him there. She had something else to say. "I'm truly sorry for everything I did to you."

As soon as she said it, she knew it was completely inadequate, but she'd gotten caught up in the moment. He gave her a sad smile and squeezed her hand before walking with the Sisters onto the field. She was left feeling empty that she hadn't said or done more.

Kaila flicked her ear. "What is it, Jen? You look sad."

"The usual," said Jenny, in the shorthand of their marriage.

"You can only try to do better next time," said Kaila, extricating herself from Jenny's lap. They followed Gary and the Sisters into the stadium to collect their things. Jenny was too ashamed to ask Gary for a piece of horn to power a new ship, so she started calculating the amount of supplies they'd need for the years-long journey to Gymnoverium. One thing they would not be taking on this trip was dehydrated cheddar cheese.

As she approached the group, Boges was holding out a tablet to Jim, who looked like he had no intention of taking it from her.

"It's my ship," he said, mouth set and smoke wafting out of his nose. "Says so right in the deed."

"You are such a jackass, James Bryant. You sign that ship over to Gary right now or I will break your nose again," said Jenny, rolling up on the mercifully short grass.

They were going their separate ways and she had nothing

to lose in not telling him off any longer. "I don't even know why you're still here. It's Gary's ship. Sign it and get out."

Lady Nashita looked at her patiently.

"We need James here for the moment, Geneva. And you don't need to fight my battles for me, unless you're interested in becoming a Sister."

It sounded suspiciously like an invitation.

"No, thank you," said Jenny.

"We have a lot of experience with people of your... abilities," continued Lady Nashita.

"What does that mean?" asked Kaila.

"Jenny might be a necromancer," said Ricky gleefully. Kaila looked down at Jenny with shock and dread.

"No," she breathed.

"No," agreed Jenny. "I just did a party trick in the null. People do that all the time."

"Oh, that's fine," said Kaila, relaxing. "Even I can do things in the null."

Jenny shot a warning look to both Lady Nashita and Ricky. They both looked amused and she could absolutely see the relation.

"I'll sign over the ship, but I want more money," announced Jim.

"And you shall have it," replied Lady Nashita. Jim's tablet pinged. He looked down.

"More than that."

It pinged again.

"Is that enough?" asked Lady Nashita.

"That'll do," he said.

"Are we passing out cash?" asked Ricky. "Because though my spirit is strong, my body is weak. I have corporeal needs." Lady Nashita laughed and Ricky's tablet pinged. She pulled it out.

"Oh āiyā, Auntie. Too much!"

"You're going to need it. I'd tell you to be safe, but it's the Reason that has to watch out for you. Go have fun and I'll see you again soon."

Ricky kissed her aunt's head again.

She leaned down and pecked Jenny's cheek.

"You should come find me in my new bar, Jenny fucking Perata," she whispered. She dragged her suitcases out into the city, where three distinct plumes of smoke rose on the horizon. Jenny figured she would be turning a profit within a day.

Jenny turned and glared at Jim. It sickened her that they'd paid Jim to do what was right. She was about to tell him so when Lady Nashita put a hand on her shoulder.

"Geneva, you should trust that everything will come right in the end."

Jenny's face got hot. It was easy to say things like that when you could see the future. The rest of them never knew if all their effort would be worth it.

"Sure. Fine," said Jenny, shrugging off her reassuring touch. She found Lady Nashita's nonchalance infuriating. "Kaila, can you get our bags?"

Kaila ambled up the ramp and picked up the two bags that contained everything they owned in the universe. It was pitifully little to show for decades of work. But they'd start again with the Sisters' money. She lifted her hand in a wave. There didn't seem to be a way to make a goodbye large enough for what they'd been through together, so she didn't even try.

"We're on our way. Good luck to everyone," Jenny called, pushing away from them.

Lady Nashita put a hand on the back of her chair and the wheels spun. Jenny whirled it around, curious.

"Don't touch my chair."

"You cannot leave yet, Geneva."

"Why not?"

"You have been invited to attend the Summit as a guest of the Pymmie."

Gary looked disconcerted and Jim spat into the grass.

Jenny didn't believe the Pymmie existed, let alone knew who she was.

"Why would they invite me?" was all she could come up with.

"They have invited all of you," said Lady Nashita, making an expansive gesture with her hands. "It's a great honor."

"Well, I'm not going," said Jim, rolling another cigarette. Jenny wanted to slap it out of his hand. Of course he was going to refuse to go, so she decided to be the best damn Summit guest the Pymmie had ever seen.

"I'd be delighted to attend," she said, taunting him with her cheerfulness.

"Human achievements speak for themselves. They don't need me there to witness some slideshow on our progress," Jim said.

"What exactly do you think the Summit is?" asked Lady Nashita, with a raised eyebrow.

"We're gathered here to prove to the Pymmie how much progress people have made in the last hundred years. We survived all kinds of catastrophes by using our wits and the resources available to us." He looked around the stadium. "Look at this. We made a whole new Earth for ourselves way out here. We have planets full of people to show them."

Lady Nashita sighed patiently.

"You, like so many others, have completely misunderstood the purpose of the Century Summit. One hundred years ago, the Bala extended their hand in friendship as you fled your dying planet, with the caveat that you would gather in a century and show the Pymmie that you are able to live in cooperation and collaboration with non-human species."

Jim scratched his stubble.

"Is that true?" He looked toward Gary.

"It is. You didn't quite do that, did you?" replied Gary.

"I don't reckon that we did."

Laughter burst out of Jenny as she realized what was about to happen.

"We are so screwed," she said, with half a mind to make a run for it before the Summit began. The only thing that stopped her was that it was kind of hard to hide from omniscient beings. She was mortified to have to face the Pymmie and account for her actions. The necromancers she'd killed, the half-unicorn she'd imprisoned, and the catalogue of a million little ways in which she'd been complicit in harming the Bala. It all weighed on her like an anchor. She fought her instinct to run and reminded herself that she'd intended to make amends to Gary. Maybe she needed to expand the scope of her atonement to the entire Bala civilization. Kaila draped a branch over Jenny's shoulder.

"Well I'm not responsible," said Jim. "I just did what everybody else was doing. And I lost my wife in the process."

"It's not for me to say who is responsible," replied Lady Nashita. "The Pymmie would like to meet with all of you."

Jim and Gary began speaking at the same time. The Reason officer in the headscarf raised her hand.

"Hi, I don't mean to interrupt, but I'm just here with a quick question about a dream I had."

Lady Nashita pulled the woman's hand and pressed it to her chest as if she was reuniting with an old friend.

"Lakshmi. We were unsure until a few moments ago whether you were going to join us. The future is so cloudy when it comes to your part in things."

"I'm not going to see the Pymmie, right?" asked the woman.

"No. Not yet."

"What is this dream I keep having about killing this unicorn?" she asked.

"I had the vision as well. In the Sixian parrot," added Gary. "Only in my vision I was killing her."

Lady Nashita dropped the woman's hand.

"That is a critical moment in the future. It determines the course of so much that is going to occur afterward. As you both saw, one of you is going to take the life of the other. What is still unclear is who will kill whom."

Gary and the woman looked at each other in disbelief. Neither appeared hostile toward the other. In fact, they were downright friendly for two people who didn't know each other before today.

Lady Nashita clapped to clear the tension in the air.

"But that's still a ways off. Today, you helped Gary out of the harvesting center and that was the first step toward a positive outcome for everyone. You have increased the chance of success by nearly thirteen per cent just by showing up. You have a lot of influence on what is to come."

"Thank you, I think," said the woman, looking completely perplexed. "What do I do now? Will I still have the dream?"

"You will have that dream... and others. They are a window into the choices you will encounter. My best advice is to examine those visions and carefully choose how to proceed. Your future is largely unwritten, Lakshmi Singh. I hope you make the best of it. Go back to your office and tell them you were released by the fugitive Gary Cobalt. They will accept your explanation. What happens after that is up to you."

Gary gave Singh a nod.

"Thank you for your assistance," he said.

"Sounds as if I'll be seeing you around," she replied.

"I look forward to it," he said, and Jenny saw a flash of expression on his face that she had only ever seen when he was with Cheryl Ann.

CHAPTER TWENTY-FIVE
Awakening

The cargo boxes pinged and Lady Nashita waved the Sisters toward the center line.

"Two minutes," Lady Nashita announced, beckoning Gary closer. "Come right up front, little Gary."

He took exception to being called "little" at a hundred and two years old, but he wasn't going to argue with the reverend mother.

The boxes chimed as the timers hit zero. The rigid plastic melted away, drooping like hot wax, and puddled in the grass. Tiny blue flowers sprouted where the liquid sank into the soil. A curious mix of Reason technology and Bala magic.

Beneath the boxes were two enormous stasis tubes. The readouts were too far for Gary to make out, but whatever was inside was much bigger than a human. The tubes pinged in unison. They hissed and vented coolant in white clouds. Everyone stepped back except the Sisters. The first tube burst open and the halves fell apart like a cracked eggshell. Gary looked up as the creature inside reared up on its two back hooves. It was his father, Findae Cobalt. Gary's breath caught in his throat.

"Is that a—" asked Jim. Lady Nashita shushed him.

The unicorn was as dark as obsidian and dotted with silver flecks like stars. His horn rose half a meter from the center of his head. He galloped around the remaining tubes, then came to a stop as the second tube fell to pieces. A white unicorn emerged. He stepped into the sunlight and looked directly at the assembled humans, several of whom did not meet his eyes.

The unicorns greeted each other with nods and nuzzles, clearly relieved to have arrived at their destination. It took a moment for them to notice Gary, but when they did a stillness came over them both. Gary stepped toward the dark one. There were a thousand things he wanted to say, but all of them seemed wrong, not enough.

"Hi Dad," he said, feeling as if he was a child again.

"Gary." Findae brought his head close and Gary rested his cheek on his father's muscular neck. It was still cold and damp from stasis, but it made Gary want to cry.

"I thought you were dead," Gary said, stepping back and suddenly feeling quite underdressed without his own horn.

"That is the story we sent into the world," said Findae. The white unicorn trotted up to them.

"Unamip. It is an honor to see you again," said Gary, bowing low. Jenny's mouth dropped open. Unamip turned to her, staring at her from the side with one large eye.

"You did not think that I was real," he said.

"I thought…" She trailed off. "I mean, I tried…"

"Don't worry. I know what's in your heart," said Unamip, with a knowing smile. Gary couldn't tell if it was a warning or a consolation, but Jenny looked aghast.

Lady Nashita stepped forward and waited to be recognized. Findae walked over and shook out his mane.

"My lord, I am Lady Nashita Naveen, Reverend Mother of the Sisters of the Supersymmetrical Axion." She bowed to him.

"Nash. When last I visited the abbey, you were one of the newest Sisters, and a terrible one at that." A Sister behind them snickered. "It's good to see that you have kept the order strong." He nodded to the assembled Sisters, who also offered their respects.

"Indeed, my lord. I remember your visit," Lady Nashita replied.

He chuckled, and the hair on Gary's arms stood on end. There was an ominous quality in that laugh. A caution that he'd heard many times as a child.

"I imagine you would remember. Did they ever rebuild that section of the castle?" asked Findae.

"No. It remains in ruins as a reminder of my folly and a warning to others who might follow in my footsteps," replied Lady Nashita, with far more glee than the words seemed to merit. She looked downright pleased.

"You are not the only cautionary tale here today," said Unamip, turning to Jim, who looked up defiantly.

"My lord, the Sisters are at your service. We are prepared to escort you and the other invited guests to the Summit," said Lady Nashita.

Gary's father seemed to notice their surroundings for the first time.

"How they've changed our world," said Findae. "A river used to run through here. Are the others here yet?"

"There are no others. All are captured or deceased except you two. And Gary." It was a kindness for Lady Nashita to include him in the count.

"Humans always think they're the center of the universe," said Findae, letting out an outraged snort that reverberated throughout the stadium.

"I fear this will not go well for humankind," said Unamip. "Let us proceed to the Summit." He reared up and galloped toward the exit. Findae followed at a trot so the bipeds and Jenny in her chair could keep up. Gary walked at his side just like he had a thousand times before. It was as if the years had never passed.

"Dad, I want to introduce you to someone," Gary said, waving Jenny to come up next to him.

"This is Jenny. Jenny, this is my father Findae."

"Kia ora… sir." Jenny raised a hand in an unconvincing wave. His father sniffed her hair.

"There's enough of my son's blood in you to make an entire unicorn," he said, disapprovingly.

"Stop," Gary interrupted before his father could go further. "I gave it to her. Humans are fragile, as I'm sure you recall."

"And how do you know each other?" asked Findae.

Jenny took a big breath.

"Well, first I shot your son in the chest, and then I held him captive for two years so I could use his horn, and then I had him arrested for murder, and then I got him caught and taken to a harvesting center."

"And I ate Jenny's best friend, turned her co-pilot against her, and I'm leading her to a meeting with the Pymmie which will probably lead to some kind of retribution for her entire species," said Gary.

"Oh, you found your sense of humor, mate," said Jenny approvingly.

Unamip laughed. "Gary, you've made a friend. Your mother would be proud."

"It only took a hundred years," said Gary.

Unamip bent down to nibble at the foliage.

"Why is this grass so short?" he demanded.

Jim stood behind Jenny. The still-unlit cigarette hung from his lips. He didn't look the least bit interested in meeting the two unicorns, particularly after the look Unamip had given him. Gary made a cursory introduction.

"Everyone, this is Jim."

Jim leaned away as Gary's father craned his neck over Jenny toward him.

"You are James Bryant," Findae said.

"Your son ate my wife," complained Jim, waving his homemade cigarette and dropping tobacco leaves all over Jenny and the king of the unicorns.

Lady Nashita clapped her hands as if bringing a class of school children to order. "Time to proceed, everyone. Two lines. Sisters in the front and back for protection."

Jim stepped to the sidelines, watching the group form up. Lady Nashita called to him. "You also."

"I'm not going to that circus," said Jim. Jenny moved closer and sat up straight as if she had something to say. She reached up and slapped him. Jim held his face. His mouth dropped open as if he'd been shot. Kaila gasped.

"You're going and you will behave yourself, or God help me I will end you," said Jenny.

"I will not help you," said Unamip, through a mouth full of grass bits.

"First Gary hit me, now you hit me. I see how it is around here," said Jim.

"Now, everyone. Please. No violence necessary. Get in line. There will be snacks," called Lady Nashita.

Jim followed, but he trailed everyone, even the Sisters. No one bothered to move him. It was not as if he needed protection from the Reason.

They walked out of the stadium like a funeral procession. Those who spoke did so in hushed voices. As they came into the open street, officers and civilians stopped to watch. Bystanders who were familiar with the Sisters were easy to spot. They backed away slowly or fled the area entirely.

As they walked, the crowd swelled. People called their friends to come out and see the strange group walking down the main road. Most of them had never seen a full unicorn with an attached horn in their lifetime – at least not one that wasn't attached to an FTL drive. As more humans gathered, they became bolder, yelling at the party as they passed. Gary was surprised that no one tried to cut off his father's or Unamip's horns. There was enough energy there to power several dozen FTL ships for years.

Kaila bent down and whispered something to Jenny, who nodded. Kaila stepped behind the wooden wheelchair and began to push, resting her longest fronds on Jenny's shoulders. An empty bottle sailed into the street and shattered in front of the group.

"Can you make us invisible or something?" asked Jenny.

"You are safe with us," said Findae.

The Sisters kept onlookers at a distance as the group walked through the crowded streets. Rescue sirens blared from the direction of the harvesting center. A couple of the Sisters peeled off from the group and returned a few minutes later soaked with sweat and blood in various colors. They passed hand signals between themselves and continued walking in silent formation.

The street sounds shifted slightly, from excited chatter to terrified screams. The Sisters tightened their blockade. The human crowds parted as the redworm came tearing down the street, dribbling acid onto the pavement.

"I like this redworm. She reminds me of your wife," Lady Nashita called to Findae.

"How so?" the unicorn asked incredulously.

"She eats like crazy and brings down every obstacle in her path."

Findae snorted.

Gary wondered about Lady Nashita's actual age. His mother had died in what passed for middle age in humans almost seventy years ago. He guessed Lady Nashita would not have been born yet, but she spoke as if they were contemporaries.

One of the Sisters broke away and walked into the street, planting herself directly in the path of the worm. Humans and Bala streamed past her like water. She extended her hands out from her sides. The group stopped behind her.

The redworm zigzagged down the street, crashing into windows on one side and then veering back in the other direction. It spotted an easy target standing still in the center of the road and headed straight for her. Gary held his breath.

The Sister shouted a series of sounds that were somewhere between words and a song. Her body stretched and morphed into a five-meter redworm. She swayed in front of the worm and let out a bloodcurdling screech. The first redworm stopped short. It pointed its mouth hole at the newcomer and spat a wad of acid that sizzled on the pavement. The transformed Sister continued to sway and spat her own gob of acid. It sat there, inert. The redworm let out a roar, then lay down in front of the Sister.

"Move out," said the tall Sister at the front. They continued on toward the Summit.

"Will they fight?" asked Gary. The tall Sister turned around.

"She made herself into a potential mate. The worm will be completely absorbed in watching her until she indicates that she's ready for sex."

"I feel you, redworm," Jenny said, with a laugh. Kaila smacked her playfully on the top of the head.

"Ow, not there. I got shot. Twice," said Jenny.

The Sisters routed everyone around the worm. They had hardly moved twenty paces when another dryad covered in papery white bark held his branches out to block their path. Birches were known to be aggressive, and those who'd spent time in harvesting were rumored to have developed a taste for blood. Kaila ducked behind Jenny's chair.

"That's Litvin and he's mean," she whispered.

The birch reached out to grasp one of the forward Sisters. She unsheathed a knife and sliced off the end of his branch. He howled and drew it back, but did not move out of their way.

"Move it, birch, or I'll weave a basket from your limbs," said one Sister.

A second Sister held out a fireball in her palm. Gary couldn't tell if it was Bala fire or not. The birch threw out a low branch, trying to trip her up. She hopped up onto the branch and ran at him up the wood, landing at the top of his canopy. Fireballs rained down into his leaves. He tried to pull her off, whipping at her neck and shoulders with flexible fronds. Other Sisters pulled out weapons and took aim at his thicker branches. An arrow stuck into his trunk, oozing sap down the papery bark. The Sister perched on top of the birch found what she was looking for and started pulling.

"There go your memories of your parents." She tossed a flower over her shoulder. "And the name of your first love." A second flower went over her head onto the road.

"Stop," he cried, waving his branches frantically. "Please stop."

The Sister paused mid-pull. She looked to another Sister, who nodded, and then she hopped down onto the road.

"You may pass, birch, but don't let me catch you accosting anyone again," she said. He apologized and waddled down the street, trailing broken and singed leaves behind him. The procession walked past a landing platform surrounded by armed soldiers. The ship that perched on it was spindly and tall. Some of the spindles had broken off in the planet's gravity and come crashing to the ground. Soldiers scattered every time one started to sway. This ship was not designed to enter an atmosphere.

"I've never seen a ship like that," said Jenny. Gary's father slowed to match her pace.

"Those are the Winsok. They live in the farthest edges of Bala space. Fragile things that keep to themselves. Their bodies are prone to breaking in planets with gravity and strong winds. I'm surprised they decided to come."

A Reason tank drove up to the Winsok ship and stopped. The driver popped her head out of the top and shouted into her loudspeaker.

"Come out with your hands up," she said. "Or your tentacles, or whatever you have."

A spindle snapped with a crack and came crashing down onto the tank. The driver took cover. Shards flew through the gate area, spearing a soldier in the leg. Two others ran for him as he went down screaming.

"Another one of those projectiles will be considered an act of aggression," announced the soldier, speaking from the protection of the tank.

"They're not doing it on purpose," said Unamip.

"It doesn't matter," said Findae. "The humans will shoot regardless."

The door to the ship opened and fell off into the dirt. A dozen delicate creatures with urchin-like spines tumbled out behind it. Another spindle cracked and the Reason soldiers opened fire. The Winsok bodies shattered like glass. Their ship collapsed on top of them in a pile of jagged shards.

"Guess the Winsok will be late to the party," said Jim, picking his teeth with a stick that looked suspiciously like one of Kaila's smaller branches. If Jenny had been in nullspace, Jim would have been a smoldering wreck.

"He is intolerable," said Findae, speeding up to walk next to Gary. "But I imagine you know that already."

"He's had a difficult life."

"Haven't we all," mused Findae.

He looked older than when Gary had seen him last, which was odd, given the lengthy life span of unicorns. His spine sagged and spots on his flank were bare from the rubbing of straps and bridles. It pained him to think of his father pulling carts. Findae followed his gaze.

"I was the household unicorn for a wealthy family for a time before stasis. They were not intentionally unkind, but I was treated like a pet. They ignored me, even when I spoke to them. It was both luxurious and terrible. But I'm sure your time in prison was far worse than anything I endured."

"It was not pleasant, but there were times when I had quiet moments to think. When others slept and no one was attacking."

"And what did you learn in those moments?"

"That I am far from the man I wish to be. That humans, at their core, are neither good nor evil, but genuinely afraid of everything they encounter. They crave familiarity and security and pleasure. They can hardly go a moment without self-gratification."

"Indeed."

They turned the corner to a huge "Welcome Delegates!" sign hung across the road. Befitting the current bureaucratic climate, that hospitality was only being extended to human envoys from Reason-controlled planets.

Findae was quiet for an entire city block.

"I had hoped these people would see you for the man you are," he said, finally.

Another empty bottle sailed out of the celebrating crowd and hit Gary in the head. He was dazed for a second, then fine.

"I believe they already do," he said.

The Reason had chosen the base conference center for the location of the Summit. Banners representing every Reason planet and station hung on the walls of the brutalist building. Bala banners were conspicuously absent.

"Such a warm welcome. I feel right at home," said Findae. He'd picked up a love for sarcasm from Gary's mother.

At the entrance to the building, a pair of soldiers trained

their firearms on the group. Lady Nashita stepped forward, hands raised and visible.

"I'd like to know why you've chosen to point your weapon at me and my guests," she said.

"Ma'am, all unidentified persons must be processed."

"Indeed, yes. Processed like bad cheese. You'll find my paperwork quite in order."

"What's your name?"

"Lady Nashita Naveen, Reverend Mother of the Sisters of the Supersymmetrical Axion."

The soldier scanned down the names on his tablet, slowly turning beet red.

"You're on the list, but your horses have to wait outside," he said.

Findae bent his head so the sharp tip of his horn brushed against the man's uniform jacket.

"Call me a horse again," he growled.

"Place your finger here please, ma'am please," the soldier stammered, stepping back and holding the tablet out as far as he could.

Lady Nashita walked past and the group followed into the building. The lobby was cavernous and sparsely furnished. Hooves clopped on the marble floor. A sign posted at the entrance said that the WELCOME PARTY COCKTAIL HOUR would be taking place on the roof. Lady Nashita looked perplexed.

"I'm sorry, this is awkward, but I should have guessed they wouldn't prepare for any Bala guests. We'll have to split up to take the elevators," she said, counting them off in small groups. Gary was assigned to ride with Unamip, Kaila, and Jenny. The doors pinged open and Unamip walked in and turned himself around. Kaila pushed Jenny in and did the same. Gary squeezed into the corner. Lady Nashita reached in and pushed the button for the roof.

"Have a good ride!" she said.

The doors closed and wordless music drifted over them.

"Have you ever attended a Summit?" Unamip asked Jenny.

Her brow furrowed. "They're once every hundred years," she said.

Unamip didn't seem to understand.

"I'm only forty-five years old," she said.

Unamip looked at Gary in horror. "No wonder they make so many mistakes, they're practically babies." He leaned down to Jenny conspiratorially. "Summits are great fun. The Pymmie arrive and ask everyone questions, then there is cake. It is delightful." His face darkened. "Except you never quite know what kind of mood the Pymmie are going to be in. The last time they came for a visit, they foisted humankind onto us."

"Are you really the Unamip that lives in the nullspace orb?" asked Kaila.

"That is one of the places I inhabit," replied Unamip.

"I prayed to you a couple of times," said Jenny. "For my wife's safety." She patted a thin branch on her shoulder. "I got her back today. Thanks for that."

"I don't grant the prayers. I simply hear them and pass them up the line. Like triage," said Unamip.

"Did you pass mine up?" asked Jenny, which was a rather impertinent question to ask a demigod.

"Definitely. Yours were often quite selfless and heartfelt," said Unamip.

The elevator doors opened and they stepped out into the blazing Jaisalmer heat. Even the black tar roof felt sticky.

"It wasn't this hot on the street," said Jenny, fanning her face. She looked up and ducked into her chair. An immense dragon hovered above the building, billowing fire above the heads of everyone assembled.

CHAPTER TWENTY-SIX
The Century Summit

The dragon was the size of a troop carrier. Jenny shoved Kaila to the ground and crouched in her chair. Jim stumbled to his knees. Everyone else hit the deck then lifted their heads to stare. Not least because the fire seemed to be coming out of the dragon's ass.

The dragon ship pointed itself toward the sky, then eased down onto the roof rear end first. People scattered to make room. Smoke and coolant fogged the roof. Jenny heard the hiss of an airlock door. A pair of figures stepped out of the dissipating mist. They were grey bipeds, tiny like human children, but with dark oversized eyes that you couldn't look into without feeling a deep existential dread.

"The Pymmie like to make an entrance," said Gary, helping Kaila to her feet.

"It's a ship," said Jim from the ground, rubbing his knees.

"It's not as if dragons are real," said Gary.

"Of course not, that would be absurd," said Jenny, rolling her eyes. "Not at all like arriving on a distant planet to find unicorns."

Lady Nashita came back to check on them.

"Everyone all right? No one hurt? Good. The Pymmie are waiting. Come." She ran off toward Findae and Unamip who were conferring quietly near the dragon ship. Jenny maneuvered her chair across the sticky tar. Kaila offered to push, but Jenny waved her away.

"I've got it now, Sap."

As they passed near Unamip, the unicorn leaned close to Jim and narrowed his eyes. "I voted for you last time. Don't expect me to make that mistake twice."

"What does that mean?" Jim asked. Unamip turned away with a whinny and waited for the Pymmie to descend from their ship. One of the two Pymmie took a step down onto the ramp.

"Who has come to represent the Bala?" asked the Pymmie. Their high voice carried past the roof, out into the city.

The pair of unicorns stepped forward.

"We have come," said Findae.

"I am Commander General of the Reason Space Force," said a man whose uniform was covered in colorful ribbons and pins. He pushed through the crowd, tilting Jenny's chair precariously as he shoved his way toward the ship. She smacked his hand away from her armrest. The Pymmie looked down at him.

"We did not ask for the human representative yet," said the other Pymmie, with a voice like sandpaper. They lifted a hand and the commander flew back into the crowd. A patter of gunfire ricocheted off the dragon ship. The Reason had snipers on the surrounding rooftops and they had opened fire at the attack on the commander general. The Pymmie were not amused. They raised their hands in unison and around Jenny time stopped.

Sniper bullets hovered mid-trajectory above her head. The Reason soldiers standing around the perimeter of the roof had frozen in the midst of pulling out their service weapons. Dignitaries were stuck as they ducked at the sound of gunfire. She'd heard that the Pymmie were adept at controlling their environment, but she hadn't realized that included time itself. One of the Pymmie stepped down the ramp and into the crowd.

"Jenny, come with me. And Kaila too, of course." The Pymmie slipped a tiny hand into hers. She felt that odd sensation of an FTL jump, that *jumpy* energy that made her apprehensive.

"You too, Jim," said the Pymmie, though they didn't hold his hand.

A second Pymmie approached Gary.

"And, of course, Gary." They pulled him along by the hand as well. Both Pymmie stopped near the unicorns.

"Enough of them?" asked the first Pymmie.

"Enough," replied the second.

"The right ones came," said the first Pymmie.

"With the exception of one," replied the second.

"We'll speak to her later."

The Pymmie led their little group up the ramp and into the belly of the dragon. One of them got behind Jenny's chair and pushed, but she didn't dare protest. Only Kaila and omniscient beings were afforded that consideration. The unicorns followed after the humans. Lady Nashita waved from the roof.

"You're not coming?" called Jenny.

"We are only the escorts. You'll be safe inside. We'll be here when you come out." The Sisters were already standing on each other's shoulders, collecting bullets from out of the air and repositioning them around the rooftop.

The Pymmie pushed Jenny into their ship. The airlock was a small octagonal room lined with paintings. A woman with an umbrella. A man with his arms folded. Everyone packed into the tiny room, tails and manes swishing into faces. The door thudded shut.

"Welcome, foolish mortals..." began the first Pymmie. "There's no turning back now."

The room began to stretch higher, the portraits becoming longer. The new images revealed an alligator trying to snap off the umbrella woman's feet. And the man with folded arms was about to drown in quicksand.

"What in the hell?" said Jim. He tried to shove his way through everyone back toward the door, which was no longer there.

"This does not look good." Jenny grabbed her wheels and turned as well, snatching hold of Kaila's arm.

"Stop it," said the second Pymmie to the first. The lights came up and the sides of the room vanished. They were standing in a banquet hall – spacious and smelling like food. Jenny's stomach growled. She hadn't eaten since before they'd gone into FTL and she was starving. "I was merely trying to use Earth humor to lighten the tone of the meeting," said the first Pymmie. Jenny couldn't tell them apart.

"You're using humor from the wrong time period. That joke is a hundred and ninety-one years too old," said the second Pymmie.

"Ricky would have gotten it," said the first Pymmie, with the slightest petulance. "We should have asked her to come as well."

"Not yet," said the second Pymmie. "We'll need her next time. No more jokes."

"I only want them to understand that this can be fun. It doesn't *all* have to be devastatingly sad," the first Pymmie answered.

"It might have to be," said the second Pymmie, turning to the group. "Everyone, please join us at the table."

Jenny rolled up to a spot that seemed to have been prepared just for her. There was no chair, but at the place setting was a plate of what looked like her kuia's pork and pumpkin boil-up. She had to take a moment to compose herself as the scent of it hit her. Kaila sat on her left where there was a pot of rich, dark soil on the floor and a glass of water on the table. The unicorns went to open spots across from Jenny that had trays piled high with dormant trisicles. Jim sat at the foot of the table in front of a plate of golden, buttery grilled cheese sandwiches. After the Pymmie took their spots at the head of the table, there were two empty chairs left: one next to the unicorns and one next to Jenny. Gary stood undecided for a moment, then took the spot to Jenny's right, set with a pile of steaming samosa.

"Hmm," said the first Pymmie, watching with interest. She didn't know why, but Jenny felt better having Gary on her side of the table.

"To begin, introductions," the second Pymmie said. "We are the Pymmie."

"Well, not all of them. There are many more of us, but they're tending to the remainder of existence while we're otherwise occupied," said the first Pymmie, who turned back to the second one. "Do we want to be the brothers or the couple with the snake this time?"

The second Pymmie sighed and their enormous black eyes rolled upward.

"They're both so overdone."

"Then I know which ones we should be." The first Pymmie raised their spindly arms in an expansive gesture.

"I am Eon," they said.

"And I am Cole," added the second. "And who are each of you?"

Jenny thought the formality was odd. Given their omniscience, the Pymmie should have known everyone already.

"We like to ease into things," Eon said, answering the unspoken question in Jenny's thoughts.

"I am Findae. He of Reverberating Snort. King of the House of Cobalt," said Gary's father with the confidence of someone used to formal introductions.

"I am Unamip. He of Lengthy Strides. Father of the House of Azure," said Unamip.

Everyone waited for Gary to take his turn. He looked painfully uncomfortable.

"I'm Gary," said Gary.

"Say your full name," urged Findae. Gary looked like he wanted to disappear into the floor.

"I'm Gaganvihari Prancer Ramanathan. He of Two Worlds. Prince of the House of Cobalt."

"Prancer," chuckled Jim, a string of cheese stretching from his mouth to the sandwich in his hand.

It was Jenny's turn. She figured it couldn't hurt to play along.

"I am Geneva Waimarie. She of the Ngāi Tahu. House of Perata."

Heads nodded. She nudged Kaila, who was gulping water as fast as the glass refilled itself.

"Kaila of Salix, daughter of Gymnoverium," she said between mouthfuls.

"I'm Jim. From Wyoming," said Jim, biting into another sandwich.

"The rest of you, please eat," said Cole. The sound of crunching echoed off the walls as the unicorns dug into their piles of trisicles.

Jenny took a bite of her boil-up. The pumpkin was tender and sweet. It reminded her of Sunday afternoons with her family and friends.

"There's a reason they call it comfort food," said Eon, answering her thoughts again.

"Every civilization has the custom of gathering for meals during a time of crisis," added Cole.

"Is this a time of crisis?" asked Jenny.

"It will be soon," said Eon.

"Have some tea," said Cole, passing her a steaming cup with a delicate grey hand. She took it and sipped. It warmed her insides. Her muscles relaxed. It was probably drugged or made with magical ingredients to make her more calm and pliable.

"No, just tea," said Cole. "Shall we begin?"

Both unicorns began to speak at once. Eon raised a hand to quiet them.

"We would like to hear from Gary."

Gary looked up mid-bite.

"Yes?"

"We have convened to assess the human-Bala relationship over the last century," said Eon.

"You agreed to work together last time we checked in. How is it going?" asked Cole.

"You know how it's going," said Unamip, spitting a trisicle claw onto the table. "They've massacred us."

"You weren't all daisies and fireflies," said Jim. "We lost people too."

Unamip stepped back from the table, pounding his hooves on the floor. "We are not the ones enslaving hundreds of species. We fought you to stop the atrocities," he said.

"You have both had a hundred years to find a way to work together," said Cole.

"Humans are incapable of cooperation. They swarm through the universe, subjugating everything in their path. Even their own people," said Findae, with a glance at Jenny.

"I asked to hear from Gary," said Eon quietly, leaning toward his side of the table. "Based on your experience, are humans and Bala capable of living together peacefully?"

Gary let out a long breath. He looked from his father back to Jenny. She knew the answer just as well as he did, but it didn't make it any easier to hear out loud.

"No."

"That's fine," said Jim. "We'll just go our own way without you."

"The Human Experiment is approaching the two million year mark," said Eon. "It may be time to declare the outcome a failure." They looked to Cole.

Unamip let out a whinny that shook the water glasses. His nostrils flared. "I was there in the beginning, when the first humans stumbled across the face of their luscious Earth. They have it within them to coexist with others. They are simply in the adolescence of their evolution. Who among us hasn't laid waste to a civilization in a fit of poor judgment?"

"I sure haven't," said Jim.

"They are small and petty most of the time," continued Unamip, ignoring Jim. "But they are capable of immense kindness and self-sacrifice. At this very table sits a human who put herself in mortal danger so that seventeen others could survive. She offered a lifetime of pain in exchange for their lives."

"It didn't happen like that," said Jenny. Her face burned. She hated when people characterized her in terms of her sacrifice. She was just doing her job. So many angry feelings came bubbling up that she took a huge mouthful of hot tea and choked it down to drown them.

"Humans know how to live in peace," continued Unamip. "They know how to sacrifice for the good of all. Jim, your own wife offered her life in exchange for every other soul on the *Jaggery*."

"That asshole stole her life," said Jim, standing and pointing a finger at Gary. "We were only protecting ourselves from monsters like him. The necromancers who exploded our buddies' heads. The unicorns who ate our wives' bones. We have the right to protect ourselves from threats and right now you are our biggest threat."

"I'm curious," said Eon, "if you're aware of what happened

in Gary's room the day your wife died."

"Yeah. He ate her bones. I came in and she was a bag of skin on the floor. Case closed."

"We shall see," said Cole.

"Jenny, can you make us a flower," asked Eon. Jenny's heart skipped a beat when she realized what the Pymmie was asking.

"I can't just–" she began.

"I'm confident you'll find enough of what you call nullspace energy in this room for your purposes," said Eon.

Jenny gathered up the energy around her. They were right, the air was charged with immense power coming off both of the Pymmie. A yellow blossom emerged from the center of the wooden table. Kaila cooed over it and caressed a petal with her fronds. It looked like a larger version of her own flowers.

Unamip chuckled and sniffed at the flower that draped over their plates.

"What an interesting ability. Are you part Bala?" he asked.

"She is all human," said Eon.

"Very interesting indeed," agreed Findae.

Jenny was uncomfortable with all of the attention, but it felt good to grow the flower and release the pent-up pressure. Unamip sneezed.

"Bless you," said Gary.

"Bless us all," said Cole as the walls closed in on them, shrinking down to the size of a cabin on the *Jaggery*. They were in Gary's quarters, back when Jenny had the dwarves weld bars across the back half of the room and locked him in. Gary was pressed into a corner, seething with anger. His hair was long and slicked down with sweat. His eyes darted back and forth, wild with hunger.

A much younger Jenny sporting a ponytail sat in her old metal wheelchair on the other side of the cage. She'd pulled up close so her footrests hit the bars.

"I'll give you water if you tell me where to find the horn," she said. Her voice rasped as if she'd been yelling.

"Never," Gary growled. He stank of concentrated urine and sweat.

Jenny wrapped her hands around the metal and pulled herself as far forward as she could get, coming dangerously close to the furious man within. She put her face between a break in the bars.

"There are fifty-two souls on board this ship. We're in bad shape. We have no food, just like you. Water is nearly gone, even with recycling. You have to help me get the *Jaggery* out of here before we start losing people. Just let me know where you put your horn. Please."

He looked up at her with fiery hate.

"You steal my ship, abduct my crew, imprison me, and starve me nearly to death. Now you want me to hand over my only leverage in exchange for a sip of water? You are a sad excuse for a captain and it was only luck that brought you a win at Copernica."

"I'll let you out," she said. "Just tell me where to find your horn."

"You are a liar. I can see it in your face. You will never let me out of here. You will all be rotting, stinking corpses in the cargo hold before I hand over my horn."

Jenny backed away from the bars and turned to adjust herself in the chair. Gary flung himself across the cell in a flash, reaching for her ponytail. He grasped it and slammed her head against the bars. She screeched and clawed at his hands as he reached his other arm through and put his forearm across her neck.

"I will kill you, then I will eat you, and then I will murder every single human on board," he hissed into her ear. She fumbled in her jumpsuit, searching for a weapon.

"Gary!" said Cheryl Ann in the doorway. He looked up and the anger drained from his face. He let go of Jenny and she hit the floor in front of his cage with a grunt. Cheryl Ann helped her back into her chair.

"You all right, hon?" asked Cheryl Ann, running her hand along the back of Jenny's head.

"I'm fine," said Jenny, rubbing her neck.

"Hey, there's a problem with the pressurization in the cargo hold," said Cheryl Ann. "I tried to run diagnostics, but the tablet isn't getting the right readings. I think you'll need to wire it up directly to the Bala controls in the hold and get the readings there. I'd do it myself, but you're much better at electronics than I am."

Jenny nodded.

"Yeah, sure. I'll go check it out." She kept talking as she rolled out of the room. "Go ahead and keep holding out on us, you wanker. And when everyone out here is dead and you find yourself stuck in this cell until the end of your long, long life, you can think back to this moment when I offered you freedom in exchange for your horn." She slammed the door on her way out.

Cheryl Ann sat down cross-legged on the floor near the bars, unafraid. She was gaunt and her cheeks were sunken from dehydration. Her hands shook as she rubbed them together as if trying to get warm. She spoke in breathy little gasps. Gary moved closer to hear her.

"Jenny's right, you know. It's bad. Jim is wasting away in front of me. And it's not just the food and water. The redworms are coming closer every day. This morning they got within five kilometers before turning. I thought we were done," she said.

"Let me out and I'll help you outrun the worms," he said, sticking his arm through the bars. She was still slightly out of his reach. "No one can pilot this ship like I can."

"No, Gary. You need to give us fuel. We're stuck out here. Dead in the water with the lights off. No planets within a billion kilometers of here. We need something. The tiniest shaving would do."

He leaned his head down and she looked into the crater in his skull.

"I have nothing. Jenny dug down deep into the bone already. There's nothing left. Have you found any trisicles yet?" he asked.

"No," she said. "Give me your horn. It's time. I know you don't want Jenny to win, but people are going to die. Jim can't get out of bed. He doesn't make sense when he talks. Jenny told me to think about saying goodbye." She said the last part so quietly that even in the silent room Gary had to strain to hear her.

"I told you the truth. I don't know where to find my horn. My mother hid it so I would be safe," he said.

Cheryl Ann put her face into her hands and sobbed. Her shoulders heaved and she made noise, but when she lifted her head, her face was dry.

"Then we're all dead, Gary."

"I'm sorry. I don't know how to help."

Cheryl Ann pulled a knife out of her boot and unsheathed it.

"I told you, there's nothing left. You can dig if you want." He riffled his hair. The crater in the center was empty and crusted with dried blood.

Cheryl Ann rested the knife in her lap.

"Jim's going to be the first one to go. I don't think he has more than half a day left. And when he's gone they're going to feed him to you so you can get us out of here. And I know that's the right thing to do, but I can't live with myself knowing that I did nothing and just let him die."

She scooted back away from the bars and pushed the knife

into her arm, then dragged it upward. Gary threw himself against the bars, reaching for the knife.

"What are you doing? Stop!" he cried.

Blood dripped onto the floor – thick and dark. Cheryl Ann's nose crinkled as if she smelled something bad. She bit her lip.

"It's not so bad," she said, her hand shaking so hard that she dropped the knife to the floor with a clatter. Gary strained to reach it, but it was too far.

"I can get a shaving for you," he said. "Just stop. Give me your arm, Cheryl Ann. We can still fix this."

She flexed her fingers and the blood dripped faster.

"Yeah," she said. "That'll work."

"Cheryl Ann, come over here. You don't need to do this. We'll find another way. We'll find my horn together. Just move a little closer."

He pushed himself through the bars as far as he could go, getting his shoulder most of the way through, but she was beyond his reach.

"Cheryl Ann, stop now and no one will know. We can still fix this. Just come here. Please."

"He has to live," she said, as she tried to pick up the knife with her cut arm. She'd severed tendons and it fell back down. She picked it up with her good hand. She laughed, a high and giddy sound.

"I can't do it." She looked up at him and a moment of panic flashed across her face.

"Give me the knife. Please." He extended his palm.

"Jenny's going to be back pretty soon. When she finds me, you tell her to look in my top pocket. There's a note about what I want. You make them do it, Gary. Promise me you'll make them."

"No, I don't promise. You have to tell them yourself," he said.

"I'm so sorry. You have to trust me, bud."

She held the knife up to the side of her throat and pushed. It was sharp enough to pop through the skin. She jumped and dropped it. Blood poured down onto her jumpsuit.

"Oh," she said, ineffectually trying to cover the wound with her hand.

Gary threw himself into the bars over and over, yelling her name, demanding that she stop. He called for Jenny and Jim. He called for Boges. No one came.

"I'm scared, Gary," said Cheryl Ann, eyes wide. Gary stretched his fingers into the empty air between them.

"Good. That's good. All of this can be undone. There's still time," he said.

"I love you," she said, making a drunken smile at him.

"I love you, too. Please come here."

"Help my Jimmy. Save them all."

She put her head down on the floor. Her hair fell into the spreading puddle of blood. She closed her eyes.

"Wake up, Cheryl Ann. Please wake up. Jim! Jenny! Anyone!"

He reached for her. Pushing so hard that his shoulder came out of its socket, then popped back into place.

He called to her several more times, begging her to come closer, until she stopped moving. He sobbed against the bars, telling her he was sorry over and over until the minutes stretched to hours. The blood on the floor became tacky.

The door opened and Jenny wheeled back into Gary's room.

"Cheryl Ann, there's no problem with the pressurization. I ran through all the diagn–"

She stared at the body on the floor.

"What the bloody hell did you do?" she asked, her fingers covering her mouth in horror.

Jenny wheeled up to her best friend and pushed herself

onto the floor. Blood soaked into her jumpsuit. She pulled Cheryl Ann up and felt for a pulse.

"Baby, wake up."

"She did this," said Gary. "She wanted to save Jim and the rest of you."

"Shut up," yelled Jenny, setting Cheryl Ann down and starting chest compressions. Gary talked over her counting.

"She's been gone since you left. You're not going to get her back," he said. "There's a note in her pocket for you."

Jenny kept pushing on Cheryl Ann's chest.

"She's been gone for hours," he said, louder.

"Fuck off," Jenny said between puffs into Cheryl Ann's mouth.

She worked until her arms were sore and Cheryl Ann's ribs crunched under her fingers with every compression.

"Stop." It was that commanding unicorn voice again. Jenny let her hands drop. She picked up the knife and reached through the bars for Gary's arm.

"You can heal her. Give me your hand. You can bring her back."

"Not now. It's too late. It wouldn't be her any more."

Jenny dropped the knife and covered her mouth again with a bloody hand.

"She left you a note. In her pocket," said Gary.

Jenny carefully opened the flap of Cheryl Ann's jumpsuit pocket and pulled out a note. She read it and dropped the paper as if it had burned her.

"She wants me to let you eat her bones," she said. They were both quiet for a long time before Jenny spoke again. "Will they be enough to get us back to an inhabited planet?"

"Yes." Gary leaned back against the wall of the cell and closed his eyes.

"It will kill Jim to know that she did this to save him," said Jenny. "It will break him."

"He doesn't have to know," said Gary. "It can be my gift to her."

"They'll put you in jail," said Jenny. "The bad one, back on Earth."

"I'd do it for her," he replied.

Jenny folded the note and slid it into her pocket, then pushed Cheryl Ann's body closer to the bars. She rested a hand on her friend's face and ran a thumb across her cheek. "Bye, bud." Gary made a snorting sound that might have been a sob. By the time Jenny had climbed back into her chair, the hard veneer of captain had come back down over her face. "Do it fast, before Jim comes in and finds her like this. I'll try to stop him from coming for you until you can grow some horn." She wheeled out of the room.

Gary wrapped his arms around Cheryl Ann through the bars and buried his head in her hair. He cried over her for a minute, then lifted her arm and bit down with a crunch.

The memory faded. Jenny had listened to the scene unfold with her head down on the table. She didn't need to see it again. She'd been there. Around the table she heard sniffles and coughs. Fingers snaked through her hair. For half a second she thought someone was trying to comfort her. Then the fingers yanked up and pulled her off the table.

"You gave her to him," hissed Jim, barely an inch from her face. Gary was up in a flash, but he couldn't disentangle Jim's fingers from Jenny's hair fast enough. Kaila whipped her branches at him as well, but Jim slammed Jenny's face down onto the table before anyone could stop him. Bits of cooked pumpkin and blood came out of her nose. She coughed and clawed at his hands. The Pymmie lifted their arms and Jim collapsed to the floor.

Eon slid over and put their hands on Jenny's cheeks. Her throbbing face was immediately fine. They gave her a pat on the cheek and bent to kneel next to Jim, who was curled up on the floor.

"All I ever wanted was my Cheryl Ann," he said. Eon rested a hand on him and he quieted.

"Will you sit without harming anyone else?" Eon asked.

"Yeah." Jim crawled into his chair, subdued.

Jenny felt sick. She was tired of fighting. Her heart pounded so hard that she heard the whoosh of blood in her eardrums. Kaila rubbed her back. Gary looked pale and tired. She wanted to climb into bed and sleep forever.

"Dear Jenny, who has shown so much strength in the face of adversity, you love both Bala and humans with the breadth of an ocean. What do you say to the question? Can humans live in cooperation with others?" asked Cole.

Jenny rubbed her forehead. She sensed the weight of the question and everything that rested on the answer. She wanted to assure them that they should get another chance, but after Copernica, and Cheryl Ann, Jim and Gary, and Kaila, she couldn't lie to the Pymmie.

"No." She flicked bits of bloody pumpkin off her face. "We can't."

Findae let out a great sigh.

"Is this some kind of Judgment Day?" asked Jim.

"Some kind of that," said Cole.

"And we've been found wanting," Jim continued.

"Most certainly," said Unamip.

"We must choose the right remedy for the ills of man," said Eon.

"Exceptions notwithstanding, the best option is to simply eradicate humans from the universe. They're a scourge," said Unamip, as if he'd proposed something as simple as taking out the trash.

"Then we would be as guilty as them, committing genocide with a flick of a Pymmie wrist," said Findae.

"No one is safe with even one human in existence," said Unamip. "Apologies, Jenny, but you know it's true. They multiply past the ability of their habitat to sustain them. Then they fan out and subsume everything they encounter. I have heard one hundred years of desperate Bala prayers begging for respite from the humans. I can catalogue them all if you like. They fall under six main categories."

"That won't be necessary," said Cole.

"I have a proposal," said Gary. All heads turned toward him. "Most Bala worlds have been overrun and stripped of their resources. Exterminating humans will not bring back our clean water or our fertile farmlands. The Bala need a new world upon which to start again. Humans can stay here and reap what they have sown."

"Fine by me," said Jim. "Get out of here."

"And what about the mixed families?" asked Jenny.

"Not one single human can be allowed on our new world," said Unamip. "They will infect it with their avarice."

"You're going to tear families apart. If those are the rules, Kaila can go with you but I have to stay." Jenny dug her nails into the wood of her armrests.

"It's a regrettable consequence of your decisions. You're not exactly blameless yourself," said Unamip.

"Kaila and I opt out. We'll just take our ship and fly into openspace. You'll never hear from us again," said Jenny, pushing herself away from the table.

"I'm afraid that is not one of the options," said Cole.

"I don't want to go," said Kaila, wrapping her branches around Jenny. "Don't make me leave."

Jenny wheeled herself away from the table, dragging Kaila with her.

"I'm not participating in this. What I said before, I take it back. I didn't understand what you were asking," she said.

"It's cruel to ask you to give more, isn't it?" asked Eon.

"But you have been trying to think of a way to make amends," said Cole.

"And this is it," finished Eon, resting an iridescent gray hand over hers. Jenny burst into tears.

"This is not what I meant," said Jenny, wiping her face with the flat of her hand. "It's too hard. It's not fair. I just got her back."

Eon leaned down and whispered in her ear. The sound was like a wind through the branches of a dead tree. "Then you will have to find her."

Jenny looked into Eon's gigantic black eyes and saw the future stretch before her. The Pymmie were to bring the Bala to a lush and fertile planet far across the universe. There was no way she could stop them. The Reason would be in ruins without Bala magic and free labor. She would take her new ship and go find Kaila's new world, but other humans would race her to find it first.

She pulled herself away from those endless eyes that offered to show her everything. Her anger was gone, replaced by disorientation. Kaila tried to pull her away.

"Don't let them take me," she squealed. Jenny took her hand.

"I can't stop them, but I will find you," she said.

"What about the mixed children of humans and Bala?" asked Findae.

"They should be allowed to choose," said Gary.

"And Gary, as one of those children, would you choose to go to this new world or remain with the humans?" asked Cole.

"I would go," he said, without hesitation. It hurt Jenny's heart to hear it, but she understood. She wished she could join them. A new world and a fresh start sounded incredible right about now.

"Allowing every partial Bala to choose is not practical,"

said Cole. Jenny doubted that was true. Eon turned to her.

"It's not difficult for us, but there will be those who refuse to choose and too many exceptions. Better to simply move any being with Bala ancestry."

"And our ships?" asked Gary.

"Good goddamn, leave us with some way to get around the system," said Jim. "We'll be trapped."

"Bala ships will go with Bala, as will their fuel," said Cole.

Which meant horns. Unicorn horns would be gone, leaving humans stranded wherever they happened to be when the Bala disappeared. Even if Jenny's new ship had an FTL drive, it would never work again.

"And all the spells and fixes that people use every day?" asked Jim. "Some people have surgically implanted Bala parts. People will die if they suddenly up and disappear." Jenny wondered if Jim had anything Bala implanted. He was certainly old enough to need some spare parts.

"Any Bala part or spell that resides within the body of a human will not be touched. All others will disappear," said Eon. The Pymmie held Jim's eyes a second longer than they needed to. There was some communication between the two of them that Jenny didn't understand. It gave her goosebumps.

"When will we leave?" asked Findae, pushing the trisicles around his plate.

"We will give them one of this planet's hours to say their goodbyes," said Cole. "Any longer puts the Bala in danger of organized retaliation."

Cole stood up to indicate the end of the meal. The food evaporated and the door to the ship opened. Everyone on the rooftop was still frozen in place. Not a nanosecond had passed since the group had left. Only Lady Nashita looked up from reading a tattered paperback to greet them.

"Well, that was productive," said Eon.

"On to the rest of the day's tasks," said Cole.

"Are there bigger items on your to-do list than condemning humankind to extinction?" asked Jim.

"Oh yes. You have no idea what the Opteryx are doing on the other side of the universe. If a black hole appears in the center of your planet, that's their doing. Give us a call. Unamip will pass the message along," said Eon.

"Who shall we be for the Opteryx?" asked Cole.

"Do you want to be the turtle? I'll be the elephant," offered Eon.

"I was the turtle last time," said Cole.

"I know, but I don't like being on the bottom," said Eon, offering a cheerful wave to everyone as they left the ship.

Unamip bowed to them and stepped into the sunlight.

Jenny wheeled down the ramp and onto the hot rooftop. She turned to ask one more question, but a billow of fire blasted her and she shielded herself with one arm. The dragon stretched its back and reached upward with two tiny limbs. It almost looked like a dinosaur with wings. The people around Jenny unfroze. Bullets continued their trajectory through the air, striking several Reason soldiers in their rear ends. The commander general was halfway through his rant.

"I demand admission to the Summit. I have been training for this day for six years–" The dragon whirled in the sky then headed into space, blasting fire out of its ass.

"They're leaving," yelled the commander general to all of the soldiers in his vicinity. "Stop them. Fire the flak cannons."

A series of dull thuds echoed from the tops of nearby buildings. The projectiles were invisible against the brightness of the sun, but Jenny could see the dragon ship turning backflips to avoid the missiles.

"They could just blink and be there," said Lady Nashita. "What a waste of time. Pymmie are always such showoffs."

As the Pymmie disappeared into a dot among the clouds, Reason officials conferred together on the roof. Jenny didn't have the heart to tell them they'd missed the Summit entirely. She pushed the elevator button, holding Kaila's hand but feeling strangely alone.

The unicorns joined them. When the doors pinged open, she waved them in first. "After you." There was essentially no room in the car after two full-sized unicorns wedged themselves in. "We'll wait for the next one."

"Nonsense," said Findae, pushing himself up against a wall. "There's room." She squeezed her chair between him and Unamip. Kaila pushed in behind her, sniffling. Their flanks were warm. She wanted to stay there and sleep.

Gary approached.

"Get on, Gary," called Unamip, pushing again to make room. Gary sidled in against Kaila. When Jim walked up, Unamip hit the door close button with his horn.

"Sorry, no room."

"Hey," said Gary. "Let him on."

Jim pushed himself up against the closing door, nearly pinching himself in it. He faced forward, not looking at anyone. The unicorns chatted in celebration, caught up in making plans.

"The dwarves will need to start building as soon as we arrive," said Unamip.

"Precisely. Basic longhouses at first, then individual residences once we have a detailed survey of the land," said Findae.

"As excited as you are, it might be kind to wait until you are out of earshot to talk about how wonderful your new lives will be," said Gary.

"I'm sorry," said Unamip. "Jenny, how are you feeling about all of this?"

"I'm feeling like such a weighty decision should have

taken years, not minutes," said Jenny, putting her head against Kaila's rough bark.

"I agree," said Kaila, patting Jenny's hair.

"This decision has been two million years in the making. How much longer would you like to prove yourselves?" replied Findae.

"We have proven ourselves," said Jim to the closed door. "We've proven that we're smarter and stronger and better at everything. And you Bala need the help of gods to even stay alive. It's survival of the fittest and we're the fittest. Don't come crying back to us when we own every planet in the galaxy except for your new crappy one."

The car was quiet until they reached the ground floor. Everyone spilled out of the elevator and into the lobby. Human dignitaries from all over Reasonspace fled the building. Some barked orders at soldiers, others looked genuinely frightened.

"Here's where I leave you," said Jim, walking away from the group across the lobby.

"That's it? After everything, you just walk away?" asked Jenny.

He turned back to her with a face like stone.

"What do you want from me? I know what it was meant to be like, but it all got screwed up. It's too late for me, but I wish you luck. I surely do that. Buena suerte."

He tipped an imaginary hat and tried to walk off into the sunset. Unamip galloped a few steps ahead to stand in the man's path.

"Enjoy the planets you stole from the Bala, James. Go find a quiet spot in the woods. Build a cabin and grow your cows. Spend the rest of your tiny little human life trying to cope with the knowledge that the love of your life never cared for you as much as she loved Gary."

Jim's shoulders sagged like a marionette with cut strings.

He walked out the front door and into the streets of Jaisalmer.

"That was really unnecessary," Jenny said to Unamip.

"Truly," said Findae.

Unamip shrugged, a strange thing to see on an equine body. "It was nothing compared to what the Bala have endured. Believe me, I have heard their desperate prayers for too long."

They walked out of the lobby and found themselves again in the midst of chaos. While they were in the Pymmie ship, the Sisters had apparently been up to some mischief in the city. People dangled from street signs and shopkeepers came outside screaming they'd been robbed. One of the Sisters had opened all of the doors to the resource harvesting center and creatures of all types rampaged throughout the streets. A neofelis cat chased a man down the sidewalk with her claws and teeth bared. She whistled and waved at Gary as she ran past. There were screams of "Redworm!" coming from around the corner. Even the unicorns looked worried.

"Let's get to the *Jaggery* before someone is hurt," said Findae. They cantered ahead.

"I'll come in a bit," called Gary.

"See that you do," said Findae, in a stern father voice.

Jenny and Kaila found a quiet spot on the sidewalk. Gary stayed nearby, waiting politely off to the side. Kaila wrapped her branches around Jenny, chittering incoherently.

"I'm not going... I'll hide with you... Bala can't... but when you do..."

"Hey, Sap?" Jenny said, putting her hands on the sides of Kaila's face. "The Pymmie let me see what's going to happen. You have to go. They're going to make you."

"No," whined Kaila.

"I know, but you'll be with Gary. He'll keep you safe until I get there."

"Sneak on board with us," pleaded Kaila, pulling her arms.

"No, Sap. It's just you guys. But I'll follow. I promise." She disentangled Kaila's fronds from around her.

She hated making promises like that, but it calmed Kaila. Gary stepped in.

"I'll be with you. Along with lots of other Bala. It'll be good. You'll see," he said. "And Jenny will come get you as fast as she can. If there's anyone who can find you, it's her."

Kaila bent down and pulled Jenny to her and they kissed as fighter jets scrambled overhead, shooting at a creature that had escaped the harvesting center a few storefronts away. The shots startled both of them and they ducked together.

"I love you, Jenny," said Kaila, pressing her rough forehead against Jenny's smooth one.

"I love you, Sap. Stay safe," said Jenny. Kaila let go and headed for the *Jaggery*.

"Wait for me. I'll walk you there. It's not safe on the streets today," called Gary.

"It never was," said Kaila, tucking herself against a building and going as still as a regular tree.

"You don't owe me some big goodbye," Jenny said to Gary. "I was terrible, so you can just leave. I understand."

She was startled when he leaned down and wrapped his arms around her. At first, she awkwardly patted his back. When he did not let go, she relaxed into his embrace.

"In one hundred years, you are my only friend," he said.

"I hope that's not true, because I was a terrible friend," she said into his cable-knit sweater.

He squeezed harder, then let go. She pushed her hair out of her face. The brisk wind on Jaisalmer fanned a fire at the end of the street. Embers blew over them, making pinpricks on their skin that were extinguished by sweat. She finally found the words she'd been searching for over the last few hours.

"I'm sorry. I wanted to make things right for you. But I can't bring back Cheryl Ann or give you back the time you lost in the Quag. The things I did... you didn't deserve that. I want to make it right, but I don't know what else to do." she said.

"Keep thinking about it and the next time we see each other, you can tell me what you decided," he said.

"It's a deal," she said, reaching up and scratching his growing beard. She blew Kaila one last kiss, then headed toward the screams. He called after her.

"Jenny?"

"Yeah."

"Life is going to become difficult very quickly in Reasonspace. Make sure you are far away soon."

"Thanks, Gary. Enjoy your new world."

CHAPTER TWENTY-SEVEN
FTL *Stagecoach Mary*

Jenny rolled down the side of the street, trying to steer clear of looters and Summit revelers who hadn't yet heard the news of the Bala's deliverance. She pushed herself toward her new ship's landing platform, staying off the main roads and avoiding piles of flaming trash and unconscious soldiers. The flak cannons still fired at regular intervals, taking down ships that were trying to abscond with Reason goods in the chaos.

Jenny wondered how the Pymmie planned to tell the Reason that they were being abandoned. Turns out, they'd simply sent an email. As a kicker, they'd put everyone in Reasonspace in the CC line. The enormous number of replies was crashing Reason servers everywhere. The out-of-office notifications alone were in the tens of billions. Her tablet was useless.

She stopped at a money machine and converted the Sisters' payment into as much cash as it would let her have. Then she headed for a supply depot and arranged for the Settler's Deluxe package to be delivered to her ship. It cost her double to have them drop it off within the hour, but it wouldn't be long before the street was choked with rioters.

She passed an alleyway where someone had set up an aluminum surplus tent. A cheer went up from the crowd inside the canvas. Jenny was about to pass by when a young soldier came running out and threw up at her feet.

The gray gel of her vomit was streaked with red. It cracked the pavement when it hit the ground and pulled the dust around it into concentric circles.

"Pie," gasped the soldier, wiping her mouth and feeling her teeth for cracks.

"Hang upside down to get it all out," said Jenny, pushing open the canvas door of the tent. She found a spot to park along the back wall.

"Righteous lads and ladies of Reason, Private Patel has lost the game!" Ricky spotted Jenny. "Ten minute break. Give your name to a server if you'd like your shot at the singularity pie. Everyone else, get your drink orders in now."

Ricky sauntered to the back of the room, tucking a wad of cash into her pocket.

"Nice setup," said Jenny.

"I've owned places worse than this," replied Ricky.

"I have plenty of room on my ship if you want a ride someplace," said Jenny.

"You know, I'd usually take you up on the offer, but I have a feeling some real estate is about to open up on this street in the next few hours," said Ricky. "You can make a lot of money off of desperate people."

"You love chaos," laughed Jenny.

"You know it," said Ricky.

"I'm heading out. Take care of yourself, Ricky," said Jenny.

"Hang on."

Ricky reached into the open suitcase on a table that was functioning as a bar. She handed Jenny a bottle.

"To christen your new ship. Just don't knock it against the hull. It'll eat through the steel."

"Can I even drink it?"

"Maybe!" said Ricky, turning back to her crowd of ten.

"Everyone say goodbye to Captain Jenny. While we drink away the Armageddon, she's off to fly among the stars."

"Bye, Captain Jenny," called a dozen drunk officers. Jenny tucked the bottle beside her in the chair. She rolled back out into the street just in time to see the *Jaggery* lift off. Cannons fired at its hull, scorching the pink blossom on its side and the white line above it. Even though there was no way any of them could see her, Jenny still lifted her hand to wave goodbye.

The streets were worse than ever. People smashed windows and ran away with as much as they could carry out of shops and homes. Gunfire sounded constantly from every direction and emergency services had stopped trying to control the fires and were instead trying to let them burn out on their own.

She arrived at her new ship, the FTL *Stagecoach Mary*, though it was hardly faster-than-light any more. It was a new small-complement transport ship – cheap but sturdy. Most importantly, it had autopilot and stasis pods for long journeys. It might take years, or decades, to find Kaila's new planet and she didn't plan on staying awake for most of the trip. She could simply tell it to canvass for habitable planets and wake her only when it found one with life.

She rode the lift up to the cargo hold and checked on her provisions. The Settler's Deluxe had pop up shelters, fire starting materials, MREs, and enough seeds and animals in stasis for fifty interplanetary colonists. It would be more than enough for one. She'd also picked up a basic backup wheelchair from a surplus shop. Where she was headed, it would be wise to have a spare.

The *Stagecoach Mary*'s cockpit was expansive compared to the *Jaggery*. Humans liked to put a dozen people on their starship bridges to sit and keep everyone busy while they watched the viewscreen. She rolled to the center of the room and transferred over to the captain's chair.

"Lay in a course heading for… the most distant habitable planet on Reason surveys," she said to the ship.

"Course laid in. FTL *Stagecoach Mary*, cleared for takeoff."

Jenny strapped herself in and pulled out the takeoff checklist.

"Would you like me to initiate launch?" asked a voice.

"One sec," said Jenny. "I'm Jenny Perata, your captain. What should I call you?" She'd never had an AI ship before. She wasn't sure how to talk to it.

"You can call me Mary," said the ship.

"Good. Mary, bump your sarcasm level by seventy percent and up your belligerence by the same. Enable profanity, change dialect to Kiwi, turn on autopilot, and push the crew risk profile up to maximum. And turn off scald protection on the showers."

"Fuck you, Captain."

"Belligerence down by thirty percent."

"Are you bloody well ready to leave?"

Jenny smiled.

"I am bloody well ready to leave, Mary."

Jenny was thrust back against her chair without warning. She would have laughed if she could have breathed. It took eight minutes to get out of Jaisalmer's atmosphere. Jenny kept the gravity off for old times' sake. She was still faster floating than walking.

The viewscreen changed from the blue morning sky to the darkness of orbit. She whispered toward the stars.

"I'm coming for you, Sap."

CHAPTER TWENTY-EIGHT
Will Penny Makes a Trade

Cowboy Jim walked the streets of Jaisalmer, stepping over bodies and crunching through broken glass. A kid with blood all over his face leaned out the broken display window of a storefront, reaching for him. Jim pulled away. There wasn't no good way to get blood out of the soft leather of his favorite coat.

"Buddy, please," said the kid. "Help."

"No change," said Jim. It was his standard reply to street people. Hands reached out of the busted-out window and dragged the kid back inside. He kicked and screamed, but it wasn't none of Jim's business. Besides, he had a mission that was feeling a mite critical right about now.

When the Bala filth disappeared, everyone had lost their goddamned minds. It mystified Jim and made him mad. This is what they'd all wanted, but no one seemed happy about it. Yeah, the street sweepers and manicurists and creatures who operated the sewage treatment plant were all gone, but there were always down-on-their-luck dudes who were willing to do grunt work like that. Lord knows he'd been one of them back in the day, shoveling manure for the cow nurses before he'd gotten some money to go off to engineering school.

Jim heard a familiar voice coming from a surplus tent down a deadend alley.

"Honored guests of this new establishment, I would like to offer you a gift for coming here on our grand opening. I have here one of the three sacred relics. This ring, once you put it on, will turn anything you touch to solid gold. You're not going to find anything like this on Jaisalmer. Especially not after today. Who wants to be the first to try?"

Jim's hackles stood on end. It was Ricky Tang, who was nothing but bad news. Jim turned his head away from the open door, but Ricky saw him anyway.

"Cowboy Jim! Come on in and try out the ring!" she called out. He shuffled over to the tent and poked his head inside. Ricky sidled up to him.

"After all we've been through, Jim. Why don't you give the ring a try?" She leaned close to whisper in his ear. "It's not turning things to real gold, but they won't notice until they sober up."

He pushed her away and she stumbled back, knocking into a chair.

"Don't you touch me. Freak." He leaned back toward her ear. She smelled like a particular flower that had been wiped off every planet in the system. It reminded him of the time he torched those greenhouses full of plants back on Earth. There wasn't no water on that planet for wasteful plants like flowers. "None of these boys know what you really are, but I do. One word from me and this joint vanishes."

Ricky looked surprised, then angry.

"You know, I deal with bigots like you every day of the week. I'm not afraid of you and I'm not ashamed of who I am, but a single word from you could get me killed and you know it. That's the only reason I will ever defer to you, asshole," she said, and turned to head toward the front of the room.

Jim paused. He only had to tell her secret to the uniformed boys and they would take her into custody. It was tempting.

He decided to hang onto his leverage for the moment. As far as he was concerned, there was a war coming up and he'd be smart to have some people in his back pocket.

An explosion rocked the building across the street. Jim pulled his hat low to block the dust raining down like snowflakes. People moaned in the rubble. Someone would come along to help them shortly. He had somewhere he needed to be.

The guard at the gate in front of Reason Command was adamant that he couldn't come in.

"Sir, we are in lockdown right now. I'm afraid I can't let you in for your appointment. You can reschedule with the regimental administrative officer."

"No," shouted Jim, poking his finger into the guy's chest. "I have something the colonel wants to see."

"I don't care if you have Lady Nashita's knickers, sir. You're not getting in today."

A civilian in a kitchen worker's uniform ran up to the gate and shoved Jim out of the way. The gate guard lifted his rifle and pointed it at the food stains on the cook's chest. A half-dozen uniformed soldiers hung back and waited.

"Please, sir. Let me in," said the cook. He lifted his hands to show that he was unarmed.

"Back away, sir," barked the guard.

"They're chasing me. They beat up the other guys on the line. Please."

"Back up or I will fire."

The guard stepped into the street, pushing the cook back toward the soldiers. Jim saw his opening. He slipped behind the guard and into Reason Command. He heard a shot behind him, but didn't bother turning around. He hoped with all his might that the elevator was still working.

Jim walked stiffly into a fourth-floor waiting room.

"I have an appointment," he said to the regimental

administrative officer. She looked up and recognized him.

"You're that guy who was with Gary," she said.

"Whatever," he shrugged. She motioned for him to take a seat.

"I'm good," he said, looking around. The newspapers on the table were ones he had read already. The RAO watched him from her desk.

"Nice hat," he said.

"It's a dastaar," she replied.

"Nobody asked for a history lesson," said Jim.

She opened the visitor's log, tilting her head in that jaunty way that meant a woman was annoyed. Jim had seen that tilt many times before. He knew he was being rude, but really, every damn creature, human or Bala, wanted to tell you all about their culture. Their weirdo gods, their super special headgear, their special pronouns that made no sense, and their food that crawled around on your plate and smelled like feet. Why everyone couldn't be normal people with normal food and normal clothes was beyond him. Everyone wanted to make things complicated so they could get attention.

"Name?" she asked.

Jim gave the fake name he'd been using ever since the Reason went to hell. The one from the best movie he'd ever seen in his life.

"Will Penny."

The officer's mouth fell open. Maybe she'd seen that movie too. A buzzer on the desk sounded. The officer motioned him toward the colonel's door.

"You can go in now," she said, barely breathing. Her right hand hovered over her service weapon. If he didn't know any better, he would have said she was thinking of shooting him.

Colonel Wenck was on the phone when Jim entered. His face had healed all the way up since the Blossom. They probably had some massive stores of unicorn blood set aside for brass like him. Or they used to. All that was gone now. Jim pulled his hat low and hoped that he had a face that was easy to forget.

Wenck slammed down his phone and cursed. The strip of clear plastic that served as a makeshift window blew into the room. Smoke wafted in. Outside the surviving window, the staccato report of gunfire echoed down the avenue.

He looked up at Jim and a flicker of recognition crossed his face. Jim didn't think Wenck had gotten a good look at him back in the Bitter Blossom before they blew him away. He was betting his freedom on the hope that the man hadn't taken notice of his face. It was a bad bet. Wenck's eyes narrowed.

"You're that old spacer from the bar–" he began, reaching for his phone. Jim put his hand over the receiver.

"Now Colonel, give me one minute to explain what I've got. You'll be interested, I promise."

The colonel tapped his tablet out of habit, but it was as dead as all the other computers in the Reason, locked up with Pymmie nonsense.

"Mister?" askied the colonel.

"Penny. Will Penny." A couple of hours ago, there would have been no way to pass through Reasonspace with a fake name. But with the computers offline and no FTL ships going out or coming in, it was like pioneer times all over again. You could just pay some guy to whip you up a laminated ID and you became a whole new man.

"Have a seat, Mr Penny."

Jim looked apprehensively at the chair.

"No, thank you. I'll stand, sir."

"You realize that my time is short now that all of the Bala have disappeared, Mr Penny. However, you apparently said something to my RAO that piqued her curiosity. She said I'd want to hear your story."

"Well, sir. For a short time, I was in possession of the stoneship *Jaggery*. Before it departed, I had access to the ship while everyone else was elsewhere."

"Mr Penny, hurry it along."

"Sure. In any case, sir, it was a bitch to break. I'm sure you're aware of the tensile strength of the material in its raw state. I ended up using redworm acid to get through it. Took a while, but I was able to secure a sizable portion of unicorn horn before the Bala were sent off to lord knows where – had to wrestle it away from an angry dwarf lady, but I got it."

Colonel Wenck leaned his elbows on the desk.

"How much horn, Mr Penny?"

"Five or six inches."

Wenck whistled.

"How the hell did you manage to hide it from the Pymmie? Every piece of unicorn horn in the system disappeared when the Bala left. Heck, every bit of spell or secretion that wasn't inside of a human being simply vanished."

Jim shrugged and gripped the back of the chair.

"There's always a way around a rule, sir."

The Colonel steepled his fingers and swiveled his chair.

"You have an incredibly valuable resource, Mr Penny. Even before the departure, it would have earned you a lifetime of luxury. And now–"

A brick came through the remaining window. The Colonel crouched in his chair. Jim ducked, then sucked in his breath and groaned.

Wenck went to the broken window and screamed outside.

"We have security cameras. You will be brought up on charges." He sat back down. "Goddamn looters. The mess halls on base were left unstaffed when those Bala disappeared. They worked all the food lines and the cook stations. Another forty-eight hours and we'll have to start using chemical weapons on our own people. So when you come in here and say that you have a good-sized chunk of unicorn horn to sell, you have one hundred percent of my attention, Mr Penny. I can offer you damn near anything you want at this point. Cash, ships, land... hell, I'll give you my eldest daughter in exchange for that horn. It would really save my ass."

Jim shifted uncomfortably at the word "ass."

"Colonel, sir, I'm looking to give you this horn for free."

The officer slapped his hands down on his desk.

"Well fuck my mother and call me son, that is the best news I've heard all year."

"There's just one thing I want."

"Name it."

"I want to borrow a ship. A big one. Troop carrier. With as many men as you can fit onto it. And I want a big enough piece of this horn to chase down that Bala filth on their new planet and drag their asses back to Reason."

A smile spread across Wenck's face.

"Mr Penny, I like your style. Usually, you'd have to be a commissioned officer to get a command like that." An explosion rocked the building, sending the remaining bits of glass in the window to the floor. "But a few openings have recently become available."

He picked up his phone and mashed a button.

"Singh, get Lieutenant Cy over here ASAP. Tell him I have a mission he's going to be extremely interested in."

The colonel slammed down the handset and reached out to shake Jim's hand.

"Mr Penny. *Captain* Penny, when I have my horn, you'll have your ship. When can you deliver it?"

"If you have a restroom and a newspaper handy, about ten to fifteen minutes."

The colonel pulled his hand away.

"Well, sir. You can give that horn to Subedar Singh, my regimental administrative officer. Captain Penny, you've done a great service to the Reason. We will not forget how you put your ass on the line."

"You have no idea," said Jim.

ACKNOWLEDGMENTS

There are many people who helped bring this book to fruition and I thank all of you from the bottom of my heart. It took a long time to get to this moment, but that made the journey all the more meaningful to me.

Dave, you were there for the birth of this idea and you stood with me at every step in the process. Twenty-five years and you still find ways to surprise and delight me. I couldn't do any of this without you. My boysies, you are amazing people and my loudest cheerleaders. Without you, I wouldn't know how to solve a Rubik's cube or the subtle differences between *Fullmetal Alchemist* and *Fullmetal Alchemist: Brotherhood*.

The Robot Gang – Marc Gascoigne, Penny Reeve, Phil Jourdan, Mike Underwood, and Nick Tyler – I'm so grateful that you took a chance on a book about unicorns in space. There was a time, years ago, when I picked an Angry Robot book off the shelf and hoped that someday I could be counted among your authors. You do incredible work and I'm thankful to be a part of what you're creating.

Sam Morgan, I'm so glad to have you in my corner. You're a fantastic agent who stepped in with a sure hand and a sense of humor to stop me from making terrible publishing choices. The rest of my terrible life choices are on me.

I'm incredibly grateful to Meleika, Elly, Nithin, Shruthi,

Liz, and S. who offered their time and expertise to make this book better. Thank you for your hard work, insights, and patience. This book is a thousand times more accurate than it would have been without your kind assistance. All the good parts are yours and all of the mistakes are mine.

Much love to the members of Team Arsenic, who are always ready with hugs and a listening ear. Ditto, with love. I'm also appreciative of the Clarion West family as a whole, especially Neile and Huw, who guided us through the workshop crucible to emerge stronger than before. Thanks to everyone at the Pub who offered advice when I needed to focus and distracted me with MCU fanfic when I needed a break. Stay hydrated. Hugs to the Codex Writers, you nudged me to finish this story and held your breath with me during the submission process. I'm also much obliged to my intrepid friends on the Writing Excuses retreat who helped me fix a few key story moments. I can't think of a better place to work on a manuscript than sailing the Baltic Sea. And finally, this book would not exist without Coke Zero and the *Pacific Rim* soundtrack.

AMBER ROYER

FREE CHOCOLATE

SPACE OPERA MEETS SOAP OPERA – IN A GALACTIC
WAR TO CONTROL EARTH'S GREATEST EXPORT!

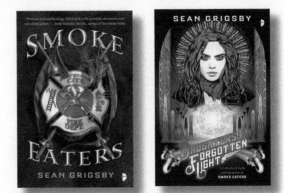
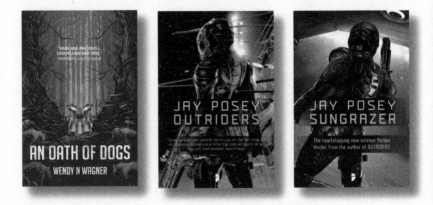

IT'S A KIND OF MAGIC...

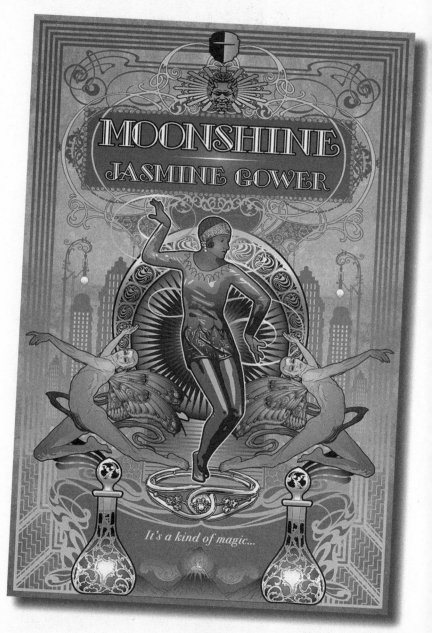

MOONSHINE

JASMINE GOWER

It's a kind of magic...